Escape from Terror
SURVIVING DREAMLAND

ESCAPE FROM TERROR

SURVIVING DREAMLAND

WILLIAM F. PENOYAR

Printed by Bookerfly Press
www.BookerflyPress.com

ISBN 978-0-9615112-0-3

Surviving Dreamland was adapted from the movie script titled The Lake, Copyright © 2011, Writers Guild of America Registration # I240278

To learn more about the author visit
www.survivingdreamlandbook.com

Printed in the United States of America

First Edition

Table of Contents

Introduction:

Uday Hussein was the ace of hearts in the US military's deck of playing cards that was provided to the soldiers soon after the second war with Iraq began in 2003. Uday was known by everyone in Iraq as a murderous thug who learned his trade from his father, Saddam. His tyrannical career began with his first killing when he was in college, and his deadly ways continued remorselessly throughout his life.

This historical novel follows both the tragic events that preceded Operation Iraqi Freedom and the courageous life and times of Lara. Born in Mosul, Iraq, and raised in Michigan as an all-American girl, she became entrapped in the near-fatal grasp of Uday and his henchmen.

Surviving Dreamland is a thrilling story that captures the hard-boiled realities of living under a brutal authoritarian regime and the terror of being caught in a helpless situation when war looms and the bombs begin to fall. Lara's triumphant survival and her tip to the US special operators succeeded in assuring the demise of two of the top three most-wanted killers during the early days of the Iraq war.

Convincing in its accuracy of detail and thought provoking, *Surviving Dreamland* races through the frequently fatal dangers that the Iraqi people faced while living under Saddam Hussein and his Ba'athist regime. It is a story of survival and bravery, but also a story of tragedy and the resilience of the human spirit.

Reviews

"*Surviving Dreamland* is a tantalizing novel from the first page all the way to the end. The story is based on true facts that actually happened and some of the fictional content happened as well but in a different manner. I point that out only because I am an Iraqi native who knows more about these facts than others do. It is a great story!" — Lee Jacob, Advisor to the Department of State in Iraq 2008 - 2011.

"*Surviving Dreamland* is a harrowing tale of an Iraqi-American young lady that survived an abduction by Uday Hussein. While a work of fiction it is also steeped with fact on the lead up to and first days of the Iraq war. It gives the reader factual insight into the daily lives of Iraqis under the Saddam Hussein regime and it also salutes the accomplishments of the special operators that provided their services. I highly recommend it!" — Sean Goad, Served in Al Anbar Province, Iraq both as a U.S. Marine and State Department Diplomat for five years between '04-'11

"*Surviving Dreamland* is a wonderful, powerful book. An irresistible storyteller, the author is able to hook you with his first few lines. Excellent research, and deep insights---all in a gripping read. *Surviving Dreamland* conveys the emotions, desires, creativity and frustrations of so many people in Iraq. This novel is based upon factual events. It is full of humanity and hope, captures some essence of the lives of men and women who were caught in the pincers of a brutal, decade-long war. Penoyar strikes the perfect balance as moving testimony to both the writer's talent and the knowledge gained from his work in Iraq with the U.S. Army, Marines, and U.S. Agency for International Development." — Jim Watson, Retired Diplomat, USAID

"*Surviving Dreamland*" is a remarkable achievement. With a background in international development and diplomacy, Bill Penoyar has delivered a thrilling novel weaving historical facts into fiction. In the final battle between the Hussein Brothers and U.S. Special Operations, I felt like I was there with an M-4 in my hands. You will not want to put this book down." — Dr. Kevin A. Rushing, Deputy Team leader, embedded Provincial Reconstruction Team (ePRT), Camp Baharia, Fallujah, Iraq 2008-2009

Dedication

This book is dedicated to the thousands of unnamed individuals who have risked their lives and dedicated their activities to the future of a safe, secure, and lasting democratic government and economy in Iraq, and to the ideals that the United States of America has always aspired to achieve as a beacon of hope to the world.

About the Author

Bill Penoyar worked for the US Agency for International Development in Iraq during 2009–2010. He assisted the US reconstruction efforts in Anbar, Baghdad, Basrah, and Erbil Provinces during his fifteen months in country. He also served as the USAID adviser for the Regional Threat Team, Strategic Operations Directorate, in support of the United States Forces-Iraq J3 Directorate from August 2009 – April 2010. While working with the embedded Provincial Reconstruction Team and US Marines at the Forward Operating Base, Camp Baharia near the Anbar provincial town of Fallujah in 2009, he learned about the rumors of Uday Hussein's activities at the former palatial lake resort that was located in the same area prior to the war. *Surviving Dreamland* was inspired by what Bill saw there. The novel began as a creative outlet to while away time in his small container housing unit room when he wasn't working with his ePRT colleagues and marines on visits to Fallujah and the nearby villages to assist Iraqis with economic and agricultural development, and governance.

Many of the characters represented in *Surviving Dreamland* were based on Iraqi, Iraqi-American, and US military colleagues whom he worked with or met in the course of his work. The description of locations which he wrote about were influenced by what he observed while traveling around the country. Some of the characters were also inspired by an Iraqi family whom Bill met while working in Iraq and sponsored when they immigrated to the United States.

Bill worked in international development for more than 30 years and in more than twenty countries on short- or long-term assignments as a foreign service officer. When home was far away, he wrote for enjoyment and, hopefully, for the entertainment or enlightenment of others. *On the Road with a Foreign Service Officer* was published as an e-book with Amazon in 2014, and *FEDSPEAK: U.S.Contracting and Grantsmanship Made Easier* was published and had limited distribution in 1985.

Chapter One:
Uday Hussein Discovers a Talent
Autumn 1984

The room had eighteen young men, all about twenty years old. Some were dressed in western clothes, though a few wore the traditional long dishdasha and had the kaffiyeh on their heads. Some had the scruffy beards of young men and others were clean shaven. It was the first day of the school year at the Iraq College of Engineering at Baghdad University, and everyone was excited and nervous. The men from all parts of Iraq: Basrah, Anbar, Erbil, Mosul, Tikrit, and Baghdad. They were grateful for the privilege of attending the college; many, whose relatives and high school friends were in the army fighting the war with Iran, were relieved that they, too, were not on the front lines where the prospects of being killed were becoming more alarming.

The professor came into the room and made his way to the front of the class. He looked old to the students, perhaps fifty or seventy, or somewhere in between. With his slightly stooped shoulders, rumpled suit, and thinning white hair, it was hard to say. Despite his tired look, his eyes were bright and he had a smile on his face. From the moment he introduced himself, it was clear that he enjoyed his work and was as excited about teaching this new class as the students were to be there.

"Welcome to the Iraq College of Engineering. You are all the sons of an ancient and famous people who began our civilization here more than 5,000 years ago. Writing and mathematics were developed by our ancestors. We have a proud past, and when you graduate as engineers from this magnificent center of learning, you will be part of a proud and glorious future for Iraq. I am Professor Talib Al-Osmany. I've taught at this college of engineering for twenty-five years. You will learn that I am very interested in having each of you succeed. Previous students have considered me a good teacher and friend. I am tough but also fair in my grading. Before we begin, please introduce yourselves.

In their turn, each of the students stood up, "Ibrahim Othman," "Abdul Al-Jabbar," "Khalid Al Abdulla," "Habib Al-Shawanna." Everyone was relaxed until the ninth student. He was perhaps a little older than the others and a bit taller. When he stood up he paused for a moment and looked around the room at each of the other students and then at the professor. He took his time, waiting for everyone to look up at him. He smiled, but it wasn't a pleasant, friendly smile. It was a cruel smile, as if he had just punched someone hard, and enjoyed the resulting pain that it had caused. It was the smile of a bully that liked having people afraid of him. "My name is Uday Hussein." Suddenly, the relaxed atmosphere of the class-room disappeared. Everyone, including the professor, began to feel uneasy.

"Welcome to my class, Uday. It is a privilege to have you with us." Professor Al-Osmay had a hollow feeling in his stomach. It was the feeling of a deep fear.

Uday continued to smile back at the professor, "It is a pleasure to be in your class, professor. I chose to take your course because you have a reputation for being one of the best teachers in the University."

"I do try to teach everyone well, and most who graduate from my class become successful in their careers. My reputation for being a good teacher and for being fair in treating everyone the same is well known. Those who work hard will succeed." As the professor spoke, Uday continued to stare at him as his smile faded. The professor felt a bit weak, as perspiration swelled up on his forehead.

"Don't worry, professor. I'll be one of your best students. You'll see." Uday's cold smile returned. "It will be a very educational year; don't you think?"

"Yes...I suppose so." Professor Al-Osmany didn't have a clue what Uday was talking about. Educational for whom? The uneasiness remained in his stomach as Uday sat down and the other students continued to introduce themselves. It was going to be a very difficult year, or worse, the professor feared. He was trapped in his own classroom, but what could he do?

Despite the drama of that first morning in the classroom, the next few weeks seemed to be normal for the students and the professor. Although everyone knew who Uday was and what his father was capable of, Uday acted as if he was like any other student. He was frequently jovial and wanted to make friends with his classmates. Of course, no one dared refuse his friendship.

Frequently, Uday would invite several of his classmates to go to the bars nearby so he would be less threatening than if he went by himself to meet women. There was always at least one big, armed companion with him, courtesy of his father's special protection forces. Uday would go out most evenings even though, true to the professor's remarks on the first day of class, the professor was tough with regard to the amount of homework that he assigned, and the hard work he expected from all of his students.

At first, despite his partying, Uday could keep up with the others in class. Within a few weeks, however, his grades and participation in class began to slip. During the second month, he was hardly in class at all. Midterm exams approached, and Uday reappeared for these. Surprisingly, he was one of the first students to hand in his test while others struggled on for quite a while longer.

Two days later, each student met with their professors to learn how they did on their exams and discuss their performance. Ibrahim and Khalid met with Professor Al-Osmany that morning. Later in the day, they were both still in the building, walking down the stairs on their way to meet other professors.

Ibrahim was not one of the best students in class, but he had worked hard. Despite the times that his studies were interrupted by "invitations" to go out with Uday, he passed the exam and had a smile of satisfaction as he walked up to Khalid, "How did you do in Professor Al-Osmany's exam?"

"It was tough, but I passed. I got an 88 percent." Khalid smiled.

"Good for you! I must have studied the hardest for Professor Al-Osmany's test, but I only got an 82 percent. At least I passed."

They were both relieved that they would continue for the rest of the semester and not have to worry about being sent into the military. "I wonder how the others did?" As they continued down the quiet hallway and walked by Professor Al-Osmany's office, they noticed the door was partially open. "Shall we stop in and say hello to the professor?" Ibrahim suggested.

"Why not?" Khalid replied. "It never hurts to be friendly with the professor." He pushed the door open further and began to walk in when they saw the professor slumped dead at his desk with a knife in his chest. On the desk was the test paper of Uday Hussein, with a score of 55% scratched out and replaced with the score of 100%. "My God! What shall we do?" Khalid began to reach for the professor, although he was clearly dead.

"Don't touch him!" Ibrahim grabbed Khalid's hand as he was reaching over to the professor's shoulder. "Don't touch anything! Quick, we need to get out of here. Don't you see what happened and who killed the professor?" Ibrahim was almost shaking with fear. "If we touch anything, they will blame the professor's death on us."

"Look at the exam on the desk." Khalid was also beginning to have a powerful knot of fear in his stomach. "Won't it be clear to the police that Uday was the murderer?"

"Khalid, Uday's exam will disappear, and they will pin the blame on us. We would make a convenient lie. The police and Uday would have their murderers and we would be dead, just like the professor." Ibrahim started to walk quickly to the door and glanced furtively into the hallway. "No one is in the hallway. Come on, let's get out of here, but first use your shirt to wipe our hand prints off the door where we touched it."

Khalid wiped the inside of the door as he stepped out into the hallway, then Ibrahim gently shut the door and wiped the outside with his shirt. Then they sprinted down the hall, down a flight of stairs, and out the door. As soon as they were out, Khalid kept running, but Ibrahim grabbed him once more. "Khalid," Ibrahim said in an urgent but hushed voice, "Don't run! If people see us running from the building, they will wonder why. We must walk as if we didn't see anything, and we must not say a word to anyone."

"Yes, yes." said Khalid. He was gasping with fear.

Ibrahim was also very upset, but he was able to appear almost calm. "Khalid, let's walk over there to the bench and sit down for a minute until you are breathing normally."

"What do you think they will do when someone finds Professor Al-Osmany dead?" Khalid was beginning to recover from his panic as they sat down on the bench, but he was still taking deep breaths.

Ibrahim was trying to think clearly despite his fear. He felt very tired, almost numb as the adrenaline began to subside in his body. "Khalid, probably nothing will happen if the guards find the professor's body when they check the building later tonight. The security forces will come, Uday's exam will disappear, and so will Professor Al-Osmany." Thinking a bit more, he said hopefully, "They will probably say that the professor died of a heart attack at his desk, or something like that."

"Yes, yes." Khalid was also trying to be hopeful. "We must act like nothing happened."

"Can you do that, Khalid?" Ibrahim wasn't sure about Khalid, and he also wondered how well he could act normal after what they had just seen.

"I think I can." Khalid's breathing was almost normal now. "I was planning to go home during this semester break. That will give me a chance to get over this."

"Don't tell your parents, brothers, or anyone about what we just saw, or it could be our death sentence. All it would take is one person saying anything about what Uday did, and we could be killed." Ibrahim was saying this as much for his own benefit as for Khalid.

The week-long midterm break was soon over, and the young men returned to the university to resume classes. Nothing was said about Professor Al-Osamy. Although people wondered what happened to him, no one dared ask. Life at the university went on. Fortunately for Ibrahim and Khalid, they had no classes with Uday in the next term, and they took extra measures to avoid being anywhere near him.

Chapter Two:
A Farewell in Mosul
Spring 1985

Spring time in Mosul was delightful. The searing heat of the summer was still several months away. There was the fresh scent of jasmine flowers as the last of the winter rains still provided refreshing and much-needed moisture to the city. Although the province looked calm and seemed prosperous, many people still had an unspoken but palpable fear about their country and their own futures. For the loyal followers of Saddam Hussein, life was very good and getting better all the time. For everyone else, life was much more guarded: trying to get along, keep a low profile, and make a living without attracting the attention of the Ba'ath Party.

Nadia was fussing in front of her mirror, preparing for an unknown future. Her long, curly black hair flowed freely on her shoulders as she put on her colorful scarf. It was going to be a very long day, and she was sitting in her bedroom, trying to think of how to make the scarf cover her hair and still show off her curls. This sort of a mindless activity helped distract her from the reality of what was about to happen. Today, her husband Omar, her baby daughter Lara, and she would visit her extended family to say good-bye before traveling to the Baghdad airport and flying to the United States.

The prospect of leaving everyone for the next two years while Omar worked as an intern at the University of Michigan hospital in Ann Arbor was a heavy burden on her at the moment. Although she knew this opportunity for Omar would definitely change their lives, probably for the better, she was not looking forward to the distance from her family and the unknown world outside Northern Iraq.

"Nadia, it's time to go." Omar came into the bedroom. She looked at him in the mirror and smiled. He was a handsome man, taller than many other men in Mosul. Although he had black hair and a mustache like so many others, his eyes had a softness and caring warmth that few other men had. His smile also was that of a gentle man, both comforting and knowing. "They're waiting for us, and we don't want to lose a moment of the remaining time that we have to visit with everyone."

"Yes, I know, Omar." She took her hands away from her scarf and got up from her chair. "It's hard for me to leave our home." She turned and looked into his eyes. Tears were welling up in hers. "This place, this neighborhood, and Mosul is our home."

Omar's smile faded, and his face became somber. "I know, Nadia. We have good memories of this place. It is hard for me to leave here also." He put his hands on her shoulders and looked into her eyes with his heartfelt love. "But, we—you and I—we made a decision that this opportunity should not be missed."

Omar had recently completed medical school at the University of Baghdad at the top of his class. As a result, he entered a competition to obtain a fully paid internship in a teaching hospital at an American university. Omar was one of only five winners. The internship included enough funding that he could bring Nadia and Lara to America also. It was an unimaginable dream that actually came true. They both recognized that some would say it was a gift from heaven. "Nawaf and the rest of your family also know that we are doing the right thing." He dropped his hands from her shoulders, held her gently in his arms and smiled again, "We'll come back here in two years, and life will resume just as we are leaving it today."

There was a cooing coming from the crib near their bed. "Lara must know it is time to go. She sounds like she's ready for this big adventure." Omar walked over to the crib, picked the baby up, and held her in his arms. Then he looked again at Nadia. "Come on, my sweet wife and mother of my beautiful daughter; let's begin the journey. Our family is waiting for us."

Nadia slowly looked around her bedroom. It was almost completely empty. All of the bed sheets had been put away, and the old wooden dresser was cleared of all her jewelry, cosmetics, and combs. It all seemed surreal. Their apartment was on the second floor. She walked past the small living room and kitchen, down the stairs, and out onto the street where Nawaf's car and driver waited. He would drive them to Nawaf's house for the farewell party that was arranged in their honor. Omar and Nadia didn't own the apartment, but it was the first home that they shared together. Leaving it was bittersweet. America held great promise, but the unknown always feels risky.

As the driver pulled away from the curb and turned the corner, the car took them past the small clinic where Omar had worked. They travelled past rows of narrow shops, each with their fronts open from wall to wall so people could easily see the merchandise inside: colorful and fragrant spices in one shop; used automotive parts in another; a dry goods shop, and a vegetable shop next to that. Nadia had enjoyed talking with the men, their wives and children who owned and worked at the shops near their apartment. They were her friends and she would miss them.

Her brothers and their families lived across the city of Mosul in the Al-Yarmuk suburb, an area with large homes and walled courtyards. Her family had been traders for years, and the business had passed on from generation to generation. This gave her family a level of prosperity and stature within Mosul that enabled them to own small estates and, for some of the men, to have multiple wives and many children. As they approached her brother's house, Nadia smiled. She was proud that none of her brothers had more than one wife, and Omar made it clear before they were married that he, too, would only have one wife, and she was the one.

Nawaf Al-Zaidan had a bright green gate and a high wall that enclosed the large yard and a large, two-story home. When the car pulled up to the gate, Omar got out. Before Nadia could hand Lara to Omar, they could hear Nawaf's booming voice from behind the wall. "They're here!" The gate flew open and Nawaf led the group of smiling people to the car, most of them Nadia's brothers, their wives and children, and a few close friends. Nadia and Omar were quickly surrounded with hugs. "Come in, come in!" Nadia carried Lara and walked with Omar as they were ushered into the courtyard. In an instant, Lara was snatched out of Nadia's arms by Nawaf's wife, Mohassin, so she could show her to the other adoring women at the party.

Nawaf was beaming with excitement, "Nadia, how is my favorite sister and my beautiful niece, Lara?" He was in his mid-thirties, about ten years older than Omar. His success showed in his body. His waistline had expanded, making his tailored trousers and shirt a bit tight. While they were talking, Nadia's other brothers joined their company. Salah was quieter than Nawaf. Although he was not as portly as his brother, he was equally as successful in business and had a big grin on his face.

"Nawaf, I am your only sister! Your beautiful niece is being a very good baby at the moment." Nadia looked toward Mohassin as she held out Lara to show her off to the others. She was with her family and could feel their love surrounding Lara, Omar, and herself. "Thank you for opening your home to our family so we can say good-bye to everyone. You're a good brother, and we'll miss you and the rest of the family very much."

Nawaf was very excited. "Omar, we are honored in many ways." He turned to another young family whom Omar did not know. "This is our cousin Ibrahim from Hillah in Babil Province, his wife Rinad, and their one-year-old daughter, Nagham. Ibrahim does business with us and represents our company in Babil, Najaf, and Karbala provinces. I told Ibrahim about your internship in America and that you, Nadia, and Lara were going to Michigan. They have honored all of us by driving all the way from Hillah, just to meet you and wish you well."

Omar said, "Ibrahim, we are deeply honored by your presence here today. If there is anything we can ever do for you, Rinad, and your daughter, let us know. Thank you very much." He and Nadia both bowed deeply and put their right hands across their chests in a show of very deep gratitude.

"Rinad, when we return from America, we promise that we will visit you in Hillah." Nadia was deeply moved by the gesture of these relatives whom she barely knew. They reminded her that family ties are deep and broad, covering distant provinces throughout Iraq. This tight sense of family and community made her proud of her people. She would miss Iraq, this ancient country, and its people, she thought. Together, it ran deeply in her blood.

Ibrahim grabbed Omar by the shoulders and brushed his cheek on both sides of Omar's face, almost as if he were kissing him, but only showing his very warm friendship. Smiling, Nawaf also grabbed Omar and proceeded with the same gesture. "Omar, welcome. Congratulations on being accepted to the University of Michigan teaching hospital and getting visas for you and your family to go to America. We're all very proud of you."

"Thank you Nawaf, Salah, and Ibrahim." Omar said, patting his eye with a handkerchief. "Nadia and I appreciate your support. I know it is difficult for the Al-Zaidan family to say good-bye to their sister so she can go to America."

Nadia looked into the eyes of Nawaf and Salah, studied their faces to lock them into her mind and heart for safekeeping, "Thanks to both of you for supporting Omar, Lara, and me. We will miss you very much." Her smile vanished of as she remembered again that they were beginning a long journey to a place far from all that she knew and cherished.

Nawaf's smile faded, "We will miss you! But we are honored that our brother-in-law, Omar, has done so well in medical school to be selected to continue his training in America. We are all proud of your accomplishments."

"It's still difficult to leave all of our family and friends, and our home in Mosul. This will always be our home." Omar said, in all seriousness.

Salah also quit smiling and whispered urgently, "Omar, you are doing the right thing. The future of Iraq is uncertain. Although we seem to be winning the war with Iran, these are dangerous times. President Saddam is draining the country of young men to fight the war. Medical doctors are being forced to serve near the front lines to care for the wounded. Any of us, including you, may be called upon to fight in this senseless conflict. Also, I've heard disturbing things about what the Ba'athists and Saddam's family are doing to Iraqis that don't agree with their policies."

"Yes Salah, I've even heard from my colleagues at the University of Baghdad that Saddam's son Uday may be involved with a murder at the engineering college where he is attending. I hope it isn't true. He's only a student. My contract with the hospital in Michigan is only for two years. Nadia and I plan to return home after my internship is completed so I can practice medicine in Mosul. *Insh'Allah*, things will be better in Iraq by then."

"*Insh'Allah*," Nawaf added. "God willing. But ever since Saddam became president it seems the country continues to go from bad to worse. I can say this only behind these walls and to my closest and most trusted family." The men were all quiet for a moment as they reflected on the sad reality. "Maybe it is only the times we are living in, due to the war. We will see."

Nadia wanted to change the subject. "We will write to you often and send pictures of America."

When he heard Nadia's voice, Nawaf quickly recovered from the dark thoughts. "Yes, but we'll be most interested in pictures of Lara."

Mohassin walked up to the group, holding the hand of her three-year-old daughter, Yasmine, as she joined the conversation. "Yes, Nadia, we want our Yasmine to know who her cousin is so that when you and Omar return home, Yasmine and Lara will become close friends."

Nadia, smiled at Yasmine. "They will be the best of friends, I'm sure of this."

Soon, the long tables that had been set up for the occasion were covered with large platters of food: roasted lamb, chicken, and large river carp on rice and garnished with steamed vegetables. There were also plates of dolma, hummus, baba ganouj, pickles, and stacks of steamy lavash flat bread, fresh out of the ovens. Wine, beer, water, and a variety of juices flowed freely as the guests reminisced about family members and talked softly about the troubles in the country. Everyone had their turn to talk with Omar and Nadia America. Many had questions about where they would live and talked about what they had learned about Ann Arbor from the friends of friends who had moved or visited there. There was friendly small talk, with loved ones who just wanted to be with them and Lara a moment longer, before they had to leave.

When everyone finished eating, Nawaf stood up on a sturdy small table and called everyone around. "Omar and Nadia, please stand by me for a moment." Lara was still being adored by several women. Nadia asked to reclaim her daughter from them and walked over to Nawaf and Omar.

"Dear family and friends, today we must say good-bye to my sister Nadia, her husband Omar, and daughter Lara. The Al-Zaidan family is very close, and it is difficult to let them go so far away. However, Omar has honored the family by graduating first in his class from the Baghdad University Medical School. He will continue bringing honor by working at the University of Michigan Medical College and Hospital. He promises to return to all of us with his family when he completes his internship and devote his services to the people of Mosul. Omar, may God be with you, Nadia, and Lara on this journey." (Everyone clapped their hands in approval).

Omar, who was a little shy in front of a large gathering, took a deep breath and cleared his throat.

He was also choking back some of the emotion that he felt at that moment, "I am humbled by all of you. Nawaf, thank you for your kind words, and your support to me and my family. It is difficult to leave Mosul and all of you. This is our home, and we promise to return as soon as we can. Nadia and I promise that our daughter Lara will know where she is from and learn about her family and friends here. Thank you."

The group gathered around Omar and Nadia to shake Omar's hand. The women's eyes glistened with tears as they hugged Nadia and said farewell to both of them. Salah entered the courtyard, "It's time to leave for Baghdad. Omar, all of your luggage is in the cars."

Mohassin came over to them with Yasmine, "Nadia, we will miss you!"

Nadia lifted Lara from where she was napping and bent down so Yasmine could reach out to her baby cousin and gently touch her cheek. "Yasmine, say good-bye to your cousin; you may not see her for a few years."

"*Mas'Allah ma*" Yasmine said quietly, "Good bye Lara."

Nadia stood up and handed Lara to Omar so she could hug Yasmine, Mohassin, and Nawaf, "Thank you for everything."

There was abrief silence. Then Nawaf spoke loudly, in part to hide the emotions that he also was feeling, "Time will pass quickly. Stay safe and take good care of my favorite niece!"

Omar gave Nawaf the kind of hug that was only for very close friends, "We will Nawaf. *Mas'Allah ma.*" It was a sad goodbye for all of them.

They walked with Salah to the waiting cars.

Chapter Three:
Hanging Out with Saddam Hussein
1986

The war was going badly for Saddam Hussein during the first half of 1986. In April his forces suffered a disastrous defeat in Al-Faw, at the southern tip of Iraq, which jutted out into the Arabian Sea. The six-month battle claimed more than 55,000 casualties. Another battle raged in the north of Iraq in the Zagros Mountains, where the Iraqi Ba'athist troops invaded Iran and began to occupy the town of Meghan. Before long, the Iranians drove them out; their American-made Cobra helicopters and TOW missiles destroyed large numbers of Iraqi tanks and vehicles and forced their retreat. Saddam ordered a second attack by the Republican Guard on July 4.but this was also defeated by the Iranians. The mounting military losses inspired the Ba'athists to call up men as old as forty-two, close the universities and colleges, and conscript all male students into the Iraqi Popular Army.

However, by late 1986 prospects were more promising. The Soviet Union and United States were both worried about the possible rise of a radical Islamist Iran. The Russians were particularly worried that Iran would side with Afghanistan in the Soviet Union's war there, and with the other nominally Muslim USSR countries in the region. The United States was concerned about the threat Iran posed to Israel's safety. Each decided to give Iraq the weapons necessary to defeat Iran and bring the war to an end. With the knowledge that the two opposing world powers at the time were going to support him, Saddam was in a very good mood. The improving situation with the war, prospects for alliances with the United States and the USSR, and increased prestige within the Arab world gave ample excuses for living large, with frequent social galas and entertaining. The recent graduation of Uday with a degree in engineering was another good excuse for an event.

All of the guests had arrived and were being escorted into an elegant dining room, where a very long table that was loaded with food and drinks. Large numbers of attendants stood behind the guests' chairs. After everyone was seated, Saddam made a fashionably late appearance, walked to the head of the table, and asked Uday to join him there. He raised his glass for a toast. When everyone was standing, Saddam smiled broadly and began his toast.

"Friends, we are gathered here today to honor my esteemed and brilliant son Uday Hussein. He has proven that he is truly my son by being the best student that the Baghdad University College of Engineering ever graduated, with a perfect score of 100% in all of his classes. He is certainly destined to be a great leader of Iraq and an inspiration for all of the people of Iraq." Everyone shouted their approval and applauded.

"Thank you all." Uday was looking good. On most evenings he would by now have a darkening shadow of a beard, but tonight he was clean shaven and feeling very smug due to the recognition from his father and the Ba'athist elite who were attending the dinner party. "I've worked hard to earn this honor, and I will work even harder for the Ba'ath party and for my father and mother." The guests cheered again and raised their glasses for the toast.

Uday walked over to the chair next to his mother, Salijiday Talfa. After Saddam lowered himself to his seat, everyone sat down. Uday was to the right and Saljida was on Saddam's left. Sitting next to her was Uday's younger brother, Qusay Hussein.

"We're all very proud of you, Son. Your father has an important position for you in the Ba'ath party." She was clearly proud of her oldest son and enjoyed the attention and respect that was given to her by all the guests and attendants. To her mind, being the wife of the most powerful man in Iraq was a very good thing.

Qusay leaned into the table toward his older brother, "Congratulations, Uday. I hope I do as well as you in college."

Uday smiled, "You will, Qusay, if you make others see your point of view. Learn from our father and me, and you also will become a great leader for Iraq as my assistant when I become president someday.

Saddam Hussein looked at both of his sons and was also smiling, "I'm proud of both of you. This family is destined to rule Iraq and all of Persia and Kuwait for many years to come. The Russians and Americans are both on our side now. As we continue to win the war with Iran with the new weapons that we'll soon have, we'll invade and conquer our ungrateful neighbor to the south in a couple of years." He picked up his glass for another, more private toast, "Here's to the Saddam Hussein family!" The four of them raised their glasses.

Uday added, "May we all live very prosperous and happy lives!"

When they finished their toast and put down their wine glasses, Kamel Gegeo, Saddam's chief servant and food taster, walked over to Saddam and leaned over to his boss. "All is prepared, sir. I've inspected the food, and I'm sure you will be pleased."

At that point, Saddam looked to the other end of the long table and admired a tall, attractive woman. "Who is she?"

"Sir, she is Samira Shahbandar, a doctor here in Baghdad. If you like, I will introduce you to her."

Saddam and Samira's eyes locked on, and they both acknowledged each other with a smile. "I would like that very much." Saddam said, with a mischievous smile.

Chapter Four:
In America
1987

The apartment was small, like most campus family housing. Omar, Nadia, and Lara had been in the United States for almost two years, and Omar was doing very well as a resident intern at the hospital. However, it would soon be time to decide their next move. Although they had always planned to move back to Mosul after he completed the two-year program, the war between Iraq and Iran, which was still raging, was not going well for Iraq. The news from Iraq was heavily censored, so the only information he could get was from the veiled language in letters from their families. They described how men of all ages from the families of many relatives and friends were conscripted into the army, then never heard from again.

As battlefield losses mounted, Saddam's only strategy was to put more men on the front lines and replace them as quickly as they fell with anyone that was out of favor with the Ba'athists. There were millions of men that seemed to fall into this category. This sad reality was weighing heavily on Omar as he sat with Nadia and Lara around the dining table of their small kitchen. Omar's command of English had improved dramatically, and Nadia was continuing to study and improve her ability to speak English and understand Americans. She listened intently and practiced speaking when shopping and visiting neighbors. At home, they typically only spoke Arabic. Although Lara was speaking a form of pidgin-English with the neighborhood children, she was learning proper Arabic from her parents at home. Neither Omar nor Nadia expected to live in the United States for long and, since Lara was still not much more than a baby, they hadn't bothered speaking English to her or correcting her on the very broken English that she was learning.

"Lara, tell your father what we did today." Lara was sitting in her high chair and Nadia was feeding her as she was speaking in Arabic.

"Daddy, we went to the pet store and I played with the puppies!" Lara was very happy with the adventure with her mom.

"Lara, that's nice." Omar said in Arabic. Then he turned to Nadia and spoke in English, "Nadia, please don't encourage her to think about a pet until we have our own home."

"Will that be back in Mosul?" Nadia was a bit puzzled but intrigued by the notion of having a small dog for Lara in their apartment back in Mosul. "Dogs aren't as popular there as they are in America."

"I don't know if we will return to Mosul when I finish my residency here." Sighed Omar, "The war with Iran is still going on, and it's going badly for Iraq. According to Nawaf, Saddam and the Ba'athists are becoming more repressive and forcing more men to join the military. If we went home, I would probably be forced to serve near the front lines."

Nadia was alarmed by this comment. "Omar, they would never send you to the front lines, would they?" She was suddenly conflicted. She didn't want Omar to be conscripted, but she never dreamed that they would remain in America more than two years. "When we go home, don't you think they would want you to serve safely behind the front lines, maybe in Basrah or in Erbil, or even in Baghdad? If you had to serve in Erbil, we would only be three hours' drive from Mosul. Wouldn't that be the patriotic thing to do?"

Omar looked at her and frowned slightly. "Nadia, this war is destroying our country. Saddam is using it to send non-Ba'athists and anyone who may not agree with his regime to the front lines. Many never return. It lets him divert attention from all the problems in Iraq, which seem to grow worse by the year. Yes, I love Iraq—as I remember it growing up. But it is not the same country anymore. Our people are suffering, and as long as Saddam and his family are in power, it will only get worse." He paused for a moment as he fortified his determination to tell Nadia something that he had been thinking about privately for the last few months but kept to himself. "Someday we will go back, but not until it is safe for us. I want to help my country without risking getting killed for my efforts."

Nadia sat for a moment without saying anything. What could she say? She thought of all the plans that she had mentally rehearsed for the last several months about coming home to Mosul and being near her brothers and their families. Not returning to Mosul had never crossed her mind. Now she realized the man she loved was confronting an ominous future, one that could lead to his death. That was not an option. In an instant, she knew what her answer had to be. "So what are we going to do?" Nadia asked cautiously, wondering anxiously about Omar's plans that would profoundly change how she might spend a very long time, if not the rest of her life.

Omar sighed in relief, and as he paused for a moment, he reflected on how deeply he loved Nadia for her calm inner strength. "I've talked with the university. They've offered assistance and support to help extend my student visa. They will also provide a recommendation when we apply for US citizenship, which we can do in three more years. I think we should stay. It doesn't mean that we will never go back to Iraq, but it will ensure that we can all live here safely and not be forced to leave. It will also mean that I will be able to open my own medical practice, so we can buy our own home.

Nadia stared down at the table as she contemplated this new reality. "I miss our families so much, Omar, and Mosul. Do you think we will ever be able to go home?"

"I know, Nadia. I also miss Mosul. Will we ever go home?" He thought for a moment. "I don't know. Only God knows. Staying here is not only best for us but also for Lara. She will always be Iraqi, but if she is also an American, her life will be much more secure and better. Maybe we will all be able to return to Mosul someday—but not now and perhaps not any time soon."

"I suppose we should start speaking English to Lara all of the time so she will do well in school." Nadia was looking into Omar's eyes and speaking from her heart. She loved Omar and Lara more than anything and knew deep in her heart that under the circumstances, this new plan was their only choice.

"She must learn English and Arabic." Omar reached over and put Lara on his lap and smiled. "Our daughter is a bright young girl. She takes after her mom. Her friends will teach her to speak English, and we must encourage this as well. We will also help her learn how to read and write Arabic so that when she grows up, she will be comfortable here in America, and, *Insh'Allah*, also with our relatives in Iraq.

Nadia smiled. "I love you, Omar. We will become an American family."

Chapter Five:
The Wrath of Uday
1988

The war with Iran finally ended in a stalemate. Both countries had the same borders as before Saddam invaded Iran in 1982. Despite the deaths of more than a half million people and a depleted treasury, he was in good spirits and distracted by his new mistress. The rest of the people in Iraq were trying to recover from the effects of six deadly years. Meanwhile, Saddam's family was busy living the high life full of debauchery, intrigue, and murder.

Uday walked into the large dining hall in a good mood. Although he was just twenty-four, his father had already made him a powerful, prestigious senior member of the Ba'ath party. His days were filled meeting with generals, ministers, and other notables as he learned the operations of the empire he assumed he would someday inherit. The occasion of this evening's social gathering was a reception honoring Suzanne Mubarak, the wife of Egyptian President Hosni Mubarak . Since the war was over, Saddam Hussein had achieved considerable prestige among the Arab League countries. Even Egypt, the country many considered the most influential in the Arab world, was showing its deference to Saddam Hussein and his family. Uday liked the deference and fear that people had for him.

He walked up to where his mother was talking with Mrs. Mubarak. They both turned to him and smiled as Uday bowed deeply. "Good evening, Madame Mubarak. It is an honor that you have come to Baghdad."

Suzanne was an elegant woman, wearing a fashionable designer dress from Paris. She was in Iraq as her husband's emissary and enjoyed the attention that she was receiving. Egypt had been ostracized from the Arab League since the 1970s, when its former president, Anwar Sadat, agreed to a peace treaty with Israel during the Camp David meetings hosted by President Jimmy Carter. "My husband sends his respects and congratulations for ending the war with Iran."

Uday bowed again slightly. "Both of our countries have reason to celebrate. I understand that Egypt will soon rejoin the Arab League.

She smiled. "Yes, Hosni has been lobbying the members of the Arab League. Although he has long been a friend of President Hussein, he asked me to extend our sincere thanks to your family for the support. We expect the Arab League to vote on our readmission next year, and we are grateful for the help from your father and the Ba'athists."

Salijda nodded in agreement, "We are honored that you came to Baghdad to visit us. Now our husbands can work together with the rest of the Arab nations to build a strong union. Please enjoy yourself and remain in Baghdad as long as you like, as our guest."

"The Egyptians and Iraqis will be strong allies in the Arab League." Mrs. Mubarak was smiling diplomatically as the Kuwaiti ambassador joined the conversation.

"Madame Hussein and Mr. Uday, please forgive me," said the ambassador. "I would like to introduce Mrs. Mubarak to His Excellency, the prince of Qatar."

Suzanne Mubarak frowned slightly and turned to Uday and Salijda, "Forgive me. I hope you don't mind that I go with Ambassador Al-Saif. I've got orders from my husband to talk with everyone I meet who may help us win the Arab League vote."

"We understand. Please go talk with the prince. Iraq wants Egypt in the Arab League as much as Egypt does." Salijda was happy for an excuse to talk with Uday privately for a moment. The ambassador's request presented a convenient opportunity for the moment she needed to have a very private and disquieting conversation with her son.

"Thank you, Madame Hussein." The ambassador bowed toward Saljida and turned to Suzanne. "Shall we go?"

"We will talk later this evening." Suzanne said, as she turned and walked toward a young man in flowing robes, standing at the other end of the very large room.

The smile on Saljida's face disappeared as soon as Suzanne turned and walked away with the Ambassador. When they were both far enough away that they couldn't hear Uday and Saljida talk, Uday asked, "Where is Saddam?" His father had been conspicuously absent from several recent ceremonies that Uday was asked to attend. He wanted to talk with him tonight regarding the Iraqi national soccer team, which he had taken an interest in.

"He is with that woman, the whore, his mistress, Samira Shahbandar." Saljida had rapidly changed from the charming hostess to a very angry woman. She felt threatened this time, by this present mistress, more than by the many other affairs that her husband had engaged in. "Mark my words, Uday, she will steal your inheritance and your rightful place as the future leader of Iraq. She is embarrassing me and has brought me great shame. Your father now spends all his time with her and rejects me as if I am nothing." Saljida knew that Uday was very easily moved to act on his anger if anyone crossed him. She was hoping this would be enough for him to develop a plan for getting rid of her tormentor. Although most of her anger and venom was directed toward Samira, she expanded her list of enemies as Hussein's servant Kamel walked into the room and began talking with one of the attendants. He looked over to Saljida and Uday, bowed slightly, and smiled.

Saljida's eyes flashed and she spoke very quietly, but with controlled anger, to Uday. "That man," she nodded toward Kamel, "is the cause of this disgrace to me, you, and your brother and sisters. He was the traitor who introduced that harlot to your father and arranged for your father to meet privately with her. He is poisoning our family and ruining your chance to become the next leader of Iraq." Uday could see in his mother's eyes that she would be happy if Kamel was dead.

When Uday was younger, he would try to hide his frequent urge to lash out for the least offence, real or imagined, against him or his family. He would control himself in public and take revenge in private when no one was looking. However, with his growing power and influence as Hussein's oldest son and heir apparent, he lost all such control. He knew that no one in Iraq would or could stop him from doing anything he wanted to do. "I will deal with him now!"

He walked over to an older man in a wheel chair and grabbed a brass-headed cane from him. Then, he walked purposely across the room to Kamel, who was talking to a waiter carving lamb with an electric carving knife.

Kamel looked up toward Uday. All the guests in the room were staring at Uday as he raised the cane and strode quickly toward Kamel. "You son of a swine! Traitor! Bastard who has ruined the family of Saddam Hussein!" Uday started to viciously beat Kamel with the cane.

Kamel, in shock and panic, vainly threw his arms in front of his face to protect himself, "Sir! What have I done?"

Uday was merciless. He swung the can like a baseball bat. The brass head first hit one of Kamel's arms with a loud thud, and the blow sent him staggering backward into the table behind him. Quickly there was another blow, this time to the side of his head, which made him spit out blood and fragments of broken teeth. Kamel slumped and sat on the floor, still conscious and in pain. He looked pleadingly at Uday. "What did I do?" It was the last question Kamel would ask.

Uday stood over Kamel and continued to beat him as he sat on the floor with his back against the table and his head bowed as if he were asleep. "Get up, you disgusting sewer rat!" Even though Kamel was unconscious, perhaps already dead from the severe blows, Uday continued to scream and whacked him again with sickening blows to the other side of his head. "You deserve to die for your disloyalty to my mother and my family."

Exhausted from thrashing Kamel and no longer feeling the adrenaline rush from the brutal caning, Uday threw down the cane and grabbed the carving knife from the table. As the rest of the guests stood in helpless silence and horror, Uday slit Kamel's throat with the knife. Blood oozed from the huge gash in the neck of Kamel's lifeless body as it toppled over and fell into a sickening heap on the floor.

Saljida watched all of this in silence. She was stone cold with no emotion while Uday dropped the knife down next to Kamel's body and walked out of the room. Saljida turned and walked out of the door behind her as the others continued to stand where they were, shocked and horrified by what they had just witnessed. Then, they also turned their backs on the deadly scene and silently walked away from Kamel, leaving the trembling attendants to clean up the mess.

The newspapers had headlines about Suzanne Mubarak's diplomatically important and successful visit and meeting with Saddam Hussein and his family. Nothing was said about the dinner party or what happened there.

Six months later at the Iraqi Embassy in Switzerland, Ambassador Al-Tamimi was nervous. "Kathryn, he is going to be here for several months."

Kathryn was also agitated. "Why did they send him here? He doesn't speak German, French or Italian. They say he is a cold-blooded murderer." The secretary to the ambassador was usually cool and calm, very professional and self-assured. These qualities and her stunning Swiss beauty got her the job as the ambassador's personal aide. However, today she was very afraid. "How do we know he won't kill us?"

"We will have to be very careful," said the Ambassador. "Tell everyone to accord Uday Hussein all due respect, but never, never go anywhere or be in any room alone with him. The cable from Baghdad said that his father told him to be on his best behavior and not embarrass him or Iraq while he's here. Let's hope that he does what he was told. I don't want anyone to take chances, especially you. Make sure you are always with another colleague while he is here.

"Yes sir, Angela and I agreed that we would always work together until he's gone."

"Good," He was very serious. "If you feel like you need one of our security guards to escort you home, that can be arranged."

"I'll let you know." There was a knock on the door and a guard announced Uday's arrival. Kathryn took a deep breath and stiffened as if she were about to be sentenced to prison. "He will not get near me," she said under her breath, just as the door opened.

The ambassador mustered all of his diplomatic charm and smiled broadly as he pretended to act genuinely happy as Uday walked in. "Welcome Uday, I understand you had a difficult six months."

Uday frowned. "Are you're referring to the punishment that my father tried to impose on me for killing the traitor Kamel? Yes, it was a bother. Fortunately, Saddam, in his wisdom, decided that I did no wrong and released me from prison as soon as he realized his mistake. Now I'm here as his servant to assist you." As he was speaking, he began to leer at Kathryn.

"Uday, this is my personal aide, Kathryn."

Uday smiled, "It is a pleasure to meet you, Kathryn."

Before he could say more, the ambassador interrupted. "Kathryn, I am sorry that your son is ill. Please take the rest of the day off so you can attend to him." Al-Tamimi was making up the story as he spoke, hoping that a son and husband would dissuade Uday from acting on any thoughts regarding her.

Kathryn immediately picked up on the ruse and said in all seriousness, "Thank you, sir. My husband told the general that he would take care of Hans until I get home." She gave Uday a cold stare, "Welcome to Switzerland, Mister Hussein." Then turned and quickly walked out of the room.

Uday began to frown again. "She is a devoted mother and wife," said the Ambassador. "She is also a very good assistant." As he paused for a moment, Uday considered his options for making Kathryn a conquest and quickly shrugged off the idea. However, he continued to watch her through the open door while she walked down the hallway. The ambassador noticed but ignored Uday's focused stare. "I am sure you will be of great assistance to this embassy and, no doubt, you will enjoy the charms of Switzerland." As ambassador, one of his most discreet responsibilities was to arrange meetings between elite members of the Iraqi Ba'athist Party and military and the most exclusive call girls in Bern. He considered his role as pimp a distasteful but necessary requirement of his job.

"Ambassador, I expect that I will be very happy with the charms that you are referring to." He said, in a matter-of-fact tone, "If the charms are not to my liking, Switzerland will have a new Iraqi ambassador."

Al-Tamimi managed another insincere smile, "You will like the charms very much." He was glad that he had already arranged the necessary services a few days earlier. "There will be two women at your apartment when you return there. Treat them well."

Uday began to smile again. "If you keep me busy while I'm here, Ambassador Al-Tamimi, you will not see me at the embassy very often."

The ambassador sighed with relief under his breath. "You will be busy," he promised. There were a lot of high-priced and very beautiful escorts in Switzerland. He had both the authority and the resources from the Iraqi treasury to do whatever it would take to keep Uday "busy" and out of the news until his exile ended.

Chapter Six:
Soccer for Fun, or a
Life and Death Situation
1992

"Daddy, where did you learn to play soccer like that? You're better than our soccer coach." Lara was growing up quickly and was very much an all-American girl. She was nine years old, and her family had comfortably settled into Ann Arbor, Michigan, where Dr. Omar Al-Mohammed was a staff member at the University of Michigan teaching hospital. Nadia had devoted herself to her family and reinvented herself as a student at the university, earning a degree in elementary education. Now she worked as a teacher at Lara's school.

Although it took a few years, Omar's hard work and regular advancement at the university enabled the family to leave their first apartment and move into a new home near the campus. The open space of the neighborhood and a yard helped Lara convince her dad to buy a black Labrador puppy which soon grew to be a very energetic and playful dog named Oliver. The community also had a large population of recent Middle Eastern émigré families, like the Al-Mohammed's, who were all football fans. That is, soccer fans, as they Americanized their terminology so others could understand what game they were referring to.

It was late summer, and the community recreation association had organized a soccer league for the children. Lara was anxious to join the team. Omar and Lara were in the front yard of their home, and Omar was teaching Lara how to play soccer as Oliver was chasing the ball.

Omar deftly moved the ball with his feet as Oliver enthusiastically but fruitlessly chased around Omar to get it from him. Then Oliver happily chased the ball as Omar kicked it toward Lara.

"Lara, when I was your age in Mosul, I loved to play football." Omar reminisced. "That's what we called it there. Your uncles, Nawaf and Salah, and I would play all the time. During high school and my early days at university, I even played on a team." He smiled and reflected on those happy times for a moment. "They were good times, and my friends said I was quite good at making goals."

Lara grabbed the ball and ran back to her dad, with Oliver chasing her, "Why didn't you keep playing?"

"Football is a wonderful sport, Lara, but I knew that I wanted to be a doctor someday. Studies were challenging, and I wanted to be the best in my class. So, I began to play football much less and dedicated myself to my studies much more." Omar lost his smile and was speaking more seriously to his daughter.

Lara pondered this for a moment, "Are you happy, Daddy?"

Omar smiled and reached out to give his daughter a hug. "Yes, Lara. I have you, your mom, this house, and a good job. Most of all, we are finally American citizens. God has blessed us in many ways." Just then, Oliver snatched the ball that was resting under Omar's foot. "We even have your rascal dog, Oliver." Omar smiled. Then he became quiet as he thought again of his past life for a moment.

"I love it here, Daddy, but sometimes you and Mommy seem a little sad." Although Lara was only nine years old, she seemed to have an insight into the feelings and emotions of others that went well beyond her years.

"We are truly blessed, and I thank God for all that He has given us. But your mommy and I still think of our time growing up in Mosul." He paused again as he thought before saying, "Of course back then, I barely even knew your mother, even though our families were friends. But I could see her playing with my sisters and cousins, and we would talk to each other once in a while when our families all celebrated holidays together. It was a happy time.

"Your uncles and I talked of all the things we would do when we grew up. You can't remember because you were so small when we moved to America, but Mosul is a beautiful city with wonderful parks. We were not far from the mountains to the north, where we would go camping and hiking. The people were more open and friendly then."

"Why did we move to America, Daddy?"

"Life in Mosul, and in Iraq, was good for us until about 1980, when I was in university." He paused again as he thought how to explain the complications of life to a nine-year-old. "Saddam Hussein had become president of the country. At first, we all thought he would make Iraq a strong, prosperous nation and would be respected as a world leader. We all supported him when he invaded Iran. But soon, things started to get worse. By 1982 Iran damaged our ability to sell oil, which was needed for the war effort and soon many families were losing their fathers and sons." Although he had shielded his daughter from the sadness of the past, he pressed on with his explanation. "My brothers Abdul and Othman—your uncles—both died in this war before you were born. Your mother and I never told you these things because you were just a child, and the memory is very painful for us. But you should know. This is why, when I was offered an opportunity to practice medicine in the United States, we agreed that we should take what God was giving to us, and the rest of our family supported this decision."

"I'm sorry, Daddy, I didn't know." Lara was saddened by what her father told her.

"It is life, Lara. You are much wiser than most children your age, and I knew you would understand this."

"I never want to go to Iraq." Lara looked into her father's eyes with the sincerity and sweetness that little girls have, "Can we always stay here? I always want to live right here."

"Your mother and I may never be able to go back to Iraq, as long as Saddam and his regime are in power." Omar reached out and held Lara's hands. "Maybe someday the country will change, and we can visit Mosul again. I hope that someday you will be able to visit your uncles Nawaf and Salah and meet your cousin Yasmine and maybe even your relatives in Hillah, near the ancient ruins of Babylon." His brief reference to Iraqi history was lost on her.

"How old is Yasmine?"

"She must be about twelve years old by now; she's a few years older than you. I am sure the two of you would become good friends if you could visit her."

Lara shrugged her shoulders and smiled. "Maybe, Daddy. For now I want to be right here with you, Mommy, and Oliver."

Omar playfully grabbed her and gave her a big hug, "Well, Princess

Lara, you have your wish. My little American princess!" Then he grabbed the soccer ball and threw it across the yard for Oliver to chase.

In Iraq, things were not going as well on the soccer field. Although the Iraqi national football team had won the Arab Nations Cup championships in 1985 and 1988, the team had not won a major title since then. After his short exile to Switzerland, Uday returned to a warm welcome from his father. When he was twenty-eight, in 1992, he became the national chairman for the Iraq Olympic and World Cup Committee, with the authority to manage as he saw fit to ensure that the team won the 1994 World Cup. The team members were nervous. Although they were still holding their own at international competitions, they were not winning championships.

"Look sharp!" Abdel, the Head Coach, was organizing the team in a row as the caravan of three Mercedes drove onto the football field. "Put your hands behind your backs and stand straight." He paused and thought for a moment before the cars were near enough for anyone except the team to hear him. Then he added, "Whatever you do, act like you are really happy. Whatever he says, cheer loudly to show you are thrilled that he is your new boss."

"I understand he can be ruthless with people who get on his wrong side." Hashim whispered under his breath as they were waiting for the cars to stop. Hashim, the team's goal keeper, was one of the better players.

"Maybe his influence will help us get the training equipment that we've been asking for," replied Qahtan, who was the lead forward on the team.

"Well, it's wise to be optimistic. Let's hope for the best." Hashim said as he straightened his back.

The cars came to a stop, and as the beefy security guards with AK-47s got out of the first and third black Mercedes, Uday stepped out of the middle car and walked over to the line of men.

"Men, this is His Excellency Uday Hussein your new manager," said coach Abdel with the biggest smile and highest level of feigned excitement that he could muster.

"Men, I am honored to stand before you today as the national chairman for the Iraq Olympic and World Cup Committee. It is my job to lead you to glorious victories on the field and to bring honor to the people of Iraq. It is your job to work hard and win. I will do whatever it takes to inspire you to win. There will be no losing as long as Uday Hussein is leading you."

Immediately coach Abdel and the team began to cheer enthusiastically.

Uday smiled broadly and motioned with his hands to make the men quiet down as he walked up to the first player. "Tell me your name and where you are from." He stood only a foot away from each man and stared directly into each man's eyes with a cold, emotionless gaze. Each member obliged with his name and city, then bowed forward slightly. If a team member was from Tikrit or Mosul, where the Hussein clan was from, Uday would smile slightly. Otherwise, he only nodded. When introductions were completed, Uday addressed the team again, "You may have heard from others that I can be very tough on people who do not measure up to my expectations. That may be true. However, I am fair, and I also have confidence that all of you will exceed my expectations." Then he turned and got back into the car as the team cheered again with all the contrived excitement and happiness that they could muster despite the fear in the pit of their stomachs.

"See, he said he will be fair and that he will do whatever it takes to help us win" said the Qahtan.

Hashim frowned. "Whatever it takes may not be what you think it is. We'll see."

Uday rarely attended the grueling practice sessions that the coaching staff developed and implemented per their new manager's direction. However, he did attend the games. Fortunately, the team won the West Asia Championship that season and Uday was pleased. However, the next season did not begin as well. After a loss in their second game, the coach Abdel cautioned the team that Uday expressed his severe disappointment and indicated that he would begin a more "hands-on" management style if the team lost the next game.

This game started well when the Iraqi team scored first. Soon, the Syrian team evened the score, and each team continued to score, tit for tat, until the latter part of the second half of the game. Then Syria pulled ahead with two scores in a row to lead by one point. A midfielder fed a pass to their forward who made a powerful shot past Hashim. The Iraq forward Ali knew the pressure was on as the team raced toward the Syrian goal and the ball was passed to him. He appeared to have a clear shot when he made a powerful kick just as his planted foot started to slip. The ball careened harmlessly outside the goal area. During the remaining moments of the game, the Syrians controlled the ball and the score remained the same. Uday was furious with what appeared to him as an intentional bad shot by Ali.

As the team filed into the locker room, Abdel pulled Ali and Hashim aside. "Ali, go to Uday's private office. Hashim, you wait here until Uday is finished with Ali." Abdel had a very fearful look on his face, and both Ali and Hashim began to worry. Nothing bad had happened to any of the players before, but now they had lost three games in a row.

Uday' office suite consisted of a luxurious private bathroom and sauna, his executive office, and what appeared to be a massage room. However, the massage table had cuffs for hands and ankles attached to it. Ali knocked timidly on the door.

"Come in." Uday was clearly in a bad mood. "Ali, I think you deliberately missed that last goal shot. Were you playing for Syria today, or Iraq?"

Ali felt a knot in his stomach, "I should have made the shot, sir. My foot slipped as I kicked the ball. I didn't mean to miss." He said fearfully.

"Go into the next room. When you are prepared, I will come in to lecture you on how to win the games for Iraq."

"Yes sir." As he entered the next room, he was immediately grabbed by two large men who pulled his shirt off of him. A third man struck the back of his legs to make him fall to the floor. They picked him up, threw him face down on the table, and cuffed his hands and ankles so he couldn't move.

Uday came into the room as Ali looked over to him with despair in his eyes. The heavy soundproof door closed with an ominous thud. "Ali, you missed the goal today. I am not happy." Several sturdy thorn branches were lying on it. Uday picked one up, studied it for a moment, and swished it in the air as if it were a sword. He had an evil smile on his face as he turned and walked over to Ali's bared back and whacked it with the branch. Ali gasped in surprise and pain. Uday could see that the thorns were already making the back bleed. "Your team is not happy!" Uday raised the branch back and whacked his back again. This time, Ali screamed out in agony. "I am being kind to you today." Uday said in a more conciliatory tone. "You are forgiven. But you will not miss another goal. Do you understand?"

Ali agreed instantly, "Yes sir! Yes sir!"

The smile returned to Uday's face as he hit Ali's back even harder, drawing more blood. The sting of each blow was intense, but now predictable. Ali did his best to control his scream, but tears were forming around his eyes. Uday walked over to where Ali could see him at the head of the table. "That was for good measure. You will not forget our little motivational speech, will you Ali?"

As Uday walked toward the back of the table, Ali whimpering quietly, "No, sir. I will play harder for the team."

Uday whacked his back again as the blood ran freely down the ragged cuts that were made by the thorns and Ali screamed again in surprise and pain.

This time in a very loud and menacing voice, Uday almost shouted, "I didn't hear you, Ali!"

With a note of desperate terror, Ali shouted back, "I will play harder for the team! I swear!"

"Good! I know you will!" Uday regained his composure. "Take him out of here." The three men took off the cuffs, but when Ali tried to stand up, he slumped to the floor in pain. The men carried him out. "The team isn't scheduled for their next practice until three days from now, so he will have a little time to recover." When you get him in the car, take him to the team barracks. Get Hashim. He's waiting in the locker room."

"Yes, sir," said one of the guards.

"And," Uday, paused for a moment as he thought of the possibilities, "when I'm done with Hashim, maybe if I feel like it, I'll have you fetch Abdel so I can provide some motivation to him."

Fear did motivate the team, which was able to win enough games on a regular basis to mollify Uday.The motivational torture continued when one or another team member displeased him on the field. However, Uday knew that if he injured his players too much, they would be worthless on the field. In October, 2003, Iraq won against Iran in the first round of qualifiers for the World Cup. All was well with the team and Uday. Then, in the final round, Iraq lost to North Korea, 2–3. The team was fearful again. By now they knew but would not speak the fact that Uday was a psychopath.

The match took place in Doha, Qatar on October 28, and the team was back in Iraq and told to muster at their home stadium in Baghdad on the following day. Curiously, on the running track not far from where they were standing, there was an open sewer hole, with the cover removed. No one paid any attention to the sewer opening when the cover was on it, but on this day it was strange that it was uncovered. Coach Abdel had the team lined up, as was customary when Uday came to talk with them. "Whatever happens today, I want you to know that I think you all performed remarkably well in Doha. We didn't win the finals, but we came very close and Uday should be happy with this."

The team looked behind Abdel. They saw the line of new cars drive onto the soccer field and screech to a stop. Uday got out of the lead car and strode purposely up to the coach, who suddenly looked anxious and nervous. Everyone could see that Uday was very angry and they all tensed up with fear. Behind him was the World Cup 1994 banner.

Uday didn't waste any time, "You lazy dogs! You have betrayed Iraq, and you betrayed me by failing even to qualify! I blame myself for being too soft on you children. Now I will show you what must be done to win next time!" Uday had watched all of the players perform at the Doha finals and noted that one of the younger team members seemed to be on the field less than the others. Uday pointed to him and his henchmen walked up to the terrified young man, threw him down and tied one end of a rope to his feet and the other end to the back of Uday's Mercedes-Benz G-Class SUV. "This lazy son of a whore did nothing on the field, and when he did play, two goals were made by the North Koreans. I want to show you what this worthless pig deserves."

Uday got back into his car and began driving, slowly at first, then faster, on the gravel track that circled the field, dragging the screaming player behind him. After one lap around the stadium, Uday stopped by the open sewer hole. The young man was bloodied and limp, but still barely conscious of what was going on around him. Uday's thugs got out of the SUV and untied him as the rest of the team looked on in horror. Uday then stepped out of the car and shouted loudly and angrily toward the rest of the team, "Throw this worthless shit into the sewer where it belongs."

The thugs dragged the man over to the hole as he screamed for his life, then threw him into it. The team members said nothing as Uday and his entourage of thugs went back into their cars and drove off the field.

Chapter Seven: Lara Is Growing Up and Uday Has a Bad Day 1996

This was Lara's first day of eighth grade and she was very much an American 13-year-old teen. The Al-Mohammed family had comfortably settled into their community. Although the memories of their family in Iraq were as strong as ever, the desire to return there had faded with time and the safety, security, and comfort they found in Ann Arbor.

"Good morning, students; welcome to eighth grade. My name is Mrs. Jones. Before we begin, let's go around the room and introduce yourselves and tell us where you are from since many of you are new to Adams Junior High School."

"My name is John Rachee, and my family moved to Ann Arbor this summer from Houston, Texas."

"My name is Lynn Chan, and we moved here from San Francisco."

"Harry Smith, from Ann Arbor."

"Lara Al-Mohammed, from Ann Arbor."

"Excuse me, Lara," said Mrs. Jones, "are you sure you're from Ann Arbor? Your name doesn't sound like your family would be from here."

"I'm from Ann Arbor, but my parents are from Iraq."

Mrs. Jones was a bit indignant, "Hah! I thought so. Lara, you're from Iraq, not Ann Arbor." Then she turned to the next student.

That evening at the family dinner table, Lara was quiet and sad. Omar noticed this. "Lara, how was your first day of school?"

"It was OK." She said in a soft voice while looking down at her plate.

Nadia was concerned, "You don't look OK. What's wrong?"

"My new teacher, Mrs. Jones told me that I'm from Iraq and not Ann Arbor. Mom, I've always been from Ann Arbor. Why did she say that I was from Iraq?"

Omar frowned a bit, "Honey, you're as much an American as Mrs. Jones. But you are *also* from Iraq. You know that you were born in Iraq, and your mom and I are both Iraqi. So, you are as much Iraqi as American."

"Is that a good thing?"

Omar considered the question for a moment, "Lara, the Iraqi civilization is 5,000 years old. Your ancestors built Nineveh where Mosul is now, the ancient walled city of Hatra not far from Mosul, and a citadel which was an ancient fortress in Erbil, 200 miles from Mosul. They were building cities in Mesopotamia and Babylon long before the Europeans moved to America. Some of our extended family is from the town of Hillah, near the Babylonian ruins. The written word, books, arithmetic, astronomy—all of these were developed in what is now Iraq long before the Pilgrims landed on Plymouth Rock. You have much to be proud of as a daughter of Iraq. But you have much to be proud of as an American. Don't let anyone tell you that you are only one or another. You are the best of Iraq and America, and we are very proud of you."

"Daddy, even though I can speak Arabic and you and Mom told me stories about when you were growing up, I feel like I really don't know that much about Mosul, Iraq, or my relatives there."

"Maybe when you finish high school in five years, things will be better in Iraq and you can visit your Uncle Nawaf and Aunt Mohassin, cousins Yasmine and Shalan, and the rest of the family."

Nadia became very concerned with the direction of the conversation, for different reasons. "Is that a good idea, Omar?"

"We'll see. The war between Iraq and Iran is over. Thanks to America and Desert Storm, Saddam Hussein and his regime are much more restricted than they were. Five years is still a long time from now. When Lara is a senior in high school, we'll ask your brothers what they think about the idea."

Lara smiled at the thought of an adventurous trip to Iraq to visit her relatives someday. "Maybe I would like that."

Omar liked the possibility also. There wasn't much bad news coming from Mosul lately. Despite the fact that the Ba'athists were still killing Iraqis with their helicopters and ground forces elsewhere in Iraq, the

American-imposed "no-fly zone" appeared to have muted the danger from Saddam and his supporters a bit, especially in Mosul, despite its very large population of Ba'athists. As long as the United States continued to make the Ba'athists nervous, perhaps it would be safe in five years for Lara to visit her extended family. "Continue working hard at school, Lara. If your uncles think it will be safe for you to visit them and you do well with your studies, perhaps as a reward for your hard work, you'll get to visit Mosul when you graduate." He smiled wistfully as he reflected on his teen years, "Time passes quickly. I remember when I graduated from high school and went off to Baghdad University. It was exciting to go to the university back then. My friends and I had many good times."

Although the situation in Iraq was relatively quiet, there was still terror. Even without wars with Iran and the United States, Saddam Hussein ruthlessly continued to brutalize the Iraqi population. Uday and Qusay both developed their own brand of evil traits.

Compared to Uday, younger brother Qusay was the lesser evil. However, he also was a cold-blooded killer to whom Saddam entrusted with the pacification of the Shiite majority in the southern provinces of Iraq after the first US Gulf War, Operation Desert Storm. It was known that he had personally killed Shiite prisoners and ordered the mass execution of hundreds, if not thousands, of men and sometimes, their families. People lived in fear. When Qusay was commanding the Republican Guard and Special Security Organization, husbands, brothers, and fathers would simply disappear. Omar and Nadia would not learn until much later that Nadia's cousin Ibrahim, from Hillah, and his brother Mohammed were two of the men who vanished as a result of Qusay's orders. This consigned Ibrahim's wife Rinad and daughter Nagham to life of poverty on their small farm in Babylon Province.

Those who died at Uday's hands suffered horrific levels of brutality and torture, for he personally derived sadistic pleasure from what he did. He was particularly known for abducting young girls and women, raping them, and frequently torturing and murdering them. He had already established a reputation for evil as a young man. When Uday was thirty-two-years old, he became much worse. Many in Iraq were willing to risk everything to see him dead.

Thursday evening, December 12, 1996 at about seven p.m., was like many other occasions. Uday drove his most recent acquisition, a new golden Porsche 911 convertible with the top down, into the area known as Mansour, near the Baghdad University district. Here many of the students would party at the disco bars and night clubs after a week of studies, even though Fridays were recognized as the Islamic holy day each week. Uday was followed at a distance by two Mercedes-Benz G-32 class SUVs with four body guards. The SUVs parked behind Uday's car in front of one of the more popular establishments, known for its large dance floor and many coeds. He got out of the Porsche and walked purposefully into the club. As Uday was entering the club, his bodyguards followed at a discreet distance. They knew the drill—and the outcome for the evening. The club owner also knew the drill. When he saw Uday walk in, a table next to the dance floor was immediately cleared to give Uday and his party a good view of all the dancers so Uday could pick his "girl friends" for the evening.

Abdul, the lead bodyguard, smiled as he looked at the dancing and observed a large selection of coeds, which his boss might be interested in. "The start of the university year is always a good time."

Uday was also looking at the crowd and noted four young women on the dance floor dancing together and enjoying their new-found freedom away from the watchful eyes of parents and relatives. "Yes, I always enjoy watching them have a good time," He replied to Abdul as he continued to watch the girls dance. Before long, he caught the eye of a pretty coed who smiled at him. She obviously was enjoying herself and the music. It only took a moment for Uday to assess his targets, get up, walk over to the group, and start dancing with the four young women. The girls let him dance with them, and when the dance ended he went back to the table where the bodyguards were sitting. Nodding in the direction of the girls, he gave the men his orders, "I think they would like to party with me. I'll meet you at the palace."

Abdul smiled and immediately replied, "Yes sir."

As the four big, well-dressed, and intimidating men walked over to the four young women, Uday watched from the table as Abdul introduced himself. "Excuse me," he said as his three colleagues surrounded the coeds, "you are very blessed tonight. Mr. Uday Hussein would like to invite you to his palace for a party." Abdul looked over to where Uday was sitting and the girls looked at him with some confusion in their eyes. Uday smiled warmly at them and they smiled back. However, one of them was hesitant and concerned about what they may be getting themselves into with this seemingly friendly but obviously very powerful man.

"This is exciting! Let's go, this will be fun!" Alla, the young lady who had first smiled at Uday, urged the others.

Nadia, the cautious one, gave Alla a nudge with her elbow and spoke quietly, "I don't know, Alla. I've heard bad stories about his parties."

Alla was too excited about meeting a son of Saddam Hussein and being very near one of the best-known men in Iraq, "Come on, we'll have a good time!"

The four girls started walking with the bodyguards. Uday got up from the table and walked briskly ahead of them to the door and outside to his parked Porsche. When the four men and young women got to the door of the club, the men formed a circle around the girls and started herding them to the SUVs.

Nadia became panicky and her face quickly changed to a look of foreboding and fear as the men started to push them to the open doors of the lead SUV. At that moment, Uday began to drive away in his Porsche when three men on the side of the street pulled AK-47s from their sports bags and sprayed the car and Uday with a massive hail of gun fire.

The guards immediately diverted their attention from the girls and pulled out their guns from under their sports coats to shoot the attackers. However, the attack was planned well; at the same moment, another car pulled up, and the three gunmen jumped into the getaway car and sped safely away before the bodyguards had a chance to fire a shot. The attackers did their work and were speeding away.

The would-be assassins made a good attempt. Uday was critically wounded, but not dead. The girls all scattered from the guards and disappeared into the night.

Several months later in a hospital room, Uday was standing in pain with the help of a walker. He was attended by a doctor, nurse, Qusay, and his mother, Saljida.

Uday, took a few painful steps with the walker. Saljida winced as she watched him suffer from his injuries, "Uday, my son, you are making good progress. Soon you will be walking and dancing again."

"The doctors tell me that you will walk again but you may not be able to dance at the disco clubs like you did before." Qusay said, "However, you have been avenged. The traitors have been captured and I've dealt with them," he added with a serious look on his face.

Wincing in pain as he took another step, Uday uttered, "They all deserve to die for what they've done to me."

"Our intelligence forces did a good job. The traitors and their families have already been dealt with, just as we've dealt with the thousands of other traitors over the last five years. We are very efficient when it comes to dealing with these people."

"I know. Saddam likes to brag about your accomplishments to me." Uday said, with a bit of cynical envy in his voice.

Chapter Eight:
Revenge

Abu Zahrar drove the old Toyota Land Cruiser with the assassination team organizer, Abu Ahmed, and the two other gunmen, Abu Sadeq and Abu Sajad, who earlier sprayed Uday and his Porsche with one hundred rounds from their AK-47s which they received from Iranian sympathizers. The names they assumed for this operation, were all pseudonyms, in order to disguise their true identities and protect their families in case anyone was caught. They were part of a very secretive Shiite Muslim resistance group, the "15 Shaaban Movement", named for the day in the Muslim calendar when the Shiite uprising began after the 1991 Gulf War.

The four very anxious men headed from the university district and traveled south, toward the small town of Mahmudiyah, about twenty minutes from the city. They turned off the main highway and sped down a dirt road to a small farm that had a small house and several outbuildings, including a shed big enough to hide the Land Cruiser. They drove it through the open door into the shed, and a moment later, the four men hurried outside, closed the door, and ran to the house.

Abu Zahrar breathed a huge sigh of relief when the door was shut behind them, "We did it!"

"*Alhamd lillah*!" the three others gasped in response. None of them could believe their good fortune; they had just killed one of the most hated and notorious members of the Hussein family, and they were alive to thank God for it.

The owner of the farm, Abdullah, was excited. "Tell me all about it!" as he offered the men chairs and hot tea. "No, wait a moment! Let me run over to Ibrahim's house and bring him here. It will only take a minute, and he will also want to know how you killed him." Ibrahim owned the farm next door. His father and brother had both been murdered under Uday's direction.

As Abdullah headed for the door, Abu Ahmed grabbed his arm. "No, Abdullah!" No one must know anything. We will only tell you because of your bravery and loyalty. If anyone, other than you, learns who we are and what we did tonight, all of us and our families will be rounded up and killed." Abu Ahmed looked into Abdullah's eyes and said with a very calm and serious voice, "Abdullah, will you swear to Allah that you will not tell anyone what we will share with you this evening?"

Abdullah, slowly nodded his head, recognizing the gravity of the situation and the oath that he was asked to make, "Yes, I swear...I understand."

Abu Ahmed smiled, "Good!" Let's sit down and we'll tell you about our adventure in Mansour." The discussion was animated as each member of the team talked about their part in the evening's activities. There were frequent interruptions as one or another member excitedly interjected his perspective on a particular instant of action of the one-minute event. Abdullah asked many questions, and everyone was happy to reply, with some embellishment, as each member's actions grew in importance and drama. By the end of a very long night, everyone was relaxed, tired, and very happy.

After they awoke the following day, during a light breakfast Abu Ahmed told Abdullah what he must do after they departed for another location, which he would not disclose to their host. "Abdullah, remember the oath that you made last night. You must not tell anyone that we were here last night or the conversation that...didn't happen." After pausing a moment to let this advice make an impression with Abdullah, Abu continued, "As soon as we are gone, Abdullah, late tonight, if possible, get rid of the Toyota. Make sure you wash it and wipe the inside to remove any of our fingerprints and drive it into an empty lot in a nearby village or drive it into the Euphrates and take a bus home." There was another pause. "Do you understand, Abdullah? If the authorities find that Toyota and track it back to you or us, we will all be killed, and probably, so will our families." He looked at Abdullah with piercing eyes, to ensure there was no mistaking the directions that he had just given.

Abdullah nodded, "Yes, Abu Ahmed. I understand completely. It will be done." After breakfast and their brief conversation, he drove them in his very old 1965 Opel Kadett to the bus station near Mahmudiyah.

The four men boarded the bus headed for Basrah, changed busses in Nasariyah, and took a connecting bus to Suq-ash-Shuyukh. This small town was on the edge of the Mesopotamian marshes, which bordered Iran. The 15 Shaaban Movement used the marshes as their base of operations. The Shiite marsh Arabs were sympathetic to the resistance, for the Ba'athists were destroying their homeland, the marshes where they had lived for centuries. Saddam had aggressively expanded the drainage of the vast watershed during the war with Iran and continued the policy through the 1990s to create lands for agriculture and oil exploration. The project created an environmental disaster, reducing the natural habitat by 90 percent over forty years and displacing most of the inhabitants in the process. However, the remaining marsh lands were still significant, and the people living there were very willing to shelter and hide the resistance fighters. They would move them on their boats from one remote village to the next in order to keep Qusay Hussein and his Special Security Organization from tracking them. The four men disappeared into the marshlands and lived to fight again.

When Abdullah returned from delivering the men to the local bus stop, he proceeded with his workday on the farm as if nothing happened. That evening, he was exhausted from the previous evening. The adrenaline from the event had kept him going during the day, but before dark, he felt too tired to think of moving the Toyota and went to bed.

The following day he woke to what would be another day on the farm. All was quiet, except for the normal sounds of his animals. All day long, he considered options for disposing of the Toyota. By evening, he decided that the time was not right for moving it from his shed. No one had come by the farm, and everything was as it had been before Abu Ahmed and his men visited. Perhaps, he thought, it would be best to wait a few days before he disposed of the car. The radio already announced that Uday Hussein had survived a terrorist assassination attempt and his brother, Qusay, had mobilized all the forces at his disposal to find the perpetrators. Abdullah reconsidered the options and decided it would be best to mind his own business and hope that the crises would pass.

After a month passed uneventfully, Abdullah began to feel some relief, even smug. He was part of a historic event and felt good about this. Soon after the visit, he began visiting with his neighbors and friends again, as he had always done. Many in the area were related by their tribal and extended families. In the immediate area, there were probably ten small farms, with an average family size of about ten including wives and children. Abdullah was the only bachelor because his wife had died young, without any children. Perhaps for this reason the 15 Shabaab Movement recruited him for their operation.

He and his friends talked about the normal things of life that affected them all—weather, family, and the latest events of the day coming from Baghdad. Abdullah was careful not to mention his recent activities or the Toyota in the shed.

One day, his neighbor Ibrahim stopped by to ask a favor, "Abdullah, my car isn't working and I need to go to town to buy some parts; can I borrow your car?"

Abdullah smiled. Ibrahim had been a good friend for years, and he was happy to help him out, "Sure. The key is where it always is, in the shed." As soon as he said this, Ibrahim began to walk to the shed a few feet away, and Abdullah panicked when he remembered what was also inside. "Oh, no!...Ibrahim," he shouted desperately.

Ibrahim was startled by Abdullah's panicked voice as he opened the shed door. On the door was the key, but when he looked inside he also saw the Toyota Land Cruiser. "Abdullah, where did you get this?" Such a vehicle, even though it was more than ten years old, would be impossible for a poor farmer from Mahmudiyah to afford. It would cost more than the income from three years of work on the farm.

Abdullah felt his stomach knotting from fear. When he saw the surprise and bafflement on Ibrahim's face he almost vomited. "Ibrahim, please shut the shed door and come into the house. I have something very important to tell you."

"You have a Land Cruiser!" Ibrahim stated incredulously.

"Come into the house now! We must talk!" Abdullah demanded in a loud and slightly threatening voice.

Once inside, Abdullah told his very good friend everything. He could not lie, and he was too unsettled to invent a story at the spur of the moment. "So you understand, Ibrahim, that we must not tell anyone of this or we all could be killed."

"What are you going to do?" asked Ibrahim.

"I've been waiting for the excitement over the assassination attempt to settle down before getting rid of the thing, but now I think I must do something. I don't want to put any of us at risk by having it in the area." He thought a moment, "Abu Ahmed did suggest that we drive it into the river." He considered the possibility, "Three nights from now, there will be a new moon, with very little light." Looking at Ibrahim with almost pleading eyes, he asked, "Ibrahim, if I drive the Toyota over the bluff at the bend of the Euphrates, near where we used to swim as kids, would you follow me and take me home?"

"You're asking me to do a very dangerous thing," Ibrahim gasped. He thought for a moment about his wife and five children, including two teenage sons and three daughters.

"Ibrahim, your father and brother were killed by the Ba'athists." Abdullah paused, trying to think of what would make Ibrahim risk his life, "Your help will contribute to the eventual destruction of the Saddam Hussein family and what it represents. My friends were able to send a strong message that the Husseins will answer for all the killing that has taken place during the last twenty years." He looked into Ibrahim's eyes, "Help me avenge the deaths of your father and brother."

Ibrahim weighed the risk and the satisfaction of helping to bring justice to the Hussein family for what they did to his family, "I'll drive you back from the Euphrates," he said slowly and deliberately.

Three days later, Abdullah opened the shed door and looked up at the sky before going inside. It was past midnight, and the sky was darker than usual. However, it was cloudless, so millions of stars provided some light even though the new moon was completely dark. "Good." Abdullah said to himself. If there was any night to drive the Toyota into the river, this was it. At this time of night almost no cars would be on the road, no one near the embankment on the Euphrates where he planned to push the SUV over the edge into a ten-meter-deep fishing hole in the narrow bed in the river. The swift current continually dredged the soft sand below, making the hole deeper.

He drove to Ibrahim's house and flashed his lights. After a moment, Ibrahim started up his old car and turned on his lights. Abdullah took the back roads as much as possible, turning left, left again across an irrigation canal, another left, then along a country road that passed large sections of open fields of alfalfa that was just starting to sprout. The road went on for several miles until he turned right onto a divided road, then took another two-lane road that would lead to the bridge across the Euphrates. The entire route would take less than an hour. When Abdullah came to the bridge, a sleepy young man was standing there. Abdullah felt his stomach twist from fear as he slowed down. The man looked at him for a moment and waved at him as if he was hoping for a ride. Abdullah ignored him and kept on driving. Ibrahim followed soon after. Both men breathed a sigh of relief as they crossed the river to the other side and drove another 100 meters to a small unpaved turnoff toward the deserted embankment where the SUV would be pushed into the river.

Abdullah worried about the young man they passed near the bridge. Why was he there at that time of night? He could only surmise that he was a local farm boy trying to get a ride home. It seemed strange that he would be there in the middle of the night, but it was not that unusual. The small dirt road turned left then right as it followed the river past several farm houses for about a mile. The stars lit the way enough so they could leave their headlights off. However the cars frequently braked to avoid ruts in the road or the occasional goat wandering around near the houses. Soon they came to a very narrow dirt trail another mile beyond the houses. There was nothing in the area other than the trail, barely wide enough for the Land Cruiser. It continued about three hundred meters to the river embankment that was approximately fifteen feet above the water.

Abdullah and Ibrahim knew this area well. As teenagers, they would take a small boat and float down the Euphrates on languid April days, before the weather got too hot. In this area the river picked up speed as its two branches passed on either side of an island and converged again at this curve. Here, the river ran fast and deep. The men got out of their cars, and Abdullah rolled down all of the windows and opened all of the doors in the Land Cruiser so the water would quickly rush in and let it sink like a rock to the bottom of the channel. The car was driven to within a foot of the embankment and set in neutral. The land was flat there, so both men got behind the SUV and pushed hard. It rolled over the edge and careened down the steep hill into the water below. The strong current grabbed it and in a moment pulled it into the channel and under the water. "*Alhamd lillah,*" both men said quietly as it sank below the surface of the water. The night was very quiet where they were.

"Thank you for helping me, Ibrahim," Abdullah said as he patted his friend on the back.

"It is finished. No Toyota, no evidence. We can both put this behind us." Ibrahim said, with a hopeful smile.

They both got into Ibrahim's car and drove slowly back to the main road. When they got to the intersection with the road toward the bridge, they looked both ways and, as with their dangerous drive to the river, no other car or truck lights were visible. Ibrahim turned onto the road and drove toward the bridge. When they started crossing the river, Ibrahim noticed a set of headlights in his rear view mirror. When he turned his eyes to the road again, they both noticed the young man with three others standing to block them. This time, the young man had an AK-47, as did the others.

An older man in a uniform stood to the right of the others, then stepped in front of their car and held up his fist signaling Ibrahim to stop. Both men panicked. What could they do? Their minds were racing to think of an escape from this trap. At the same moment, the car that pulled up behind them stopped and four Special Security Organization men stepped out with their guns drawn and pointed at them. Even if jumping off the bridge was an option, it was too late.

"My corporal, Abdul, told me that he saw you drive by here an hour ago in a Toyota Land Cruiser." Abdul nodded with a stern glare that was much different from the sleepy look that he had when they crossed the bridge earlier. "He said that he watched your tail lights blink off and on as you turned off the road and headed up to the curve of the river," the older man said.

Abdul smiled and interjected, "The night is dark but it was easy to follow your taillights, even from this distance." Clearly, Abdul was beginning to realize what he had done and how it might influence his career with the Republican Guard.

"My name is Colonel Afzhal." I am under the direction of Qusay Hussein. He instructed the Republican Guard to post men at every possible check point in Iraq to look for a white 1985 Toyota Land Cruiser. It was the escape vehicle for the attempted assassination of Uday Hussein." What color was the Land Cruiser that you were driving, and where is it?"

Ibrahim and Abdullah stood silent for what seemed like a very long time as the seven men who surrounded them all raised their guns and pointed at them. Abdullah finally spoke with a firm but resigned voice, "I drove the Toyota. It is white."

"Where is it?" the Colonel insisted.

Abdullah paused again, knowing that he was facing imminent death, "It is in the river. It was not mine, and I asked my friend to help me get rid of it."

"Who owned it?"

"I don't know. It was abandoned on my farm."

"We are going to drag it from the river, and if it matches the description of the assassin's getaway car, you will be charged as a traitor to Iraq and dealt with accordingly."

"My friend knew nothing. I asked him to help me get rid of the car, and he did!" Abdullah said in an almost tearful voice.

"Your friend is an accomplice and is as guilty as you. We will trace your friend's car registration to where both of you live. Then we will round up the other accomplices and bring all of you to justice."

"There were no other accomplices! Just me, I swear!" Abdullah pleaded.

"You can tell your story to his honor, Qusay Hussein, later today. His office has already been notified, and preparations are being made for him to meet us this afternoon." The colonel looked at both of the men and shook his head, "Take them to Mahmudiyah!"

Immediately, Abdullah and Ibrahim had their hands cuffed behind their backs and were shoved into the police car behind them. As the car drove off the bridge, a Republican Guard Toyota Land Cruiser with the colonel and young Abdul pulled in front of them. A truck with the rest of the men pulled in behind to form a caravan. All three vehicles turned on their flashing lights and sirens in the middle of the night, announcing in their way that this group was very important.

The caravan arrived at the police station in Mahmudiyah at about six a.m., and both accused men were thrown in a jail cell. By ten a.m., divers were able to find the car in the river and confirm the age of the Toyota but noted there was no registration or plates. At about the same time, Ibrahim's car was traced to his home, and the Special Security men were able to ascertain that Abdullah lived nearby.

The Special Security men took over. Abdullah and Ibrahim, each in their turn, were brought into a room next to their jail cell. The script was the same for both men.

"Who are your accomplices?"

"I didn't have any," said Abdullah.

"Liar!" Whack! A brass-knuckled fist crashed into the side of his jaw, breaking three teeth.

"Who gave you the Toyota?"

"I found it on my farm. I don't know," Abdullah mumbled from his bloodied mouth and broken teeth.

"Liar!" Another blow came to the other side of his face, this time near his eye. Blood was soon pouring from a jagged gash.

The pummeling of both men continued for three hours until the midafternoon, when Qusay and his entourage of four trucks and twenty heavily armed men arrived. As he walked into the police station, all eyes turned to him, and the men stood at attention. Abdullah and Ibrahim were dragged into the room and held up by their tormentors, since they could no longer stand on their own.

"Bad, bad men," Qusay said in a low, menacing tone as he looked at both of them. "Who are your accomplices that tried to kill my brother?"

"We've been asking them this question for the last four hours, sir. They won't tell us," said the colonel.

"Well," Qusay paused a moment for effect, "we know where their homes are. Probably their families and the neighbors next to them were all in on this traitorous action." Qusay paused again. "Let's all go there and gather them up. Perhaps we will get an answer if we have them all together."

"No! They don't know anything!" both men pleaded as they were dragged out of the building and loaded into the back of a truck, along with five armed guards.

Soon the caravan stopped in front of Ibrahim's house, and the men burst into his home and searched his farm to gather up his wife and children. Within a few minutes, they were all standing in front of the house, looking bewildered, and were horrified when they saw their father and Abdullah barely kneeling, thoroughly beaten and bloodied.

Meanwhile the other trucks and men fanned out to the nearest five farms. They gathered the families and workers that were found in the area and brought them back to where Qusay and the rest were waiting.

As the thirty frightened and confused people—men, boys, women, and children of all ages—were dragged from the trucks, Abdullah and Ibrahim continued to plead: "They had nothing to do with it. They don't know where the truck came from!" Abdullah, in desperation, began to add, "There were four of them. They were all named Abu. I took them to the bus station, and that was the last I saw of them. I don't know where they went to!" He begged, "Please let everyone go! They had nothing to do with this! I am the guilty one!"

Qusay had his revolver in his hand and walked up to Abdullah. "Bad, bad man," he said calmly as he pointed the gun to Abdullah's head and fired at point-blank range. Abdullah fell over, dead. "Well," Qusay paused again, "what is your name?"

"Ibrahim." He was looking at his family, friends, and neighbors,."Sir, please, they had nothing to do with this." He was sobbing. "Abdullah told you the truth. The assassins came to his farm house, left their getaway car there, and disappeared on a bus the next day."

"Why would these men come here, unless they had collaborators?" Qusay paused again, "I think many of you have been collaborators in this hideous crime against Uday, and you all must pay the price." He raised his pistol again, shot Ibrahim in the back of the head, then walked toward his car. When he got into the car, started it, and opened the window, he gave one last order to his men: "Kill them all!" As he sped away, the remaining henchmen lined up the thirty innocent men, women, and children and opened fire with their AK-47s, murdering them all within a minute after Qusay's departure.

Qusay explained the search and destruction of the alleged ring of assassins to Uday and his mother. Despite his pain, Uday smiled. "Qusay, I'm glad you're in charge of the security forces. You are very good at your job." Then he thought back to his mother's comment about dancing in the clubs of Baghdad. "Yes, Mother, I'll have private disco parties at my Dreamland palace near Fallujah."

Chapter Nine: Back in Business

Uday slowly recovered from his wounds. Although his body was now weaker, his evil personality had only grown stronger, as manifested in his search for sadistic and heartless pleasure. Due to his injuries and the ascension of Qusay as Saddam Hussein's trusted heir apparent, Uday withdrew from the center stage that was Baghdad. In 1999, he preferred his Dreamland palace and resort complex, "*Ard al'aham*" in Arabic, that was located about forty miles from Baghdad, on the outskirts of Fallujah. His palace was on an island near one end of a picturesque lake. A large swath of land surrounded the lake and contained many small one- or two-room cottages, a large area for camping, and an open-air nightclub and disco bar. At night many strings of festively glittering lights reflected off the lake, which was just beyond the large, outside dance floor. Before Uday began frequently staying at the palace, the estate was primarily a business interest for the Hussein family, promoted on Iraqi TV as "Dreamland." It was a pleasant area, which attracted families to it as a vacation resort. When Uday realized that it was conveniently located less than an hour from the Mansour District of Baghdad, he decided that "Dreamland" offered the most convenient, least public palace for him to pursue his interests. Despite his near-death experience there, Mansour was his favorite area to troll for young coeds.

Iraqi coeds were not his only prey. Uday enlisted his large staff of trusted henchmen to attract a variety of women for his pleasure from near and far. At the time, the countries of the former Soviet Union were near economic collapse, and many young women were attracted to Iraq by the promise of good-paying jobs.

Uday certainly enjoyed the variety of women. Despite his injuries, he was not inhibited about dancing at the Dreamland disco. Most of the time, he was in the mood to take whomever he liked from the dance floor to his palace bedroom on the other side of the lake. No one who refused ever lived to tell about it.

It was early May; the evening air on the lake was still comfortably warm but not too hot for Uday to host a party with his bodyguards. It was attended by ten very attractive women who had arrived the previous week from Ukraine and Russia. They came to Iraq with the promise of jobs on the Dreamland estate as housekeepers, cooks, and receptionists. When they arrived, they were told to rest for a few days to recover from their flights. Several days passed, and they still had not been directed to their new jobs or told what their responsibilities would be. Six days after arriving, they were bored with their situation and becoming a bit suspicious and anxious about why they were there in the first place.

The invitation to attend a party at the disco hosted by the son of Saddam Hussein lifted their spirits. They were especially enthusiastic when they were given a choice of several new, attractive, sexy-looking Western evening gowns to wear at the party. Since Uday was hosting this party, they anticipated meeting a variety of interesting guests but were quickly crushed when they were escorted to a few tables by the dance floor. Uday, whom they had never met before this evening, and several of his very large and not particularly attractive friends were the only other attendees. They were all offered strong cocktails and were soon talking among themselves, pretending to have a good time. Uday and his men watched from the small bar at the other end of the dance floor and sipped on their drinks as they watched the young women. Uday took his time to consider his options for his first conquest of the evening.

Despite the unusual situation, the women were in a lovely location. The surrounding area was well landscaped, with date palms and many colorful bougainvillea plants. Although the disco was not impressive, the view across the lake toward the setting sun was breathtaking. The disco's location was interesting. It was at the end of a lagoon that was almost enclosed on both sides by what appeared to be narrow land-bridges; these were connected by a fifty-foot wooden bridge that appeared to have a gazebo-shaped cage. The cage was part of a curious contraption connected to a hoist that could move it into and out of the lagoon. The women realized that Iraq was already a very curious place for them, and their strong drinks helped them enjoy the view and ignore the cage. They just assumed that it was used for fishing or other such sporting activity.

"Where did you find them?" Uday asked his "chief acquisition specialist," whom he liked to call Igor. He was a former Communist Party enforcer in Russia who needed a new job after the Soviet Union collapsed. He moved to Iraq and made his credentials known to the right people among the Ba'athists. Before long he found a new boss with the same ruthless instincts as his previous employers. Uday and Igor developed a good working relationship, well suited for Uday's various requirements.

"They're from Ukraine and Russia, and they were cheap! I told them they would come and live very well working for you in a palace." Igor smiled, as he stood next to his boss, who was sitting at a table, sipping his third Scotch. The women were all dancing among themselves, enjoying popular Russian and Ukrainian music that was selected especially for this evening.

Uday was also smiling, "Did they know what kind of work?"

"No sir," Igor chuckled softly under his breath. "I thought you would enjoy telling them yourself."

"I think I will join the fun." Uday said, with a small grimace as he slowly stood up from his chair and limped over to where the women were dancing. The DJ who was managing the recorded music knew the drill. When Uday got up, it was his cue to end the music so the women would return to their tables and make it easier for Uday to walk over to greet each of them. As the women sat down, they looked at the man limping toward them, and wondered who he was. Clearly he was in some pain, and one of them could not help staring at him as he slowly made his way to their table. She also caught Uday's eye, and he decided to sit down next to her.

"Welcome to my home," He said to all of the women at the table. Then he looked directly at the woman sitting next to him, "I am Uday Hussein. What is your name?"

"Tamara Stetsenko," she said shyly. Tamara was about twenty years old, about five feet six inches tall, with dyed blond hair, and very pretty.

"Nice to meet you, Tamara. How do you like Iraq?"

Tamara knew only a few words of English. Uday couldn't speak Russian, so they both struggled to communicate in the one language that both knew a little. "I never seen anything like it. No beautiful place like this in Ukraine, in middle of desert. We only arrive last week and you treat us like special guests," Tamara said with a thick Slavic accent.

"I'm glad you like it here." Uday nodded in the direction of the DJ, who obediently started another Ukrainian song. "Will you dance with me?"

Tamara smiled and got up to dance. Uday also struggled a bit to stand up and began to dance with her. She frowned again. It was clear Uday was crippled and "danced" in a series of awkward, unnatural jerks. She danced with slow, languid moves, but she could not help staring at him; although she tried to look happy, her smile was forced. She was clearly not enjoying herself. Uday noticed this and stared at her coldly. He stopped dancing in the middle of the song, and the music stopped with him.

"You don't like my dancing?"

Tamara frowned and looked embarrassed. She lowered her gaze to her feet and said nothing.

"Perhaps you would like to see my moves in the bedroom?"

She was startled by this statement. Although she didn't understand him very well, "bedroom" was in her English vocabulary. "Sir, I am very good cook. I was told that you have job for me here in your kitchen."

"No, I have a better job for you. Let's go, and I'll show you."

Her eyes widened with fear. "No, sir. I am a cook. That is why I am here!"

Uday was instantly enraged by her protestations, "A cook! I'll show you what we will cook tonight!" He grabbed her arm and, instinctively, she pulled it away from him.

He gave her a very cold stare and turned to his nearest bodyguard. "Take her to the cage, and we will all watch what gets cooked up when I'm not happy!"

Two beefy bodyguards grabbed Tamara's arms and walked her around the lake to the gazebo-like cage. She seemed like a very small puppet as she was dragged by the two men. The evening was growing steadily darker as the setting sun glowed red in the sky.

"Turn on the lights so our other guests can see the meal for the fish!" Uday shouted. The rest of the women looked at Tamara and were horrified by the scene.

Spot lights focused across the lagoon and onto the gazebo as the men began walking on the land bridge toward the wooden bridge with Tamara. Until then, Tamara had futilely devoted all her attention and energy to breaking loose from her tormentors. When they reached the wooden bridge, she saw that the middle of the bridge did not have a gazebo. It was a cage with a rope tied to the top of it and wrapped around a pulley. The rope was twisted around a cleat on the bridge to keep the cage from dropping into the water. Tamara realized that she was in life-threatening danger and began screaming and kicking the two men.

The women at the disco were all forced by the guards remaining with Uday to watch. All of the men had pistols in their hands and menacing looks on their faces. The women, numb with fear, obediently turned to watch in horror at what was about to happen to Tamara.

The two men with Tamara forced her into the cage and locked the door. Tamara was screaming and crying, "*Pajalusta*! *Pajalusta*! (Please! Please!) *Yah ne hotchu umeret*! (I don't want to die!)"

Uday yelled in a very loud, almost maniacal voice to Tamara and the distraught women, "Tamara, you will feed the fish tonight!" He turned to Igor and spoke in Arabic: "Tell the rest of them in very clear Russian that unless they are my very good friends and do exactly as I say, they will join Tamara and the fish."

Igor repeated Uday's words to the girls in Russian. They looked at him with anguish. Some of them began to cry quietly. Tamara was screaming as the men untied the rope. Immediately, the cage slowly began to drop into the water. She continued to scream as she sank with the cage into the water until the cage disappeared and there was silence.

After a moment of silence, except for the soft whimpering of a few women, Uday looked at all of them coldly. He seemed like a worker at a slaughterhouse, looking at a new herd of sheep entering the pen. "Let's party!" he said, very deliberately, leaving no doubt that he was to be obeyed, no matter what. The music started up. The women looked at him, looked at where Tamara and cage once was, and slowly, half-heartedly started dancing again with forced moves, knowing that their lives depended on it.

Chapter Ten: High School in Michigan 2000

"What did you think about the class assembly today?" Danny was a tall, lanky, and thoughtful teenager with slightly long shaggy brown hair. He was well liked at school and was active in sports and several of the clubs. He was also a good friend of Lara and their other buddy, Melanie. They had known each other since elementary school and lived in the same neighborhood. Since they had frequently walked to and from school together for the last several years, there was a strong friendship between them.

"I don't know... it was OK." Lara answered. "It's nice to be a senior this year and have the principal recognize us." Lara had grown to be a very bright young woman who excelled both in academics and sports, where she was the captain of the Pioneer High School women's soccer team.

"It seemed like only a short while ago that we started high school." Melanie was the artistic one of the three. She was in all the theatrical productions, either on or behind the stage. She was also a gifted alto in the choir.

"It was kind of scary that the principal was already talking to us about when we graduate and that we should start making plans for the future." Danny was pondering the uncertainty that lay ahead.

Melanie smiled, "Well, we're all going to the University of Michigan, right?"

"I thought you wanted to go to New York when you graduated and live with your older sister there for a while," Lara chimed in. "Remember,

Broadway was calling you? What about your dreams to be an actress? You were pretty good last year in the school play. Everybody thinks you have a lot of talent."

Melanie was still smiling. "Yeah, I know. I would love to be on Broadway, but my parents really want me to go to U of M. They say it makes a lot more sense for me to be a lawyer, like my dad, than to be a starving actress. And they're right."

Lara shook her head as she accepted Melanie's change of plans, "What about you, Danny?"

Danny was looking down at where he was walking and thinking of his future, "Yeah. I'll go to the U of M—if I get accepted. My grades are OK, but not great."

"Don't worry, you'll get in," Melanie said with some encouragement. "Lara, what about you? You've always been on the honor roll. Are you planning to go to the University of Michigan? With your grades, you can probably go anywhere you want to."

"I may not go to a university next year at all." Both Melanie and Danny stopped walking. They were surprised by this response. Lara was on track to be the valedictorian of her graduating class. Her dad was a well-known doctor at the university, and there had always been talk of her following in his footsteps.

Danny was incredulous: "Lara, You're nuts! Why not? I know both of your parents expect you to go to a university. They've talked about it for as long as I've known you and your family."

"Yes, I know. They want me to go, and perhaps become a doctor, like my dad. But, you know we have relatives in Iraq, in Mosul. My mom and dad have been talking to my relatives there. My aunt and uncle have offered to let me live with them for a while to learn more about Iraq and our family. I don't know. This past summer, I've been giving it a lot of thought."

"Can I go too?" Danny became much more animated, thinking about an alternative to more classrooms. "I'd rather go live in a foreign country for a while than to college. Four more years of textbooks and lectures isn't my idea of fun."

Melanie had a very different attitude, "Lara, you must go to the University of Michigan with me! I was hoping you would be my roommate!"

"I'd like that," Lara said, looking seriously at Melanie. "But I've heard a lot of nice things about Mosul. My uncle, aunt, and the rest of my extended family all seem like really wonderful folks based upon the phone calls and e-mail we get from them. Plus, I have a cousin there, Yasmine, who remembers me from when I was a baby. She really wants me to visit her. We write each other often. She's almost like the sister I never had. I'd really like to get to know her."

Lara, how many kids your age get an opportunity to go live in a different part of the world, right out of high school?" Danny said with a big smile and a twinkle in his eyes, "I think it would be a wonderful adventure."

Lara smiled back. Then her look became more introspective as she began thinking again of this very serious decision that she would have to make. She walked down the sidewalk with her friends with her. They were all quiet as each of them considered their own future and what it may bring. Lara turned off the sidewalk and up the driveway to her house. She turned to say good-bye, "Well, I don't know what I'm going to do. See you two tomorrow."

Both Danny and Melanie stopped for a moment. "Bye." Then they continued to walk on toward their homes, in silence.

Later that evening, Nadia, Omar, and Lara were sitting at the dinner table. Both parents were in a good mood. Although Lara was always happy to spend time with her folks, this evening she was a little more reserved and less talkative than usual.

Nadia smiled as she passed the platter of roasted chicken to her daughter, "Well, Lara, how was the first day of your senior year?"

"It was good, Mom. But the principal said that my class should begin to think and talk about what we're going to do when we graduate from high school."

"What do you want to do, Lara?" Omar could tell that something was troubling Lara.

"Well, I definitely want to go to the University of Michigan eventually, but I told Danny and Melanie today that I may want to spend time with my relatives in Mosul first."

"Hmmm. What did they think of that idea?" Omar could sense his stomach tighten a bit. Lara's answer would have serious consequences for her future during the next few years. He was comfortable with whatever Lara decided, but he was also conflicted. Certainly a year with her relatives in Mosul would be a valuable life experience that should not be missed. However, he would dearly miss his daughter. Even though things were better now in Iraq, there was some risk.

"Melanie thinks the idea is really stupid, but Danny thinks it would be a lot of fun." Lara said this with a perplexed look. She was seeking an answer from her parents, knowing that the decision would have a tremendous impact at this stage in her life. Omar continued to gaze into her eyes and repeated calmly, "What do you think, Lara?"

"I don't know Dad. Part of me really wants to go directly to U of M, but there's another part tugging at me to accept Uncle Nawaf and Aunt Mohassin's offer to live with them for a year. I don't know what to do."

There was an awkward silence for a moment as everyone pondered the gravity of the discussion. Soon, Nadia joined in this discussion, "Well, honey, you don't have to decide right now. Your father and I will support you with either decision."

Lara began to sigh in relief at the prospect of postponing this conundrum until another time. However, this sense of relief passed in an instant when Omar spoke again, "That's right, dear. But I think if you do go to Mosul, you'll always remember that experience as one of the best in your life. You never want to look back on your life and say, 'I should have done this or that.'"

"Omar, leave Lara alone!" Nadia responded with a bit of tension in her voice, "We agreed that this would be her decision."

Lara looked first at her mom, then her dad, and held her breath for a moment waiting for what would be said next. Omar looked at his wife as he thought about her softly spoken but firm position. Then with slight resignation, he turned to Lara and smiled gently, "You're right, dear. I'll try to keep my preferences to myself. Give it some thought, Lara. We'll support you either way. I promise."

Lara breathed a sigh of relief, and smiled broadly. "Thanks, Dad and Mom." She thought for a moment and changed the subject, "This year is only beginning. Did I tell you that our soccer coach thinks our team has a good chance at winning the championship this year?"

Omar was beaming with pride for his daughter. "Well, with the best women's soccer team captain that Pioneer High School ever had, I'm not surprised." The drama of the past moments passed quickly, and the family returned to the same easy banter that was usual at the Al-Mohammed home.

Autumn went by quickly. Lara continued to excel in her studies and began to plan for the spring soccer season with the women's soccer coach. Melanie was excited about her role in the school's production of *Sound of Music*, and Danny was just happy that he was getting decent grades that semester.

The three friends were all in a good mood as they walked home in the snow in early January 2001 after winter break. They were relaxed and talked about the good time they had during the holiday season and the fun they expected to have during the final four months of high school before graduation. Soon they were at Lara's house and she invited them inside to warm up for a while. As they came through the front door into Lara's home, Nadia greeted them with a big smile, "Lara! I'm glad you're home. This letter came in the mail today from the University of Michigan. I think it's an acceptance letter. Go ahead! Open it!"

"Congratulations!" Melanie was also excited with the news. "Open it, Lara!"

Lara opened the letter and read it to everyone: "Dear Ms. Lara Al-Mohammed, The University of Michigan Board of Regents is pleased to inform you that you have been accepted to begin your freshman year in 2001. Congratulations!"

Nadia was bursting with pride and hugged her daughter, "Congratulations dear! I'm so proud—your father and I are both so proud of you!" She was beaming with happiness.

"I knew you would be accepted!" Melanie said with a big smile. Then she also hugged Lara.

Lara was excited about the prospect, and sensed that her decision on whether to go to Iraq and visit relatives or go to U of M had resolved itself with this acceptance letter. It was clear that the right choice would be to go to the U of M with Melanie and probably many of her other classmates. She was giggling with enthusiasm, "Now we can be dorm mates, like you said."

Suddenly, Melanie became quiet and stared at her best friend for a moment. Lara could immediately tell that something was not right. After an awkward moment of silence, Melanie said softly, "I'm not going to U of M next year."

Both Lara and Danny were stunned by this news, "What are you talking about?" Lara was more than stunned. In a moment, the compass pointing the direction she would be going was smashed.

Almost at the same time, Danny stated his opinion in a loud voice, "Melanie, you're nuts!"

"Well, I didn't know how or when to tell you, but...I'm going to New York next year to study theater arts," Melanie said, blushing a little at how her choice became known to her good friends. She had decided some time ago and had been thinking of how she would break the news to them. Somehow, she figured that there would be a perfect moment to inform them. This was certainly not what she had in mind.

"When did you decide this? Why didn't you tell me you were thinking of this? Who am I going to get for a roommate now?" Lara asked, with some anger and frustration in her voice.

"My sister kept telling me to apply to school in New York." Melanie began her reply. "She said I could stay with her. We both worked on my dad and mom, until they finally agreed to let me try it for a year, since I'll have a place to stay. It was tough for my dad to agree to this, but he said he wanted me to 'get it out of my system,' so if I decide it isn't the right thing, then I'll be more focused at U of M. I ... I think it is the right thing. We'll see. I'm excited and relieved that I could finally tell all of you .... I'm also sorry that I told you in this way. I was hoping that I could break it you more gently."

Lara quickly got over her anger with Melanie, although this news turned her plans upside down. She hugged Melanie. "Congratulations! I knew that's what you really wanted to do. I'm glad you will get to follow your dream!" She was excited for Melanie, but she already had a knot in her stomach, because her moment of certainty had just come undone.

Nadia turned to Danny, "What about you, Danny? Are you going to the U of M?"

Danny looked at everyone sheepishly. After a moment of silence he responded, "Well, I guess this is the day of surprises. Nope, I plan to join the Marine Corps."

Lara's life became completely unraveled at that moment, "Danny! You can't do that! Who am I going to go to U of M with? Why are you joining the army? My two best friends are deserting me!" Within a ten-minute span of time, from planning the fun of their last semester when they were walking to the house, to the devastating news that her two best friends were going their separate ways in only a few months, she was, for a moment, an emotional wreck.

"Well, both of you know that I'm only an average student." Danny continued, "Even if I would have been accepted at U of M, which I wasn't, I'm not really that interested in going back to school at this time. After basic training, the Marines said they would send me to Europe. I've always wanted to see another country. They also said that, once I figure out what I want to do, they'll send me to school. It seems to be the right thing for me to do at this time."

Melanie smiled at him. Then, after a moment of thought, gave him a more serious look, "You know Danny, the army also goes to war sometimes."

"We haven't had a war since Desert Storm ten years ago," Danny replied optimistically. "Thankfully, things have been quiet since then. Hopefully they'll stay that way while I'm in the service."

Lara was still in a melancholy mood, "My two best friends are leaving me! I was counting on both of you joining me at U of M. This isn't going the way I thought it would."

"Cheer up, Lara." Danny smiled with sort of a brotherly look, "The good news is that none of us are going anywhere until this summer. My enlistment date won't be until July."

Melanie put her hand on Lara's shoulder, "And I won't move to New York until August. We still have more than six months together. Cheer up!"

Lara forced a smile, "I'll be OK. Even if we aren't together next year, we'll still be best friends, right?"

Danny and Melanie answered at the same time, "Right!"

Melanie added, "We'll always be best friends." Danny nodded in agreement as he discreetly whisked away a tear in his eye. He knew as they all did that this was a solemn moment that marked a transition in their lives. Very soon, they would no longer be schoolmates and relatively carefree teenagers. Instead, each in their own way would have to accept the daunting responsibility of becoming young adults.

Nadia could sense what these three young friends were thinking but continued to act as if all was well: "I am so happy for all three of you. Lara is going to U of M, and Melanie and Danny, both of you are following your dreams. God be with all three of you!"

Danny and Melanie started moving toward the front door, "See you tomorrow Lara. Congratulations!"

"I'll see you tomorrow," Lara said and added wistfully, "I wish that I would also see you with me at U of M."

Danny turned and replied with a half-hearted smile, "You'll get over it, Lara. Remember, we still have a lot of time left before the end of the school year. See ya." Then they were gone, into the snowy night.

Lara looked very tired as she turned to Nadia, "Mom, this isn't going according to the plan. What am I going to do?"

Nadia gave her daughter a gentle hug and smiled in a way that only mothers can do when consoling their children, "Honey, you will go to U of M, like you wanted to do. It will be a whole new experience for you."

Lara sighed and looked at her mom with a deep love and affection that they shared, "Yes, I guess so."

Later that evening, Omar was reading the papers that came with Lara's acceptance letter to U of M while Nadia watched TV. Lara was up in her room doing homework but was having a hard time focusing on anything other than the afternoon's news: her acceptance by the U of M, and subsequent announcements by Melanie and Danny. As she came down the stairs, Omar looked up from the papers, "Lara, the university is having a reception for students and their parents that live in the Ann Arbor area next week. We should plan to go to this."

Lara walked into the room and plopped into a chair for a few moments while she collected her thoughts. Omar was watching with some concern. She usually had more energy and purpose than she was demonstrating then. She seemed more like a forlorn Raggedy Ann doll that had been tossed into the toy box. She was clearly unhappy. "Dad, is it still possible to go to visit my relatives in Mosul?"

Nadia's attention immediately switched from the television to Lara as she gave her daughter a puzzled look. Omar was also a bit surprised by Lara's question. This was not the response he had expected. "I think so, Lara, but why? You've been accepted to the U of M. This is what you've said that you wanted to do for the last three years."

"I know, Dad. I do want to go to U of M. But, I've been thinking. Melanie is going off to New York City, hopefully just for a year, and Danny is joining the army. It won't be the same without them around. We've been friends since elementary school."

This discussion was certainly not what Nadia had expected either. She tensed up with some fear about the prospect of her daughter going to Iraq. "Lara, you have lots of friends, and you'll make many new friends when you start college. What are you talking about?"

"Mom, I know that I'll still have a lot of friends. But both Melanie and Danny are doing something they really want to do. And they're doing it right out of high school, before they lose the chance to explore their dreams and try something different. I've been thinking about what you and Dad told me about our relatives in Mosul and about Iraq. Maybe I should go there after high school to see for myself what it is like. I've always wondered about what it was like for the two of you when you grew up there. If Uncle Nawaf and Aunt Mohassin still think it's OK for me to live with them for a while, then I think I should go before I start college. I think the U of M letter says that I can enroll later than next September, if I want to.

Omar looked down at the acceptance letter. "Yes, Lara. I think I read somewhere in the documents that you have up to five years of the acceptance to enroll. So, you have time. Nadia, what do you think?"

Nadia looked at both of them and sat there for a moment while she thought about the possible consequences of her response. She was very conflicted, wavering between worry about the safety of her daughter and a desire for her to meet her family in Mosul. It was a tough call. "I don't want Lara to go." She paused for a moment more to collect her thoughts, "But I also know that it would be wonderful if she could meet Mohassin, Yasmine, Shalan, my brothers, and our other relatives, and Omar, to see where you and we grew up."

Omar struggled to contain his excitement about this change of heart from Lara. "Hmmm, I don't know Lara." He thought a moment. "It has been relatively peaceful in Iraq for the last few years. I'll ask Nawaf and Salah if they think it's OK for you to visit them." His face lit up with a big smile as Lara waited in suspense for his approval, "If so, it will be fine with me."

"Dad and Mom, you're the greatest! Thank you!"

The next four months flew by after the fateful discussion. Lara's soccer team made the state finals, but didn't make it to the championship game. She also graduated from Pioneer High School with honors.

Her senior year was quickly over, and a bittersweet summer began as Lara, Melanie, Danny, and their other friends spent as much time as possible hanging out together before each one left to follow their destiny. Since Lara had the most flexible schedule, she followed the advice of her parents and waited until the weather had cooled a bit in Mosul.

"Did you remember your airline ticket and passport?" Nadia quizzed her daughter as Omar drove the car to the airport.

Nadia knew she had them in her purse, but checked just to make sure, "Yes Mom."

"Where are all of the cards for Nawaf, Mohassin, Yasmine, and the others?" Nadia asked.

"Also in my purse."

"Make sure you hide them in the bottom of it, and don't let it out of your sight." Nadia continued anxiously. "You know there is money in each of the envelopes with the cards."

"I know, Mom, I've got all of the envelopes at the bottom of my purse, and you already told me to keep it under my arm all of the time. The purse won't get away from me." Lara acted as if she had traveled all of her life, although she was also nervous. This was her first time taking an international flight since she left for the United States as a baby with her parents. All of the family vacations since then were in a car. Also, although she was looking forward to the relative independence of living far from home, she knew that she would miss her mom and dad very much.

"Where is the money that we gave you?"

"I have enough in my purse to cover possible emergencies until I arrive at Uncle Nawaf's in Mosul, and the rest is in the money belt that dad gave me, strapped to my back."

Omar smiled. "OK, Nadia that's enough of the inquisition. Lara is a smart young woman and she'll be fine." He was proud of her daughter and excited for her to meet his and Nadia's extended family. He was also worried that his pride and joy would soon be in a different place and culture that was very foreign to her. However, he never showed his concern to either Nadia or Lara. He believed this trip would be a good experience for Lara and didn't want to give either of them any cause for additional misgivings. "You'll be fine, Lara," was all he could say at the moment. Saying this also helped him overcome his own worry.

The rest of the drive to the airport was quiet. Each of them was in their own thoughts for the few remaining miles. Omar parked the car and helped Lara with her three large suitcases. Although the airline only allowed two with the price of the ticket, the third bag was required for all of the other gifts that Omar and Nadia wanted Lara to deliver to their relatives.

"Lara, have Uncle Nawaf call us as soon as you get there."

"Yes, Mom."

"Give everyone a big hug from your dad and me."

"I will, Mom." They were all in line at the check-in counter. Soon Lara was presenting her ticket and identification as the bags were weighed, ticketed, and put on the conveyor belt. They all walked slowly to the security station, and then it was time to say good-bye.

Nadia was trying, unsuccessfully, to hold back the tears in her eyes as Lara gave her a big hug. "Mom, don't cry. The year will pass quickly and I'll be home before you know it." She was also trying to hold back her tears. She braced herself a bit and turned bravely to Omar, "Dad, I'll miss both you and Mom very much. This is a good idea, isn't it?" It was too late to change her mind, but she wanted reassurance.

"Lara, you will cherish this next year for the rest of your life. You never want to look back and say that 'I should have, would have, could have, but didn't.'" Omar was also fighting his emotions and looked into her eyes, "This is the best time in your life to have this adventure. Everything will be fine. You'll see. As soon as you arrive in Mosul, you will be welcomed into the family that has always been there, but never had the chance to know you."

"Thanks, Dad." Lara stepped back and looked at both of her parents before entering the security gate and her journey, "Thanks to you both," she said as she looked one more time into her mom's eyes, then turned, went through the gate, and was gone before she lost control of her emotions.

Chapter Eleven:
A Mosul Wedding

There was excitement in the large villa of Nawaf Al-Zaidan. His daughter, Yasmine, had completed her studies at the University of Baghdad, and it was time for her to marry a suitable young man. Consistent with family tradition, the prospective husband had to be preapproved by Nawaf, his brothers, and his wife Mohassin. The process for an arranged marriage typically required a lengthy evaluation of young men, based on their known qualities, families, and status, followed by very carefully orchestrated introductions of appropriate candidates to Yasmine. A further complication was that the families of the young men must also approve of Yasmine and her family.

Frequently, a young man would be introduced to a number of suitable women, based upon the recommendations of his family. He had a vote in the process, so if the young lady didn't meet his expectations for some reason, he could ask his family to keep looking for another prospective bride. Depending on the men and women, and their family connections, this process was often frustratingly long as one or another suitor or family member didn't agree with the arrangement. When this happened, the process began again and possibly again, until either an acceptable match was found, or the selection of appropriate candidates was depleted. Occasionally the result was a very frustrated, unhappy, and unmarried young man or woman.

This didn't happen often, but it could. Occasionally, one or both suitors met with and rejected almost all available candidates. When families were about to give up hope that they would ever find a happy and suitable match for their son or daughter, the young man and woman would became desperate and decide to accept any marriage arrangement just to be done with the process. It wasn't a great way to start a marriage.

In the best possible situation, both families were already familiar with each other and the children from each family were already friends. Then, if all went well, the process could be quite easy and produce a happy outcome for everyone, especially the young man and woman. Nawaf, Mohassin, and Yasmine were hopeful that this would be one of those happy outcomes. Yasmine's older brother Shalan was about the same age as her prospective husband, Aziz Al-Atwan, and was also pleased, for they had all known him and his family since they were young children.

Omar was right when he predicted that Lara would immediately feel the love of her extended family. Since she already spoke fluent Arabic, she quickly became comfortable in her new home and the city of Mosul. Before leaving Ann Arbor, she worried about the more conservative dress codes and culture in Iraq compared to America. When she arrived in the cosmopolitan provincial capital of Nineveh Province in the summer of 2001, she was pleasantly surprised. Although most women preferred head scarves when they were in public, others were comfortable without them. Her parents had always imposed a dress code at home for Lara, including loose-fitting clothes and more conservative dresses than many of her high school friends wore, so she didn't feel out of place walking with Yasmine and the rest of the family in Mosul.

Five months passed quickly as Lara was introduced to all of the relatives and friends. She was "the niece from America" and treated like a royal guest. Although she sometimes felt a bit overwhelmed by all the warm and loving attention from people who had been strangers a few months earlier, Lara gratefully accepted their generous hospitality.

Yasmine and Lara became the best of friends and developed an almost sisterly fondness for each other. They could have passed for sisters. Although Omar and Nawaf were about the same height, Lara was about two inches taller than Yasmine. Because of her high school sports, she was stronger and walked with more of a confident swagger than Yasmine and all of the other young women that she met. Nawaf and Mohassin told their friends that this was due to her "American" upbringing.

During this time, Yasmine confided to Lara that she secretly loved a young man from a family that had long been friends to the Al-Zaidan family. When they were small, they played together all of the time. Their friendship continued through the years. When they became young teenagers, Iraqi propriety dictated that they could not be alone with each other, but they continued to visit during special holidays when friends, family, and neighbors would meet at social events. They lost contact when Yasmine began her studies at the nursing school at Baghdad University and Aziz went to the prestigious Iraq Military Academy.

Coincidentally, soon after Lara arrived in Mosul, Yasmine saw Aziz again, when he was visiting his parents while on leave from the Iraqi Army. He had grown taller and more handsome than Yasmine remembered, and her interest in him was immediately reignited.

Aziz was on leave for only a week, but during that time, Yasmine began to frequent the family's roof top patio hoping that she would be noticed if Aziz bothered to look up at her house from the street when he visited his friends in their neighborhood. She also urged Lara to join her in frequent walks over to the neighborhood where Aziz lived. They always ensured that their strolls passed Aziz's parents' house as often as possible, even though it was about a kilometer away from the Al-Zaidan home. Within a few days, Aziz did notice Yasmine and was equally smitten, for she had grown into a beautiful young woman. When they first fixed their stares on each other, even without words both of them clearly knew that they wanted to be with each other.

During the next several months, during the Eid festivities after Ramadan and a few other opportunities when Aziz came home on leave, the families did get together for social occasions. The two young people took advantage of these rare opportunities to exchange notes and occasionally talk with each other within view of everyone but far enough away that their discussion couldn't be heard. It was during their last encounter that Aziz pledged his love to Yasmine and declared that he would ask her hand in marriage. Yasmine was overcome with joy but had to rein in her happiness so that her parents and others wouldn't notice anything unusual. This was in December. The following day Aziz returned to his duties in the army.

It didn't take long for Yasmine's excitement to get the better of her self-control. Soon Lara knew, and then the unusual outbursts of giddiness and giggling between the cousins piqued Mohassin's curiosity. Mohassin immediately approved when they confided in her, and quickly everyone, even Nawaf, knew the poorly kept secret. Happily, he also approved. However, since Abdullah and he were such long and close friends, he thought it would be fun to play a game with him.

"That's a terrible idea! How could you do such a thing to Abdullah and poor Aziz!" said Mohassin when he told her his plan.

"Daddy! No!" Yasmine exclaimed. Lara and Yasmine just stood dumbfounded, not knowing what to say.

Nawaf smiled mirthfully, "Abdullah and I are very good friends. That's why I can do this and not expect an immediate reaction from him. He will want to consider my hesitation when I tell him that I want to think about it and consider other suitors for Yasmine." Nawaf began to chuckle as he thought about it, "Besides, how dare Aziz propose to my Yasmine without talking with me first!" His smile continued to get bigger: "He deserves to be made nervous for several moments, at least."

Shalan started laughing. "Dad, it's a great idea! Since my uncles will be there, they'll all play along. It will be great fun."

Mohassin and Yasmine looked at Shalan sternly. "Abdullah knows you very well, Nawaf. He'll look at your eyes and know you are kidding."

"Well, ladies," Nawaf said to his wife, daughters and Lara, "the charade may only last for a few moments, but it will be enough to scare Aziz ... and I think that's not a bad thing."

Shalan continued to grin and shake his head in amusement. "Come on, Mom, Yasmine; it will only be a joke and everyone will remember it, in a good way, for a long time."

Yasmine still had a scowl on her face as she glared at her father and brother. However, Mohassin, who was accustomed to her husband's good-hearted but sometimes slightly wicked humor, began to smile gently. "OK, Nawaf. Yasmine, Lara, and I will play along with your game when we go to talk with Hana. It's lucky for you that Aziz's mother has the same weird sense of humor as you. She will play along with this sport as a way to get back at all of the jokes that Abdullah has played on her over the years."

Both the Al-Zaidan and the Al-Atwan families were known as fun-loving people who enjoyed a good laugh. Perhaps that's why they were such good friends.

In accordance with tradition, the women in the family began the formal process. Mohassin and her sisters visited with Hana and her sisters to discuss the possibility of a marriage between Aziz and Yasmine. There was no delay in their very positive approval. Mohassin also discussed Nawaf's idea for playing a game with Abdullah and Aziz. Hana lit up with a smile when she heard this, "Of course! What a great idea. I hope Nawaf and the others can keep straight faces. I know they will all have a hard time holding back a good laugh."

Yasmine drew her lips tight and stared at Hana and the other women.

Mohassin smiled. "Good. I know Nawaf will be pleased that all of you will play along with his silly game. Remember, not a word to Abdullah, Aziz, and the others."

Hana gave Yasmine and Mohassin a hug, "We'll soon all be one big happy family, and Nawaf's joke will be talked about for years. I can't think of a more fun way to bind our two families together."

Aziz would next visit Mosul in late January, 2002. A few days before Aziz returned home, Nawaf received a call from Abdullah, indicating that he had a matter of very grave importance to discuss with him and his brother. He asked if it would be acceptable if he came over the following week, accompanied by Aziz.

Nawaf acted as if he didn't have a clue about the subject of important discussion but he readily agreed to a meeting. The next few days were filled with excitement, particularly among the women. Nawaf met with his brother Salah, Salah's wife Walla and son Othman, and his other brothers and their families to brief them on the purpose of the meeting and his plans for it. Everyone supported the match, and all agreed that to the best of their abilities, the five brothers and their grown sons Shalan and Othman would act surprised and concerned about what was going to be proposed.

Nawaf and Salah knew that after the offer was made, everyone would enjoy looking back at the drama as they pondered this important decision. They would pretend at first to disapprove, trying to increase the suspense and make Aziz and his father nervous about the outcome for a few moments before agreeing to it.

The day and time arrived for the meeting. The extended Al-Zaidan family was gathered in the front entry way that also served as the formal drawing room for meeting with visitors. The room was large. On either side were comfortable, low, velvet covered sofas with long low tables in front of each. In addition to the sofas, the room also contained six comfortable chairs. There was enough room for a party of eighteen people to sit comfortably. Since the two families had known each other for many years, Nawaf wanted the meeting to be informal. There would be plenty of room for the Al-Atwan men, Nawaf, his four other brothers, Shalan, and Othman to sit and discuss the matter of "grave importance" that Abdullah had referred to. Yasmine, Mohassin, Walla, Lara, and some of Yasmine's close friends waited and listened behind the door of the adjoining kitchen, out of sight of the men.

The family was talking in hushed voices, speculating on how the expected request would be made, when Othman peeked out past the thick curtain on the front window. "They've just entered our front gate!" he said excitedly. Immediately Yasmine and the other women rushed into the kitchen.

"There's more than just Aziz, Abdullah, and his brother Azzam!" Othman said in a slightly panicked voice. "Many, many more!" Othman could see a steady stream of men and teenage boys streaming through the courtyard gate and gathering around the front door. Nawaf and Salah looked at each other with some concern.

"How many?" asked Nawaf.

There was a long silence. Then Othman reported in a matter-of-fact fashion, "The last man just came through the gate and they closed it. I count about thirty."

Nawaf smiled and let out a sigh: "That's a lot! I was hoping it wouldn't be much more than that, but I was expecting much less. Abdullah and Aziz are trying to make a good impression." Just then, there was a knock on the door. Nawaf said softly, "Othman, stood by the door waiting for his father's signal to let them in. Remember our plan. Whatever is said, keep a straight face and try your best to look like you disapprove." He smiled broadly again at Salah and Othman. Then he forced a stern look onto his face as he motioned Othman to open the door.

Soon there was another knock and, as the door opened wide, Nawaf stood in the doorway, "*Ahlaan wasahlaan bikum*! (Welcome!) *Alssalam ealaykum*. (Peace be upon you.) " Abdullah, and Aziz smiled and walked in as Nawaf, Salah, and Othman moved away from the door and toward the sofas on one side of the room. Nawaf, his brothers, Shalan, and Othman moved quickly to the other side of the room in front of the sofa facing Aziz and his father. Aziz looked a bit nervous as everyone watched the other men and teenage boys enter the room and flank him and his father. Abdullah smiled and nodded to each person as he motioned them to move to one or another side of where they were standing, directing the more revered older family members to stand in front of the chairs that were there. Nawaf motioned to Othman to move the chairs nearest where he was standing to Abdullah's side of the room. Clearly, there was not enough seating for everyone, and he wanted to ensure the senior members of the Al-Atwan clan would be able to sit down. They were all dressed in either formal traditional robes or western business suits.

After everyone entered the drawing room, Nawaf slowly sat down: "Abdullah, Aziz, gentlemen, please sit." As Abdullah sat down, Aziz and the others also took a seat. The remaining men stood and looked at Nawaf and the others. The Al-Zaidan men were not doing a very good job of maintaining their serious demeanor now. They were facing a very large group of men and were not quite sure how long they would be able to conduct the charade that they had rehearsed, before one or more of the Al-Atwan clan would get angry.

"Thank you for agreeing to meet with us." Abdullah said with a very serious look on his face.

"Abdullah, we've been friends for years. It's always a pleasure to see you and your family." Nawaf waved his hand toward the table in front of Abdullah. Bottles of water, a pot of hot tea, cups, sugar, and cookies had already been placed there for the primary guests. "We are humbled and honored by your visit and by the attendance of so many members of your esteemed family. Please forgive me for my lack of hospitality. We only expected you and Aziz. Excuse me a moment while I request more refreshments."

Nawaf started to stand up when Abdullah began to speak, "No need to do that, Nawaf. We are only here for a short while, to ask you, Salah, your brothers, Shalan, and Othman a very important question."

Nawaf sat down and slowly took a deep breath as he resumed staring seriously at the two men across the room from him, blocking out all of the others. "Abdullah, this seems like a very serious matter. What is wrong?"

It was Abdullah's turn to express a serious concern. He had assumed that Nawaf would have been briefed by Mohassin and Yasmine about the purpose of the meeting, so he thought the discussion would be very short and simple. "Nawaf, I think you know why we are here. Our families have been friends for many years. We have watched our children grow up together, and now it is time to think about grandchildren." As

Abdullah spoke, Aziz fixed his eyes on the table, trying to avoid making eye contact with his hosts across the room. He was doing his best to hide the mounting stress that he was feeling as the seconds passed.

Nawaf continued to pretend that he didn't know the reason for the visit: "Abdullah, what are you talking about?"

Aziz could feel a knot in his stomach and closed his eyes for a moment. "Allah, please help my father say the right words, and please guide Nawaf and Salah to say yes," he silently prayed.

"Nawaf, your daughter Yasmine has come of age. She is well educated and has just graduated from Baghdad University. My son Aziz has also come of age. He's worked hard, graduated as a lieutenant from the academy, and is already serving in the army." As Abdullah began speaking, Aziz opened his eyes and looked across the room at Nawaf and the others, all of whom had frowns on their faces. However, Aziz noticed that his friend Shalan's face was contorted as if he was struggling to keep from smiling. "We, my son, brothers, esteemed relatives, and I, humbly beg you to consider allowing Yasmine to marry my son Aziz. He will make a very good husband and honor both of our families."

Nawaf forced himself to shake his head in a negative gesture for a moment as he pretended to think about it.

Aziz started to panic. The seconds passed silently, and small beads of sweat appeared on his forehead as he looked pleadingly at Nawaf. Shalan looked up at the large group in front of them. Many had lost the smiles on their faces and began to look agitated. Some showed hints of anger in their eyes. He also began to have a knot in his stomach, as he wondered how much longer the suspense in the room would last. It seemed that the room crowded with more than forty men was quickly getting very hot and there was no air.

Nawaf looked at his brother, "Salah, what do you think?" He paused a moment more to increase the drama. "Aziz is just beginning his military career. Perhaps we should meet with the other families who are suggesting their sons to us for Yasmine."

Aziz feared he might faint from the tension that he felt and the thought that he could lose Yasmine to someone else. Abdullah frowned, but waited quietly for his friends to continue their deliberations.

Salah, who had been observing all this drama with a forced frown, could no longer continue the game: "I think Aziz will be a good husband for Yasmine. His family is well known among our tribe. This will unite two very important families here in Mosul." His frown turned into a big smile with a twinkle in his eyes. Shalan and Othman started to giggle under their breath as the Al-Atwan clan collectively sighed in relief.

At that moment the men could hear the women whispering excitedly in the other room. Nawaf changed his expression from frown to smile: "My brothers and I accept your proposal. Aziz and Yasmine shall be married!" Immediately, the other men in the room clapped their hands and started shouting happily, "*Alhamd lillah*! Praise be to God!" The family room erupted with the joyous and loud song that Arab women make at weddings and other happy occasions. "Lulululu!" was heard as a chorus of approval and excitement from the women in the kitchen.

Everyone stood up and started filing by Abdullah and Aziz to shake their hands and give them big hugs. Nawaf also stood up. "It appears that everyone approves." He smiled as he gestured to the happy sounds coming from behind the wall. Soon Nawaf, Shalan, Salah, and Othman were also on the receiving line of hugs, and cheek kisses from the men of the extended Al-Atwan family.

Finally, Aziz spoke up as he bowed and raised his right hand toward his heart as a gesture of gratitude. "Mr. Al-Zaidan, I swear to you that I will take good care of your daughter and protect her to my dying breath," he said seriously.

Nawaf smiled and looked Aziz in the eyes. "I know you will, Aziz. I know you have always been fond of Yasmine. Her mother and I are pleased that you want Yasmine as your wife. I pray to Allah that your dying breath will not be for many, many years after you have given us many grandchildren and great-grandchildren."

It was a happy moment for both families and an exciting time for Lara as she thought about how much she enjoyed celebrating this occasion with her new-found family. She was experiencing a fulfillment that she never thought she would realize when she first decided to visit Iraq.

The wedding was scheduled for early May, before the heat of summer became too unbearable. Both Aziz and Yasmine looked forward to their respective prewedding parties that would be held in the Al-Atwan and Al-Zaidan homes. Aziz and his friends joked, told funny stories about their adventures together as they were growing up, and sang popular songs well into the evening. Yasmine and her friends did much the same, but also applied the fashionable reddish henna dye to Yasmine's forearms and hands. In Arabic and Islamic culture, henna was believed to be a plant from heaven. Due to its heavenly origin, the dye was frequently applied to both the groom and bride as a symbol of their connection to heaven.

The wedding party was held in a park by the Tikrit River in Mosul. Several hundred people attended the celebration, including the extended Al-Zaidan and Al-Atwan families, their business associates, and other friends.

It was a pleasant day, with a slight breeze from the river carrying the smell of lilac trees. The Al-Zaidan family spent a small fortune on the event with a sumptuous buffet that stretched along a thirty-foot table that included mountains of rice, several perfectly cooked lambs and goats, chickens, fresh giant carp, cooked vegetables, and fresh fruit.

Yasmine was radiant in her white dress that was imported from the United States, with help from Lara and her parents, who provided it as a wedding gift to their family. Nawaf, Mohassin, Shalan, and Lara were all dressed in conservative but fashionable western attire. All of them were busy talking with different groups of guests from Mosul and distant relatives from Anbar, Babil, and other provinces. Lara was surprised at how extensive the Al-Zaidan family was. It was also interesting how the family was inter-connected by many marriages to the extended Al-Atwan family. Even more surprising was how many of these relatives could trace their lineage and multiple offshoots of their family to the other families for more than three or four generations, going back well over one hundred years of family history. The families were intertwined, with both Sunni and Shia members. It appeared to her that the differences and attitude regarding whether a relative was one or another sect was about as nominal as American families that consider Lutherans, Methodists, and other Protestants as close relatives. She reflected on how most American families do well to trace their immediate family back one or two generations, having lost much of their history before the families immigrated to the United States.

Although Lara was an honored guest in the Al-Zaidan home, she was not a member of the wedding party and arrived to the event with some of Yasmine's friends. Although she knew Aziz from a distance, she had only learned all she knew about him through discussions with Yasmine. She had also never formally met Abdullah, only hearing his voice during the meeting with Nawaf in the family drawing room. Soon after she arrived, she made her way to where Yasmine and Nawaf were talking with Aziz.

"Lara!" Yasmine almost shouted in her excitement to see her cousin walk across the crowded park. "Aziz, I want you to meet my American cousin that I told you about."

Aziz, smiled and bowed as Lara walked up to the small group, "Lara, I am honored to meet you. Actually, I feel like I already know you. Yasmine has been telling me all about you and your family. Welcome to Mosul."

The notion of bowing when being introduced was a new custom for Lara. She started to hold out her hand for Aziz to shake, as her father had taught her to do in America when being introduced to someone. However, she quickly switched gestures to a bow, "Aziz, I also think I know you already. I am so happy for you and Yasmine. I know the two of you are perfect for each other."

"How do you know they'll be perfect for each other?" Nawaf asked with a smile on his face, "You've just met Aziz."

"Uncle Nawaf, I just know." She paused a moment to think how she would explain this, "Women just know these things."

Nawaf, continued to smile as he shook his head; his experience as a married man told him that there was no point in arguing this logic. "Well, I'm sure you're right, may Allah be praised."

"Nawaf, who is this young lady that you've been hiding from us? I didn't know you had another daughter." Abdullah was talking with another group of guests when he first saw Lara and walked up to introduce himself.

"Abdullah, this is my niece, Lara. You may have seen her as a baby with my sister Nadia and her husband and your classmate, Omar Al-Mohammad, before she and Omar left Iraq for America in 1984. Omar was able to complete his residency in Ann Arbor, Michigan and became a doctor in the United States. Lara grew up as an American and is a U.S. citizen, but she is still our Iraqi niece. Omar and Nadia didn't want her to lose her Iraqi heritage and asked that we be her guardians and live with us for a while."

Abdullah bowed toward Lara. "Ms. Lara, I'm honored to meet you. I grew up with your father and uncle Nawaf. You come from a brave and honorable family and must be very brave yourself to want to come all this way to Iraq and spend time here." He paused a moment and a look of sadness came over him. "Lara, I'm very sorry for the attack on the World Trade Center. All of my family was very saddened by this attack. Most Iraqis want to be friends with America. Criminals like the ones who attacked America are terrorists. But their actions make many Americans and others afraid of all Arabs, including Iraqis. I hope Americans know that we Iraqis had nothing to do with this terrible thing."

Lara bowed again and moved her right arm to her chest as a gesture of heartfelt gratitude, "Thank you, sir. Most Americans don't think the Iraqis had anything to do with the attack. Most believe it was Al-Qaida, Osama bin Ladin, and the Taliban in Afghanistan."

Abdullah smiled and then changed to a look of fatherly concern, "Why did you decide to visit Iraq during these troubled times?"

Nawaf couldn't help wanting to impress his friend, "She must like it here because she asked if we could help her attend a year or two of college in Iraq before she returns to America."

Lara continued: "When my father and mother suggested that I come to Iraq for a visit, I thought it would only be for a short time. At first, I didn't want to do this. But, many of my high-school friends said that I should visit Mosul so that I could return to America and tell them what the country is like. In Ann Arbor, where my home is, I have many Iraqi-American friends. They were also raised in America. Their parents and relatives would tell us about the many wonderful things they remember when they were growing up in Iraq, during the 1960s and 1970s. After being here with Uncle Nawaf and Aunt Mohassin, I felt like, somehow, I belonged here. Then when Uncle Nawaf offered to help me attend my first year of university, I couldn't say no to such a generous offer."

"So, you like Iraq now that you've been here for a while, even with our troubles?" asked Aziz.

Lara looked at him as if he was one of her friends in Ann Arbor, "Aziz, I've only lived in Mosul and visited some of the antiquities of Nineveh with Yasmine and her family. However, I've already grown to love this place and the people that I've met here. They are kind and very giving. One other thing, it's kind of strange actually. Although I grew up in America, I feel very connected to this country; its culture and history. I love America, but I really feel at home here in Iraq and look forward to spending another year here. The only thing that bothers me is that I've noticed many Iraqis seem very sad all the time, and afraid of General Saddam Hussein." Then, in a very American, slightly immature and direct way, she asked, "Aziz, you're in the army. Should people be afraid of General Hussein?"

There was a moment of stunned silence in the group as Aziz pondered his response to this very highly charged question.

Abdullah also tensed up. To keep his son from the awkward question, he immediately directed his attention to Aziz and Yasmine. "You two have made our families very proud. May God bless you always."

Aziz and Yasmine expressed their thanks for Abdullah's blessing by bowing slightly toward him. "I am honored to be your daughter-in-law and will do my best to honor and please Aziz," Yasmine said solemnly.

"Yasmine, you have always been well liked by my wife and me. Even when you were a child, we always hoped that you and Aziz would be joined in marriage."

Although he had already been briefed on their plans by Mohassin, Nawaf was waiting for an appropriate opportunity to formally ask, "So, Aziz, what are your plans now that you have taken our daughter from us?"

"I've been assigned to the President's guard in Baghdad. The army has provided us with a small flat, and we will move there. Hopefully, Yasmine can also find a job at the hospital." Yasmine was smiling as she thought of the exciting new life she was going to have with Aziz in the heart of Baghdad. Another moment passed as Aziz quickly considered possible responses to Lara's question. It was not a question that any Iraqi would ever ask in private or public. Under the circumstances, he took a very mature and diplomatic approach. He ignored the question entirely and, like his father, changed the subject with a compliment and question, "Lara, you're a very perceptive and mature person. Which university are you planning to attend? Mosul or Baghdad University like your cousin Yasmine?"

The serious demeanor produced by her question evaporated, and she was once again smiling as she looked at her relatives, "Uncle Nawaf already knew that you and Yasmine were planning to move to Baghdad, so he talked with my father and mother and they allowed me to study at the Baghdad Women's College for medicine. It is in the same district where you and Yasmine will be living.

Nawaf had a slightly panicked look on his face. Although he and Mohassin had discussed helping pay for her education, he hadn't mentioned the possibility of having Lara move to Baghdad.

Mohassin's face was troubled as she looked at Nawaf: "Nawaf, are you sure this is a good idea?" Lara immediately sensed that she may have said too much.

"With my new son-in-law in the Iraqi Army watching over my daughter and niece, I am sure they will both be fine."

Everyone smiled in agreement. The party continued well into the evening as the families became reacquainted with friends and relatives from Mosul and other provinces and cities in Iraq. They were honored to have perhaps twenty relatives from Nawaf's maternal grandfather's side of the family that drove several hundred miles from the city of Hilla in Babil Province. Months later, everyone still talked about the wonderful time they had at the Al-Atwan and Al-Zaidan wedding party and how happy Aziz and Yasmine were on that magical evening under the stars with their many loved ones in the park near the Tikrit River.

Chapter Twelve: The United States Enters the Picture July 2002

Summer was a more relaxed time at Fort Bragg. Although the North Carolina army base was known for its all-business approach to training, especially for special operations, it also offered many activities during nonwork hours, especially for families, creating the easy ambiance of a large summer camp. The soldiers stationed there were encouraged to participate in the frequent sporting events and take their families and friends to the concerts, picnics, and other activities offered at the housing communities and the larger facilities on the base.

The thousands of soldiers stationed there were always focused on their mission in the event of a war or other crises in the world. However, their immediate concerns were closer to home. The war in Afghanistan had begun, but it was limited primarily to long-distance bombing, courtesy of the Navy and Air Force. There were some ground operations but these hadn't affected many of the Fort Bragg Special Operations personnel by June 2002. There was a premonition that before long, much more would be asked of the US military, something that would affect everyone living in or near the fort. It was late June and there was still a relative calm. People were enjoying summer and the many benefits that were on offer at the huge military base.

July 3 was a Wednesday. That afternoon, Joe and his team were told there would be an all-hands meeting for his team and others on the following Monday, after the Fourth of July holiday weekend. It was clear that something big was going to be discussed, but there was only speculation on what it might be.

Joe Keith was a major and the senior team leader for his Delta team that included himself and eleven other men who were part of the US Army Special Operations Command (USASOC,) which was a component of the Joint Special Operations Command (JSOC). In his early thirties, he was based with his wife and two young sons at Fort Bragg for the last five years. During this time, he rose through the officer corps as he trained and proved himself on many assignments with the First Special Operations Command. He spent a large portion of his time away from home on training missions and, less frequently, on assignments in Bosnia, Kosovo, Haiti, and other hot spots around the world. When he was home, he had a good relationship with his wife and kids.

After a pleasant four-day weekend, Monday arrived and he was on his way to the conference room when he met Paul and Tim, two of the senior members in his team. Paul was the team warrant officer and assistant team commander. Tim was the Non-Commissioned Officer-In-Charge. Sergeant Major Tim Jones was one of Joe's best friends and the go-to guy that everyone on the team trusted for his common sense and good advice.

Tim transferred from the marines to the army when he was offered the opportunity to train for and join the Delta Team Special Forces. Gunny Jones had served two tours with the marines. Although he liked the camaraderie there, the marines didn't have special forces like the other branches. There was plenty of competition for the army's Delta Team, but Tim submitted his application and was accepted. Tim was an E-7 gunnery sergeant with the Marines and had distinguished himself in 1995 when he and his unit helped rescue an Air Force pilot who was shot down in hostile territory during a peacekeeping mission over Bosnia. Gunny Jones's reputation earned him recognition within the marines and the attention of army recruiters, who were able to offer him the career opportunities he wanted. The men in Joe's team came to know the first sergeant simply as Tim. Joe and a few of the others still occasionally called him "Gunny." He was respected as a natural leader, was one of the best shots in the command, and could diagnose and fix any weapon that the team used, even in the worst field conditions. The men on the team all knew that for marines, "Gunny" was a term of respect for those men who earned it. The name seemed to fit Tim and he didn't mind.

"I wonder what's up?" Tim asked. "They've never called all of these special forces teams together at one time. Could we be on our way to Afghanistan?"

Joe had also been pondering that. In recent months, their training was in more arid regions of the country. Although no formal messages were shared with the teams at Fort Bragg, there was a lot of talk and rumors among the men. When they walked into the non-descript building, it was clear that all the Delta teams in the USASOC and other JSOC teams from around the country had also been invited to the meeting. There were service men in US Navy, Marine, Air Force, and Army uniforms walking toward the same destination. Joe and his squad was among a group of approximately 240 other very fit men in the auditorium also taking their seats and chatting casually with each other.

"They haven't told us anything." Tim answered his own question. "It's going to be something big, whatever they have in mind," he said in a matter of fact manner. In front was a podium and behind it on the wall were the emblems for the Navy SEALs, Army Delta Force, and the Air Force 24th Special Tactics Squadron. An army general and athletic looking man in civilian clothing stood at the podium in front of a large map of Iraq. "Gentlemen, I hope all of you had a good weekend. For many of you who left your homes from elsewhere in the country to meet with us today, welcome to Fort Bragg and the Joint Special Operations Command. You've been invited here to begin training for and become part of a highly classified mission. President Bush directed that we create a team made up of the best of the best soldiers from all branches of the service. You've all seen the news that this administration believes Saddam Hussein is developing weapons of mass destruction that will be used against our friends in the Middle East, and against the United States. Although the UN Monitoring, Verification, and Inspection Commission's work in Iraq is still in progress, we want to do our own research. Your teams have been selected to do that research. The code name for your mission will be 'Task Force 20.' Our colleague, standing with me, from the CIA Special Activities Division, will brief each team on where you will concentrate your reconnaissance activities. SEALs, you will work in the southern region, 24th you will cover the western provinces that border with Iran, and Delta Force, your focus will be on Anbar and much of the central region, the northern and north-central provinces." The general passed his hand over the various regions on the map as he spoke. "Now, I would like to introduce you to our partner in this adventure, whom you will know and address only as Charlie"

A man with the face and build of an athletic 40-year-old, but with white hair that belied his youngish appearance stepped up to the podium. He engendered the respect due to someone who had seen and done much in his career. "Thanks general. Gentlemen, we will begin training tomorrow in Washington DC. There you will meet other team members who will help supplement many of the briefings you'll attend by providing far more detail based upon their personal experiences. These men are Iraqi-Americans who were born and grew up in Iraq, then emigrated from there within the last twenty years. They were recruited from their civilian lives in the United States for their knowledge of the language, people, and the geography in the areas where your teams will be assigned. After four months of training with you in DC and in the field, they will travel independently to Iraq and begin their own reconnaissance before you arrive. They'll be your guides and help provide cover for you when you are there."

After Charlie's brief statement, the general concluded the meeting, "That is all for today, except for picking up your orders and plane tickets on your way out the door. Tell your families and friends that you will be on an assignment for the next several months. Beginning now, we cannot allow you to have any conversations with them regarding this mission until further notice."

Joe frowned and turned to Tim, "That was to the point. I guess we're not going to Afghanistan." He paused for a moment. "This will be hard on the family. They've become used to having me around for some of the time. It's been good while it lasted."

Gunny knew Joe's family and understood his friend's concern. Long deployments helped end his marriage. He managed a stiff smile. "They'll be OK, Joe. Alice has been through this drill with you before. She'll hold things together while you're gone."

Joe slowly nodded an affirmative. "Yes, she will. I was gone nine months in 2000 on the Kosovo peace-keeping mission. She wasn't happy, but she didn't complain." Then he smiled, "She sure was happy to see me get off the plane when I came home."

That Monday was a very short work day for Joe and Gunny. Soon after the meeting, the five teams of the Special Operations Group received orders and plane tickets. Then they were dismissed for the rest of the day so they could pack their gear and say good-bye to their families. On Tuesday morning they would depart for a training center near Washington DC, where they and the other elite military teams would meet to begin cultural and situational training.

Alice smiled as Joe came through the front door, "That was a short day. I'm on the way to the pool with the boys. Do you want to join us?"

Joe looked at his wife and smiled with approval. She was already in her bathing suit under her summer dress. He stood looking at her for a moment while she waited for an answer.

Alice was a pretty woman. They met in college and were married soon after they both graduated. He decided after his sophomore year that a desk job working with his father in a small accounting firm, or any other white-collar career, was really not what he wanted to do. He applied for the Army Reserve Officer Training program when he began his junior year. After one year of training, he decided the challenges of the army and collegiality of the people he worked with suited his personality. By then, he was on track to graduate in a year, and with a job and career already determined, he asked Alice to marry him. She had no hesitation in saying yes. His time in the army passed quickly, and when they were assigned to Fort Bragg, it was sometimes hard for him to believe that they had already been married for more than ten years. He still thought of her as the most attractive woman he had ever known.

"Well?" asked Alice as the boys came down the stairs with their suits on and towels in hand, "Do you want to go with us?"

Joe had been standing still and looking at her for longer than he thought. His mind was racing from how pretty she looked in her summer dress to the news that he would have to share with her that day. Her second question broke his momentary contemplation. "Uh, yeah. I'll get my suit and be right with you." He bounded up the stairs to their bedroom to change while Alice gathered the boys and headed out of the house to the car.

Time was short, and Joe knew more than the rest of the family how important this last relaxing time with everyone would be. He began to think about how he would explain his departure early Tuesday morning and his mysterious disappearance for three or more months to Alice and his sons. Different scenarios were considered and set aside. "I'll sort it out after our time at the pool," Joe thought as he gathered his suit and towel and went to the car.

The day was pleasantly warm and the boys were quickly in the pool, followed by Joe and Alice. They frolicked around as Joe would toss one, then the other son into the air as they laughed and pleaded to be thrown upward into the air by their strong dad to come down quickly with a big splash, again and again. Soon, the boys became distracted by their friends and swam away from their parents to play with the others. Joe and Alice smiled as he then swept Alice off her feet and held her in his arms as he would a little girl. He held her close for a moment. “Joe! We’re in a public pool!”

“Yes, I know. But, I haven’t held you like this for a long time.”

When he let her go, she stood up and gave him a hug and kiss, and smiled. “Let’s go sit in the shade.” When they were sitting down, she asked, “So what was that meeting about this morning?”

It was an innocent question, and very reasonable. Joe didn’t usually have early morning meetings that segued to the rest of a day off work. Although he should have anticipated her question, he hadn’t. He was caught off guard. He had to pause for a few moments to collect his thoughts.

Alice could sense his playful mood fade away, and she became concerned. “What is it, Joe? You’re not going away again, are you?”

Joe paused a moment more. “Yes, Alice. Let’s talk about this when we get home and the boys are outside playing.”

It was Alice’s turn to be contemplative. “OK” was all she said. The rest of their time at the pool was relatively quiet as each of them was deep in their own thoughts, pondering how their lives might change in the near future.

Later in the day, the boys were visiting their friends, and the parents had time to talk. “Alice, my team and others have been ordered to begin training for another mission.”

“Are you going to Afghanistan?”

“No. I can tell you that much,” Joe said, with no hesitation.

“Good. So why can’t you tell me where you’re going?”

Joe had to think about this for a moment. It was July 2002 and the drum beat of war with Iraq was still months away. “Honey, this is one of those times when I just can’t tell you anything more. I’m sorry.” Usually, Alice was vivacious and happy, in constant motion. At that moment, she looked small and fragile, her energy and joy drained out of her. Joe reached out and hugged her in silence. “I’m sorry that I have to leave you and the boys for several months, and...”

Alice pulled away from Joe’s embrace. “Several months! Joe!” She fell back into his arms with a whimper and tears in her eyes. This was not the first time that Joe had left for lengthy periods during previous assignments, but it was the first time that she had no advance warning and no explanation from her husband on where he was going, or why.

“I’m sorry,” Joe said again as he looked with sadness into her eyes. The last eighteen months had given them a reasonably long stretch of quality family time together at Fort Bragg, and he wanted the status quo to continue indefinitely. He took a deep breath and assumed the stoic strength that helped him define himself as an elite member of the US Army. "Alice, it's my job. We both knew that this normal life together with the boys wouldn't last forever. I do what I do because I feel good about working with my buddies on the team, helping others, and the challenge of giving really bad people the justice they deserve." He paused as Alice looked at him with a frown. "I don't know what I would do for a career if I wasn't working with my team."

Alice stepped back from their embrace and stiffened her back as she regained her emotional balance. Then she looked at Joe with a straight face that hid her true feelings, "Yes. I understand. The boys and I have been through this before, and we can do it again," she said, half believing it herself.

Joe hugged her again. "Alice, I turn thirty-three in six months and will have twenty years with the army in less than seven years. By then, I'll be too old for this type of work, and we can think of something that will keep me home with you and the boys. What do you think?"

Alice smiled faintly and shrugged. "That would be good. What can I do to help you get ready?" she asked as Joe pulled out his empty duffle bag from under the bed.

The following day, after arriving in Washington DC, Joe's Delta Force team gathered in a government building classroom with the rest of the Fifth Special Forces Group who attended the Fort Bragg meeting the previous day. Charlie and several other men stood in front of the classroom. "Good afternoon, men. I hope all of you had a good flight this morning. Welcome to the George P. Shultz Foreign Affairs Training Center. You will spend the next four weeks here learning about Iraq's history, geography, economy, political structure, and the different cultures and religious beliefs of the people. We will cram a lot of information into this limited time. The men standing with me will introduce themselves to your individual teams after we break from this general meeting and go into separate classrooms. These men will be your most valuable instructors during the next several months, and your most valued colleagues when you arrive in Iraq."

After introductions, the teams were assigned separate classrooms where they learned more about their new colleagues, and a hint of where they may be going to after training was completed.

Joe, Paul, Gunny, and the team went to their assigned class room. At the door was a man who appeared to be about forty. He was in a business suit and had the appearance of a successful businessman. He was smiling and shook the hand of each team member as they entered the room. When everyone was seated, he walked up to the front of the classroom and introduced himself. "Gentlemen, I've been looking forward to meeting each of you since I was recruited to join your noble work. My name is Hakim, which means 'wise' in Arabic." He smiled. "I think my parents were perhaps too optimistic," he said as a self-effacing joke. "I escaped from Iraq in 1991, soon after the Desert Storm war. I am from Mosul, but unlike many from that city, I was not a Ba'athist. Saddam Hussein and the Ba'athists wanted to crush the uprising that was encouraged by President George H.W. Bush after Desert Storm. Unfortunately, things did not go well with the uprising. Hundreds of thousands of Iraqis, mostly Shia and Kurds who were not clearly aligned with the regime, were considered a threat. When I had the chance, I escaped over the mountains to Turkey and made my way to the United States in 1992. Saddam is responsible for the deaths of millions of my people and ruined Iraq. It is time for him to go and I want to do my part to make this happen.

I grew up in the region where you are going. When I was a boy, my father, brothers and I would go camping in the desert and the mountains in Nineveh Province. I know the area well, and I know the people. I will train you on their customs and history, and I will be your guide when we are there."

Joe thought to himself, "Now it begins..."

Chapter Thirteen:
Baghdad University
September 2002

The oppressive heat of summer was beginning to give way to a more comfortable though still warm September in 2002 when Lara was enrolling for the fall semester at Baghdad University. Nawaf and Mohassin drove her from Mosul that morning and were met at the university by Aziz and Yasmine, who had an apartment nearby. This was a time of new adventures for Lara and all of the young women who were leaving their families for the first time to begin their adult lives as college students. New students explored the dorm rooms and met their new roommates and classmates for the first time. Excitement was in the air, and the campus was buzzing with enthusiasm.

Mohassin was unusually quiet during the drive from Mosul. She was deep in thought, concerned for both her daughter and niece. Yasmine and Aziz had been living in Baghdad since the wedding. Yasmine's absence from their house was difficult for her. Now she was losing her niece and surrogate daughter as well.

Nawaf picked the young married couple up from their apartment, and the five of them drove to the campus, parked the car, and walked toward the dormitory. "Lara, we will miss you in Mosul. Are you sure you want to go to school here in Baghdad instead of the University of Mosul?" Mohassin shared her concern and impending loss.

"Aunt Mohassin, I'll only be a few minutes from where Yasmine and Aziz live. Look at how busy this campus is! Yes, I want to spend my first year of college here. It will be exciting!"

Nawaf and Aziz decided it would be more appropriate to look for a place in the shade while the women explored the new living arrangements. "Remember, Lara, you are here to study and pass the courses necessary for you to transfer to the University of Michigan next year, like we promised your mother and father."

"Yes, Uncle Nawaf. I'll study hard and do well in my classes. But I think that it will still be a lot of fun," she replied with a hint of a smile on her face, betraying her enthusiasm and excitement.

Yasmine smiled, "Father, remember how frightened I was when I entered the university? It appears my American cousin has no fear. I think she'll be fine. Aziz and I promise to check on her at least once a week, and she is only a phone call and ten minutes away from our place. Did you see all the restaurants we passed during our walk here? We'll have plenty of opportunities to meet every week." Yasmine and Lara turned and started toward the dormitory door, almost skipping with their excitement, followed by Mohassin, who was much less enthusiastic.

Nawaf turned to Aziz, "Well, Aziz, I think this place is off-limits to us. Let's sit on the bench over there, under the shade. We may be waiting for a while."

When the women entered the dormitory, Lara's enthusiasm was diminished. The paint on the walls was faded and showed the years of wear by thousands of students. The linoleum floors also needed replacement, in some places worn so thin that the concrete flooring underneath showed through. Each floor had a common lavatory and shower room that, to Lara's American sensibilities, seemed a bit small for the forty women on her floor who would be sharing it with her. It also looked barely clean enough to be tolerable, lacking the cleanliness of almost any American restroom or the dormitory facility that she visited on the University of Michigan campus. Fortunately, she was more taken with the excitement of the moment and the prospect of meeting her new roommates.

When they arrived at the door of her room, they could hear some laughter. Yasmine knocked and asked in Arabic, "We have another roommate for you; may we come in?" The door was immediately opened and three smiling young women were standing there, looking at Lara, Yasmine, and Mohassin as they walked in. It was a small room with a window and two bunk beds for the four of them. A small desk with a lamp and chair was positioned at the head and foot of each bed, with two very small closets on either side of the door. Thankfully, an overhead fan was also in the room.

"We're sorry to interrupt. I think I'm supposed to be in this room also," Lara said to the other women, speaking in Arabic with a slight Mosul accent.

"Hello, my name is Eman. Don't be sorry. We all just arrived and were introducing ourselves." Eman was dressed in a fashionable but conservative western blouse and loose-fitting slacks. Lara took an immediate liking to her.

"My name is Babra." Babra was slightly shorter than the others and also wore western attire, but a colorful hijab loosely covered her head. She seemed a little shy and perhaps a bit nervous about her new environment.

"And my name is Eleah. My family lives in Haditha, and Babra is from Hilla. Eman is from Mosul." Eleah wore the most traditional women's clothing for Iraq, with a black hijab and long flowing dress. She also had a brilliant smile that radiated warmth and a trusting heart that also endeared her to Lara.

"Eleah, you're such a talker!" Eman said. "Before long, Lara, Eleah will probably share her entire life story with you."

Eleah pretended to pout for half a second. Then she returned to her beaming smile, "Well, I just like people to feel welcome." She looked at Lara and bowed as an expression of friendship. "The more they know about us, the more comfortable and welcome they will feel. Where are you from Lara?"

"First, let me introduce my Aunt Mohassin and cousin Yasmine. They're from Mosul. I'd like you to guess where I'm from," Lara asked playfully.

"Well, your accent isn't exactly from Mosul. You must be from some other northern province, perhaps Erbil or Tikrit?"

Babra began to smile as she entered the game, "You don't have an Anbari accent. I guess you're from Sulaymaniyah."

Lara returned the smiles: "Thank you for the compliments. Actually, I'm from Michigan in America. I wanted to learn how others thought my Arabic was."

"No!" Eleah exclaimed, "You don't sound American at all. How exciting, to have an American living with us!"

Mohassin was standing next to Lara as the introductions were being made, but then she moved slightly in front of her niece in a discreet but defensive gesture, "It's nice to meet all of you. Please do me a favor, though; don't let others know that Lara is from America. Not everyone in Iraq is interested in or likes America as much as the three of you do."

"I promise." Eleah bowed slightly and raised her hand to her heart as a gesture of respect for Mohassin. "Lara's secret is safe with me. But I do want to learn all about America. Maybe someday, I'll get to visit there."

"I've heard so much about America. Can women there really work in any profession and pick their own husbands?" Eman asked. She had an uncle that lived in Los Angeles and also dreamed of visiting America someday.

Lara laughed, "Well, women certainly work in many professions and are even managers and company presidents. Since I haven't been looking for a husband, I don't know if I can choose who I would want. I suppose some women get to pick but I think most of the time, the men do the picking.

Eman frowned, "You mean the fathers and uncles?"

"No, I mean the young men who women meet when they are also studying at universities, or later in the work place. Usually men and women end up picking each other. I think in some ways it's much more complicated in the US"

"How can men and women meet at work? I knew more women were allowed to work in many professions that only men work in here, but I thought they worked in separate areas." Babra was very interested in all this new information.

Lara smiled, "I'll tell you many things about America, but please don't let others know, OK?"

"We promise," Babra said as Eman and Eleah nodded in agreement. "It would be wonderful to have the freedom to meet many different men and choose the one to love, who also loves me. I think my family is already beginning to make plans for who I will marry.

Yasmine emphasized Mohassin and Lara's request: "It is very important that you keep Lara's secret. We never know who is angry at America and would want to hurt any American, including Lara, if they could."

All three roommates turned solemn for a moment and vowed to honor this request. It was clear they understood the reason for this secret and importance of keeping it.

"Well, I can tell you that after my husband Aziz and I secretly pledged our love to one another, his father and uncles met with my father and uncles to ask permission for him to marry me." Yasmine changed from seriousness to happiness, "It was all very formal and romantic. I'm very happy."

Mohassin smiled, "Your father and I and Aziz' parents always knew that Yasmine and Aziz would marry."

"Momma! You never told me this!" Yasmine seemed genuinely surprised.

"When you and Aziz were small and played together, it was clear to both of our families that the two of you should eventually marry. Aziz's mother and I would frequently dream together that this would happen. And it did!"

"Aunt Mohassin, I had no idea that you were involved with the matchmaking!" Mohassin was happy to share her secret: "Who do you think gave the idea that Aziz and Yasmine should marry to Nawaf and Abdullah? It was Aziz's mother and me!

"Well, I hope my parents make the right choice for me like it seems you did for Yasmine and Aziz." Babra's parents were from a traditional clan in the Babil Province, and she was quite sure that she would likely not know who her husband would be until after an arrangement had already been made.

"You will meet Aziz when we all go out to dinner together. I'm sure you will like him." Yasmine was always happy to talk about Aziz. She had never been happier in her life.

"It's clear that you're in love, Yasmine," Eman said. "We look forward to it. Lara, your American secret is safe with Eleah, Babra, and me. Right, Babra?

Babra smiled, "I still think that Lara is from Sulaymaniyah." Eleah also nodded in agreement.

"Good!" said Mohassin as she looked at Yasmine. "We must get back to our husbands." Both Mohassin and Yasmine hugged Lara, and Mohassin wiped a tear from her eye as the turned to walk out the door. Then Mohassin looked back one last time, "You will take care of our Lara for us?"

Eman, Eleah, and Babra all bowed slightly and in all seriousness said, "We will, don't worry." With that assurance, Mohassin and Yasmine walked out to meet their husbands.

"Lara, can we help you move your things into the room?" Eleah asked.

"Thanks, Eleah, I know I'll like living with you, Babra, and Eman. This will be an exciting year. My things are in the lobby."

Impulsively, Eman hugged Lara, "Let's go! When you settle in, we'll all go together to explore the campus and area around the university. I've seen a lot of shops and restaurants and can't wait to visit all of them." It was clear to Lara that she would be very happy with her three new friends.

While the women were in the dormitory, Nawaf and Aziz were sitting on a bench outside the dormitory talking about very different matters.

Although he had known Aziz since his birth, the dynamic had changed, and it was time that he got to know the young man better. It was a tough transition for Nawaf to change from the judgmental father of any potential suitor of the daughter whom he loved dearly to become a compassionate father for this new son-in-law. The task, as he saw it, was to build a bond of trust and understanding between them instead of a suspicion based on his concern for Yasmine. "Do you like the army unit that you're with, Aziz?" Nawaf asked in a fatherly sort of way.

"Yes sir. You've seen the nice flat that they gave to Yasmine and me to live in. The army is treating us very well." Aziz was also aware of this new and different relationship with Nawaf. He always respected him as an elder and a wise man. However, the seriousness of Nawaf's question indicated a more equal, man-to-man discussion about life.

"I know, Aziz. The army does provide a good salary and housing for you and Yasmine. This is all good. But do you feel comfortable with your job as a security guard for President Hussein and his family?"

Aziz was puzzled. "What do you mean, sir. Of course I feel comfortable and very proud that I have such important work. President Hussein treats our unit very well."

Nawaf was looking across the expanse of lawn in front of them when he began the conversation. Then he turned to look at Aziz: "We are all proud of you. I just wonder...."

"Wonder what, sir?"

"There have been rumors." Nawaf was a little nervous about having this conversation, but he reasoned that Aziz was now very much part of the family, so he could be trusted. "I'm sure you've also heard them; that President Hussein, his sons Uday and Qusay, and the entire Ba'athist regime is afraid of almost everyone else in Iraq. They don't treat everyone as well as you and the special security guard unit that you are part of. I've heard of abductions, mass killing in other parts of the country, and even talk of Uday taking university girls from this area for who knows what? I've heard from a few other fathers in Mosul that their daughters have told them of the disappearances of some of their classmates when Uday was known to be visiting local restaurants and discos. The classmates disappeared and were never heard from again."

The direction of Nawaf's questioning made Aziz nervous. "Respectfully, sir, I've never heard of such things. Please don't speak of this again. I've pledged to protect President Hussein and his family. This includes reporting any scandalous talk about them. I did not hear anything you just said. I must never hear such things. Please sir."

"Yes, Aziz. I understand." Nawaf sighed. "Let's talk about happier things. So, you and Yasmine like your new apartment. Do you think it is big enough for a family?" He brightened up at this thought and smiled.

Aziz was also smiling at the change in subject and the direction of this new conversation. "Yes sir. You saw our place. We have an extra bedroom for a child when God grants one to us."

"Good! Mohassin and I are looking forward to grandchildren. You can start anytime." Nawaf said half-jokingly.

"We also look forward to it, but we want to wait one year to give us time so Yasmine can practice what she learned at the university. By then, I will be promoted so we will have more money for a family. Also, we want to have more time so we can keep an eye on Lara for the year that she is here in Baghdad."

"Hmmm. I guess that's OK." Nawaf thought to himself that Aziz was indeed becoming a responsible young man. He was pleased. "No more than a year of waiting. Agreed?"

"Yes sir. Yasmine and I both promise." Aziz had already been dreaming of the future he described and was very happy to share this with Nawaf. Both men were in a good mood.

"Agreed! Good! So, in addition to protecting our dear president, your other most important job will be to keep Yasmine and Lara safe in this big city of Baghdad."

"Yes sir. I promise to protect them with my life!"

There was a brief pause in the conversation and a cloud came over Nawaf as he became serious again, "Well, I hope you will never be in a situation where you will have to do that. Your family, Lara's father and mother, Omar and Nadia, and Mohassin and I all have a lot of confidence in you and are very proud of what you are doing. Just know that these are dangerous times. America is accusing Iraq of having weapons of mass destruction, and President Hussein, his sons, and the Ba'athists are probably very concerned and anxious about this situation. Sometimes people do crazy things when they are concerned and anxious."

Aziz frowned. "I understand what you are saying. I believe that President Hussein is a very strong leader and will protect all of us, and Iraq."

Nawaf and Aziz stood up as they both saw their wives leave the dormitory building. "Let's hope so." Nawaf turned and locked onto Aziz so they were staring at each other. "Please be careful and keep Yasmine and Lara safe. As a parent and father, it is my job to worry about such things."

Aziz forced a smile to show his confidence. "Don't worry, sir. They will be safe with me." He looked away from Nawaf toward Yasmine and Mohassin as they walked out of the building to join them, "Ahh," he sighed in relief for another change from the seriousness of the moment, "here they come now."

Before the two women met up with their husbands, Lara came running out of the dormitory to catch up with Yasmine. Before they arrived at the park bench where the men were standing, Yasmine and Lara were laughing and talking with one another. Mohassin walked ahead of them and was noticeably more assured of the situation than before she entered the dorm a half hour earlier. "Nawaf and Aziz, it appears our Lara has found a new home." Mohassin finally broke into a smile, indicating her approval of Lara's new home and friends.

"My roommates, Eleah, Eman, and Babra, will be wonderful!" Lara enthused. "Eman is from Mosul. They are all very nice. I think we will have a lot of fun together."

"Just remember your parents are sending you here to study so you will have no problem going to the University of Michigan when you return home. Not to have fun." Nawaf said with all seriousness.

"Oh, father. Lara will study hard, but she can also have a good time at the university and here in Baghdad with us." Yasmine was looking at Nawaf. Then she turned to her husband, "Right, Aziz?" Aziz smiled, "Of course! We'll plan to get together for an evening at least once a week."

"It will be great fun!" Lara added. "I'm excited for the school year to begin next week." She looked at her aunt and uncle. "Yes, Uncle Nawaf, I promise to study hard and be at the top of my class. You and Aunt Mohassin have been so wonderful to me. I really appreciate everything that you and my parents have done to allow me to spend a year at the university here."

"I'm sure that you will do very well, Lara." Nawaf remained serious, "Please call us and write to your parents often so we all know that you are fine and working hard."

"I promise. Thanks again for everything. Have a safe trip home. Aziz, Yasmine, I'll see you on Thursday." Lara gave each of them a big hug, "I love you all, but Eman, Eleah, Babra, and I are planning to go for a walking tour of the campus and the surrounding area." She started walking back to her dorm. They watched her leave. She turned one last time to wave good-bye, "I'll be home to Mosul in a couple of months for our first break."

Yasmine called back, "Lara, remember, Aziz and I will meet you in front of the dorm at seven this Thursday evening. Aziz says he has already picked out a restaurant that he thinks you will like."

"It's my favorite," Aziz called out.

"I can't wait! I'll see you then. Gotta go!" With that she turned and ran up the sidewalk toward the building.

"I think our Lara is on her way," Nawaf smiled. "Can I take the three of you to dinner before Mohassin and I drive back to Mosul?"

"Sounds great, Dad. Aziz will even let you pick the place."

"Your choice, sir," Aziz turned to Nawaf, "and, I'll remember our discussion."

Nawaf smiled as the three of them began to walk toward the car. "Thanks, Aziz."

"What discussion?" Yasmine asked.

"Oh, nothing dear. Just man talk," Aziz answered.

Nawaf smiled again, "Yes, Yasmine, nothing to worry about. Just man talk."

Mohassin shook her head, "Hmm! Get used to it, Yasmine. I've learned over the years that husbands like to have their 'man talk.' Usually, it amounts to nothing."

Nawaf added with a chuckle, "Maybe, but we think it's important."

Chapter Fourteen: Back in the USA

During September of 2002, the anxiety of September 11, 2001 was beginning to recede in the collective memory of many Americans, like a bad dream. People were buoyed by the prospect that the war in Afghanistan had begun in earnest. Everyone was optimistic about the anticipated destruction of Osama Bin Laden and Al Qaeda in a few weeks or months, along with the Taliban, which was equally as abhorrent to American sensibilities. Despite the lingering grief for the victims of 9/11, most folks had recovered a sense of normalcy despite some background noise coming from Iraq. However, based upon the proven firepower and capability that the US military had demonstrated in Afghanistan, people were comfortable that Iraq did not pose much of a threat. If it did, the United States would destroy Saddam Hussein's military in a repeat of the very short 1991 Operation Desert Storm war, which had lasted less than two months.

The football season was in full swing, and many American families had settled in on a Sunday afternoon to watch the Pittsburgh Steelers play the New England Patriots. Hal Smith and his two boys turned on the TV, and while surfing the cable channels, Hall stopped on the news for a moment to hear President Bush talk about the imminent threat to the United States posed by Iraq and the weapons of mass destruction that Hussein may be hiding there. President Bush was speaking from the Oval Office of the White House in somber tones, "Saddam must understand that if he doesn't disarm, for the sake of peace, we, along with others, will disarm Saddam Hussein" Hal thought that was interesting, but not interesting enough to miss the beginning of the game. He resumed pushing the channel button on the remote.

Chapter Fifteen:
The Newlyweds
November 2002

Aziz and Yasmine, married for almost six months, had settled into a comfortable and happy routine in Baghdad. Yasmine enjoyed her work at the Child Protection Teaching Hospital within the Saddam Medical City.

The United Nations Security Council sanctions against Iraq that began in 1990 were devastating to much of the country. High rates of malnutrition, lack of medical supplies, and diseases from lack of clean water were reported. As a result, the infant mortality rate in southern and central Iraq had more than doubled. Despite these daunting statistics, the hospital complex where Yasmine worked was largely sheltered from the devastation that was occurring elsewhere in the country.

The Saddam Medical City was a huge complex containing twelve medical institutions or specialized hospitals. The size of the complex, quality of care, modern equipment, access to medical supplies, and the credentials of its medical staff had no equal in Iraq. It was reserved primarily for the military and the Ba'ath Party elite. It was also available to members of the regime's favored tribes, which included many families from near Tikrit in the Salah ad-Din Province, where Saddam's tribe was. Others were as far away as Mosul.

Members from these tribes who were in the Presidential Guard and Special Republican Guard, their families and relatives were also recipients of the services provided by the hospital complex. Saddam imported large numbers of young, uneducated tribal men from Tikrit and his childhood village, Al-Ujah. Most came from other parts of the Iraqi Sunni Arab countryside and a few trusted Shiite areas to provide his family and regime with extensive protection services. Young men from tribes who were considered friendly to the regime were encouraged to join the armed forces, where they enjoyed speedy promotion.

Even though much of Iraq was suffering from the policies of Saddam Hussein and his regime, the complex was not as stressful or overworked. The quality and quantity of the staff was robust and the services provided were the best in the country.

The location of the complex along the Tigris River was pleasant. Yasmine could conveniently and safely walk to work from their apartment nearby. All of her colleagues in the pediatric ward were women whom she had become very fond of working with. A few of the older doctors were mentors for her professional development. They were experienced wives and mothers, and didn't mind providing her with useful advice as she grew in her marriage with Aziz. There were several nurses about the same age as Yasmine and they were like sisters to her, discussing their husbands and lives as only close friends would be comfortable with sharing among one another. Sometimes, the number of children that required attention and the distressed parents who needed reassurance weighed heavily on Yasmine. However, most of her young patients did get better and this gave her the enthusiasm for getting up every day to go to work.

The route from the hospital to the apartment took her past several small markets, where she usually bought groceries to prepare meals for Aziz and herself. Although it took several weeks for her to develop a shopping and cooking routine which did not interfere with her job and time with Aziz in the evenings, she quickly learned which shop had the items that she was looking for on a particular day. This knowledge reduced her shopping time considerably. Fortunately, Mohassin raised her daughter to be a fine cook and housekeeper so Yasmine had no problem taking on these responsibilities in the tradition of all Iraqi women and wives.

Aziz also enjoyed his work with the President's Guard. His enthusiasm and attention to details earned him recognition among the more senior officers. According to gossip among his peers, this would soon lead to a promotion from second to first lieutenant. The prestige, salary, and other benefits associated with his work in this elite branch of the Iraqi Army allowed Aziz to enjoy a status that was well above most of his friends at home in Mosul. It also provided the means to take Yasmine, and occasionally Lara, out to dinner at nice restaurants conveniently located near their apartment and Lara's dormitory.

Although the three of them agreed to meet at least once a week, it soon became clear that Lara's busy campus life and the busy lives of Yasmine and Aziz limited their small dinner engagements to a more occasional basis. The increased time alone with Yasmine was a happy arrangement which Aziz appreciated most. The two of them would go out to dinner or some other evening activity as least once a week. Frequently, in the early evenings or on their days off from work, they would go for long walks along the Tigris just to hold hands and talk.

November was one of the better weather months in Baghdad. The rains typically started in December and the temperatures were usually very comfortable: not cool, but not warm either. Just right for evening strolls.

"Yasmine, isn't the breeze coming from the river nice?" Aziz was making small talk one evening as they walked on a trail in a carefully manicured park near the Tigris and their apartment.

Yasmine smiled. She didn't mind his engaging questions. "Yes. It was a long day at the hospital today. It's nice to be outside enjoying the night air." She moved her hand slightly to touch his as they walked, and he responded by holding hers. It was quiet as they walked and they both enjoyed the moment and each other, the gentle squeeze they gave each other's hand spoke for them.

"Yasmine, I've been thinking." Aziz finally said after a few minutes of silence. "What do you...?" He was a bit hesitant as he considered what he wanted to suggest to her.

"What do I what?" asked Yasmine. This type of question was unusual for Aziz. She made light of it, "What do I think about the man in the moon?" she smiled as she looked up at a full autumn moon.

"No." Aziz smiled a little. Her response helped him relax a little as he proceeded with his proposition, "You know, Yasmine, the guys in my unit are saying that I may be next in line for a promotion."

Yasmine stopped for a moment and looked at him. "Aziz! That's wonderful! When will this happen?"

"I don't know. It may only be a rumor, or the guys are just joking with me. But, if I did get a promotion..." He paused and took a deep breath, "What do you think about, maybe, we try to have a baby?" There. He said it, and sighed with relief that this very important suggestion he had been contemplating for the last several weeks was out. Thanks to the modern facility where Yasmine worked, she had the knowledge of and access to modern birth control, which enabled them to plan their family much more than most people in Iraq.

"I thought you told my father that we were going to wait a year, until we could afford a larger apartment?" Yasmine was quizzing him, but inside she was about to burst with excitement.

"Yes, I did say that, but Yasmine, if I get the promotion, we will be able to get a larger apartment as soon as one becomes available. If we start trying now, it probably won't be several months before we know if you're pregnant. Even if it takes several more months for you to begin to show, we'll have our new apartment by then. I think your father and mother won't mind." He said this quickly, racing to the conclusion so he could hear her response.

Yasmine impulsively gave him a big hug. She was also dreaming of having a baby but, because they both had committed to wait a year, they were using family planning supplies available at her work. "I can't wait to have a baby!" She was so happy with the thought that a few tears formed in her eyes as she looked at him.

Aziz was relieved. Then the magnitude of their decision to begin a family began to concern him. He wanted to discuss this with Yasmine for a while. However, now that they were both in agreement, he began to think more strategically about the timing for this. "Yasmine, I want a family as much as you, but...let's wait, at least until I actually have the promotion. Is that OK?"

Yasmine smiled demurely as she looked into his eyes. "Yes, Aziz. That's OK. I don't think we will be waiting very long." She said confidently.

It was a touching and love filled moment for both of them. They hugged again, this time both had tears of emotion in their eyes. Then, they turned toward their apartment building, quietly hand in hand, enjoying the evening and the company of each other more than ever.

Chapter Sixteen: Semester Break and a Visit to Mosul January 2003

Lara's first semester flew by. Her initial fears that she didn't understand Iraqi Arabic well enough to follow the lectures and keep up with the extensive required readings were unfounded. She did fine and attained grades ranging from the top 15% to 5% in her classes. Not bad for an American, she thought.

No time was lost in establishing a close relationship with her roommates. Although her background and experiences were substantially different from theirs, they were all a bit surprised at how similar their views on life were with regard to young men, love, and the long-term prospect of marriage and having families. Near term, they wanted to do well at the university so they could become working professional women. They all enjoyed the student life on campus and the many different restaurants and night clubs nearby. Yasmine and Aziz joined them for a night out about once a month. However, most of the time the young married couple preferred to spend time only with each other.

Saddam Hussein and his regime of thugs remained in control and seemed to enjoy brutally asserting their total power over everyone outside their inner circle of very loyal henchmen. However, the country did enjoy substantial secular freedom. Women, especially, enjoyed the liberties taken for granted by many of their sisters in America and Europe. Baghdad, more than most of the provincial capitals and other larger cities, had relaxed views on dress codes, drinking, and movement without male family escorts to ensure that single daughters and sisters were never alone in public. This freedom included risks that women anywhere in the world faced with regard to unwanted advances, or worse, from men. But it was a risk that the young cosmopolitan Iraqi women were willing to accept. This was as it had always been, except in Mosul, for Lara. However, this freedom was very new to Eman, Eleah, and Babra.

They were cautious about this change in their lives from the traditions of their home communities. Lara, as the less risk-averse American woman, was their role model. Using Lara's example, her roommates quickly embraced these new freedoms. They were still naïve and shy around men, preferring to talk and (at night clubs) dance among themselves than risk an encounter with men they did not know. Much of their family and religious upbringing served them well in this regard because it helped them avoid risky encounters. However, with each other they did enjoy the opportunities and freedom of movement that Baghdad offered.

The semester break lasted two weeks which was enough time for most students to go home to visit their families and get some much-needed rest from the full schedules at the university. Eman's parents drove to Baghdad to take her back home for the break and Lara was able to get a ride to Nawaf and Mohassin's home with them. It was a pleasant and quiet time, which Lara enjoyed. Her aunt and uncle were like surrogate parents to her, and they considered her like a daughter as well.

Since Yasmine was in Baghdad, Mohassin and Lara spent a lot of time talking about Lara's adventures at the university and, of primary interest for Mohassin, how Yasmine and Aziz were getting along. Lara assured her many times that they were very happy and very much in love. Mohassin smiled every time when Lara said this, but she could not help but asking the same question, in different ways, two or three times a day.

The rest of the time, they went shopping together, and Lara was pleased when Mohassin offered to teach her how to prepare special family recipes for the evening meals. Previously, Lara did not take much interest in this aspect of domestic life, but now it offered a pleasant and interesting diversion from everything she was doing in Baghdad.

She was also able to call her mom and dad several times and reassure them that she was fine and enjoying her time at the university.

"Yes, but how are the courses? I want to be assured that you are going to be able to transfer to the University of Michigan with no problem when you come home," Omar asked more than once during the week.

Nadia was on the other house phone and added, "Lara, it's just that we miss you. Even though we know you are safe and our family is watching out for you, we still worry about you and want you to do well at the university while you're there.

"Mom, Dad, I'm studying hard and am near the top of my class for several of the courses."

The other end of the phone would be quiet for a moment as Omar pondered his daughter's assurances. It had been eighteen months since she left home, and he missed her a great deal. The initial excitement of having her visit Iraq and family there had worn off for both Nadia and himself. They were both anxious for her to return home to Ann Arbor. "Lara, I'm sorry to be so concerned about this." He paused again, "It's just that your mom and I are really missing you and want you to do well at the University of Michigan. If you study hard now in Baghdad, your efforts will certainly help when you enroll at the U of M."

Lara was a bit contrite and appreciative of her dad's concerns at the same time. "I know, Dad. I am studying hard and doing well. My grades show this. Don't worry. I'll continue working hard this year, but I hope you and Mom don't mind if my friends and I enjoy our student life also." She said in an even, matter-of-fact tone.

Omar sighed again and smiled. He remembered long ago when he was also enjoying life in his freshman year. "OK, Lara. You're right. We know that you are doing well and we're very proud of you. Keep up the good work. Please don't enjoy student life too much while you're there. Your mom and I can't wait to have you back home with us in five months."

A tear came to Lara's eye when she thought of her parents and the home she missed. "Dad, Mom, I also miss both of you very much. I promise that I'll continue working hard on my studies. I'm really enjoying Baghdad University, but I'm also looking forward to coming home next summer."

"Good!" Omar and Nadia said at the same time. Then Omar continued, "Keep up the good work, make good friends, and enjoy the rest of your time there. Perhaps after you graduate from U of M, you can go back to Mosul and Iraq."

Nadia added, "Just be safe, dear. We can't wait until you're back home with us!"

"OK Mom, Dad, I will. I love you." Lara said her good-byes, hung up the phone, and brushed another tear from her eyes. "I really do miss them," she thought to herself.

Mohassin was watching and listening silently as Lara talked with her folks. When the phone conversation was over, she knew that Lara was a bit sad, about both missing her home and the prospect of leaving the other family that she had come to love and her Iraqi friends that she made in Iraq in only five months. Quickly changing the somber mood, she smiled and gave Lara a big hug, "Lara, we're so glad to have you here with us during your break. We'll be sad to see you return to Baghdad today."

Nawaf was in the drawing room reading but had also heard Lara's side of the conversation and came into the kitchen where the two women were talking. He also wanted to brighten the mood with a smile, "Lara, we're already looking forward to your next visit with us. Don't stay away very long. The university seems to be going well with you." He paused for a moment and changed his smile to a more serious demeanor, "We and your parents are very proud of your excellent grades from last semester."

"It's always nice to come home. This really seems like home, and you are like my parents." She gave each of them a gentle hug. "Uncle Nawaf and Aunt Mohassin, thanks again for helping me stay in Iraq this extra year so I could do this."

"We're glad you could do this also. I think you will have good memories of Iraq when you return home in June." Nawaf said, "Just be careful in Baghdad. I'm afraid that America's President Bush may really start a war, even though President Hussein says we don't have any weapons of mass destruction and the United Nation's team still hasn't found anything."

"Uncle, America would never attack another country based only on suspicions. It's not the American way." Lara was very sure of this. "I'll be OK. You'll see. Nothing bad will happen. I'll complete my studies this next semester. Then, after a nice visit with you in May, I'll finally return home to my mom and dad."

"I hope you're right Lara. Just be careful. Since you're getting good grades, I guess it's OK if you also have a little fun."

"I am having fun!" Lara beamed with enthusiasm. "Aziz and Yasmine have become part of the Eman, Eleah, Babra, and Lara social club. All six of us get together as often as we can. Baghdad is such a wonderful city. It is so much more cosmopolitan than sleepy Ann Arbor. We are planning another outing in two weeks. Aziz says it will be to celebrate Ramadan Revolution Day."

Nawaf frowned, "I don't think that's anything to celebrate." The Ramadan Revolution in 1963 set events in motion that led to the emerging power of the Ba'ath Party and Saddam Hussein. At that time, it was rumored that thousands of people were killed for being suspected communists and other dissidents.

"Uncle! You're always so serious. I don't even know what it was about. It's just an excuse for the six of us to get together for a nice evening out." Lara was still smiling about returning to her friends and life in Baghdad. Nawaf decided not to dwell on the unpleasant bit of history at this time and offered a weak smile in return.

"Nawaf, don't you remember when you were young? I'm sure they are just looking for a reason to get together," Mohassin interjected.

Lara continued, "Plus, Aziz and Yasmine don't have to work on February 9, so we can all stay out a little later than normal."

Nawaf became serious again and reached out to hold Lara's hands gently, to ensure he had her attention, "Just be careful."

It was time to go and they walked out to the courtyard and Nawaf opened the front gate to the street. Lara gave her aunt and uncle one more hug, "We will be careful, Uncle Nawaf." She glanced through the gate and saw Eman's family car turn the corner to their street, "Here comes Eman and her parents to take us back to Baghdad." Quickly she grabbed her suitcase that Nawaf had set out by the door earlier, "I love you both and will see you again soon. Bye!" She took a few steps toward the gate as Mohassin and Nawaf both called out, "*Alssalam ealaykum* (Peace be on you), Lara. Study hard, stay safe and out of trouble, and have fun—in that order."

Lara grinned as she walked to the car and Eman's father, who had gotten out of the car to help Lara put her suitcase in the trunk of the sedan. She called back, "I promise. *Ealaykum 'an alssalam* (Peace be with you also)." Then, she turned to see Eman standing next to her. They greeted each other with a quick hug and got in the car. Soon the car turned the corner, and Lara was gone.

"Somehow, I'm more worried this time," Nawaf said with a frown. "I guess I shouldn't be."

"It's your job to worry for all of us," Mohassin replied. "Don't worry; we'll see her, Yasmine, and Aziz next month, and everything will continue to be fine.

"*In sha' allh,*" Nawaf said quietly.

Mohassin agreed with her own prayer, "*In sha' allh.*"

Chapter Seventeen:
The End of Normality
January 2003

It was about a six-hour drive back to Baghdad. The trip was quiet except for some small talk about the planned activities for the new semester. Eman's father was driving the family car, and to pass the time, he quizzed Lara on what she thought of the frightening talk coming from President Bush. Lara provided him with the same assurances that she gave to Nawaf. The notion of a conflict with America was not possible according to Lara's way of thinking. Besides, she was sure Iraq had no weapons of mass destruction. She had been in Iraq long enough to know that the country loved rumors and conspiracy theories. To her knowledge, there were not even rumors of such weapons in Iraq. No doubt, the UN team would make this clear to the world within a few weeks.

As they approached Baghdad, it started to rain. Soon the downpour turned the fields and empty areas into pools of soft mud. Lara noticed some cars on the side of the highway, up to their hubcaps in the sticky-gooey stuff.

"Why are those cars off the road?" Lara asked.

Eman's father was concentrating on his driving and had slowed the car down to almost a crawl. "During the dry season, the dust blows across the roads. When the rains begin, as they just have, the dust becomes very slippery, and many people continue to drive much faster in these conditions than they should. Hopefully those drivers stuck in the mud will learn their lesson."

"There's been very little rain until now," Lara said. "I've never seen it rain this hard in Iraq."

"It's like this in the Anbar and central provinces of Iraq, usually from mid-December through sometime in March. The rains started later than usual this year."

Lara looked out the window and saw another hapless driver with his car and family stuck along the side of the road. "I sure wouldn't want to be out there in this mess."

"In the desert villages, when it rains like this, people have a difficult time going anywhere." Eman added, "When you're walking in this, your feet will sink to your ankles, and the suction of the mud makes each step a challenge."

"Well," Lara sighed, "I'm glad we're in the city."

The drive took longer than usual, so they arrived to the dorm after dark. Eman said her good-byes to her parents, who were traveling to another part of the city to stay with relatives before returning to Mosul. Lara and Eman made their way to their dorm room to meet their other roommates and good friends, Eleah and Babra, and begin another exciting semester in January 2003.

Chapter Eighteen:
Looking and Lusting for Women
February 8, 2003

The sun was almost setting over the lake at Dreamland, one of Uday Hussein's favorite palace and resort complexes in Iraq. The lake was shaped like a giant creature with two legs, a distorted head, and a long arm that was bending over a small person on her back in a helpless position with one leg and foot extended and the other foot in the air. The head of the small person had a tiny neck created by two small earthen walkways jutting out toward the middle of that part of the lake. They were connected by a thirty-foot bridge that still had the disguised cage in the middle. An island in the middle of the bigger portion of the lake formed the outline between the giant's head and arm. It had an attractive arched bridge that connected it to the mainland. The road from the bridge continued on the island for about 800 feet and was shaded by large palm trees. Near the end of the road were several small cinder-block cottages with brown stucco exteriors. The cottages were located behind a very large stately home. Many in Iraq would call the home a palace. It was approximately twenty thousand square feet: 100 by 100 feet square and two stories, each with spacious fifteen-foot ceilings.

The land surrounding the lake was shaded by palm trees and included parklands with many more cottages, smaller cabins and family campgrounds. The entire complex of Dreamland had originally been created as a private recreational area for Ba'ath party members and their families. The complex enclosed approximately two square miles and was located about five miles from the city of Fallujah, in Anbar Province, a region that had strong support for Saddam Hussein and his regime.

The complex was home to a cadre of very trusted gardening, maintenance, housekeeping, and kitchen staff, an army tank company with a complement of soldiers and support staff, along with an elite special force of bodyguards. Their mission was to cater to Uday's requirements and whims when he was there and maintain the complex for close friends and Ba'ath party elite when they were invited to stay in the cottages and cabins. The house was Uday's private domain and the second floor, especially, was visited by only a few members of the cleaning staff, who were sworn to secrecy on what was there.

It was rumored that it included a well-equipped gym; a very large bathroom complete with showers, sauna, and large whirlpool bath; and a refrigerated room for cooling down after a workout. Probably Uday's favorite room was a massive bedroom complete with an ornate king-size bed and dresser, large mirrors on two of the walls, a large closet replete with his several official military uniforms, sporting outfits, and other dress and casual clothes, another closet with skimpy women's clothing in various sizes, and a smaller closet full of sadistic-looking instruments for which only Uday had the key.

The Dreamland property had been reserved exclusively for Uday during the week before the Ramadan Revolution Day celebration so he could entertain some of his father's political friends and their families. When the guests departed on the day of the celebration, he would have the place to himself. This would provide the requisite privacy for his other, more self-centered and very secretive activities.

The air was comfortably warm later in the day and cooled slightly as the sun set over the lake. Uday summoned Ali, his senior bodyguard, to bring his new Lamborghini to him and gather the other guards with the four high-end Mercedes SUVs to the front of the house. He was in the mood for some fun near the University of Baghdad district known for a lively night-life and many, many young women. It was a great night to enjoy his new car and live the life of a debonair and sought-after playboy, which he imagined himself to be.

Uday always enjoyed driving his latest sports car at dusk along the highway from Dreamland to Baghdad. This latest addition to his collection had a custom paint job with a large metallic gold racing stripe that accented the high-gloss red finish on the rest of the car. Since the stripe was his idea, he immediately liked it very much. The divided four-lane Route 1 highway to Baghdad was very good and mostly straight all the way to the city. The local police, National Guard, and a lead Mercedes with some of his guard staff cleared all other vehicles from the road for about ten miles in advance of Uday so he could drive as fast as he wanted with no obstruction or interference from other traffic. He had taken delivery of the car a few days before, and with his official entertaining duties out of the way, he was ready to entertain himself. The average time to drive from Dreamland to Baghdad University for most people would be slightly more than an hour. However, Uday was not like most people; with others clearing the way, it took him only about thirty minutes while cruising along at 120 miles an hour, slowing to safer speeds only when he reached Baghdad.

When he arrived at the restaurant and night-life district where he typically went to look for his evening entertainment, he and his lead car were approximately ten minutes ahead of his caravan of guards. Rather than go into the nearby nightclub immediately, he waited in the car and enjoyed the envious stares of the university students, particularly the coeds, as they admired his car and smiled at him. Probably none of the passersby knew who he was, but they were certain he was an important person, probably someone powerful within the country who expected deference and perhaps deserved a healthy dose of fear. He and his new Lamborghini waited at the curb long enough to attract the attention of the few others who did know him, and they made certain to keep their distance.

Soon the other three Mercedes SUVs pulled up behind him. When he saw the SUVs turn the corner in his rear-view mirror, he slowly got out of the car as six of his bodyguards got out of theirs and walked up to meet him. With his beefy companions, Uday slowly made his way down the street with a slight but noticeable limp. The others slowed their pace to walk with him.

He was in a good mood, contemplating what the evening would have in store for him as he talked to his men, "I wanted to celebrate earlier this week. It was nice to enjoy some time with Abid Hamid Mahmud and his family, but I was glad when they left this morning so we could come here." Uday smiled and sighed with contentment for a moment. Abid Hamid was his father's personal secretary and right-hand man. He was also his brother's top aid for overseeing the Iraqi Special Security Organization. Although Uday and Qusay liked and respected each other as henchmen for their father, they were also rivals aspiring to take over their father's position one day. Uday considered his time with Abid Hamid as an investment in the future. "It is Ramadan Revolution Day! On this day in 1963, my father helped overthrow General Abd Al-Karim Qasim and begin his path to become president of Iraq! It is a good excuse to have a party at Dreamland!"

Ali smiled. It was always much better when his boss was in a good mood, but his collegial friendship with Uday was strong enough to ask questions that others only thought about. "Sir, aren't you a little worried about the Americans?" All Iraqis were aware of the provocative, even threatening statements made by America's president and his staff.

"Why should I be? The United Nations investigators have been looking for our mythical weapons of mass destruction for two years, and they still haven't found them." Uday stopped for a moment and pointed across the street to a large white truck with men unloading cases of beer for the nightclub next to it. "There's one of the 'mobile biological weapons labs' that Bush's puppet Powell talked about on TV the other night. The UN will demonstrate to everyone we have no weapons of mass destruction, and Bush will look like the fool that he is."

At that moment a handsome young man dressed in his Iraqi Army lieutenant's uniform approached. It was Aziz with his wife Yasmine, her cousin Lara, and their friends Eman, Eleah, and Babra walking toward the restaurant near Uday's car. The young women were typical of many young University of Baghdad coeds. They were attractive, full of life, and happily enjoying the evening with good friends. It was a festive evening in Baghdad, and they were in good spirits as they walked up the street toward Uday and his bodyguards. When they walked by Uday, he became very interested in the five women and turned toward them as they stepped around the other men. At that moment, Uday smiled and nodded silently to his men as the group of young people began to walk by the Lamborghini and the SUVs. Their walk slowed slightly as they admired the shiny new vehicle. Uday turned to Ali and spoke quietly, "I think those young ladies would like to go to a party with me."

One of Uday's men immediately walked up behind the festive group, "Young ladies, this is your lucky night. Mr. Uday Hussein has invited you to a party at his Dreamland palace."

Aziz, Yasmine, Lara, and the others turned to see who was talking to them. They were startled to see the men confront them. Uday smiled and bowed slightly as he and Ali stepped over to stand in front of Aziz and Yasmine. Some of the girls smiled in puzzlement. It was clear that the man with the limp owned the Lamborghini, and the notion that they might be meeting a very famous person in Iraq momentarily intrigued and interested them.

Aziz knew exactly who he was talking, to and his stomach knotted in fear. "We are honored, Mr. Hussein, but we must refuse." He reached over to grab Yasmine's arm to protect her: "My wife, her cousin, and friends all must get up early tomorrow for work and classes at the university," nodding at Lara and the others.

Uday smiled. "I was not inviting you to the party, lieutenant—only the others." He gestured with a wink and smile toward Yasmine, Lara and the others. "And I cannot leave out your wife. She must go with us also."

"No, sir!" Aziz was terrified and his voice rose with his level of fear and concern for the women he had sworn to protect. "They cannot go with you!" Immediately, he began to turn away with Yasmine's arm firmly in his hand. "Lara, you must come with us!"

Lara started to follow Aziz and Yasmine as the other girls looked confused. Before the trio could take two steps, one of the men grabbed Lara. They all stopped as Uday stepped very close to Aziz and looked threateningly into his eyes, "Lieutenant, do you know who you are talking to? I am Uday Hussein, the son of your president and commander in chief. You will not argue with me. They will all come with us now!"

Another bodyguard pulled Yasmine away from Aziz as four of the men grabbed the wrists of the other girls. Aziz was in total panic, "No! You can't do this!" he said this as he pushed Uday aside to reach for Yasmine, knocking him to the ground in the process. Ali helped Uday to his feet as two of the others grabbed Aziz. The others were frozen in fear.

Uday was enraged. "Traitor! You will soon learn what happens to traitors." He looked at the women as Yasmine began to cry in horror. "Take them to Dreamland! I will be there later."

Yasmine, Lara, and the others were terrified as they were forced into the SUVs and the doors were quickly slammed shut. Yasmine was sobbing as the car waited at the curb. She tried to open the window as she screamed to her true love, "Aziz!"

The car they were in waited for a moment so Yasmine could clearly see through the window that two of the men held Aziz by his arms as Uday stepped back three feet from him. "I'll show you what we do to traitors!" Ali handed Uday his pistol, which he examined for a moment as he slowly pulled the slide to load a cartridge. He took a moment to enjoy the drama of it all. Then, seemingly in slow motion, he lifted the pistol and shot Aziz in the heart, killing him instantly. Uday was satisfied. "Get rid of the traitor. I'll see you at Dreamland tomorrow." Then, as if nothing had happened, he and Ali walked down the street to another night-club knowing, beyond doubt, that Uday would have a conquest or two that evening.

After the driver and his partner heard the shot while Yasmine, Lara, and the others were looking through the car windows and sobbing hysterically, they began to pull away from the curb. The remaining men picked up Aziz's dead body, dumped him into the back of their SUV, and drove off in a different direction.

The SUV with the five terrified women drove at the speed limit on the less-traveled Highway 11 from Baghdad to Fallujah and Dreamland. When they arrived at the entrance to the large compound, it was lit only by the moon, stars, and a few lights in the large house, about a mile from where they turned off the highway. Lara could only see small buildings along one side of the road and large fields of trees. It appeared that they were in a deserted village of some kind. Soon they went over a slightly arched bridge and drove a short distance farther to the rear of the house with the lights. The back doors of the SUV were opened by National Guard soldiers. The five women were firmly pulled from the two rows of seats behind the driver and escorted to a small cottage behind the big house.

The front door had a bar across it and a padlock that firmly secured the door. When it was down, the door was sealed shut, even if the force of ten men pushed it from behind. Near the door was a window, which Lara noticed had two vertical bars embedded into the walls above and below it. She guessed it was about three feet by three feet, or probably a square meter. Although they were too afraid to put up any resistance and complied with the soldiers' directions to enter the cottage, the men purposely grabbed each one of them in a manner that would have been avenged with an instant beating, if not an honor killing by fathers, brothers, and other male family members, if they were touched that way when they were escorted around the shops near their homes. Clearly the thugs were enjoying their unchecked opportunity to take advantage of the situation. They had worked for Uday and his brother long enough to observe and adopt their sordid practices.

Once inside, the single light in the small living and dining area was turned on to reveal a very worn sofa, upholstered chair, small square table, and four wooden chairs. There were smaller windows on either side of the room in addition to the front window. These windows didn't have bars, but they were higher on the wall and appeared to be too small for a person to fit through. Each window had heavy curtains hanging on either side. Despite the shocking events of the evening, Lara was focused enough to observe and begin to consider opportunities for escaping. "Well," she thought, "at least we can close the curtains for privacy."

When they entered the room, Yasmine immediately collapsed onto the sofa in exhausted, heart-wrenching crying. She could control her emotions during the drive to Dreamland out of fear that her weeping would prompt Uday's two men to summarily shoot her and the others on a darkened strip of the highway. However, once inside the cottage, she could no longer contain her utter despair. This startled the guards, and one of them pulled his pistol out and pointed it at her.

"Stop this noise, or I will shoot you now!" he said with a very firm, assured voice. Even if he knew of the trauma of the girls' evening in Baghdad, he probably couldn't care less about it. Typically the young women brought to Dreamland late at night were very frightened, but they were usually subdued and frightened enough to comply with the soldier's commands in a silent, dazed manner. Yasmine looked at him and immediately took a deep breath to try to stay silent as he stared back at her with the gun still pointed in her direction. Instinctively, Eman and Lara each took a step slightly in front to protect her. The gun was then pointed at them, and everyone was silent for a long moment as the soldier considered what to do next.

"You have been invited here as guests of His Excellency, Uday Hussein." He paused for effect, not realizing that the women already knew very well who had kidnapped and sent them there. "This will be your living quarters until Mr. Hussein chooses to send you away." He paused again, as if he were thinking through the lines of a carefully worded script. "Mr. Hussein wants you to know that you will be well cared for here, as his guests. Tomorrow a delicious meal will be delivered for you in the morning. During the afternoon, you will be escorted to the women's section in his home to wash and prepare yourselves for a very enjoyable evening with him at his private club on the lake. There are several very well-stocked wardrobes for each of you to select an evening dress that you think Mr. Hussein would like to see you in." He stopped again and, satisfied that he had their complete attention, put away his gun, although the other soldiers had their hands on their gun belts, at the ready. "You will want to please Mr. Hussein. He is very generous to young women such as the five of you if they make him happy."

Lara, Eman, Babra, and Eleah all remained standing and stared at him in silence. Yasmine quietly slumped her head forward and covered her face with her hands. The men opened the door and began to back out of the house as the spokesman offered one final threat: "One last thing. Do not think about attempting anything that will make Mr. Hussein angry. He can be very generous, but if any of you make him upset...well, Allah be with you." With that advice, he shut the door, and they heard the soldiers lower the bar and lock it into place.

The main room had a small sink and hot plate on a bench bolted to the back wall. The hot plate looked like it had been used plenty of times, based upon the baked on grime that covered some of it. It was plugged into the single outlet on the wall. Beyond the wall was a small bedroom with a single double bed to the left-hand side, and a bathroom to the right, which consisted of a typical Middle Eastern toilet with porcelain foot treads on either side of a hole in the floor and a water hose attached to a pipe near it. There was also a small sink with a single dripping faucet. Lara observed this and was thankful that at least there was running water. The bathroom had a small window, and the rear wall of the bedroom had another square-meter window with two bars embedded into the stucco on the bottom and top of the window opening.

"What are we going to do now?" Eleah asked the others. Yasmine remained seated, silently rocking and softly crying in long deep breaths as Lara, Eman, and Babra thoroughly searched through each room.

The cottage was made of cinder blocks, with a concrete slab for a floor. Solid walls were also covered with a stucco that was particularly thick along the windows so that the bars were firmly embedded into it. The four girls walked into the bedroom. Babra walked over to the window and tried pulling on one of the bars to see if she could make it move. Nothing happened, so Eman began helping her, also without success. Meanwhile Lara and Eleah looked at poor Yasmine. She appeared to be very small on the sofa. Eleah walked over and sat down next to her to provide some comfort. Lara shook her head in sadness, but stiffened her resolve to find a way out of the situation. "Someday," she thought, "Mr. Uday Hussein and his people will get what they deserve." She walked into the bedroom and saw Babra and Eman struggling with the bar. She went back into the other room, grabbed a wooden chair by the table, brought it to where the two were working, and suggested that they arrange themselves so that Lara could stand on a wooden chair and grab the bar with two hands while Eman grabbed it in the middle and Babra grabbed the bottom. "OK, Babra, you pull the bar toward the middle of the room. Eman, you help her, while I push the bar toward the window." They all pulled and pushed as best they could but nothing happened. Then Lara pulled with Eman's help, and Babra pushed. Still, the bar remained firmly in place.

After a few more attempts, they gave up, exhausted from the terrible evening and their fruitless efforts. They agreed to call it a night and find a place to sleep in a place with one bed, a sofa, and a stuffed chair for the five of them to use. When the three of them walked back into the living area, Yasmine was asleep in a sitting position, leaning on Eleah, who had also dozed off. Eman brought another chair from the table and collapsed into the upholstered chair, propping her feet up on the wooden chair. "You two share the bed tonight. We'll trade places, if we're still here tomorrow night," she said as she tried to make herself as comfortable as possible.

The others turned off the light and walked into the darkened bedroom, with the help of the ambient light shining through the windows from the big house. "Maybe we'll be back in Baghdad by tomorrow night, after we meet Mr. Hussein," Babra said hopefully.

"*In sha' allh,*" Lara said quietly. She was not as optimistic.

The following day, February 9, was an unremarkable date except for the fact that it would be forever burned into the memory of Lara and her friends because of Uday Hussein and his henchmen. They had a fitful night of sleep. When the time the sun began to rise, they were all so tired that a deep sleep overcame them. They remained sleeping until later in the morning when a loud banging and the sound of the bar being lifted from the door woke them up. A large breakfast of freshly made bread, a variety of chilled fruits, eggs mixed with meat, and juice and coffee was delivered to them. They hadn't eaten much the day before, anticipating a nice dinner that had been terribly aborted. During the past fourteen stressful and exhausting hours, they had not given much thought to food. So when the breakfast arrived, they were ravenous. Despite their lingering anger because the meal was provided by the staff of a tyrant, they ate all of the large portions provided to them. Later in the day, two soldiers escorted them into the large house that contained a section on the first floor reserved exclusively for women. There they were met by four women soldiers, not much older than they were, and directed to a shower room where there were all the cleaning supplies necessary to prepare themselves for the planned meeting with Uday, described the night before. The wardrobes contained a variety of dresses in an array of sizes. All of the outfits were designed to be sexy. There were a few outfits with a blouse and skirt combination. The women soldiers spoke very little while their charges were getting ready. However, when it was time to select their evening attire, one repeated the warning from the night before, "Choose wisely. Mr. Hussein is expecting that you will make him a happy host this evening. Your outfit will help inspire his appreciation for you. If you choose something that displeases him, it may go badly for you."

Lara, Eman, Babra, and Eleah selected one-piece dresses that would have been very fashionable in expensive European night clubs. They did their best to find the least alluring. However, considering their options, they all looked very attractive. Yasmine found a blouse that was one size larger to ensure that it was loose enough to disguise her shapely figure. The skirt was attractive, even though it was the most conservative offering available.

When the soldiers saw them, they only glared. They did not hint whether they thought Hussein would like or dislike their appearance. When they were ready, the five young women were escorted back to the cottage to await their fate.

At about five p.m., as promised, the women were escorted to the Dreamland disco in the SUV by the two men from the night before. There was still plenty of daylight, so Lara and the others had a much better look at the lake and surrounding area. Although there was a park-like quality to the well-manicured lawns, palm groves, and other shrubbery, they could see several discreetly placed Soviet tanks parked across the lagoon near the island palace. They also observed the appearance of an armed camp, with small groups of soldiers positioned along the way. The SUV drove slowly around the side of the lake, but the distance was short, perhaps half a mile. Soon they arrived at the two-story art deco building with a large patio area overlooking a lagoon that narrowed and was connected on both sides by a foot bridge before opening up to a larger portion of the lake. The sun had another hour before it would set over the lake, in front of the building facing the setting sun, it had a patio adorned with many strings of festive colorful lights, creating the illusion of a small and exciting night club. They could see the arched bridge and the island where Uday's house was on their left. The guards from the previous night and a few additional men, all with sidearms or AK-47s, were organized on the perimeter of the patio.

When the SUV doors opened, the women got out and were escorted to the patio. They were offered seats at a table arranged so the five of them could face the lake and observe the remaining rays of sunlight picturesquely lighting up the sky and water. It was still the rainy season, so there were clouds in the sky, and the orange-tinted dust from the surrounding desert area helped enhance the different shades of light and color that they were beginning to witness. Despite this setting, they all had a knot of fear in their stomachs, not knowing what would happen next. The unsmiling men with the guns made the situation more ominous. Cocktails heavily laced with alcohol were served to them as they waited for their tormentor to arrive. They waited for about a half hour, sipping sparingly at their drinks as the sun began to set. Lara noticed in the distance that more armed men were lurking in the shadows beyond the disco and along the lake.

The more Lara looked around, the more she thought the entire compound looked like an armed camp. Finally, she noticed the Lamborghini with Uday driving around the lake. Within a couple of minutes, he arrived at the disco followed by two black SUVs with bodyguards behind him. As he walked onto the patio, she could sense from his expression that he was not happy. Immediately all of the men snapped to attention, and, Ali who walked to the side and a few steps behind his boss, shouted to the women, "Stand up and greet your host!"

Although they saw him arrive and walk toward them, they were startled by Ali's very loud and authoritative command. They quickly stood up in his direction, but perhaps out of fear, they all stared downward to avoid eye contact as he walked up and carefully studied each of them, as if he were reviewing a line of young recruits. His interest was not on their attire. He had a certain approach to introducing women to Dreamland that worked quite well for him. His interest was to identify his first conquest and instill fear on the others. Frequently, the approach he took with the first woman was sufficient to instill fear in both her and all the rest. However, if the first woman was the slightest bit uncooperative, his approach in that situation still had the desired effect.

Although this review only took a minute or two, it seemed like it was a very long, frightful time to Lara and the rest of them. "Look at Mr. Hussein!" Ali ordered. They all looked in his direction, and he returned a cold stare, momentarily looking into the eyes of each very frightened coed and Yasmine.

The National Guardsman who had waved the gun at them the night before pointed toward Lara, "That one," he pointed toward Lara, "seems to think she is their mother and protector. Last night and today, they all followed her instructions. When we ordered them here this evening, they wouldn't move until she told them to follow us."

Uday walked in front of her and studied her carefully once again. Lara was very attractive in her summer dress. She looked straight ahead toward the setting sun as Uday carefully considered the guard's recommendation. "Perhaps," he said, thinking that would indeed be a pleasure to subdue her. He could tell she had spirit, and breaking such women always enhanced the excitement for him. However, he already knew which woman he would take first. He turned away from Lara and stepped to her left to confront Yasmine, who was standing next to her. "I've already thought about this on my way from Baghdad." He looked at Yasmine with a sneer. "I want this one. She and her now deceased husband dared to challenge me last night. Now, I want to see how she behaves without him by her side to," he smiled at the irony of his next comment, "well, to defend her." Still smiling, as he reached for the top of her blouse, "He's not here to defend her tonight!" His hand paused for a moment. Then with a fast pull downward, he ripped her blouse to expose her bra.

Yasmine stood still, looking down in complete despair. She had seen her beloved Aziz killed and now she was being totally humiliated in front of her cousin, friends, and the leering men. The other women were also looking down, embarrassed and afraid. Eleah and Babra began to sniff softly, trying to hold back their tears and anguish for Yasmine. Uday reached into his pocket and pulled out a small knife, opened it, and pointed the blade at her throat, gently lifting her chin up so she would be looking at him. He held the knife there for a moment and slowly drew the knife down to her bra and with one very deft swipe downward cut it in two to expose her breasts . Uday continued to take his time as he admired what he saw, and surmised that it was good for the morale of his men to enjoy Yasmine's helpless situation as well. He looked into Yasmine's eyes, "Did the men tell you that it's a bad idea to challenge Uday Hussein?" His voice grew louder as he said this and simultaneously reached down to her skirt and pulled it so that it fell to her feet. "Tonight, you will celebrate your new freedom from being married by joining me in the palace." He said this with a more even, but sincerely threatening tone in this voice.

These moments were always interesting for him. Would his victim meekly and fearfully accept his offer or not? It was a win-win situation as far as he was concerned. If she accepted his offer then, good. He had a lot of very unconventional ideas on how to take revenge with her in his bedroom because of the dead young lieutenant's audacious attempt to protect her from him. If she said no, then it was always enjoyable for him to crush a strong-willed woman.

Yasmine stood there in misery and shock, looking at the skirt around her feet on the ground. There was another tense moment of silence. Then Uday's voice rose in anger again, "Now you will come with me to the palace." He reached over and tightly grabbed her wrist, "You will come to the palace with me now!"

Yasmine looked up at him and spit in his face. "You are the devil! I will not go with you! I would rather die!"

Lara and the others all stood there looking in silence and disbelief that this was happening.

Uday dropped Yasmine's wrist and calmly wiped his face with a handkerchief. "As you wish."

As soon as he finished saying this, she felt a strong hand grip each of her arms and looked to see two of the guards pull her in the direction of steps leading to the side of the lagoon. She quickly tried to turn in one direction and saw Lara and the others standing helplessly as she was being marched forcefully along one of the earthen walkways toward the small bridge at the neck of the lagoon where it connected to the larger body of water. She began to scream desperately and struggle with the two men, going limp so it would be hard to pull her along, and when that didn't work, she dug her heels into the hard, sharp stones on the path trying to slow their progress. The men simply picked her up by her arms so she didn't touch the ground at all as they walked onto the bridge until they came to the cage that was hoisted on a large rope next to it. The cage had an open wire gate and the floor was aligned evenly with the bridge on the lagoon side. Yasmine began screaming and kicking with all her might as she realized what was going to happen to her.

The men dropped her and she fell to her knees with a thud in front of the open gate. Then, as both men quickly lifted her from the back, she was tossed into the open cage. As Yasmine slowly got to her feet, facing the disco, she could clearly see Lara, Eman, Babra, and Eleah looking at her, crying and begging Uday to stop the men. Six of the guards with Uday circled behind the women to ensure they would not turn away from what they were about to witness. It all became silent for Yasmine as she stood in shock and despair, looking at her cousin and friends, as if everything was a very bad dream that she would wake from if she could only scream loud enough. Then she was thrust back to the terrible reality when she heard Lara scream, "No! You can't do this!"

Yasmine felt her feet lift off the cage for an instant, as the guards let the rope lose so the cage would drop to the water. She saw the women wailing and trying to turn away as the guards forced them to look in her direction as the water quickly rose to her waist. The cage continued slowly but relentlessly to sink lower, and soon her head was only part remaining above water as she tried helplessly to lift her entire body to the top of the cage, trying for some miracle that would keep the cage from sinking. The last thing she heard was Lara crying out, "No! No!... Yasmine! Stop! Stop Pleaaaase....."

Everyone at the disco looked on, either in morbid satisfaction or horror, as Yasmine continued to scream hysterically and thrash about in the cage trying to keep above water as it continued to sink. The remaining light from the setting sun was gone, and there was only the sound of splashing as the cage sunk to the bottom of the lagoon. Then there was silence.

Lara was crying uncontrollably, as were the other three coeds. Uday shouted, "Silence!" With this command, fear once again gripped each of them. They stopped crying and held in their sorrow with very deep breaths, trying as best they could to be silent. Doing otherwise could mean they would be next to face the cage.

Guards were still standing directly behind each of them when Uday stepped over to within two feet of Lara and, with a very evil look in his eyes, smiled with a false charm. "Since your cousin was not cooperative, I am sure you will be." He looked at the guard behind her and commanded, "Take her to the palace."

The guard and two others were quick to respond by grabbing her and started toward one of the SUVs while the remaining men corralled the others and began walking them to the other vehicles behind Uday's car. Uday, with Ali at his side, began walking more slowly but deliberately up the small hill to his car. Near the Lamborghini, a National Guardsman, accompanied by two others, stood at attention. When Uday walked up to him, the soldier handed him a cable from his father, "Sir! The president just called. He wants you, Qusay and the rest of the Revolutionary Command Council to meet him at the Ba'ath Party conference hall near his Al-Faw Palace in Baghdad at once."

Uday was angered by this unexpected interruption of the activities he anticipated for the rest of the evening, but realized what this was about and had no choice but to control his anger and shout to the men with Lara and the others, "There's been a change in plans. Take them all to their quarters behind the palace! I will be back in a few days to spend time with each of them." When he began to get into his car, he shouted out one more statement, which would be taken as an order: "Especially that one!" The lighting behind the club was sufficiently well-lit so that everyone could see Uday point toward Lara. Although Lara's back was to him as she was being shoved into the SUV, she knew who he was referring to, and so did everyone else.

Before the drivers in the SUVs could start their engines, Uday and the two trailing SUVs roared down the lake road toward the gate of Dreamland and toward the Al-Faw Palace complex that was his father's retreat.

Chapter Nineteen:
A Time of Worry
February 9, 2003

Within one hour of leaving Dreamland, Uday and his entourage arrived on the very large Al Radwaniyah Presidential Complex near the Baghdad International Airport about twenty minutes from downtown Baghdad. The compound encompassed the Qasr Al-Faw palace, a sixty-two-room building with a very large, impressive domed atrium near the center of the complex, on one of many large interconnecting lakes fed from the Tigris. Near Al-Faw were multiple large villas, two of which were exclusively for Uday and Qusay. About two miles away was the nearly completed "Victory over Iran and America Palace" and across the lake from the palace were the Ba'ath Party House conference hall and a movie theater. Nearby was Saddam Hussein's private zoo containing a variety of African animals; from time to time he and his family, including his grandchildren, would hunt them for sport. There was also a park for his grandchildren, complete with mini-houses that looked like ones in a *Flintstones* cartoon.

Al-Faw wasn't the largest or most frequented of the ninety-nine palaces that Saddam Hussein built in the country, but it was just as elaborate as the others, with plenty of gilded ornaments. The entire complex was very attractive and well maintained despite Hussein's lack of interest in the place. Uday counted his villa near Al-Faw as one of his favorites. Uday and Qusay would occasionally visit and cruise the lakes on their smaller house boats, entertaining friends and Ba'ath Party officials.

Late that evening, Uday had other things on his mind. He sped directly to the Ba'ath Party House where Saddam, senior Ba'ath Party Members, and generals from all branches of the Iraqi military were gathered in the large conference room. When he arrived in his Lamborghini, two soldiers snapped to attention and one opened the car door as the other stood by to escort him into the building. Uday walked with his limp to the front of the room, nodding to the others as he took his seat next to Qusay and the most senior ranking generals and members of the regime. Near the podium, he saw his father talking with his uncle, Saddam's half-brother Barzan Ibrahim Al-Tikriti, the leader of the Mukhabarat, the Iraqi intelligence service. Saddam noticed Uday enter the room, and they briefly made eye contact as he was talking with Al-Tikriti. It was clear that both men were very serious. A moment later, Saddam stepped to the podium.

He began by reading from a script prepared for him and placed on the podium, "The Americans are gathering forces at the Kuwait border." He paused for a moment and looked slowly at everyone for effect, "They are unloading ships and parking their tanks, and other hardware outside Kuwait City...thousands of tanks, Humvees, and troops, and enough provisions for a real war with us. Our intelligence service says that Bush has recommended that the UN investigators leave Iraq as soon as possible." Saddam stopped again and looked up from his script. Then he began to address his audience directly, without looking at the paper in front of him. "We must prepare for when the Americans attack us. There is no doubt that Bush intends to invade Iraq regardless of what the UN investigators tell him." He stared at the generals sitting in the front row with Uday and Qusay. "Cancel all leave and put our troops on full alert. Evacuate the Ministry of Defense and other strategic buildings in Baghdad. When they do attack us, they will start by bombing there first. Move each of your operations to the locations outside of Baghdad that were built for another attack. After you meet with your officers and make final preparations for war, I want to meet all of you back here in about two weeks. There are probably American spies everywhere, so we will let you know the date and time of the meeting at the last minute. It may be our last meeting together for a while, and I want each of you to provide me with your plan of action when the Americans attack us. You are dismissed." Immediately everyone in the room stood at attention and the military officers snapped a brisk salute as Saddam returned the gesture, turned and walked to the side of the short stage to speak individually with a few of his closest circle of advisers.

Soon the others left the room, and Saddam turned to Uday and Qusay, "When the Americans do invade, they will be looking for all of us. I don't want you at the meeting I just talked about. Go to Tikrit and Mosul. There, our family and tribal sheiks can identify safe houses where you can hide. Stock the houses with plenty of weapons and supplies, and don't go back to your palaces until this crisis passes. The Americans will certainly begin by bombing the ministry buildings in Baghdad and our palaces, as they did in 1990."

Both sons bowed slightly, "Yes sir."

Saddam nodded in silence, satisfied that they knew the threat and would do everything possible to defend the family and themselves until this next encounter with the Americans was over. He began to turn and walk toward Al-Tikriti when Qusay added, "Stay safe, Father."

Saddam stopped for a moment and, in a rare instance of actual humanity, he turned and gave each of his sons a short embrace. "I will. You do the same," he said, looking at each of them in the eye. He turned again and walked briskly away to begin strategic planning with his intelligence adviser.

"Those damn Americans," Uday said quietly to his brother. "That devil Bush junior and his father always did want to destroy us and Iraq."

When Uday and his entourage sped away from the night club, Lara, Eman, Eleah and Babra were quickly pushed into the SUV and driven back to the cottage. The girls were in shock from what they had just witnessed and were unable to express any emotion. They simply complied with the silent shoving of the guards as if the entire process was an out-of-body experience. The short trip was without incident, and the girls were soon in the small living room behind the locked and barricaded front door, with three guards posted around the cottage. After peeking from behind the heavy curtains that were pulled tightly in front of the living room window to assure themselves that no more trouble would befall them that evening, they sat down and remained silent or cried softly to themselves as they slowly recovered from the shock and trauma of watching helplessly as Yasmine was murdered. Before long, the adrenaline drained from their bodies, and in silence, they each found a place to lie down and go to sleep.

Bang! Bang! The loud knock on the door startled them awake the following morning, February 10. They could hear someone unlocking the latch on the bar across the door, un and in a moment it was opened. A young man who was a servant at the palace walked in with a tray of eggs, fried fish, fresh hot bread, and coffee from the palace kitchen. The two guards looked in from the door and stared as the girls sleepily sat up with their clothes in disarray. Clearly the guards were thinking of something other than breakfast. The servant that delivered the food turned and walked out as the others slowly followed and barred the door once again.

"When will they let us go?" Babra asked quietly as she began to wake up, "We have exams in a week." Her question was to no one in particular, but it was on each of their minds.

"I don't think they plan to let us go," Lara replied in a matter-of-fact tone.

The others gazed at Lara blankly as this possibility was considered. "They must let us go!" Eleah was sitting bent over, with her forehead resting on her hands. She was almost in tears. "Our families will be worried, and we will be shamed!

Eman had a little more control over her emotions, but like the others, she was completely despondent. "We have already been shamed by Uday. We will all die. Just like Aziz and Yasmine. At least they died with honor."

Lara shook her head and sat silently with the others for several minutes as they all pondered their situation. After a while, she stood up and shook off her sense of helplessness, walked over to the door as the Eman, Babra, and Eleah looked at her quizzically, and started banging on the door and yelling in desperation, "Let us go! You can't keep us here! We've done nothing wrong!" When she started this, the others were horrified at what might happen next.

Within moments of Lara's banging and yelling, they could hear the door latch and bar being lifted, and a guard walked into the room with his revolver drawn. Another guard had his AK-47 pointed at them. Angrily, the guard with the revolver began talking to them, "You are here because Uday wants you here until he returns. It may be tomorrow or next week, but he will be back. Then he will resume the party, and you will all bring him pleasure. Or else you will join your friend in the lake. Now shut up!" In an instant he left, and the door was slammed shut and the bar came down with a loud thud.

Lara walked back to her chair and collapsed in tears, as the others also began to sob quietly and mournfully at the fate that was just presented to them.

Chapter Twenty:
Learning about Iraq
February 15, 2003

It was a cloudless evening at Ali Al Salem Air Base about twenty-three miles from the Iraqi border in Kuwait. Joe and his team were lined up along with four other Delta Force teams on a landing strip in front of a black US Air Force Lockheed MC-130H Combat Talon One plane. Each soldier had over 200 pounds of gear, including the 130 pounds for the parachute pack and rucksack containing all-weather clothing, gear for desert camping, and the essential tools of their trade: weapons, ammunition, body armor, helmet and face shield, the thermal gear they were wearing, and oxygen bottles that were essential for their 30,000-foot trip from the plane to their landing zones.

The five teams with twelve men each were standing at ease as Joe looked into the dark sky. Though the moon was bright, the stars were still magnificent in the desert sky.. However, this intensified the magnificence of the stars above them. The weather was a comfortable 70 degrees Fahrenheit, but they were dressed in much warmer clothes for their journey that night, especially the minus twenty-five-degree temperature and wind chill they would face during the first minutes of free fall after the plane's doors opened over the landing zone. As Joe gazed at the stars, deep in his thoughts, he was startled from his reverie when the brigade's executive officer called out, "Attention!"

The general, whom Joe recognized from his meeting at Fort Bragg, walked up to the formation of soldiers. "At ease," he called out to the men.

"All of you have worked and trained very hard for this moment. I know it's been a difficult seven months, especially with regard to the essential secrecy that each of you had to maintain in your communications with your families. In time, everyone will know what you've been working on during this difficult time of separation.

You all have the deck of playing cards showing the most wanted regime members and have probably memorized their names and faces. Although we are not at war, we still want to know where these men most likely will be when a war begins. Your job at first will be to locate any prospective safe houses where these individuals may go to when the shooting begins and lock in the coordinates of these targets for later. Then we want you to locate and identify specific military targets so that when you are notified, you can ID them with your lasers once the bombing starts. Your squadron commanders will brief each team separately on your other mission, which will be to search for evidence of the weapons of mass destruction that our United Nations colleagues seem to have a difficult time locating. Any questions?"

Tim snapped to attention and asked, "Sir, when will the shooting start?"

"Sergeant, unfortunately I can't provide that information to you at this time. You'll know when the time comes," the general replied, knowing that providing that information could compromise the entire war effort if any man was captured. "Stay invisible. Be safe, and good hunting." As he said this, he stepped back, stiffened up, and saluted the men.

The executive officer yelled, "Attention!" All the men instantly snapped to attention and returned the general's salute. Then he turned and walked toward his waiting Humvee. "At ease!" was shouted again as team commanders, including Joe, stepped out of formation to brief their team members with the information that they had received only a few hours before.

"Men, we will be dropped near the small town of Hatra in northwestern Iraq. You all know that Hakim completed teaching us his portion of the Iraq cultural training program three months ago. At the time, we thought he had returned home. However, I learned today that he left the US last month and traveled to Iraq. He will meet us 100 meters in front of the ruins at grid coordinate GB24319 and take us to a safe house near there. Enter the grid coordinate into your GPS compasses. We will aim for the same place when we jump out of the plane." Joe paused for a moment while everyone locked the essential information into their electronic compasses.

"Once we've rested up, Hakim will take us to the Mosul area and help us identify and mark the grid coordinates of the houses of Saddam's relatives, who may offer him or his family refuge when the time comes. We only have seven nights to survey the city. I understand there are only ten places they may use in our area of operation. When we arrive in Mosul, appropriate clothing will be provided to help us blend in with the population. While there, we will store our kit and sleep in a safe house that Hakim has identified for us. It is strategically placed near the areas where the possible targets are located. On March 6, Hakim has arranged to take us to an area in the southwestern region of Nineveh Province near the Syrian border. There is reason to believe that this area has hiding places for sarin poison in aluminum tubes used for chemical bombs. Our job will be to find these and lie low until we are told to plant a laser beam on them for the Navy pilots to lock onto."

He paused for a moment and smiled, looking at Tim. "Gunny, that's when we'll all know the war started." Tim smiled back and nodded his approval. "From there," Joe continued, "we'll make our way back toward Mosul where we will eventually meet up with the US Army 101st Airborne Division. Saddam is from Tikrit in the Salah ad Din Province, just to the east of Nineveh Province. So we may get lucky and find one or two high-value targets in the deck of cards that you all have." He paused a moment, then asked in a louder voice, "Men, are we ready?"

The team yelled back, "Yes sir!"

When he heard their enthusiastic approval, Joe ordered, "Grab your gear men; let's explore Iraq!" They each grabbed their equipment and began walking to the open rear doors of the C-130 as the pilot started the engines.

Soon they were in the air and climbing to 35,000 feet. The plane was heading toward five separate drop zones above northwestern Iraq where each team would jump at designated places to meet their Iraqi guides and begin their respective missions.

The men were sitting in canvas web seats and strapped in with harness-like seat belts. Their gear sat in the middle of the aisles of the two rows of seats that faced each other and stretched from the bulkhead near the cockpit to the decompression chamber and the doors that opened in the back of the plane. The seats were uncomfortable, but all of the men had flown often enough to adapt. For them, a crowded, cramped, and uncomfortable ride was all just part of the job. The flight from Kuwait to the first drop zone in Northern Iraq would take about three hours.

The special operators were using the new Modular Integrated Communications Helmet (MICH) communications component. This had been integrated with their specially designed helmets in 2002, while they were still training for deployment to Iraq. The men immediately appreciated the versatility the new technology offered. The multichannel communications capabilities to talk with the other men in the team and with nearby command centers were integrated with noise suppression to protect their hearing from bomb blasts, gun fire, and other deafening combat noises. The headset cord could connect to one or more radios. The MICHs were also capable of talking on a dual radio channel with a press-to-talk button. With this system, the men could plug into another radio with many more active channels. The headset speaker systems could also monitor separate radio systems. The men used the dual channel radios to listen for guidance from the plane's flight master and pilot and to communicate with each other. Although the men had their MICHs in place to protect their hearing from the roar of the plane's engines, the communications capability was turned off until it was time for their drop to conserve the system's battery power.

Some men tried to get a little rest by shutting their eyes, while others simply looked at each other, deep in their own thoughts as the time passed. They all acclimated to the additional oxygen they would for the jump by taking breaths through their oxygen masks, which that were temporarily connected to the plane's oxygen tanks. Finally, the jump master motioned to the men to turn on their MICHs and to the team nearest to the decompression chamber to unbuckle their seat harnesses and stand up. "First drop. Team One, get ready! Doors open in nine minutes!"

The team leader disconnected his face mask from the plane's oxygen supply, connected it to the oxygen bottle strapped on his chest, and stood up. The rest of his team followed, carefully helping each other strap on their parachutes, survival gear, backpacks, weapons, and ammunition. They checked each other to ensure everything was in place and secured for the often-practiced but always dangerous departure from the plane. When each man was thoroughly checked over by his partner, he would complete a final check on his own gear. After he completed all preparations and was confident that he was ready to go, he gave a thumbs up. When the entire team finished signaling to the jump master and team leader, the final countdown began before the equally dangerous free fall in subzero temperatures until they opened their parachutes and could guide their landing to the preplanned drop coordinates. "Five minutes! Can you all hear me?" The team leader talked into his MICH over the din of the plane's engines. The members of the team raised their right hands with thumbs up, indicating that the communications system was working. Then they put on their night vision goggles that fit with their oxygen masks to form a seal around their faces, protecting them from the subzero temperatures outside. The jump master opened the decompression chamber door where the men entered before opening the side door near the back of the plane.

When the last man went through the chamber door, the jump master shut and sealed it to protect the others from the instantaneous suction of decompression and the subzero blast of night air as the plane descended to 30,000 feet for the drop. The red light on the chamber wall facing the rest of the soldiers indicated the plane door was still shut. Inside the chamber, the red light was also on as the team inside gave each other one last check to ensure everything was in order. The pilots leveled to the designated altitude and started the countdown in the chamber as the plane lined up to the exact drop coordinates. The light changed to yellow, and a second series of lighted numbers appeared in the chamber: ten, nine, eight, seven, six, five, four, three, two, one. The door to the plane opened as the light turned green. Within ten seconds, the twelve men were out of the plane and free-falling at 120 miles an hour toward their destination. The plane door closed, the red light came back on, and the plane climbed back to 35,000 feet and flew to the next drop zone.

Thc flight route was a loop north of Baghdad, over areas near Samara, Tikrit, Kirkuk, Sulaymaniyah, and Mosul. Teams were dropped at about fifteen minute intervals, so Joe and his team had over an hour before their turn as the last jump team. Finally, the jump master looked at Joe as he stood up and called out, "Team Five!" Joe and his team of twelve men stood up and began the drill that they had practiced for more than a hundred times in their careers with the army; they had honed their skills even more during the last seven months of training, since July 2002. Soon the red light in the chamber changed turned yellow and the countdown began.

"Here we go," Joe thought silently to himself as he stood at the door in front of his line of men. He was focused on the door as it suddenly slid to the right into the wall of the plane as it opened. In an instant, he stepped forward and was free-falling into the night. Below, he could see a thin cloud cover that he was racing into.

His MICH headset was on, so he could hear, "Manny out, Bob out, Jordan out, Nick out..." Soon he heard with relief, "Tim out." Tim was the last of the twelve-man team to leave the plane and was safely clear of it, falling with him and the others toward the darkness below. Joe and the others could see the speed, altitude descent, and GPS coordinates reflected in their face shields. They used this information to maneuver through the clouds during their rapid descent, much like Superman, as they positioned themselves for parachute opening. At their speed, they only had two minutes to get into position. The numbers on the shield were racing as Joe extended his right arm to veer right, then his left arm to zero in on the GPS position that he needed as he soared downward. The plane dropped them at approximately two miles east of the landingdrop zone, so as he fell, he was aiming for the coordinates and accounting for the mild winds, which could take them dangerously off course if they were simply in free fall. At 10,000 feet, Joe was at the GPS coordinate but his trajectory zoomed him past it. He immediately pushed his right arm forward and pulled his left arm to his side to go into a tight downward spiral. Within twenty seconds and five thousand feet above the earth, he was back over the coordinates and at the proper altitude to pull the cord and open his chute. With a jerk of the parachute lines slowing his forward and downward descent, Joe was soon able to take a breath of relief and look around for his comrades. They were all soon in view, and within seconds they were opening their chutes and controlling their lines so that they would all land within two hundred feet of each other. He also saw, off in the distance, another parachute floating down that was delivering more of the gear that they would need for the next few months. Soon he also observed a car racing across the desert toward where the gear would land. Joe smiled. "Good, that must be Hakim." He thought to himself.

The darkness of the night quickly gave way to the dim outline of the earth that was fast approaching as Joe and the others navigated to their destination. All he could see were the outlines of some walls and a vast empty landscape with a few lights perhaps two or three miles from where they were going to land. The ground was rushing up on him now, and he prepared for landing. The landing zone was well chosen—flat and free of big rocks or holes that could be dangerous to men hitting the ground with all their gear at a running pace. He eased the velocity of his decent and shifted it into a horizontal instead of vertical momentum. In a moment, he was at full stop and caught his breath, as he lifted his face shield above his helmet, took off the oxygen mouthpiece, and stowed it into his jacket. He looked around and was relieved to see Tim and the others landing and doing the same.

He could see the headlights of a car in the distance and quickly disconnected his parachute, dropped his backpack and stripped off his thermal gloves, coat, and pants to his much lighter weight desert outfit that he wore underneath. Although he had worn a protective face shield and extreme weather gloves during the jump, his hands and face were still numb from the cold. As he fumbled with the gear, his hands and fingers quickly warmed up and became more nimble. By the time he had the gear off and piled between the approaching car and his now prone position, his hands and senses were sharply focused on what everyone hoped was Hakim. Their training taught them to err always on the side of caution and consider worst-case situations. He was preparing for what could be their first deadly encounter. The other men were making the same speedy transition from diving Supermen to shadows in the night.

Within a minute, everyone had dropped to the ground near where they landed and prepared themselves and weapons for what may be an unplanned firefight. Joe looked through the night vision scope of his rifle. The car had dipped behind a small hill in front of them and reappeared a moment later, only a football field away from where they were quietly waiting to see if it was Hakim. Although he assumed it was his colleague, he and the others didn't want to take a chance that some unknown Iraqi would emerge from the car, who happened to see the parachutes as they approached the ground.

The car stopped quietly, the headlights were turned off and a small light inside the car was turned on and off six times. Joe could barely make out through his scope that there was only one person in the car. The flashes of light were Hakim's signal that the area was empty except for him. He opened the door and the night vision scopes enabled all of the team to recognize their friend, who was going to be their guide, interpreter, and protector in Iraq.

Hakim began to walk slowly, with his hands in the air toward what appeared to be black boulders to the right of his car. Although he was quite certain that the boulders were his team, prudence suggested that he should approach men that he knew were in the shadows cautiously. When he was within 100 feet, he spoke just loudly enough for them to hear, "*S'Allam Allaehkum! Wahan Assallam*! (Welcome!)" he said.

"Hakim, it's us," Joe replied quietly as he and the men rose to their feet.

Hakim let out a sigh of relief. "This way!" he said as he hurried in the direction of the ruins. It wasn't safe to be standing around in the open. Perhaps others had seen the parachutes and decided to scavenge for what was falling near there. When Joe was parachuting within 200 feet of the ground, he had noticed off to the left of where he was about to land what appeared to be old, destroyed buildings. They slung their backpacks and other gear back on their bodies, grabbed their weapons, and started walking briskly to catch up with Hakim and his car. As they approached the ruins, they noticed the buildings were ancient; the men soon learned they were the ruins of a very old complex of Assyrian and Roman buildings. In moments, they were behind the wall of the first ruin, then Hakim turned on his flashlight and slowly led them down some stairs, pointing the light from side to side as he went. When he reached the room below, the men waited behind him as he looked around the room with his light. It was completely empty, but he still took a little time looking carefully at the corners to ensure it was safe. When they all entered the room and turned on more flashlights, they saw what may have been a two-thousand-year-old store room.

"What were you looking for, Hakim? It doesn't look like anyone has been here for a long time," whispered Bob, one of the communications sergeants.

"It's not people that I was worried about," said Hakim. "It's the snakes."

"What snakes?" Manny, a weapons sergeant, asked, with a bit of concern in his voice.

"Well in this part of Iraq, they're mostly vipers. One is sand colored and about two feet long, and the other is more spotted and six feet long. They're both poisonous," Hakim explained.

"The sand-colored one is called a Field's sand viper and the Lebetine viper is the other one," Nick, the team's operations and intelligence sergeant, advised his colleagues. "Probably you won't have to worry as much about the Lebentine viper because it likes rodents and is more common in areas where there's a lot of grass or farmland. He's the one that can kill you with a high dosage of venom with primarily hemotoxic effects that will cause intense pain before killing you. Since there isn't any grassland near here, I think the Field's sand viper is the one we may see lurking in cooler areas near or in the buildings. It is sand colored and has a black tip on its tail. This guy can also put you in a world of hurt, but the good news is that it's slow, and as long as you don't bother it, it won't come after you."

"Well," Pete, one of the weapons sergeants sighed as he put down his weapon and began taking off his back pack, "that's encouraging—I think." Pete was one of the weapons sergeants with the capability to operate and maintain every weapon used by the team.

Nick continued with his herpetology lecture, "The other good news is that in this part of Iraq, we won't have to be too concerned about the saw-scaled viper. This little critter is only about twenty inches long but is the most lethal in the world. When he bites you, expect to die from massive internal hemorrhaging and bleeding from your mouth to your butt." Nick paused for effect and smiled with the satisfaction of knowing these tidbits of information may be useful for his comrades, "The good news is that these guys only like southern Iraq, not where we are." The others were silent for a moment as they considered Nick's comments.

Joe quickly changed the subject and held out his hand to Hakim, "It's great to see you!" Joe spoke for the team.

"Hakim, what is this place?" Tim asked.

"This was the fortress city of Hatra. It guarded the two main caravan routes connecting Mesopotamia with Syria and Asia Minor 2100 years ago. At the time, the fortification was immense. The city was guarded by two city walls. When an enemy crossed the first wall, he'd still be faced with a moat and the second wall. Maybe someday, instead of fighting Saddam, we can visit this place as tourists," Hakim said hopefully.

"*In sha'allh*, Hakim. God willing. It's really good to see you again. What's next?" Joe asked. This was the first time that any of them had ever been in Iraq. Although they attended plenty of lectures on the country and read a few history books, they were relieved to have a knowledgeable and trustworthy friend as their guide during this mission.

Hakim smiled at their welcome. He finished his moment of hopefulness regarding the future of Iraq, "*In sha' allh*," he replied quietly, then continued with the plan that he had been working on for the last month. "First, we need to retrieve your cartons of MREs and extra ammo that are still in the desert. I saw the parachute land about 300 meters left of where the car is. When I leave tonight, maybe a couple of you can help me load it into the back of my car and we can bring it back here."

"No problem," volunteered Tim. "Jason likes to eat a lot. He can help us."

"When it comes to food, I'm always happy to help out," Jason smiled. In addition to being one of the bigger men on the team, he was also one of the two medical sergeants. The carton contained 300 packages of meals ready to eat (MREs) and other supplies, some of which would be hidden near Mosul for later in their deployment to sustain them until they met up with the 101st Airborne.

"You can stay here and rest until tomorrow afternoon when I return with an old bus that I bought," Hakim continued. "It was pretty beat up, but mechanics have done a lot of work so the engine and transmission are in good shape. Typically, men buy these and use them as a business, taking people back and forth from Mosul to the smaller towns and villages in Nineveh province. The bus will have a rack on the roof, and we'll put all of your gear on top and cover it with a heavy tarp cover. I'll also bring clothes for each of you to wear. We will look much like any other bus with laborers going to Mosul from the villages for construction jobs in the city."

The men nodded in approval, "Good," said Joe. "This fits with the plan I was told before leaving Kuwait. Saddam has distant cousins living in Mosul. Several are wealthy, with large villas, or for Mosul, small palaces. There is a chance that Saddam or his relatives may go to one of these places to hide when Iraq is attacked."

Hakim continued, "Mosul is about fifty-five miles from here. We'll go there first, and while things are still quiet and relatively easy to move around the city, we'll check out the places where Saddam's relatives live. Then we'll head across the desert to Baa'j. I have some cousins that live in Baa'j and talked with them and some other villagers in the area. According to them, the Iraqi Army has been visiting something between them and Sinjar about twenty miles northwest of their town, not far from Route 47, which heads east toward Sinjar, Al Tafar, and on to Mosul. There's also an unofficial border crossing about twenty-five miles due east of Baa'j, where a Syrian road ends, and on the Iraq side of the border, there's a road that runs north to Route 47."

"Since there's a border crossing of sorts, is there a lot of traffic in the area?" Joe asked.

"Probably, most of the traffic will be headed toward the border. Many families have been streaming into Syria lately," Hakim noted. "The location of the suspected WMD facility is somewhere within thirty miles between Baa'j and north of Sinjar. I'll park the bus and stay with my relatives while you continue into the desert from there. I've found a spot where you can store your supplies near an abandoned barn. You can use the barn to hide during the day and as a base camp while you explore the area. It has a water-well with a hand pump near a tool shed in the back. I think you will appreciate the water-well."

"Sounds good to us." Joe said. Any questions so far?" Joe asked his men. A few shook their heads no.

"Isn't it a little risky with all of us riding in a bus?" Paul asked. Paul was second in command of the team and a chief warrant officer.

"The alternative is to get at least five cars and trustworthy drivers that would be necessary to take all of us and your gear" Hakim frowned. "I don't think that's an option. It's a long walk in the desert if you want to go anywhere. I don't think that's an option either."

"Hakim is right. The bus is the best way to go. I think we'll be just as safe, and more comfortable on the bus," Nick stated.

"The bus is the best way to go," affirmed Joe. "We have a lot of ground to cover for the next couple of weeks and breaking into smaller teams to travel around will only complicate the mission. We learned before we got on the plane in Kuwait that we would search for WMD. It will be interesting to see first-hand what Saddam has been hiding." he continued, as he and the others began removing their equipment and preparing for some downtime and sleep.

Tim agreed, "It will be a pleasure to ride on the bus instead of marching through a lot of desert with all of our gear."

Colin, another weapons sergeant on the team, was a bit nervous about traveling around Iraq in the comfort of a bus. On previous missions, the team had either traveled quietly and stealthily at night or was transported to their destinations by stealthy helicopters. "Won't we be a bit obvious in broad day light, sitting on a bus?"

Nick replied, "By the time we all get on the bus tomorrow afternoon, we'll have two-day-old beards, and we'll look more like men from the villages as time goes on. Right, Hakim?"

Hakim nodded his head affirmatively, "Don't worry, Colin. When you see the new wardrobe that I'll bring tomorrow for all of you to wear during the next few weeks, you'll agree that no one would give you a second look. Remember the training on how to blend with the locals? Just walk with a slight slouch, don't look anyone in the eye, and don't speak when we're within earshot of anyone. If you all follow these rules, we'll be fine. I'll do all the talking."

"Hakim knows what he's doing. Like Tim said, we'll be in much better shape and probably much safer traveling quickly on a bus than walking at night through the countryside," Joe added.

"Tim, Jason, let's go get the cartons and bring them back here," Hakim urged. "Tomorrow morning, all of you can repackage the boxes of ammo, MREs, and any other gear that came down in the cartons. We need everything to look like boxes of construction tools and building materials when you're finished."

"No problem," Joe affirmed.

"I've also made arrangements for safe house locations in Mosul for our reconnaissance mission this week, and a different location northwest of the city for our return after the WMD mission."

"Thanks, Hakim, for all you've done for us already." Joe spoke for the entire team. The men had already removed the bed rolls from their packs and were preparing for some much-needed sleep. "We'll take two-hour shifts to keep an eye on things. The sun will be up in about an hour. Since Hakim will return tomorrow afternoon, this should give all of us time to rest up and get ready for Mosul."

"There may be a couple of buildings here that still have a portion of a flat roof remaining, or at least the remains of a second floor that could offer some protection. I suggest that you guard the perimeter from one of these. The land to the south and northwest of here is all desert for 100 kilometers, so I don't think you will need to worry too much about those directions. However, the northeast direction is toward the village of Hatra and city of Mosul. The southeast is in the direction of Anbar Province and Ramadi, so you will want to keep an eye on those areas."

"Thanks, Hakim. Tim and Jason, go with Hakim to bring the cartons back here. Pete, Phil, and Colin, see if there is any building with a roof near here and set up watch there. It's about 0500 now. At 0700, Jared, Paul, and I will relieve you. Tim, Nick, and Manny will be next at 0900, and Bob, Jordan and Jason will take the 1100 to 1300 shift," Joe directed. Jared was the team engineer sergeant, responsible for a wide range of disciplines, from demolition and construction of field fortifications to topographic survey techniques. Phil was the other communications sergeant specializing in the operation of every kind of communications gear, from encrypted satellite communications systems to old-style high-frequency Morse key systems. Jordan was the other medical sergeant.

"That will work fine," Hakim said, as he reached into his pants pocket. "Before I forget, here's a fully charged Iraqi cell phone with my number programmed into it, and a small battery pack for recharging. The land-line phones haven't been working well lately, but the telecom network seems to be just fine. If you need me for anything, call the number three times, and hang up each time after three rings. I won't answer the call, but I'll know it is you and will come to where ever we last met as soon as possible. It's not very high-tech, but at least it's a backup plan in case your plans change. Otherwise, let's stick to our agreed plans before we go in separate directions each time. I expect to return here at about 1300 with your new-old clothes, your supplies, and the bus. Be ready."

"Thanks again, Hakim. See you then," Joe said. Hakim nodded to his friends, turned, and walked out the door with Tim and Jason.

Joe turned to Pete, Phil and Colin, "Take your camouflage netting with you. It's still dark, but within an hour the sun will be up and you'll need the netting for shade and concealment from anyone flying overhead."

The three men stepped out into the night. It was just before dawn, which allowed them to look around the ruins to find a suitable watchtower without worrying too much about being spotted from a distance. Fortunately, within two hundred meters, there was a two-story structure that had an opening to the second floor. It was suitable enough, but the ladder to the second floor was long gone. They had their night vision goggles on and started looking around. There were several piles of large building stones lying near the perimeter of some of the buildings that must have fallen down over the last two thousand years.

Pete walked out the door. The others followed and started picking up the larger building stones that were roughly cut in approximately one foot squares. They carried them into the building and placed them below the opening. The men worked silently and soon a pyramid-shaped pile was taking shape. The low ceiling of the first floor would place the opening within reach of the men with perhaps three or four rows of the stones piled on top of each other. As they were walking out the door to scavenge for the last row of stones, it occurred to Pete that they should remember what Nick had been talking about. He was about to express his concern to the others when Colin let out a loud, startled, "Shit!" from around the corner of a nearby building. The men quickly grabbed their M19 Glock pistols and ran to the corner of the building. Silently, Pete looked around the corner as he began raising his pistol for action, then he saw Colin standing three feet away from the stones and looking at them with his hands on his hips. "Damn, there's a snake behind those," as he pointed to the loose assortment of stone blocks in front of him.

Pete and Phil put their pistols down and started laughing quietly. "I was just about to warn you about snakes," Pete said, "I guess I don't need to now." The three of them carefully walked up and peered behind the stones that hid the snake. It was a curled-up sand viper that, without the night vision goggles, would have been almost impossible to see in the dark. It wasn't moving. "Nick was right. These guys don't move much, thank goodness."

"He didn't have to move; when I saw him, he scared the crap out of me," Colin said smiling and shaking his head.

"It's a good thing the Iraqis aren't snakes, or we'd really be in trouble," Phil joked.

Within a few minutes, they gathered the remaining blocks required to create a platform high enough for each of them to climb to the second story of the building. It was open to the clear, star-filled sky, with a partial half wall of blocks that offered protection and provided a means to hang their camouflage netting over them. They fashioned their net-like covers and positioned themselves to view the various fields of vision indicated by Joe as the first rays of dawn lit up the eastern sky.

"I wonder what those big black shadows are over there." Pete was looking toward the south east.

Phil had the western half of the perimeter to watch, and it was very dark in that direction. "It looks pretty empty over here," he said.

Colin was looking toward the north east and could only make out the scattered ruins of foundations. Just then, the first rays of day light appeared, and both Colin and Pete began to see the ancient city of Hatra appear before them. It was like a mirage at first, slowly becoming clear and very real with each passing moment, as more light came from the rising sun. "Wow! Phil, you've got to see this!" he spoke softly.

Beyond the nearby foundation ruins and the low building where Joe and the others were sleeping, there were large and majestic structures. Some appeared to be about fifty feet high. The pale morning sun gave the buildings a soft, honey-colored glow. As the sun began to climb into the morning sky, Colin and Pete were both in awe as they saw a myriad of arches and columns that were still standing. All three men were looking through their rifle scopes, scanning their areas of responsibility. Phil could only see the road that Hakim drove on to meet them and the area where they had landed a few hours before. The entire landscape was barren except for some patches of green in the distance. Despite Colin's suggestion to take a look in the other direction, Phil wanted to ensure his area was secure. At the moment, there was nothing moving in his direction.

"I'll trade places with you for a while, Phil. The view in our direction is magical," Pete said as he began to crawl over to Phil's position, staying below the walls that surrounded them.

"Thanks. It's all clear over here." Phil rolled over so that Pete could position himself at the opening of the wall where he had been, then crawled over to where Pete was. "Unbelievable! I've never seen anything like this," he exclaimed as he peered through the break in the wall and saw before him the large arched buildings, vaulting up to create big entryways shaped as if two flaps of fabric were pulled apart to open a tent door. There were statues of long-forgotten gods, men, and a few women in every direction. Most were still standing. Some had lost their limbs, which were lying near them, and other statues had fallen over, along with column pieces and other large building stones. The entire area was large, approximately one mile in diameter. The building where the men were perched was on the far western portion, near what appeared to have been a long wall that encircled what remained of the ancient city. The men rotated their positions every fifteen minutes and were pleased with the views that kept evolving with the changing light as the sun rose higher in the sky. The unexpected show made the time go by quickly.

When it was almost time for their watch to end, Pete talked into his small transmitter to Joe. "Joe, you won't believe this place," were his first words when he connected with Joe. Colin and Phil could hear Pete's side of the conversation. "No, there isn't anyone in this area but us. We're 200 meters to the southwest as you come out of the store room. You will see a standing one-story building with a half-wall on the second floor. We're up here and there's an opening from the ground floor. We'll see you soon."

Within a few minutes, Joe, Paul, and Jared came out of the low building nearby. They walked quickly and stealthily toward the building.

In a moment, they were inside on the ground floor. "How's the view?" Joe asked from below.

"Come on up and take a look," Pete replied quietly. "Phil, Colin, and I have been enjoying the view for the last hour."

Joe was already on top of the pile of stones, placed his weapon on the second floor, and lifted himself up. As he picked up his weapon and looked over the wall in a crouched position, he understood what Pete was talking about. "Paul, Jared, you guys have got to see this." He was as impressed with the ancient ruins of Hatra as the others. Soon the three of them were in position, and the first shift descended through the floor.

When they were on the ground and about to walk out toward the store room, Pete cheerfully called up to the new shift, "Enjoy!" Soon they were back in the cool shelter of the storeroom as the others stirred from their sleep.

"Did you see anything?" Tim asked.

Phil smiled as he laid out his bedroll, "You bet we did. It's all good"

Tim was still half asleep and was satisfied that it was all good. At the moment, he was more interested in catching a few more hours of sleep than learning what was so good about it. Soon all the men in the storeroom were sleeping as Joe and his small team continued the watch. They too were awed by the ancient city of Hatra. Joe thought to himself that someday, when it would be safe to explore the area, he would like to come back and perhaps bring Alice and the boys to this place on holiday. Perhaps, he thought wishfully, this war would be as short as Operation Desert Storm. If it was, they could all visit here in a couple of years, when his boys would be old enough to appreciate the magnificent ancient history that Iraq had to offer.

The sun continued to rise in the sky. Although it was still February, the coolness of the night was quickly giving way to the warmth of the day. Before their shift was up, they were all glad that the camouflage netting was providing modest shade. Their shift ended, and the next three men replaced them. The stillness of the area was occasionally interrupted by the movement of a circling hawk in the cloudless sky, and a small flock of sheep in the distance off to the left of the empty road, about a mile away. Certainly, there was a shepherd with them, but he was nowhere to be seen, even with the high-powered lens of a sniper rifle scope. The 1100 to 1300 shift was the most difficult in the noonday sun. By then, it had become very warm, and a slight breeze had kicked up some dust that was blowing past the last team that was looking out through the walls. Jason was watching the northwestern area as the dust seemed to be stronger out toward the distance where the road was. He peered through his scope and alerted the others, "I think something's coming down the road." Soon he could see an old bus passing the sheep and continuing toward where they were. "I think it's Hakim," he said, then added, "other than the sheep, there's no one else around."

"That's good," said Bob. He started talking into his headset, "Joe, we think Hakim is on his way. There's an old bus heading toward us."

Joe replied, "Good, keep an eye on the bus and don't betray your positions until you're sure it's Hakim. All of our personal gear is ready, and we're just finishing up with the repackaging of the stuff in the carton."

Bob relayed the message to Jason, as he kept his rifle pointed at the driver's side of the bus with his finger off the trigger. In a few minutes, the bus slowed to a stop next to the ruins of the city perimeter wall and twenty feet from the store room. He could see the driver inside was Hakim, "All clear," Jason announced.

Bob spoke into his headset, "Joe, it's Hakim. We're on our way back to the storeroom." As he said this, Jason and Manny quickly took down the camouflage nets, rolled them tightly, and put them into the containers that Pete, Colin, and Jared had left for them earlier in the day. Then, in an instant, they were down the hole and returned to the others. As they approached the storeroom, they saw Hakim coming from the other direction with a large bag walking to their cellar hide-out. Soon they were all safely below, as Hakim emptied the bag of old clothes on the floor.

"Based on the list of all of your measurements that I took with me when I left the US, I tried to find suitable attire for your stay here in Iraq. I hope you like them," he smiled. The men looked at the garments that were strewn on the floor and began picking through them and holding them up to each other to see which piece of clothing would fit which man.

"Well, Hakim, it's clear that you were not shopping at the nearest Macy's," Manny joked. Soon the men were stripping off their military garments and pulling on the mixed pieces that were available. When the transformation was complete, the elite special ops team was gone, and replaced by twelve very poor-looking laborers from some village. The two-day beard growth, which they all had, completed their disguise. The men quickly packed their gear and put everything except their sidearms into their packs and the bags that Hakim also had on the bus. These were concealed under their new-old clothes.

"OK men, let's load up and begin our tour of Iraq." Joe directed. The bags were hoisted onto the large roof rack of the bus and securely covered and tied down. Hakim even had strapped a couple of cages of live chickens with the other luggage, for effect and perhaps an evening meal or two at their next location. When everything was secured, Hakim counseled them again on how they should act on the bus, "On our way to Mosul, we may be stopped by the police or army. It will be a good idea to pick up a few passengers that are also going in the direction of Mosul, to make the bus seem even more local. Everyone is nervous about what the US may do, and they are suspicious of everyone." He looked at Joe to see what he thought of this idea.

"Hakim, I think for our first time out, it would be safer if we avoid any possible contact with others. We'll spread out on the bus so that we don't look like we're all traveling together," Joe counseled.

"OK," Hakim nodded. "Don't forget to avoid eye contact with anyone else. If we get stopped, I've got all the necessary papers, and I'll do all the talking. Some of you can pretend that you're sleeping and the rest of you can look out the window or wherever, as if you've been through the drill many times before and are bored with the process."

Hakim paused for a moment as the men were quietly pondering the prospect of confronting an inquisitive Iraqi soldier when Pete broke their contemplation: "Don't worry, Hakim, we've been in the army long enough to know how to be bored."

The others smiled. "Yeah, Pete, we've all been bored plenty by your long-winded and lame jokes," Jared quipped back.

"The trip to Mosul is about three hours from here, so we should arrive at our first safe house in the south-east part of the city around 1630." Hakim continued, "It is actually a vacant house my uncle owns. The good news is that I've asked if I could use it for a few days while friends from Ramadi were in town. He told me any friends of mine are friends of his, especially if they're from Ramadi. He's had the water turned on so you all can get cleaned up."

"Good!" said Joe. "I was beginning to worry that people would know we were coming from a mile away because we smelled so bad."

The ride to Mosul began uneventfully. Although the bus drove near the local town of Hatra, which was only a mile away from the ruins where the men spent the previous night, it appeared that no one had any interest when they drove by the turn-off to the dirt road leading into the town. The bright afternoon sun made the bus very warm, but the soft breeze through the open windows was pleasant as the men watched the countryside pass before them. The barren ruins of Hatra and sparse grass leading over the first hill toward Mosul soon changed to more grassy areas where the winter rains gathered in low-lying fields between the gently rolling hills. The only life visible as the bus drove by was a small group of goats with their newborns playing among them.

"Look at those kids," said Manny. "They can't be more than two weeks old."

"They're goats," Nick corrected.

"Kids are young goats," Manny corrected back. "I guess you didn't grow up on a farm."

"Hmmm," Nick replied," I guess I just lost some credibility as the intelligence officer on that one."

"That's OK. You impressed me last night when you told us about the snakes. No doubt Colin thinks you have credibility," Manny responded, poking some fun at the notorious snake event that Jared was happy to share with the others earlier in the day.

Colin just smiled and looked out the window as the bus rolled on. An hour passed, and the small hills became more green and populated with sheep, goats, and a few cows as more villages were passed. "So, Nick, what do you know about Hatra? Pete, Jared, and I were amazed as the sun came up this morning and we saw all those old buildings near us."

Nick perked up from a half sleep. He was an avid student of ancient history, among other things, and was reading a book whenever he had the opportunity. Next to learning, his second biggest pleasure was sharing what he knew with others, particularly if they were really interested in what he had to say. "Hatra began as a small Assyrian trading post between the ancient Parthian city of Ctesiphon on the Tigris River near Mesopotamia and Antioch, near the Mediterranean Sea on the border between Syria and Turkey. It is about 2,500 years old. During the early centuries, it was developed with Greek, Roman, Parthian, and Persian architecture as each empire occupied it. It was...uh oh," Nick was just warming up for a lengthy discussion of these empires when Hakim began to slow the bus down to stop at a police checkpoint. Immediately, all the men on the bus feigned a total lack of interest on what was going on. When Hakim stopped and opened the door, a police officer entered the bus and looked with a frown at the men who were going to Mosul to earn some money to take back to their villages. He spoke with Hakim for a moment or two as he looked at the papers presented to him. Hakim provided a few dinars tucked in with the papers to speed up the process.

Outside, an officer walked around the bus, occasionally looking under it and at the men sitting inside. He was not impressed with what he saw, and seemed only to be going through the motions, with no interest or concern that anything was suspicious. After less than five minutes, Hakim started the bus again and they were on their way.

"Thanks, Nick," Colin said quietly. "You can tell us more later." He and the others began to look out the windows, relieved that the drama was over and they were safely on the road again.

There were three checkpoints along the road to Mosul, and the men became accustomed to assuming their role as day laborers. However, they were always relieved each time the bus started moving again. Although it was about 145 kilometers (88 miles) from Hatra to the southeast section of Mosul where the safe house was located, it took more than the three hours that Hakim estimated.

Before the arrival of Joe and his team, Hakim made a point of driving the bus to the safe house and parking it next to his Toyota sedan. He also introduced himself to the neighbors, indicating that he was the nephew of Mohammed Tareq, whom they all remembered. It was clear that Mohammed was well known in the area and well liked. Hakim explained that his uncle was letting him stay at the house because he was starting his bus service to the villages. Soon Hakim and his bus became familiar in the area, and no one paid any attention to his coming and going.

When the bus was still on the last open stretch of road before Mosul, the men were getting anxious about their new location. "Hakim, before we get to another checkpoint, what can you tell us about Nineveh?" Paul asked. "I know it's mentioned in the Bible, but I don't know much about it."

Hakim was happy to provide the men with more historical context. "Mosul is the second largest metropolis, after Baghdad. It's located approximately 90 miles from the Syrian border and is a prosperous trading center with a large middle class and strong economy and is known worldwide for being near the ancient city of Nineveh." He began, "Paul, you're correct about the Old Testament of the Bible. Nineveh is discussed in the books of Isaiah, Jonah, Nahum, and Zephaniah; unfortunately, most of the references were regarding prophesies of doom and destruction. It was also a major crossroad for trading and war. Inhabited for approximately

8,000 years, it evolved into a city-state with perhaps 5,000 people by about 3,000 B.C., complete with an Assyrian king and a temple for worshipping Ishtar, the goddess of love."

"That's interesting," Colin smiled. Since he was one of the single men in the team, anything regarding love and goddesses was interesting to him.

"During its long history, the city was governed or conquered by the Persians, Medes, Babylonians, and others in its early years, and the Ottoman and British empires in more recent centuries," Hakim continued. "Iraq and Mosul became a semi-independent kingdom from 1921 until 1958 under the influence of the British for much of this time. A military coup in 1958 and series of short-lived governments eventually descended into what we have now, the autocratic and brutal dictatorship of Saddam Hussein and the Ba'ath party. Thankfully, during much of the Ottoman and British eras, scholars studied the historical significance of the ancient buildings and cuneiform writing that was abundant in the area and preserved them. Some of the artifacts were stolen or purchased by the British and ended up in their museums. However, the scholarly studies they conducted are still appreciated and a source of pride for the Iraqis."

When the bus reached the outskirts of Mosul, Hakim explained, "Except for a small area in the center of the city, it's very dark at night due to the oil embargo since 1993 which limited funding for adequately maintaining the power grid. This resulted in the rationing of electricity for most of the population in the evening. Lacking any other option, most people go to bed early and rise with the sun the following day."

The ride through Mosul after sunset was quiet. When they arrived at the empty house, it was already dark and the men quickly unloaded the gear from the roof. Hakim gave them a quick, tour of the old cinder-block and concrete house. It wasn't big, but as Hakim promised, it did have running water, which made the men very happy. It also had a storage room below the first floor, where the men could stow their gear and rest when they were not scouting the locations that were identified as likely safe houses for Saddam Hussein and his family. Fortunately, the house was located in an area that was interspersed with empty lots used for the local goats and chickens, and for the boys to play soccer. It was far enough away from the neighbors to ensure a level of privacy, as long as the men didn't have their flashlights on at night and stayed hidden during the day. After everyone settled into the store room that evening,

Hakim showed them a map of Mosul and the surrounding area with ten red circles that represented locations that Saddam and his family might consider as safe houses. Routes were discussed to determine the best options for avoiding questioning eyes or possible confrontations with police and others. Reconnaissance at night was the best approach. The men trained long and hard to work silently in the shadows and remain virtually invisible to others.

Joe organized the twelve-man team into four three-man teams that would scout the red circles in a different area each night, marking GPS coordinates and taking digital pictures of each place. Their guidance was to write down their thoughts on whether the houses looked like good candidates as safe havens, based upon the same criteria that Hakim used to hide them. The schedule for departing their safe house would vary. Sometimes, Hakim would take two teams to an area in the bus and go with one or another team if he thought the location had real potential as a safe house for members of Saddam's family. Other times, he would take one team in his car and accompany them.

The requirement to keep a low profile ensured that most nights, more than half of the men would simply stay in the house and stand watch for three-hour shifts while one or two teams checked out the circles in Mosul that Hakim marked. It was February 16, and their next objective was to be in Baa'j by March 6. This gave the team sufficient time to be careful and do a thorough job as the men all settled into a somewhat tedious but critical preinvasion routine.

Chapter Twenty-One: Palace Captives

"When will they let us go?" Eleah said, apropos of nothing anyone was talking about. "We've been here three weeks! Maybe Uday is not coming back?" She paused for a moment and looked toward the ceiling, "Please God! ... But what will happen to us?"

Lara, Babra, Eleah, and Eman had been imprisoned in a small cottage behind Uday's palace on the island in the middle of a lake since February 8. They were well-treated prisoners, with three acceptable meals delivered by Uday's palace staff every day. Their captors' routine included loud banging on the door each morning at six a.m. Breakfast was delivered at six-thirty. The guards would usher them outside to walk around the perimeter of the island, but not over the bridge, for about an hour before the day became too hot. The guarded walks took them past the side of the island where they could not miss seeing the wretched disco bar and cage where Yasmine died. Lara quickly learned where this stretch of the walk was. She would always look down as she walked by, trying to avoid any reminders of the terrible two nights when Aziz and Yasmine were brutally murdered by Uday Hussein. The condition known as post-traumatic stress syndrome, or PTSD, was relatively unknown to most people other than combat veterans at the time, but Lara and her friends felt its symptoms as they could not help playing over and over the recurring incidents of horror in their minds.

When their walk rounded the front of the palace and the girls looked in other directions, they would also try to focus on the beauty of the orchards and meadows that had been planted and cared for. They would go crazy if not for the small pleasure of seeing the parklands surrounding the lake and dreaming that someday they would escape this terrible situation and breathe safe and free in another place. Lara knew it would be home in America. Eman, Babra, and Eleah could only imagine such a place based upon what Lara had told them.

Thankfully, the February weather was still cool enough so the cottage did not get unbearably hot inside. Unfortunately, each day seemed to drag on slowly, and Eman scratched a calendar on the bedroom wall behind a window curtain so they could keep track of the days. Except for Eman's scratches on the wall, each day was identical. During the first days of their captivity, the girls were quiet as they processed the terrible events they witnessed. This put them all in a semi-dazed frame of mind. Their families, university, and the situation they were in were unconsciously blocked from their thoughts as they went through the motions and the monotonous routine day after day.

This state of shock lasted until late February, when they began to discuss their circumstances and, for lack of anything else to talk about, to relive good memories of their first semester and visits with their families. Sometimes one or more of them would break down, sobbing as the pleasant memories jarred again and again with the cruel reality of the present. This process, though, was cathartic. It helped them pass through the grieving process they all experienced. Slowly they started to think clearly, especially about plans for their escape.

"Did you notice on our walk this morning that there were fewer trucks and soldiers around the lake?" Lara asked one day after their walk around the palace.

"Yes, it's interesting that on the first evening, I counted five tanks protecting the palace on the other side of the bridge. Now there are only two," Babra added as she peeked behind the front room curtain, and out toward the palace. "The guards are not going away, but there aren't any visitors at the palace either."

Lara stood up, walked to the bedroom window in back of the house, and peeked quickly through the bars on that window. "There's only one guard back here now. Last week there were three." She walked back into the living room where the others were. "It's time to plan our escape," she said decisively. Then, with more conviction as she looked toward the bedroom, "We need to escape."

Later that evening, the girls were in their bedroom. They started to take turns peeking out the window to see if the lone guard would leave his post for a break every now and then. It was almost dark outside, but there was just enough light for the four of them to take a wooden slat from under the bed mattress and wedge it behind one of the vertical window bars and in front of another one. Eleah had been peeking out the bedroom window, watching the guard posted out back. Before long, he lit up a cigarette, and glancing over to the cottage, assured himself that everything was normal. Eleah could see the lighted tip of the cigarette move toward one side as the guard walked around the corner, and she could hear him talk with one of the other guards. After almost a month of imprisonment, the girls had learned that the casual level of guard duty at night was also part of the routine.

Soon, Babra was standing on a chair trying to pull the bar inward while Eman was pushing on the wooden slat on the other end to exert more inward pressure on the same bar. They discovered that the bars were hastily installed in their cottage windows and sealed tight with a thin layer of mortar. The idea was to break the grip of the mortar on the bar by applying enough force at the base of the bar.

"It's moving a little bit!" Babra said with an excited whisper.

"Lara, help me push on this a little more." Eman was pushing as hard as she could and noticed that something was beginning to move. Lara stood beside Eman and with the palms of her hands pushed as hard as she could as well.

Whack! Crash! The slat broke at the bar they were pushing, and the force shattered the window behind it. In an instant, they could hear the front bar go up and the door open as the other guard ran around back with his flashlight in one hand and a pistol in the other. The living room light came on, then the bedroom light, as the men quickly walked into the bedroom with their AK-47s held waist high and pointed menacingly at them.

"Where do you think you're going? Uday ordered that you are to stay here until he returns. If you try to escape, you will all die!" It was clear the guard was almost as frightened by the attempted escape as the girls were by getting caught. He aimed the gun at Babra, who was still standing on the chair.

"No!" Eleah cried in alarm and desperation, "We must go back to our university and to our families! No one knows where we are! Let us go!"

"If you're dead, they will never find you." The guard turned his gun on Eleah.

"Please don't shoot," Lara pleaded, when the guard turned his gun toward her. "We won't try to escape again."

Both guards continued to point their weapons as the guard with the flashlight and pistol directed the others: "We need to fix this window. There's glass everywhere." The three of them knew that if the young women escaped and Uday returned to find them gone, all three would be summarily executed on Uday's orders.

"Abdul, Uday will be really mad when he comes back and learns that we killed one of them, especially that one," the third guard said, nodding his head toward Lara.

Abdul considered this for a moment and lowered his gun as he continued to stare at Lara and the others. "Get some of the staff from the palace to come out here and help barricade the window. Then go tell Ali and Yousef to get dressed and come here with their weapons. The five of us will guard this place tonight. Tell the staff to use some of the sandbags that were filled for the front of the palace to pile beside the back wall so they cover the broken window."

The second guard ran off on his errand, and Abdul continued to wave his gun back and forth menacingly as he backed out of the bedroom toward the front door. When he reached it, he quickly lowered his gun, stepped out, and slammed the door shut. The bar came down across it with a thud. The girls were recovering from their close call with death when they heard voices and saw people through the bedroom window. Lara recognized one of the young men from the palace as he was stacking the sandbags behind the bedroom wall so they would reach high enough to cover the window opening. Two guards with AK-47s looked on from a distance. "Why were sandbags made for the palace?" she whispered as he piled a bag in front of the window. She guessed that the sandbags in front of the palace were another sign that something was going to happen soon.

As he piled the next bag precariously on the stack, almost covering the opening of the window, the young man answered, "The Americans are preparing to attack us. We will crush them of course, but we want to protect the palace in case they try to bomb it." The bags were hastily stacked on top of each other. Although Lara was still shaken by their close encounter with the guards, she surmised that if they could dislodge the bars, they could probably push on the top bags to make the pile fall over and away from the window when and if they had the opportunity to make an escape.

As she was contemplating this, the teenage soldier who was guarding that side of the cottage spoke up, "If any of you try to escape again, you will all be shot!" Now that his comrades had once again made the girls cower, the teenager was emboldened to make it clear that he was in charge.

Chapter Twenty-Two:
Reconnaissance in Nineveh Province
March 5, 2003

Joe, Paul, Jared, and Hakim were conducting their last reconnaissance mission in the suburbs of Mosul, moving around cautiously to ensure they would not be seen. Lying low on a small hill, they looked through their night-vision binoculars to see a walled villa on the corner of a street with only a few other villas on it. "We're looking at the residential area of Al Yarmuk. That is the villa of Nawaf al-Zaidan. He is a distant cousin of Saddam Hussein," Hakim said as he pointed to one of the other villas. "That is the villa of his brother Salah on this side of the street and four houses toward us."

"Why do you think Saddam would come here?" Joe asked.

"I don't know if he would come here." Hakim replied. "He is a distant cousin to this family. But the Hussein family is a distant cousin to many of the other families between here and Tikrit. Saddam, or his sons Uday and Qusay, may go to any one of the palaces and villas that we looked at." He paused for a moment and then concluded, "You never know."

"OK, Paul, do you have the coordinates for this place?" Joe asked as he turned to his warrant officer and designated number two leader in the team command structure.

"Yes sir," Paul confirmed as he punched a few number keys on his GPS, "it's in the system." He hit the send button and it was encrypted and sent via a satellite to Operations Command.

"OK, Hakim. Where next?" Joe asked.

Hakim smiled, "Saddam has many cousins, but that was the last place in Mosul that Saddam would consider suitable for himself or his family."

"Good. I'm ready for a change in scenery. It's almost dawn. Let's get back to our basement and get some sleep. Tomorrow night, we'll head toward Baa'j to find those WMDs." The men looked through their binoculars one more time. They got up to walk down the back side of the hill toward their dirty Toyota, away from the quiet neighborhood they were investigating.

The sun was just starting to brighten the sky when Nawaf al-Zaidan departed the walled courtyard of his house on his way to a business meeting in Baghdad. He was going to meet with business colleagues in Baghdad, and he planned to check on Yasmine, Aziz, and Lara. Typically, one or another of them would call at least every two weeks, but it had been almost a month since Nawaf last heard from them. He and Mohassin were worried. Although it was a busy time for the three young adults in Baghdad, he and his wife should have received a call from them by now.

When Lara first arrived at the university, they would receive phone calls at least once a week. However, as the school year passed, the calls became less frequent as life in the big city became busier for them. He also knew the national phone company had become much less reliable during the last year, and it was frequently difficult to make calls to, or receive them from Mosul and other parts of the country. Nawaf assumed that no news was good news, but it was unusual not to get a phone call for so long. After his business meeting, he planned to stop by the hospital where Yasmine worked and surprise her by taking her out to lunch.

It was about a three-hour drive from Mosul to Baghdad on the highway, and he needed to get an early start that day. As he turned onto the street in front of his home, he looked up toward the east where the sun was just coming up over the hill that separated his upscale neighborhood from the traffic activity of Mosul. Twenty-five years earlier, when he and his brothers decided to buy the land and build their homes in this quiet area, the city seemed much further away. The hill was a pleasant place to climb in the early evening with his family to enjoy dinner that Mohassin would prepare. They would all enjoy the night air as they looked out over the lights of Mosul that shone brightly a few kilometers away.

"Strange," he thought to himself, as he happened to see four weary village laborers getting up from their sleep in the early morning light and disappear down the other side of the hill. It was unusual to see anyone unfamiliar in the area. "I'll have to tell Salah and the others," he said, talking to himself. Lately, the entire country was tense with the threat of war with the United States. The last thing they needed were a few men from some local village bothering them.

It was about dusk the following evening, March 6, when the men loaded up the bus and began their journey to Baa'j.

"We'll miss our Mosul home," Pete joked. "When we finish our visit to the country, will we be returning to our city home?"

"I think we'll be going somewhere else where we will lie low and relax until we meet up with the 101st Airborne." Joe said. "Hakim, where is it that we're going to when we come back to Mosul?"

"Actually, we will drive around Mosul and go about twelve miles northeast of the city, toward the mountains. It's an old building that I'll tell you more about when we're finished looking for the WMD," Hakim replied. "When I dropped all of you off on the night we arrived at the house, I continued to our future residence with the carton of extra MREs and other material that Joe said you won't need until we're finished in the country."

The men accepted this vague answer, knowing that the lack of details increased the security of all of the teams working in northern Iraq. It was the military way of protecting them after their respective reconnaissance missions were completed. Sometimes too much information at the wrong time could be dangerous.

The men looked scruffy, with longer hair and three-week-old beards. Their limited exposure to Iraqi men from Mosul and laborers from villages gave them a better understanding of the mannerisms of most Iraqi men, and how to mimic them to some degree. Although none of the team smoked cigarettes, several began to carry a pack. When they were in a public area, one or more of the men would light up in order to blend in better with the locals. They were more confident about the ride to Baa'j than they were from Hatra to Mosul.

"There may be more checkpoints this time," Hakim cautioned as they began the trip. "The army and local police have been ordered to check anyone that looks suspicious." The confidence that Joe and the others had before they departed the safe house quickly evaporated. Instinctively, each man checked his pistol underneath his loose-fitting jacket. Fortunately, the March evening air was still cool enough that such outer garments were common and provided good cover for the small weapon each man carried with him. "Don't worry," Hakim continued. "I've seen how you all act when you are around my countrymen. You'll be fine. Just don't look anyone in the eye and don't say anything. I'll do the talking." Hakim provided these instructions before, but they were worth repeating. Without traffic, the trip from Mosul to Baa'j would normally take about two hours on the main roads. However, the route that Hakim had chosen was not as direct and zig-zagged on poorly maintained small one- or two-lane roads most of the way between small villages. It was a couple of hours longer, but he expected they would encounter fewer checkpoints along the way. He informed the men that they should expect them near the villages, where they would likely be manned by local police who would rather be home in bed instead of the more disciplined army regulars.

Joe counted six checkpoints along the way. Each time most of his men pretended to be asleep as a local constable would stop the bus, knock on the door and step up to Hakim, who would show him some documents, always tucking a few Iraqi dinars in with them. There would be a flash of light pointed around the interior as the officer took a brief, cursory look around to see the men sleeping or looking out the windows. Then he would step out and wave his hand to Hakim, indicating that he could move on. It was past midnight when Hakim finally drove through the very small town of Baa'j. He drove about four kilometers further down the road, turned onto a dirt road, which was more like a rutted trail, and stopped at a small abandoned barn that was near the foundations of another structure, perhaps a farmhouse that had been leveled for some unknown reason. The barn was about five hundred meters from the main road. It had all four walls and most of a roof. It wasn't very big, perhaps ten by fifteen meters, with a wide barn door on one end and a smaller door on the other. There were three pens on each side. A water well and a smaller building that seemed to be a tool shed were behind the building. "I'm sorry. It's not much," Hakim began."I wanted to give you privacy but also ensure you had access to water. The hand pump on the well out back works. Although the water has a bit of a taste to it, I think with your water purification tablets, it will be fine. Also, the shed over there has a wooden floor with a small hole dug out under it. I think the former owner may have used it to hide his gun or some other contraband. You may want to consider expanding it so you can hide your excess gear until you need it."

The men were looking around, getting accustomed to their new, more humble accommodations. "Thanks, Hakim. We've had worse places to spend time in." Joe said, reflecting back on their desert training in the United States. "It looks like the farmhouse was leveled. What happened to the owner?"

"He was killed by Saddam's thugs in 1997. The rumor in Baa'j is that he was somehow involved in the attempted assassination of Uday Hussein in December 1996. I'm not sure how that could be, since they rounded up and killed a group of men and their families somewhere south of Baghdad near the Euphrates. Maybe he had the bad luck of being related to one of them."

"I'm sorry," Joe said.

"It's the way it is in Iraq," Hakim continued. "Actually, I don't recommend that you stay here too often. There are other farms nearby. Before you arrived, I saw some boys kicking a soccer ball down by the road." He pointed in the direction they just came from. "I suggest you use this place sort of like a depot for your extra stuff and take the rest with you."

"With us...where?" Tim asked.

Hakim pointed out past the shed toward the northwest. "I was told the trucks and equipment that may have the WMD are in that direction. The road we were on continues near there toward Route 47 and Sinjar, about twenty miles from here, where it intersects with the main road toward Mosul. I haven't been near where the WMD are rumored to be. I understand that not even the folks from Baa'j can get near enough to see what is going on. But, I think if you head northwest in that direction, toward the town of Sinjar" as he pointed again, "you will probably come across whatever is out there within eight to fifty kilometers, or five to thirty miles from here."

"So, Hakim, I'm still not sure where you think we should stay," Tim asked again.

"Well, out there," he pointed again, "in the desert."

Joe took over the conversation. "Hakim is right. We can't stay here. First of all, we don't know how long we will be in this area. All we know is that when the war comes, we will be among the first to know. In the meantime, our job is to find the WMD."

"Based upon the satellite images, Hakim is pointing us almost in the right direction. Tomorrow morning, I'll get a better visual fix on where we are and be able to map out the most direct route to where images indicate that the trucks, buildings, and missiles are located," Nick volunteered.

"We'll take advantage of the night," Joe continued. "Paul, you, Jason, and Phil go, check out the shed, and if there is a hole under the floor, start making it deeper. We'll take enough food and supplies for ten days in the desert and leave the rest hidden in the hole. At least the weather is still cool enough that we won't worry about the heat. You" he began, nodding to Nick, "Jared, and Pete head due north from that corner of the barn, into the desert." He said as he pointed to the northwest corner of the building. "Take your gear and find a suitable bivouac about one kilometer due west of the back of the barn. Start preparing a site where we can take cover during the day under the camouflage nets. Bob, Jordan, Colin, Tim, Manny, and I will stay here until 0300 to get some sleep. Then we'll carry the rest of our stuff; help Paul, Jason and Phil with theirs, and meet up with the rest of you. We'll finish preparing the bivouac before dawn. Then we can all rest during the day. Tomorrow night, we'll begin our search for the elusive WMD that may be out there."

"OK gentlemen, let's go dig a hole," Paul began removing a heart-shaped tool from his rucksack and unfolded it into a small shovel.

Nick and his small team picked up their gear and started out toward the shed and the empty space beyond, "See you soon, Hakim. We look forward to your next tour." In a moment, Tim, Jared, and Pete disappeared into the night.

"Thanks again, Hakim, for everything," Joe reached out his hand and Hakim clasped it in friendship and camaraderie. "When the action starts, we'll all know it. When it does, we'll meet back here as soon as we can."

"Be safe," Hakim replied. "I'll have a nice visit with my uncle's family for the next few days, until we meet up again."

Joe speculated on their next travel back to Mosul, "According to the briefings we received just before coming to Iraq, we expect that all hell will break loose when the US invades. The expectation is that all of Iraq, including all of the armed forces, will be in panic and not very concerned with who is traveling where in the country, as long as they're not wearing a US uniform."

"I'll have the bus fueled up and ready to go, with some spare jerry cans of gas, and wait for you to signal me with three calls after the war begins with the phone that I gave you in Hatra. I'll meet you here on the night after you signal me." Hakim said, "I expect there won't be any checkpoints on the day after the war starts. Everyone will be focused on the border with Kuwait, where the US began the attack last time."

"Yes. That's what I'm thinking. We'll head back to Mosul and see what trouble we can get into next," Joe smiled. Hakim turned and walked back toward the bus.

"Oh, one more thing, if you need to meet with me before the war starts, give me five calls. I'll know that you want to meet me here the following evening, and I'll just be driving my cousin's old white Toyota pickup truck." Hakim turned again, stepped onto the bus, and drove back onto the road toward his relatives in Baa'j. He looked forward to a few more days of peace and quiet with some of his relatives before the invasion would begin, and the prospect of returning to his family in California in only a few more weeks.

At sunrise on March 7, Nick checked the image that he had on his small computer and drew the direction toward the expected WMD location with the mapping software. The day began with clear blue sky and a brilliant yellow colored sun rising in the east. After his calculations were made, he crawled under the camouflage net and back into the hole that was dug the night before and where Joe, Pete, and Phil were sharing the space with him. There were two similar holes strategically arranged as points on a triangle, with sand colored cloth swatch netting covering each of them. There were four men in each hole. The schedule was the same as when they arrived that first night in Haditha. Three men would rest while one man would have his rifle intently looking through his scope and sweeping a 180-degree perimeter so that his field of vision would overlap the watchmen in the adjacent points of the triangle to ensure a 360 degree guarded position.

Since it was still early in March, the nights were still a bit longer than the days. Nick and the others were thankful for this. The men would spend their time sleeping, keeping watch, or just sit around talking. The day was quiet and slow, as the sun rose in the sky to its zenith and slowly sank lower toward the western horizon until dark.

They were all experienced with the tedium of waiting, either in lines at the various bases where they had been stationed back in the United States, during training exercises, or on past deployments, when at times they would spend days in cramped quarters waiting for an encrypted message before striking a designated target, or for the weather to break before moving to another location safely. Despite their years of conditioning for this sort of thing, it was always boring and the least enjoyable military activity for any of them. The adrenaline rush each man experienced when the action started was what made the tedium and the hard, seemingly endless training, and the separation from families and friends all worthwhile. Among themselves, they agreed that the adrenaline rush was the driving force that kept them motivated, but it was something that they would not admit to their wives if they were married. It was the excitement of being at the tip of the spear, where the most intense, efficient, and adrenaline-producing action was in the U.S. military forces. That action induced a sense of pride associated with being part of an elite team, and it made all the tedium and the other occupational activities and dangers of their work acceptable.

When the first star became visible in the sky, the men came out of their daytime shelters and gathered around Joe, Paul, and Nick. "Good evening, men. I hope everyone had a nice sleep in our new home away from home," Joe began with a smile. "Nick, what's the plan?"

"According to the last best image I have on the computer, we need to head northwest. Hakim was about right in his guess on where the WMD may be. I think if we walk in this direction for about ten miles, we will see what is going on." Nick pointed toward a small hill as he spoke with confidence. "Caveat emptor," he cautioned. "The computer image didn't show much, but it is clear that something is there, including what looks like a truck and a bunch of long pipe-like things, which could be missiles of some sort. There is a dirt road to the location, and it is clear that some construction took place. The intel I received is that there may be something hidden underground or in a bunker buried in one of the nearby hills.

"OK. Nick and I will take the lead. Pete, Jared, Colin, and Manny, take the right flank. Paul, Jason, Jordan, and Tim, take the left. Leave your MICHs around your necks and turned off. I think it will be quiet out in the desert," Joe continued. "Let's go for a walk."

The men hoisted their packs with MREs and water for the next eight hours, ammo for their various weapons, and communications and specialized equipment unique to each man's military specialty over their body armor vests. They checked their Colt M4A1 carbines and weapon accessories, including the grenade launchers that made them more versatile, and started following Joe and Nick at about ten-foot intervals.

The night sky was full of stars and the bright glow of a crescent moon so the men had good visibility for their journey.

Manny and Tim brought up the rear, and as they often did, the two men started talking about what they saw and were thinking. The friendly banter was not intended to be profound. It was simply a way of passing the time and taking their minds off the fact that they were each carrying about sixty pounds of gear and protective armor, walking in a strange new place. The March night air was cold in the desert even though it was in the high 70s midday. In the desert, the temperatures quickly dropped to the 40s or lower after sunset. "Sure is quiet out here," Manny observed. "It's nice."

"Yeah," replied Tim. "It's the desert, Manny. What do you expect?"

"Well, I figured we'd hear an animal or something."

"It is nice," Tim agreed. "Sometimes it gets so quiet and peaceful at nights. When I'm not on patrol and just lying back and looking at the stars, I can almost feel a connection." Tim continued to walk in silence.

"A connection with what?" Manny asked. "Are you talking about God?"

"I don't know. I was raised in a Christian home, so I guess I'm a Christian. But, you know," Tim paused again, "I've seen a lot of bad stuff in the world. I'm not sure what I believe anymore." They walked a while longer in silence, looking around and listening for some sound as they went. Occasionally, they looked up into the black sky, a waxing crescent moon, and more stars than they ever observed in the night skies above North Carolina or most any other place in the U.S.

"Well, I was born a Catholic, and I'll probably die a Catholic," Manny volunteered. "I suppose that I never thought of any other religion."

"Nothing wrong with that," Tim replied. "I was raised as a Baptist. Everyone in my family is a Baptist. They're all good people and they have a strong faith in their salvation through Christ. I think that's great. But..." Tim paused again as they walked up another small hill and focused again on their surroundings and what may be on the other side. Soon they were following the team down toward more open desert with nothing but hard pack sand, small rocks, and patches of grass.

"But what?" Manny urged Tim to continue.

"It's hard to say. You know, when you're taught all your life to believe something, like the love of Christ and salvation, and the power and might of God, ..." Tim paused again and Manny remained quiet, letting Tim collect his thoughts on this very complicated, but as far as he was concerned, very important subject. After a while, Tim continued, "You know Manny, I've seen a lot of stuff, "he repeated. "Sometimes I have a hard time understanding what Christ was talking about...." He was quiet again as they walked toward another hill, "Manny, do you mind if we talk about something else?"

"Sure, Gunny. It's none of my business anyway," Manny replied. "It is an interesting subject. We don't have to figure it out tonight." Manny also wondered about his faith from time to time. Not that he didn't have a rock-solid Christian belief—he did. But he had read enough of both the Old and New Testaments of the Bible to question scripture in many places. It certainly was an interesting subject and on long assignments like this, when there wasn't much else that hadn't already been discussed with his comrades, religion was something that remained open to a variety of ideas and philosophies that the team was not opposed to discussing.

Manny had heard an old World War II veteran say, "There aren't any atheists in foxholes." At the time, he wasn't sure what that meant, but as he continued in his career in the military, he appreciated the meaning that was behind the statement.

The men trained and went on very challenging missions so many times together that their bond of friendship and respect transcended each other's different points of view when it came to faith. It was clear that they all had a strong faith in God, and the possibility of a heaven. However, each had his own different interpretation of how it all worked. Manny's real name was Emmanuel. However, he preferred using the less formal Manny, and sometimes, his buddies called him "Reverend", especially when he was engaged in a discussion of this sort. It was a good-natured moniker they gave him, but it certainly applied. He was careful not to dwell on the subject too often or with too much authority or conviction. However, he frequently was the one in the group to turn to on this subject when the tedium of waiting, which occurred often enough in their line of work, would get to the point that his friends were happy to talk about religion or anything, just to break the monotony and boredom.

The team had been walking about an hour from the position of their dugout positions, roughly seven kilometers. Tim began to calculate in his head how close they might be to the suspected WMD location. Hakim had driven the bus five kilometers from Baa'j to the abandoned barn. From there, Nick and Joe directed the men to go another kilometer into the desert where they set up their bivouac. Hakim also said that the suspected WMD site was fifteen kilometers from Baa'j, if they walked in a straight line from their bivouac to where Nick thought the first site would be. However, based on the indirect route they had taken, first to the abandoned building, then to their bivouac, and now toward the first location, he guessed that they were within perhaps ten kilometers of their destination.

Tim and Manny were both looking around as they walked in silence through a relatively long flat area when, near the crest of the next hill, Tim saw Nick stop and point toward the right as he spoke to Joe. Immediately, Joe held up his right arm and made a fist, which was the sign for everyone to stop where they were. Then he motioned for the men to put on their MICHs and waved for them to come up to where he and Nick were. As the men started again in his direction, he made another movement with his hand reaching up, then pushing downward, signaling that the men should bend down as they neared the top of the hill. Joe turned again and got down to his knees and flattened himself on the ground next to Nick. In their turn, the men spread to the right and left of Joe and dropped to prone positions and peered through the night vision scopes on their rifles to see what was in front of them.

"It's not what I was expecting." Nick was the first to express the obvious, which the others were thinking. About one kilometer from where they were laying, the men could see a truck that appeared to have been abandoned, an old trailer that may have been used for a bunkhouse, some pipes scattered around in no particular order, and not much else.

"Is this what the satellite images indicated was a possible site of the WMD activity?" Joe asked. He already knew that it was.

"Yeah, it looks like something was going on there at one time." Nick put down his binoculars. "What do you want to do, boss?"

Joe continued to look through his binoculars, sweeping his vision from right to left and back again to determine if anyone was in the vicinity, or for any other sign of recent activity. "I don't see a thing." He slowly stood up and grabbed his rifle. "OK men, let's go see what is there. Tim, you, Manny, Jason, and Bob, go right. Paul, Colin, Jordan, and Jared, go left. The rest of us will go down the middle. You all know the drill. Stay low. Look for anything or anyone that may be there and at first site, let us know. If we all determine there are no threats, we'll meet at that truck." All the men had their MICHs on so they could communicate with each other for more than a mile.

Paul and Tim both nodded and started in their separate directions in a crouched position as the others fanned out behind them and followed. Joe, Nick, Pete and Phil started down the small hill, zig-zagging, crouched and silent as they went. They moved quickly. Although they stopped frequently to assess their surroundings and possible danger, they all closed in on the truck within a few minutes. When they were within 100 meters of the truck, Joe held up his right hand in a fist again to signal everyone to stop. He and Nick once again raised their night vision binoculars to inspect the surrounding area to ensure it was safe. After a very careful study of the situation, he lowered his binoculars and waved everyone forward. The area was silent, as were the men. They walked toward the truck with their rifles at the ready in case there were any surprises.

The men noticed deep ruts in the ground as they stepped on the soft sand that had blown through and covered them. There were also pieces of pipe fittings and scraps of metal scattered around. Jared and Phil stepped over other, longer sections of pipe. The men noticed that the truck was old. They could see from a distance that the door to the trailer was open to a dark room. A quick check revealed that it had been a bunk house that was now full of sand and possibly some critters that they decided did not require further investigation. There were only shards of rotted tire treads sticking out from under the rims of the truck that were partially buried in the sand.

"OK, I guess we're the only ones here," Joe continued, stating the obvious. "This truck is ancient!"

"It's a 1959 Chevy truck," Jason offered confidently. "My dad used to fix old cars and trucks in his garage when I was a kid. I remember when he had one of these towed in from the junk yard. It took him more than a year to bring it back to life and get it cleaned up. I don't think he got much money for it when he finally sold it at a vintage car and truck fair, but he sure took a lot of pride in how much people admired it."

The others nodded in approval. Jason was proud of his dad and occasionally repeated his story about the garage and fixing up old cars and trucks. One thing was certain—Jason knew his vintage vehicles. Joe and the men began inspecting the truck as Nick pondered the situation. "I don't understand why there is nothing here. The satellite photo I saw clearly showed the truck, building, the pipes, and what appeared to be activity here and a few other locations within twenty kilometers north and west of here."

"OK men, let's look a little closer around here. Perhaps we're missing something." Joe said as he was kicking the sand with the toe of his boot. "Maybe if we move the sand around a little near this truck and where the pipes are scattered, we may come up with more clues."

Paul gathered three others near him, "Let's start over there where the pipes are farthest away from the truck." He pointed in the direction he had begun to walk, where 100 meters in front of him lay several three-meter sections of pipe.

Tim talked to the three closest to him, "We'll start over here." He pointed 180 degrees from the direction Paul and his team was walking, toward where they had descended the hill and about eighty meters away, where some other broken pipes and fittings were sticking out of the sand.

"I'll start kicking the sand behind the truck and the rest of you each take a side or the front and do the same." Joe started kicking the sand as he moved left about ten meters, then right about twenty meters; stepped forward and then worked his way left again for about thirty meters before repeating the process toward the left. He wasn't sure what he was looking for, but since they were there, he surmised that they should at least see what was near the surface of the sand, if anything. Since the war hadn't started and it was clear that this area was not part of a battle zone, he was certain there were no buried land mines to be concerned with. "Leave no stone unturned." He thought to himself as he went back and forth.

The men worked in silence as they continued moving closer to where they would eventually meet up. Paul and his team were about ten meters away from intersecting with Joe's team when Colin stopped and kicked his foot into the sand a little harder. "I think I found something." He called to the others. Everyone stopped for a moment and looked up.

"Jared, help Colin clear the sand and tell us what's there." Paul directed. "The rest of us will keep kicking the dirt."

As the rest of them resumed their search, Jared and Colin quickly moved about six inches of wind-blown sand from a metal plate that was about one meter square and at least two inches thick. "We found something, but we're going to need more help lifting this metal plate. It must weigh at least 200 pounds." Colin called out as he and Jared were struggling to lift one side of the heavy piece of metal. Immediately the others went over to help move it from where it was placed long ago. Soon, it was lifted up and moved away from what was a concrete lined hole about one meter deep. They could tell it had a concrete floor because of the smooth, even layer of sand that covered it. Sticking up through the floor was about a six inch diameter pipe that rose vertically for about a half meter, and had a cap welded over it.

Immediately, Jared recognized what they unearthed. "It's a well-head that's been capped off."

Based on this information, Nick began to solve the mystery. "When we were still back in the States, I looked at a lot of satellite images of this place and everything within 100 miles of here, including the area inside Syria. The nearest oil field with pumping stations in Iraq is about 30 miles east of here near the town of Tal Afar and the nearest fields in Syria is north-west about 40 miles near Al-Hasakah." He said pointing toward the west of where they were. "About twenty miles inside Syria and for about fifty miles running north and south, there are about fifteen small oil and gas fields in that area. Some with oil rigs on them. It appeared from the satellite photos that many of the fields were abandoned, with a few structures or pipes remaining. Probably, about the time the oil fields were discovered fifty or sixty years ago, the oil companies were searching this area."

"It looks like they found something here." Paul surmised.

"Maybe, but I'm guessing they didn't find enough to make it worthwhile." Nick continued. "Even if there was only a little gas or oil that they were able to pull out of the ground, it probably wasn't enough for them to invest the money in developing a full-blown drilling and pumping operation here." He stepped back from the hole and looked at the others. "What they did was to cut off the pipe and cap it below ground level so they could protect it with a cover, in case someday they decided to take another look."

"Makes sense," Jared said. "I had an uncle that lived in Titusville, Pennsylvania near where they first discovered oil in the eighteenth century. He told me that around that area, there are lots of capped pipes sticking out of the ground where others had drilled, hoping to strike it rich. It's a bit of an environmental problem because in some places there's some gas leaking from the pipes and lots of abandoned pipes and other junk that was just left behind when drillers moved on." Jared looked down and kicked a piece of pipe fitting. "Over the last century, they've cleaned up most of the mess, but in some small patches of farmland, you can still see some of the remains of rusted oil derricks and other equipment."

"Well, gentlemen, that's what we're looking at here." Nick concluded.

"OK, men, time to go home." Joe directed. "This was a learning experience. Tomorrow night we'll check out another location on Nick's list."

"This was the closest place on the list. According to the GPS coordinates that I have, there are four others in the area north of here," Nick volunteered.

"Did the satellite images all show a broken-down truck and pipes?" Jared asked, half joking.

"Actually, two of them didn't have anything except for clear indications that earth had been moved and roads had been created to get to the locations." Nick said with a bit of embarrassment in his voice. "When we were reviewing all the satellite images for Northern and Western Iraq, there were a number of locations that showed some activity had taken place, but we were told that the WMD could be buried in underground bunkers, caves, or anywhere. So any remote location like this, which had clearly been occupied for a while and showed enough disruption to the natural terrain such as roads, carved up hill-sides, or what-ever, required further investigation."

"First light will be in about two hours," Paul reminded everyone. "We better head back to our comfortable holes in the desert."

"Paul's right." Joe confirmed, "Let's get back under the camouflage nets and get some sleep while it's still reasonably comfortable in the early morning. Then we'll make a plan for checking out the remaining four locations." As he began walking in the lead along with Nick, he smiled, turned and called back to the rest of the team, "Maybe we'll strike pay-dirt at one of them."

When the men returned to their bivouac, it was just getting light on the morning of March 8. Nine of the men got as comfortable as possible for sleeping, and the remaining three took positions for the first two-hour guard shift. By midafternoon, all of the men had at least six hours of sleep and plenty of protein and carbohydrates from their MRE packs. Tim was positioned as watch for his team in their protective hole. A light breeze was blowing in his face, and he enjoyed the moving air since it had been still for most of the day as he peered through his scope toward the western desert. He looked up into the sky to see if there were any clouds and was surprised to see the sun had changed from its normal brilliant yellow to orange.

When he observed this, he could hear Jason in the southwest hole of the triangular bivouac exclaim, "Holy shit!" Immediately, Tim pointed his rifle and scope in the direction that Jason was focused on. Jason usually avoided such words that were so common in the military.

A wall of orange sand was coming toward them. At the moment, it appeared to be about five kilometers away and towered about one thousand feet into the sky. The wall seemed to stretch all the way across the horizon. "Holy shit!" Tim thought to himself. By then all eyes were peering through the camouflage netting at the slowly moving wall. They could clearly see boulders in its path disappear entirely as the wall enveloped them.

"It will be on us in a few minutes. Seal your weapons and your communications and computer equipment in your carry cases, cover your faces, and hunker down. It shouldn't last more than a few minutes, but we're going to get a lot of sand dumped on us while we're in it," Joe advised his men. Quickly they followed his orders and did what they could individually to cover their faces, put on their helmets, and button their loose collars around their necks. Their training had talked about the notorious dust storms of Iraq, but this was the first one they had witnessed.

Soon it was on them. Moments earlier, they could clearly see their hole-mates. When it came, everyone became a dusty blur to the other and the camouflage netting over the other holes disappeared entirely as the dust and sand moved over them. It wasn't a fast wind, like the storms in the United States. The wall moved in a slow motion with barely a noise as it passed. Quickly the sand started weighing down the netting. Tim watched as the lines holding the camouflage in place became tight from the added weight, and he wondered how long they would hold before the anchored stakes would pull from the loose ground and let the netting collapse on top of them. He looked at his watch and noted that the cloud of sand had been with them for about five minutes. "I hope this doesn't last much longer," he thought to himself.

A moment later the haze began to clear as the wall began to move past them. Everyone remained still for a few moments more, slightly dazed by what they had just witnessed. The netting had collapsed slightly, making the space in each hole a little smaller, and for some reason it felt hotter than before. "Climb out of the holes, men, and dust yourselves off. Let's see if there's any damage," Tim could hear Joe tell everyone.

When they crawled out of the holes, each of them was covered in a thick layer of dust and sand. It was in their hair under their helmets, and despite their best efforts to seal their clothes around their bodies, they could feel the sand and dust on every inch of their skin. They started brushing the sand off their uniforms as they watched the backside of the wall slowly recede toward the east. The entire event, from first sight of the wall until they climbed out of their bivouac, took about twenty minutes. It was after six p.m., and the sun was getting low in the sky. "As soon as it gets dark, let's take the netting down and shake off as much sand as we can. In the meantime, inspect your equipment. Clear the sand as much as possible from everything and, if necessary, clean your weapons. After dark, and after the netting is removed, we'll shovel out the loose stuff and make our holes a little deeper and perhaps more comfortable," Joe ordered.

It was clear to him that the men were in no position to take showers or otherwise clean the sand and dust off their bodies. Later in the evening, he sent teams of three back to the base camp, a kilometer away, and as two stood guard, each one in turn would use the pump and water well to thoroughly rinse away all the sand and grime. This process took most of the night, but all twelve were cleaned off and back to the bivouac before dawn. They all agreed that without a good rinse, courtesy of the well, they would have been miserable for the next several days. If the holes were a little deeper and perhaps a little more spacious, Joe surmised, perhaps they would also be a little more comfortable.

Later that evening, Joe, Paul, Tim, and Nick mapped out their strategy for visiting the remaining four locations on Nick's computer map. Nick described what he knew from the briefings he attended before they left Kuwait and what he could read from the computer maps and images. "There are only one or two satellite images for each of the first three locations. Each one has a single dirt road and what appear to be some buildings nearby with large piles of rocks and moved dirt, indicating that there may be something underground. Perhaps missile silos, caches of poisonous gas or other weapons of mass destruction that are buried or in caves on the sides of hills that are adjacent to the buildings. Unfortunately, the images are not clear enough to indicate if Iraqi military units are also hiding in the areas. Each location is progressively further away from our bivouac. There is one about six miles northwest of here. Then in about a straight line going north from there, the next is eight, twelve, and then twenty miles from here, west of the small village of Bara. The fifth and last area does appear to have a few trucks and buildings with what appears to be a large cache of pipes or missiles carefully stored in rows, and other activity." As he said this, he handed the small computer with the map of the region to Joe. It identified the five potential WMD locations, including the first that was visited already.

Joe studied this for a minute. "What is the terrain like from here to each of the other locations?"

"The next three have terrain similar to our walk last night, only further. Unfortunately, for the last and farthest one, in addition to being thirteen miles further from here than the others, we will also have to cross Route 47 and a few small farms in our path," Nick replied as he pointed to the area north of 47 and west of Bara village.

As Joe pondered this, Paul offered a suggestion. "Well, the fifth looks like the most likely location for the WMD based on what Nick says. It's also the furthest and, because of the potential for being spotted by a farmer or when we're near the road, we'll have to be more careful than walking around in the middle of the desert. Maybe we should go to the next three first. Then we'll go back to the barn to resupply, get cleaned up, thanks to the well and pump, and connect with Hakim, before making a two-day trek to the last location.

Tim smiled, "I like that idea. Especially the cleaning up part; even with my rinse tonight, I'm already feeling like the sand is getting under my skin and I'm sure everyone else is feeling that way too."

Joe looked at his colleagues and thought a moment more, "OK. Paul has a good idea. Tonight is March 9. Assuming there are no more major dust storms in the next few days, we'll look at the next three locations between now and March 13. We'll go back to base camp on March 14 to check in with Hakim, resupply, get cleaned up again, then head for our last WMD destination and check that out on March 15."

The team liked the plan. They were trained to endure long periods of uncomfortable conditions in the desert. However, they were always happy when the hardship was broken up with at least a day of relative comfort. An opportunity to clean up, thanks to the well near the barn, was a real morale booster.

Nick's description of the next three prospective WMD locations proved to be correct. Each one was much like the first. Despite the lack of real evidence indicating they wouldn't find any WMD, the men searched each area thoroughly by checking for hidden caves in the side of nearby hills. When they kicked the sand in their systematic check for underground bunkers, they always found a hidden abandoned wellhead at each one.

On the night of March 14, the men packed up their camouflage netting and carefully filled in their three holes so there would be no tell-tale sign that they were there and returned to the barn. There was a small Toyota pickup truck parked beside it. Thanks to the cell phone provided by Hakim, and the five unanswered calls that Joe made on March 13, Hakim was waiting for them when they arrived. He was sitting on the floor with a sack next to him when Pete and Colin quietly sneaked up to the window and door of the building and peered into the dark corners with their night-vision scopes, which enabled them to look around corners without being seen. They quickly confirmed that it was Hakim inside and waved to the rest of the men that all was well. When the men entered the barn, they greeted Hakim as a long-lost friend. Fortunately, there was still enough light from the waxing three-quarter-moon to allow them to see each other without resorting to flashlights. "It's good to see you, Hakim," Joe said as he shook his hand. "What's in the sack?"

"Well, I didn't know why we were meeting, since everything is still quiet in Iraq, but I figured if you wanted to see me, I might as well bring some roasted chickens, fresh bread, local honey, dates, and other fruit from a couple of the small Baa'j markets. You'll also find a couple of bars of soap and some shampoo."

Spontaneously, Tim picked Hakim up with a big hug, "You're my man!"

Hakim was surprised by the hug but smiled at the real gratitude that Tim and all the men expressed to him. "So why are you here?"

Joe explained the results of their first four visits to the alleged WMD sites and their plan to move camp the following evening in the direction of the fifth, and possibly the most promising, location.

"Nick is right. You'll have to travel more carefully in that direction. You saw the farms along the road as we arrived here from Mosul. There are more along small dirt roads in the northern direction, where you will be headed. The road that you'll cross is the one that leads to a couple of official and unofficial border crossings with Syria. Lately, due to the concerns everyone has about a US invasion, there has been a lot more traffic on that road because families are leaving the country to stay with relatives in Syria, and others are bringing in supplies to stockpile for when war does come."

"What do your relatives think of the situation?" Jordan asked.

"Do they know why you're visiting them?" Nick added.

"Let's sit down and I'll tell you the situation. Help yourselves to the supplies," Hakim said as everyone removed their gear and sat on the floor, except Tim, Manny, Jason, and Bob, who took positions at the windows and door for the first watch. "My cousin knows that I am here to support the overthrow of Saddam Hussein," Hakim began. "He's not a fan of the Ba'ath party and Saddam in particular."

"Why is that?" Jason queried.

"Unfortunately, Saddam and the Ba'athists are only interested in their Sunni and tribal brethren and actually fear the other groups as threats to the regime. Anyway, my cousin's family is not Sunni, but he's in a predominantly Sunni region. He lost his grandfather during the Iraq-Iran war, and his father was taken out into the desert and killed because he was targeted as a potential troublemaker after Desert Storm. His family always resented Saddam and will be happy when the Americans get rid of him."

"Does he know that we're here?" Joe asked.

"He only knows that I'm working with a group that will help overthrow the regime. He understands the risks of knowing too much and hasn't asked any other questions, but he does like what I'm doing, whatever he imagines that to be. He lent me his pickup truck that I drove here with this evening."

"That's a relief," Paul said with a sigh. "It's good to see you, Hakim."

"No problem. Is there anything else I can do for you gentlemen? I should be getting back to my cousins before it gets too late," Hakim asked as he got up off the floor.

The others stood up with him. "No, Hakim. Thanks for the food and supplies. They're a welcome treat," Joe said. "We just wanted you to know our plans before we go back into the desert. I think there will be a new moon on about April 1. I don't have a clue when the war will start, but since there won't be any moon visible on April 1, I'm guessing that may be a good time to start one."

"Good guess," replied Hakim, "I hadn't thought of that, but I wouldn't be surprised if you're right."

"OK. Be safe, my friend, lie low, and someday, when you think the time is right, tell your cousin thanks from us. Unless there's an emergency, we'll contact you with the three short calls on your cell phone on the night before we return here," Joe said as Hakim grabbed his light jacket and headed for the door.

That evening, the men made the most of their time in the barn and water well resort, taking more leisurely bucket showers with the soap and shampoo provided by Hakim. They were also able to shake out much of the sand from their gear and repack everything, along with additional ammunition and enough MREs from their storage hole under the shed for their next ten or more days that it would take them to go to the remaining potential WMD site and back to the barn to meet up with Hakim and his bus sometime after April 1.

At about one a.m. on March 16, they began their fifteen-mile northwestward journey toward their destination and set up a bivouac in a rock cropping on a small hill where they had a 360-degree view of the surrounding area at about six a.m., about one kilometer from the road and nearly a mile and a quarter from the nearest farm buildings. Although the ground around the rocks was more firm than the sand in their previous location, they were able to dig one large hole deep enough to have adequate cover for all of them to comfortably hide under the netting. When the first glimmer of sunlight gave Joe and his team a better view of their temporary surroundings, they were satisfied to see they were far away from any grazing land where the local livestock were roaming among the grass lands in the valley near the farm and road. Although there was a risk of being discovered, they were hopeful that the farmer would not have any reason to climb the rocky hill where they were. The early morning chill in the air also signaled the location of the other farm houses nearby, because they could see the smoke rising from the cooking fires as the families were preparing their morning meals. The men noted four different smoke columns. Based upon their distance from the bivouac, Nick estimated that the closest was on the opposite side and to the north, about a mile away. There was another column of smoke about two miles away and directly in line with their planned route toward the next site.

"The satellite map indicates there's a small dirt road off this main road that winds around the other farm and behind it. We can see where the farm house is. What we can't see is whether or not there is fencing around the perimeter of the property and how large an area that may be. I guess we'll find out tonight," Nick advised.

"Well, we'll have to figure out how to get around it then," Joe said, "Tim, you and your team take the first watch, and the rest of us will try to get some sleep. At least these rocks may offer us some cool shade for part of the day."

The men settled in for an uneventful day. When each team had watch duty, they noted a steady stream of traffic traveling in both directions on the road. Occasionally, several Iraqi Army trucks would pass by in the direction toward Mosul. Fortunately, the grazing goats and sheep on their side of the road remained far away from their position. On the opposite side there was a small herd of livestock with a man and boy watching the animals, near the road and directly in line with their desired route for the evening. Behind the goat-herders, the land rose again to another small hill that blocked the view of the more distant farmhouse beyond that. It appeared that the top of that hill was much closer to the road, but it had a steeper and more difficult climb to the rocks at the summit. Although the goat-herders were a concern to the men as they stood watch during the day, by late afternoon the man and boy with their charges began to move slowly down the very straight road that led toward Syria in the west and disappeared in the direction of the unseen farm. That evening, storm clouds began to gather in the sky and Joe smiled. "Luck is on our side," he thought. The clouds and the diminishing light of the moon added to the darkness as the sun set. Traffic on the road also diminished until, by eight p.m., a vehicle drove by only every few minutes. Without any words, the men began to prepare their gear and themselves for the long and potentially risky night ahead.

"What's the plan, boss?" Tim asked.

Joe had been thinking of a plan during the day. "OK, I don't think we should all cross the road together as a team," Joe began.

Pete smiled as he thought of a stupid joke, "But why did the team cross the road?" Some of the other men and Joe also smiled at the old and dumb chicken joke, for all knew the answer was "to get to the other side." Frequently, the men welcomed weak humor as a way to relieve tension when the threat of danger increased on their missions.

"The team will get to the other side to see what WMD they could see," Joe continued with the moment. Then he became serious again, "We'll do this in our teams of four. I noticed a flat rock on the hill on the opposite side." He pulled out his laser light that was used for marking targets for the fighter pilots to fix on when they made bombing runs, and pointed it with his night scope in the direction of the opposite hill, quickly locating and fixing on the rock he was referring to. "Look through your scopes. Can you see the rock that I've marked with the laser?" He asked.

The men pointed their rifles in the direction where Joe's gun was pointing and quickly identified the target. "Paul, when your team nears the road, we'll be watching from here to see if lights are coming from either direction. When there are no lights, I'll turn the laser onto the rock. This will be your signal to get across the road and begin climbing toward the rock. If you see lights or hear road noise as you're climbing up the other side, make yourselves invisible. No doubt the drivers and everyone in the vehicles will be more focused on the road than on the dark hills on either side. As soon as you're halfway up the hill, we'll send Tim and his team down to get positioned for the next crossing. Once they're across, Phil, Pete, Nick, and I will start down the hill. Paul, once you're at the rock on the other side, we'll rely on the four of you to shine the light on the rock when you see from your side that it is all clear."

"Yes sir," Paul said as his team prepared to move out.

Phil and Pete were positioned looking toward the traffic lights coming from opposite directions of the road. As the clouds continued to gather and night became darker, each spotter whispered, "All clear." The men traveled quickly down the hill, stopping and occasionally flattening on the ground when they saw headlights coming from either direction. Because of the necessary interruptions in their journey, it took them more than thirty minutes to get within fifty meters of the road, where they lay in a small drainage ditch waiting for Joe's signal. They looked like four rocks from the road.

Everyone on the hill continued to watch through their scopes as Phil and Pete whispered again, "All clear." Joe pointed his laser at the rock and immediately, the four dark figures emerged from the ground and sprinted across the road and began their climb up the hill. The traffic was slowly dwindling so their need to stop and take cover was less as they hurried up the hill on the other side.

When they were nearing the halfway point to the summit, Joe looked at Tim. "Get ready." Tim, Manny, Jason, and Bob were already prepared to move out. When they heard the "All clear" from Phil and Pete, they were on their way. As they neared the road and before they dropped to the ground, the "All clear" from the spotters was spoken and Joe aimed the laser again. He could see that Tim noted this, and his team continued over the road and began their climb up the other side. Joe scanned his scope up and down the mountain and saw that Paul's team was close to the top of the hill and rocks where the laser was pointed as Tim moved slowly and steadily toward them. He also felt the first drops of a light rain fall.

A few moments passed as another two cars drove by and the rain continued. Joe decided it was time to go. "OK men, when Phil and Pete give us the 'all clear,' we'll head out. Let's get ready to go." The men loaded up their backpacks, ammo belts, and weapons and prepared to go. Soon the signal was given, and the men began their way down the hill as the light rain continued.

As they moved forward, Joe noticed the ground beneath his boots was getting more slippery as the water mixed with the light sand on the surface and turned it into a filmy substance. The others were spread out as they descended the hill, but they all noticed the same thing and slowed their pace accordingly to avoid falling. Every time there was a headlight, they would kneel in the slippery goo rather than lie prone and try to look like rocks, hoping the drivers were more interested in staying on the equally slippery road than the views along the darkened hills on either side. When they finally neared the road, Joe was relieved to see that Paul had his laser pointed at the rock, and Joe's team quickly crossed the road together. As they were almost on the other side, Nick began falling as he slipped on the tarmac. "Whoa!" Pete exclaimed as he saw his colleague begin to lose balance with all of his gear and fall toward him. In an instant, he was able to lean into Nick's fall to keep him from hitting the ground hard. The sudden sideway motion made them both fall on top of each other in a small puddle. About then, Joe could see lights coming from the east, about two miles away.

"Are you guys all right?" Phil asked as the two men started trying to get up with their gear.

"Yeah. Just startled, that's all." Nick said, as Phil and Joe helped their two colleagues onto their feet.

"There's a car coming, let's get off the road and out of sight!" Joe said in a tense voice as he pointed to a nearby out cropping of large rocks and began moving in that direction. "Get down and be ready." Quickly the men moved to the rocks and tried to blend with them. They could see from the slowly brightening lights that the vehicle was moving at only about 10 miles per hour and there were two more sets of lights behind the first one. "Take the safety off your weapons," Joe ordered.

It seemed like slow motion as the lights continued to get brighter and light up the road in the direction that they were all looking. Soon they could hear the sound of the vehicles and, instead of cars, they were trucks. "Damn." Joe thought as he continued to stay motionless in a prone position, with his chest lying in the wet mud. As the first truck began to pass, he noticed the next one was right behind it, then another. It seemed like an eternity before the three trucks passed the men's position and continued down the road. When the red tail lights were finally out of sight, the men got up and tried unsuccessfully, to wipe off some of the mud that had stuck to their body armor and uniforms.

"Yuck!" Pete exclaimed!

Joe shook his head, "Yeah, we all agree. At least Pete and Nick aren't hurt and we all survived the passing convoy without incident."

Pete smiled, "Can we turn around now and go back to the barn so we can get cleaned up?" It was another joke and they all knew he was kidding.

"Nice try, Pete. Not this time. Let's climb the hill and meet up with the others. Maybe tomorrow will be a better day." Joe said as he adjusted his gear and put the safety back on his weapon. They began the slow climb to the top of the hill. Paul assigned two of the men to continue their look out for road traffic while Tim, and the others began to prepare their new bivouac, including a light tarp under the netting, to keep some of the rain off of them.

By the time they were all situated in their new position the rain had stopped and the skies were beginning to clear so the men could look up to see plenty of stars but only a small sliver of the moon. The night temperatures were still cold in the March weather. The others shared their thin thermal blankets with Joe and his team as they huddled together, so the cold and their damp clothes wouldn't conspire to give them hypothermia. It was a long night and they were all glad to see the first sunlight and the warmth that it would soon produce.

As the men continued with their watch rotation, Joe, Paul, Tim, and Nick plotted their approach to the next WMD site. Their plan had been to climb over the hill that they were presently sitting on, and continue for another three miles. But the weather didn't cooperate. It was March 17 and they still had about twelve miles, around the western side of a much larger hill in front of them, to arrive at their destination. During the night, they all learned that, in addition to being slippery, the rain soaked desert turned into a thick mud. They would be walking in a landscape with approximately 100 pounds of gear, supplies, weapons and ammo that would make them sink into the wet desert about two inches and hold each step of progress for a moment before letting go before they could take another step. It was not the best condition for walking stealthily as soldiers who were members of the army that everyone knew would soon be invading their country.

When the sun began to rise, so did the smoke from the breakfast fires at the farms. Joe, Nick, Pete and Phil stripped down to their skivvies and laid their still damp uniforms out to dry under the netting with the quickly warming sun. Nick soon spotted the farmhouse that was beyond the hill they were bivouacked on. Beyond the farm, there was a much larger hill that stretched east and west for at least several miles and appeared to be at least several hundred meters, or a thousand feet above the valley. "That's Jebel Sinjar," advised Nick. "The highest elevation is about 1,700 feet, but we'll take the trail around the western side, about three miles in that direction," he said pointing west, "then over toward Bara and the suspected WMD location."

There was no fencing around the farms to keep the livestock in, which was good. He could see that it was a large operation with several pens of sheep and about ten men and boys taking care of them. As the morning progressed each man would take his assigned herd in one or another direction, including the location where the sheep and herders were by the road. Another was at the bottom of the hill they were on, in the direction that the team wanted to go, approximately five hundred meters from where the men were hiding in their bivouac. The man watching the herd nearest their location did not seem very interested in his surroundings and only mildly interested in his sheep. The sheep grazed nearby but the man walked directly to a rock that was apparently his familiar resting place, near where he could gather some branches from a dead tree and start a small fire to brew water for his morning tea. Every hour or so, he would get up from his resting place and kept moving around the rock in order to take advantage of its shade from the sun. Occasionally, he would stand up to survey the location of the sheep, ensuring they were all within 100 meters of where he was. Satisfied that all was well, he would settle down again to drink his tea, smoke cigarette, have lunch, and in the heat of the day, take a nap. As the day progressed, the team could see the ground change slowly from a dark brown indicating the wetted earth from the rainfall to a lighter brown as it began to dry.

"I understand that it will take three to five days for this ground to become completely dry." Nick advised. "Since last night's rain was fairly light compared to more severe storms that happen in this region, I suspect this will be reasonably dry in two days."

"Swell." Tim sighed. "I hope we're not stuck here for the next two days."

"Actually considering the muck that we will have to walk through tonight, even if it is less gooey than last night, staying here until everything is dry is a nice thought." Joe began. "But it's not an option. We need to check out the last site by March 19 – tomorrow night."

The quiet tedium and boredom of the day under the camouflage netting was welcome that day as the men rested, cleaned and checked their weapons and prepared themselves mentally for the long, potentially difficult night ahead. Late in the afternoon, the herders and their sheep began their slow walk back to the farm pens and house for the night. Soon the small sliver of a moon appeared in the sky, along with the bright red star that was Mars near it. Within an hour, it was completely dark with the stars shining through patches of clouds that continued to drift by.

The men prepared their gear and at about 10 p.m., Joe gave the order to move out in their groups of four, moving in quiet, zig-zagging paths, skirting the perimeter of the sheep pens and farm house by a half mile as they made their way beyond the complex to begin their walk around Jebel Sinjar. The clear air, thanks in part to the previous night's rain that cleared all of the dust, made it easy for the team to keep an eye on each other and where they were walking to ensure no one would have an unfortunate fall due to the remaining slippery low spots and rocks.

Although the ground underneath their feet was a bit soft when they started out, the men discovered that, as the evening wore on, and the air got colder, the ground began to stiffen more so that it became easier to pick up the pace. By one a.m., March 18, the men were about seven miles closer to their destination. Joe stopped the team for a momentary break. "Nick, how much further do you think we have to go?"

"Based on my GPS coordinates and the pace that we've been doing so far, we need to travel about five miles before we are within the area that the map says the last location is situated in. We've been averaging about three miles an hour, but that's because we've been slowed a bit by the muck and the zig-zagging precautions as we passed through the remaining farm areas. If we can pick up the pace from here on out, to maybe four or five miles an hour, we should be near our destination in less than two hours."

The men were already feeling the exhaustion in their thighs and backs due to the weight of their gear and slogging through the still damp muck. The thought of a rest crossed all of their minds.

"I think we should go for it." Tim volunteered.

Joe smiled. "Well men, what do you think?"

"I'm ready for a good work out tonight." Jason said. Quickly all the men nodded in agreement.

"OK, let's keep on walking." Joe said, "It will be nice to get to our destination tonight so we'll have more time to dig a nice hole for ourselves, and check out our new surroundings."

The men were motivated by the fact that they were on their way to complete this phase of their mission and the prospect of, perhaps at last, finding the proof of weapons of mass destruction that everyone in the United States expected were in Iraq. By 0300 on March 19, the men could see a faint glow in the distance that would likely be the military base and WMD depot that was being protected there. When the team crested the next hill, the glow was brighter, but lights were still not visible. Joe, Nick, Paul and Tim looked at their surroundings to determine whether to move closer to the lights, or to bivouac near where they were.

"There isn't much out here to provide cover for us." Tim frowned.

Paul kicked the ground with his boot. "Yeah, and his stuff is pretty rocky. I think it would be hard to dig a deep enough hole for all of us and not make it look like there was some major excavation work going on for the bivouac."

Nick was looking at his computer topographical map of the area and Joe surveyed the distance with his night-vision goggles. "It appears that, in the valley between this hill and the next, there is a small wadi that may provide an opportunity for some cover. Also, the ground there will be more sandy and easier to dig a hole in."

Joe didn't think much of this suggestion. A wadi was typically a dry stream or river bed that only filled up when it rained. It didn't seem like a good idea to dig a hole and hide in a place that could potentially be under water if there was another rain storm. "I'm not interested in getting wet again, along with the rest of the team. However, Paul is right. There isn't much up here that would work for us. Let's go down to the wadi and scout around there to see if we can find something above the water line that would offer some good cover.

The men made their way down into the valley and started walking along the wadi. It soon became clear that the ground there was still wet and muddy from the rain that fell two nights previously. "This won't work." Joe said. "We'll have to move a bit closer to where the lights are coming from and hope that we find something up that hill." He pointed to the next hill crest in the direction of the lights.

Soon they were on the other side of the wadi, with only one minor incident when Jared stepped into what he thought was a small remaining puddle of water and discovered that it was much deeper as he sank up to his ankle in the thick goo-like mud that still remained there. After Colin and Jared helped extract Jared from the mud hole, Joe directed his men to fan out across the hill as they made their way to the top. "Stay low, we don't know if the Iraqis are watching this area or not. We also don't know how close we are to their military base. Look for clusters of rocks, or any other formation that we may be able to use as a basis for some camouflaged shelter. Turn on your mike and earphones. If anyone sees something that may be a good possibility for shelter, let me know, and we'll take a look."

The men formed an arc of about a quarter mile and began their way up the hill. They walked slowly, as they kept an eye out for the possibility of Iraqi guards in the area, contemplated and rejected several possible bivouac locations. Fifteen minutes passed as they began to near the crest of the hill, with no promising locations noted. Then, Colin could be heard on the headphones. "I think I've found something!" His voice sounded excited. Joe, Paul, Nick and Tim quietly made their way to where Colin was standing. Near him was a small cave carved out of the side of the hill. The sides of the cave were made of rock and the opening was wide enough for one man to crawl in without his rucksack on his back.

"OK, Colin, you found it. Stick your head inside and let us know what's there." Joe directed.

"Thanks, boss." Colin replied. "If there's anything good in there, it's mine."

Joe and the others smiled. "It's a deal," Joe agreed.

"Especially the snakes," Jared cautioned and joked with Colin at the same time.

"Oh, yeah. I forgot about the snakes." Colin took off his backpack and got on all fours to crawl in with his flash light in one hand and pistol in the other. He paused a moment thinking of Jared's comment. "Do any of you want to be the first to check this out?" When the others shook their heads no, he moved slowly at first as he carefully looked in every corner and possible snake hiding place to ensure it was completely empty. In a few moments, he was all of the way inside.

"This must have been some temporary quarters for shepherds. There's a fire pit and some trash including cigarette butts and empty rice sacks. It's not big, but I think seven or eight of us could cram in here with our stuff." Colin whispered into his MICH, so the others could hear. Clearly, this was not the ideal situation for a bivouac, Joe thought. There was no way to get out if the men were found out by the Iraqis. Also there was no way, other than the opening, to look out and see if anyone was approaching, and the opening was facing down the hill, away from the military base.

"Not great." Paul said as he was thinking the same as Joe. Tim and Nick were watching the dark shadows of the men approach the crest of the hill.

"Joe, I think you should call the men back here before they get too close to the top of the hill." Tim jolted Joe from his bivouac dilemma.

"Men, drop down in place." Joe said into his MICH. Immediately, he could see the eight others get down in a prone position as they awaited further orders. It seemed as if the men just disappeared into the ground. Joe had an idea. "We'll see if there are four to eight locations near the crest of the hill that would be suitable, if modified with a shallow hole and camouflage netting, for one or two men to stay in and keep an eye on the military base. The men will stay on watch for the entire day, and be relieved after the sun sets and before the sun rises. The remaining men will stay in this hole and rotate in and out to the look-out posts. What do y'all think?" Joe looked at Tim, Paul and Nick for an affirmation of his idea.

"It's as good as any idea that I could come up with." Paul said.

"I think I'll go up to the top and look around first." Joe said. "Colin, you can come out of your new home now, if you want." Joe whispered into the cave. Then he spoke into the MICH, "If any of you on the hill are near a place that could be made into a one or two man camouflaged bivouac, let me know, and I'll come take a look. I'll shine my laser beam at a rock where I'm standing. If you think you have a good location, shine your laser at where my beam is pointing and we'll be able to find you." In a moment he was pointing his laser at a rock and soon, five other lasers were pointing at his red mark. "OK, Nick you follow that one, Paul, you take that one, Tim, you follow that, Colin you take that one, and I'll follow the one from over there. Do you think all of you can find your way back to this spot?

Nick looked at his GPS and called out the coordinate. "It is XY28942 in your GPS. Got it? Just follow your way back to this coordinate and you'll find your way back here."

"Help the men with the lasers dig a good camouflage bivouac for one or two men. The first watch until six a.m. will be Jared, Jordan,

Tim, Jason, and Bob. The rest of us will take the second watch from six a.m. until dark and we'll continue to rotate on and off from there." Joe directed. He began his walk up toward the source of the laser light he was following and the others did the same. When he got to the soldier with the laser, he discovered it was Jason.

"Hi Joe, welcome to my patch of the hill." Jason said as a greeting. "You can see there's already a bit of a hole here, and I can make it deeper. Or, just up there, on top of the hill, there's a boulder, and it appears the ground there is also soft enough to dig a hole and cover it with a net."

"Let's go take a look." Joe said as he began to crawl on his stomach to the location that Jason pointed out.

When he made his way there, with Jason close behind, he could see the source of the lights in the distance, about a mile away. The lights were shining on a large area that contained several semi-trailer trucks and trailers. Two of the trailers had twenty foot containers with no visible indication of what may be inside them. The third trailer had what appeared to be a large container with a door, which looked similar to the dilapidated container bunkhouses they saw at the other locations. Near the trucks were what appeared to be stacks of long pipes, perhaps missiles, or the aluminum tubes that contained poisonous chemicals or biological agents used as WMD. They were about 25 feet in length and perhaps two feet in diameter. Unfortunately, the stacks were pointed away from them, in a direction that made it difficult to determine for sure what they were. Joe couldn't make out whether they were missiles, pipes or something else through his binoculars.

"I can't really determine what the containers are for on the back of those trucks, or those are missiles near them. We'll get Nick to give us a better idea of what we're looking at when the sun comes up." Joe looked around where they were on the hill. There was a relatively steep incline from the valley below toward where Jason and his bivouac would be. This would make it difficult for anyone looking up to see beyond the crest of the hill.

Except for the few trucks, trailers and stacks of missiles that were illuminated by the lights, there was very little else in the area which would indicate that the Iraqi army had established a fortified camp that would include guards and other military hardware. Joe was interested in what they would see in the daylight. His team would make every attempt to conceal them-selves and lay low, to avoid detection. However, he was cautiously optimistic that the Iraqi Army was more concerned about protecting their border with Kuwait in the south of the country, leaving few men in the rear guard on the Syrian border to protect what may turn out to be very few, if any WMD installations. He was satisfied that the risk to his men was sufficiently low that they could do the necessary to remain undetected until they moved on to meet up with Hakim in a few days. It was clear that this was the better location for observing the activity when the sun was up. "We'll make the bivouac here, Jason. Can you keep a low profile and dig a suitable hole for two men, prepare the netting, and stay here to keep an eye on things until six a.m.? Nick and I will relieve you then, and you can make your way back to the new home that Colin found for us."

"Yes sir." Jason said, as they walked back to his original location and picked up his shovel from his nascent hole in the ground. "This ground is relatively easy to dig through. I'll have a nice big hole for you and Nick to enjoy next to the rock in no time."

"OK, I'll see you in a couple of hours." Joe turned on his GPS to get the coordinate that Nick provided, and began making his way back to the cave.

When he arrived at the cave, he was greeted with a question from Nick, "Any luck?"

"Yeah. Jason has a good location with a view of the area with lights. He's preparing a hole and netting there." Paul, Colin and Tim were also listening as Joe turned on his microphone to talk with the others still near the crest of the hill as he turned his laser light on once again pointed it at a rock so the others on the hill could see the light from where they were on the hill. "Pete, Phil, Jared, Jordan, Manny, Jason and Bob, turn toward where we had the laser light marker on a rock earlier, and look for the same light now. Jason, turn your laser on and aim it toward the rock that I'm lighting up again. The rest of you, follow Jason's laser beam toward his position on the crest of the hill. Jason's location will be the center look-out bivouac. The two men closest to Jason on either side of him, point your laser lights toward the rock."

In a moment four other laser beams were pointing down from the top of the hill to cover the beams from Joe and Jason's lasers. "OK, those will be the other four lookout locations. The other two men will use the GPS coordinates that Nick provided to walk back to where the rest of us are, by the rock. Jason and the other four men, prepare a comfortable bivouac to settle into. At six a.m., just before sunrise, the rest of us will relieve you. Everyone except Jason, you can turn off your lasers now, dig your holes, make them as deep and comfortable as possible and keep an eye on things with the two flanking positions guarding this side of the hill and the others, including Jason, keep an eye on the activity under the lights. Hopefully the rest of the night will remain quiet. Y'all will be happy to know that Colin located a comfortable place for the rest of us to stay out of sight, and get some sleep before we relieve you in a couple of hours."

The lasers were turned off and, within a few minutes, Bob and Phil, began to emerge nearby as they followed their GPS compass to the new base camp. "Did we win the prize?" Phil joked in a soft voice as he neared their location.

"Sort of." Joe replied. "Phil, stay out here with me to see if you have any signal on your radio with HQ. Colin, show the other men into our new home for the next couple of days."

"Be happy to." Colin smiled as he pointed the way to the small opening of the cave. "When I get in, pass your gear to me, and then come on it. The cave is big enough for all seven of us, and our gear. The only downside is that it doesn't come with an en-suite bathroom."

Bob frowned, "Well that stinks." The men smiled at the bad joke.

"Nothing new for us happy campers." Nick replied.

"The good news is there are those big rocks not far from here that you can visit, and there is room in the back of the cave where we can dig a hole." Joe advised. "We'll only be here for the next two hours before we relieve the others on the hill before daybreak. Nick and I will take Jason's bivouac, Paul, Tim, Phil, and Bob will each relieve the man in one of the other bivouacs that are being prepared for you. We'll take the day shift and the others will relieve us after sunset, which will be seven p.m. this evening." The men nodded their understanding as Joe continued, "This is March 18. Tonight, some of us will go down to the WMD site, to get a better look at what those lights are shining on, and assess the level of Iraqi military and WMD in the area." Then we will hunker down until Phil and Bob get the signal that the fighting has begun and we learn what our next assignment will be."

"Sounds good to me." Colin said as he got on his knees and crawled into the cave. Silently, Bob took off his back pack and other gear as he prepared to hand it in to Colin. A few of the others took a short walk away from the area to do their business, not wanting to stink up their new home. Phil set up his radio and began manipulating the dials in an attempt to gain a signal.

"I'm not getting anything, and there's no indication that any messages have been sent to us." Phil advised Joe.

"OK. I just wanted to check. Beginning with our shift in the bivouacs this morning, you and Bob can alternate every four hours on checking your radios and continue doing so until we hear from Command on what our orders are."

"Yes Sir." Phil confirmed. Soon they were all inside and made themselves as comfortable as possible for their short sleep.

The cave was dark, dry, and had a comfortably cool temperature. Although Joe was typically a light sleeper, the quiet and relative comfort conspired to give him a much needed deep sleep until his watch alarm began to wake him up. It took the alarm about a minute before Joe was finally fully awake. "OK men, time to start the day. Let's get up and head up the hill to our daytime shelters, so the others can get some sleep." Slowly, the others started moving, and in silence, each man gathered his gear and shoved it out the cave hole to prepare for their shift as guards and protectors for the others.

When they were all assembled outside of the cave and donned their gear and weapons, Joe briefed them on the plan for the day. "Paul and Tim, each of you take the two flanking bivouacs, Phil and Bob, take one on each side of the middle bivouac. Nick and I will take Jason's bivouac in the middle." As they nodded their understanding, Joe turned on his mike and pointed his laser light once again at the rock. "Good morning gentlemen, I'm glad you had a quiet couple of hours gazing at the stars and lights below. We're ready to take your place. Please point your lasers to my laser mark on the rock and keep it there until each of us show up to relieve you. Then, we'll do the same with our lasers to guide you down the hill to Colin and your sleeping accommodations."

Immediately five laser beams were pointing to Joe's marker. He turned off his laser, "OK men, let's begin our day shift. Since we're all tired, Nick and I will take the first four-hour watch duty while the rest of you sleep or relax. Then Bob and Paul will take the watch until two p.m., then Phil and Tim until six p.m. I figure we'll all be awake and ready to head down the hill by seven p.m."

"What about me?" Colin asked, feeling a little left out of the day watch activities.

"You're the big winner today, Colin." Joe said, since you found the cave, I'll leave it to you to show the men in. You can take the first four-hour watch looking from the hole down this side of the hill while the others sleep. Then break up the remaining watches into two hour shifts for each of the men. Tonight, we're going to check out the WMD, and we'll need you and Pete, as our weapons sergeants on that mission."

"Yes sir." Colin smiled. He was getting used to the comfort of the cave, could use some more good sleep, and was already looking forward to the night ahead. He and Pete were well liked and appreciated as exceptionally good men to have on missions that require stealth behind enemy lines. The mission to check out the WMD was such a mission. It was the type of assignment he liked most about his job.

Joe and Nick turned and started up the hill, following Jason's center laser beam and the other's followed their lasers until they reached their colleagues and daytime destinations. Within fifteen minutes, the watch rotation was completed and soon Joe and Nick settled in, with their rifles and scopes trained on the trucks, equipment on the flatbed trailers, and missiles nearby.

"What do you think Nick?"

"It's any one's guess what the two containers on the trailers contain. The third one appears to be a bunk house. Nick confirmed Joe's assessment. "The missiles stacked nearby look a lot like long pipes to me, but I could be wrong."

Joe was a bit unhappy with Nick's assessment regarding the missiles, but happened to agree with his prognosis. "I was kind of hoping they looked more like WMD of some kind."

"Well," Nick paused for a moment, thinking of possibilities, "I'm just telling you what I think. However, there is an outside chance they're the WMD that we're looking for. Those flatbeds may contain the launchers for the Russian SP-300, which NATO calls the SA-10 Grumble missile systems. The original version of the S-300 system which became operational in 1978 was used as air defense systems. Back then, the system was used as a country air defense system. The S-300PT unit consisted of surveillance radar, fire control system and 5P85-1 launch vehicles, which could be in those containers. Usually there is a low-altitude detection radar for targeting and shooting down planes. I don't recall how big these pieces of equipment are, but they may be in one of the containers. A launch system could be in the other container. We know the Russians did sell some of these systems to Syria, Iran, and Egypt. Perhaps, the Iraqis bought some of these and repurposed them as platforms for WMD missile launchers. I don't think so, but maybe those are really missiles stacked near the trucks." Nick paused again. "Or, maybe not. Another possibility may be that the containers are factories to make the chemical agents for the warheads on the missiles for biological warfare."

Joe frowned. He was always impressed with Nick's knowledge of military minutia, and his ability to go into detail on things that most people had never heard of. Nick was also accustomed to his matter of fact, way of providing such information in a manner that still left Joe without a clear-cut solution to his problem. "Maybe or maybe not. Nick, that doesn't help me decide if it's worth the risk to send a small team of men down there to check it out tonight."

"Sorry." Nick thought for a moment about Joe's dilemma. "We were told to search for the WMD. That could be WMD."

"Yeah. It could be." Joe pondered this for a few minutes as they continued to look through their powerful rifle scopes at the trucks and material nearby. "Yes. They could be, but we really won't know for sure until we go down there and check them out." Joe and Nick both smiled at the final conclusion.

"Well boss, we were sent here to make sure." Nick affirmed Joe's decision. "Who's going to do it?"

"You will lead the team, along with Jared, Pete, and Colin." Joe replied. "Your intelligence knowledge and Jared's knowledge of engineering will provide the expert confirmation, one way or the other, and Pete and Colin are the best men to cover your back."

"Yes sir." Nick felt good about Joe's decision. It reaffirmed his self-importance to the team and Joe, and like everyone else on the team, it was the type of work that he most liked to do.

Chapter Twenty-Three: Operation Iraqi Freedom Begins March 19, 2003

Before the shift for the night watch in the fox hole bivouacs began, Joe called the men on the day watch down to the cave for a brief meeting before sending the night watch up to take their place. As the entire team gathered around Joe, he began to describe the plan. "There will be a full moon tonight with only a little cloud cover so be careful." Joe gazed at the sky for a moment as the last glimmer of daylight shining on the clouds disappeared. "Nick, Jared, Pete and Colin will take a little walk to check out the WMD area to validate Secretary Powell's assertion that the U.S. is justified if and when we attack Iraq so that these weapons are destroyed. Jason, Tim, Manny and I will go with you down the hill and take up positions behind the large boulders that are there to provide cover for the reconnaissance team as they make their way toward the lights and the equipment there. The rest of you will take up positions in the bivouacs so you can watch our backs. Nick, do you have anything that you would like to add?"

"Before we got on the plane in Kuwait, we all watched Secretary Powell address the U.N. on February 5. I kept his speech on my computer. According to the information provided to him, the Iraqis have a missile brigade that, at least a couple of months ago, was based outside Baghdad. The brigade had a number of disbursing rocket launchers and warheads containing biological warfare agents. It is assumed that these have been moved to various locations, in western Iraq. The US has firsthand descriptions of biological weapons factories on flat-bed trailers, pulled by trucks, perhaps like what we've all been looking at for the past eighteen hours. The trucks, with the factories behind them, are easily moved and were designed to evade detection by inspectors. In a matter of months, they can produce a quantity of biological poison equal to the entire amount that Iraq claimed to have produced in the years prior to the Gulf War. Secretary Powell presented drawings of the truck and rail car-mounted mobile factories, which were provided by reliable sources inside Iraq. Based upon the drawings, the CIA has provided us with some detail regarding what the tanks, pumps, compressors and other parts look like and how they fit together." Nick paused for a moment, "The trucks, loaded flatbed trailers, and long tubes that we've been observing from the hill all look similar to what Powell described."

Joe smiled for a moment then became serious. "Gentlemen, Nick is proving again that we have our own WMD. Nick's steel trap of a mind and his ability to recall this level of detail will annihilate any mere mortal in a game of Trivia Pursuit or any other mind game." The men chuckled at this kidding at Nick's expense.

Nick smiled and took this as a good natured, compliment. "I only have a bit more to add." The men were once again attentive as they prepared for another short course on Iraqi military hardware. "There are at least seven of these mobile biological agent factories. That means that the mobile production facilities are very few, perhaps eighteen trucks that we know of. There may be more. Here's the critical bit of information, and the reason why we must accurately identify what is in the WMD area. These factories can produce anthrax and botulinum toxin. They can produce enough dry biological agents in a single month to kill thousands upon thousands of innocent people. The stuff is the most lethal form for human beings."

Nick's message sunk in with the men as they pondered the consequences if they didn't accurately ID what was near the bright lights on the other side of the hill. "OK men, if there are WMD like what was described by Secretary Powell and Nick, despite what appears to be minimal security there, Nick and the others may possibly be walking into a well concealed installation with much more danger than we've estimated, based upon what we've been observing. Nick, Jared, Pete, and Colin, when you get near the area and are still outside the lights, I'll leave it to you to determine if there is a significant risk based upon your observation of additional Iraqi forces. Otherwise, we'll stick to the plan as I've laid it out to all of you. Good luck." With that, the entire team headed up the hill either to take positions in the five fox-holes, or to proceed down the other side to the unknown danger that may be there.

Nick and his team began their stealthy maneuvers toward the bright lights and the WMD area as Joe and his team fanned out and quietly descended the hill. When the others covered about half the distance to the trucks, they took up positions on the ground and behind whatever cover was afforded about five hundred meters from the bright lights. Quickly, they each assumed positions for resting their rifles on the ground or rocks so they could carefully calibrate their scopes to ensure accurate, if not pin-point shots at the guards if necessary. Soon four rifles were trained on the guards while three other rifles were sweeping slowly back and forth, as the men looked for other Iraqi personnel that may threaten the others who were quickly moving toward the lighted area. All they could see were three guards sitting around a camp fire cooking their evening meal, smoking cigarettes not far from the truck that was in front with the bunk-house container on the trailer behind it.

The reconnaissance team used all the skills they learned during many months of training, practiced, and used since they joined Delta Force Special Operations. Joe used his binoculars to track Nick and his team while the others had their rifles trained on the guards and looked for other threats. "By the book." Joe thought to himself, as he watched his men approach the lighted area. Nick and the others were not taking any chances with their approach. Unless the guards were really observant and watching their area of responsibility very closely, they would have a hard time seeing the four men quietly get closer and closer to the trucks and stacked material nearby. Joe noted that the guards seemed to care less about their surroundings and what may be going on, other than the conversation they were having with one another.

Joe could see his men fan out, just beyond the perimeter of the lights. Nick and Jared circled around behind the trucks while Pete and Colin provided cover behind two large boulders. Strangely, there were no other Iraqis in the area.

The men silently made their way behind one of the flat-bed trailers that was the last in the row of trucks and trailers, and farthest from the guards. In a few seconds, they were directly behind it and discovered that the back of the container that they observed from a distance was covered by tightly drawn canvas, nailed around the edge of the box to hold it in place. Jared pulled out his knife and carefully cut a two inch slit in the middle of the canvas so they could see what was inside with their night vision scope. "It's drilling equipment." Jared whispered to Nick with some disappointment in his voice. He could see carefully secured stacks of drill bodies, drill heads, and string components. They moved to the next trailer and container and cut a similar slit so they could peer inside where they saw smaller cardboard boxes with labeling from American drilling equipment suppliers. "Drilling safety equipment, down-hole tools and machining equipment..."

"OK. I get the idea." Nick whispered. "Let's check out that stack to see if they're really pipes or actually the WMD missiles that we're looking for." They quickly walked over to the stack of material. Upon close inspection they determined that the "missiles" were definitely drilling pipes manufactured in China.

"Do we need to check out these boxes?" Jared whispered as he pointed to the two wooden boxes next to the stack of pipes.

"No. We've seen enough. The Iraqis wouldn't be moving around WMD and oil field equipment." Nick surmised. He and Nick had already been in the area about five minutes, and the longer they remained within the range of the lights, the greater were their chances of being discovered. The guards were still talking by the fire, but they had been there for a long time, and he didn't want to push their luck. It was also clear that there were no other guards or Iraqi Army missile systems operators anywhere in the area.

In a moment, they vanished back into the darkness and were soon leading Pete and Colin back toward the hill. Joe watched the entire mission from his position on the hill and was relieved that it was a quiet event. When the guards remained by their fire during the last hour, he was reasonably convinced that they were not guarding WMD. When he saw the team making their way back to the hill, he signaled his team to climb back up the hill also. Soon all of the team were either manning the bivouac fox-hole positions or back at the cave. "I was able to watch your movements. I'm guessing there's no WMD. What did you learn?" Joe asked as they arrived at the cave opening.

"The good and bad news is that we didn't find any WMD." Nick began.

"We opened the back end of the two large boxes and discovered everything related to drilling equipment." Jared interjected. "The so-called missiles are actually drilling pipes, although, even up close, they sort of looked like missiles."

"Although we could have attempted to investigate the boxes next to the pipes and the other container trailer, I thought it wasn't worth the chance of being discovered, so we headed home." Nick explained.

Joe nodded his head approvingly. "I agree. Since there were no other Iraqis that you or we saw other than the three by the fire, I think it's safe to say this is a staging area for a drilling operation and not a WMD launching site. If it were, we certainly would have seen a lot more Iraqi Army personnel and systems specialists.

"Shall we call it a day?" Nick spoke for his team. Although it ended happily as a quiet search mission, the adrenaline rush associated with a prospective fire fight, which is always possible in enemy territory, was very real for them. As the excitement of the last hour began to wear off, the men were feeling tired and ready for a good sleep.

"By all means." Joe smiled as he waved his hand toward the cave opening. "Thanks, men. We have the validated information that we can report back to command when they contact us. Now it's a matter of waiting for them to give us the word."

While the Task Force 20 Delta One team was in process of completing their mission to determine if WMD was in the north-western part of Iraq, the U.S. Navy was expecting the order to begin the invasion of the country. Aboard the USS *Donald Cook*, an Aegis destroyer in the Arabian Gulf, a group of missile control officers and sailors were gathered to hear final instructions from their captain. "Ladies and gentlemen, Operation Iraqi Freedom is about to begin. You've all been training hard for this first offensive since last summer. Now you will have the chance to put your training to good use. We just received orders to destroy the enemy's headquarters and suspected locations in and near Baghdad where Saddam, his sons, Ba'ath party members, and the senior Iraqi Army staff are likely to be staying. You have your targets. Be precise and decapitate the head of the Saddam regime, Ba'ath Party, and the Iraqi Republican Guard so we can end this war before it begins. God be with you."

The sailors returned to their stations and the lieutenant in charge of the missile control room asked each member of the missile launch crew to call out the coordinates of their assigned targets. Each sailor called out his or her assignment as the lieutenant checked his list and confirmed, with an "Affirmative."

The last target on the list was called out by Fire Controlman First Class Sandy: "Our group will be hitting the buildings that are in Saddam's palace complex near the Baghdad airport.

"Affirmative," called out the lieutenant. "We've been authorized to use the number of salvos needed to get the job done. Let's pray this will be a short operation like Operation Desert Storm was in 1991."

Sandy turned to her colleague that was also assigned to target the complex. "Our target is the Ba'ath party headquarters near one of the palaces of Uday Hussein, Saddam's oldest son."

Second Class Fire Controlman Baker took a big breath and let it out slowly as he began to type in the coordinates of their target. "I wonder if anyone will be in the building tonight. With the Tomahawks, we've got enough fire power to flatten most any building."

"It would be good if there were some of the senior Ba'ath party members there" Sandy replied, "but I guess we won't know until our troops finally get to Baghdad and can assess what kind of success we actually had. One thing is certain. Since it's near the airport and Saddam's palaces, they'll have all their defense systems trained on us."

Baker smiled. "I expect the Iraqis will have a lot more to worry about than we do."

At about the same time the captain of the *Donald Cook* was giving the order to proceed with the attack, about one hundred Ba'ath party members and a cadre of the elite Iraq Republican Guard General Officers were gathering in the auditorium of their headquarters about three miles away from Al Faw Palace, where General Saddam Hussein was presently residing. They were summoned to present Hussein with the final preparations for the expected invasion by the United States.

"Hello Abdullah, we haven't heard much from Bush in the last few days. Maybe all of his threats are just political talk?" General Nabil greeted his old friend and comrade in arms as they entered the auditorium.

Abdullah sighed, "I don't think so. Bush really believes we have weapons of mass destruction, plus I think he wants the Americans to think he's a macho president. A war with Iraq will make him a war-time president. He probably likes that idea."

"Well," Nabil replied, "I've deployed my troops outside Baghdad and ordered my men to take their weapons, change into civilian clothes, and return to their families. I want them to be prepared to fight in small groups at a later date if the Americans roll over us like they did in 1991. I think we will be more effective resisting them this way, rather than presenting a united force that the Americans can crush with their superior numbers and weapons."

"Don't let Saddam hear you say that!" Abdullah whispered nervously. "He would have you shot as a traitor."

"I don't think a strategy to save my men to fight the Americans and win the war is traitorous. I recall studying how the American colonies won against the British by using similar tactics," Nabil whispered back.

"Yes, but like Bush, Saddam has a huge ego, and your strategy doesn't fit with his notion of a brave and united Iraq National Guard that stands its ground and crushes the Americans when they invade.

"Well, Abdullah, I hope cooler heads prevail and the Americans don't attack, so we can return to some normality."

"With our dear General Saddam, I doubt if we will ever have the normality we both knew as young soldiers thirty years ago."

"Now you're talking like a traitor." Nabil smiled at the sad irony of Abdullah's statement.

"I'm just tired of this constant war or rumors of war," Abdullah sighed again as they worked toward their seats, and he patted his colleague on the back.

"Well, my friend, we can only hope for the best. It's getting late. I thought General Saddam was going to talk to us tonight."

Meanwhile, at his Al-Faw palace Saddam Hussein was looking out over the lake from the third-floor balcony toward the lights of the Ba'ath Party headquarters building. He had just completed giving his immediate staff their instructions and was smoking a cigarette when his aide interrupted his moment of quiet, "Sir, the generals are gathered at the headquarters, and they're waiting for you to speak to them."

"Yes, Hassan. I know. Let me finish this and enjoy the view for a moment. I don't think I'll be back here for a while after tonight." Saddam turned again to admire the quiet view over the lake. The lights from the headquarters reflected brightly on the calm water.

"I thought you were planning to return here next week, after visiting Tikrit," Hassan replied with a bit of concern in his voice.

"The Americans will attack soon, Hassan. They have been too quiet for the last few days. After they do attack, it is hard to predict where any of us will be for the next several months."

Hassan was a young officer, barely in his twenties. His uncle was a cousin of Saddam's, who got him the job as aide when the general visited Al-Faw. His assignment had nothing to do with his very limited understanding of the dangerous situation that his country faced, and a lot to do with his idealistic opinion of General Saddam Hussein and the Ba'ath party, which had been very good to his family. "Sir, I'm sure we will defeat the Americans when they attack. We just received a call from headquarters; our generals are waiting for us to hear you inspire them to beat the enemy and tell you what plans they've made to repel the invaders.

Fire Controlmen Sandy and Baker were tracking the missiles headed for the Ba'ath party headquarters in the *Donald Cook* mission control room as Sandy watched her monitor and called out the last seconds of the missiles flight before impact, "Thirty seconds before impact...fifteen seconds..."

After gazing for another moment at the quiet shimmering of the lake and the lights of the headquarters on the other side, Saddam took one last drag on his cigarette, "OK, let's go meet the men who will protect us from the Americans." He turned from the lake and took a few steps into the palace when a thunderous BOOM! BOOM! threw Saddam and Hassan to the floor as the missiles crashed into the party headquarters. The two men lay on the floor for a moment in shock, then slowly rose to their feet and looked out to where the Ba'ath Party headquarters had been, where now a blazing fire emanated from the super-heated rubble. The beautifully shimmering reflections on the lake had been replaced by what looked like the fire of hell.

Back on the ship, the lieutenant was looking over the shoulders of Sandy and Baker to watch the screen in front of them. "Well, it's begun. I pray that it will be a short war."

The ship's captain was also in the Command Information Center and watched as the sailors worked professionally to do their job. "After we find the WMD and roll over Saddam and his thugs, the Iraqis will welcome us as their liberators," he said to his men and women, then, quietly to himself, "God willing, the war will be over by this summer, if not by the end of the year."

Chapter Twenty-Four: A Close Call with Death

The morning of March 20 was quiet on the Lake Baharia compound near Uday's palace. Lara and the others slept in more than usual. Babra was the first to wake up and noticed how quiet it was. While the others were still sleeping, she walked into the small living area and peeked around the curtain near the front door. The sun was up, and only a few soldiers and staff were talking with each other and milling around nearby. The position of the sun indicated that it was later in the morning than usual. She wondered why they had not been awakened by the loud banging on the door that signaled a new day and ushered in a servant from the palace with their meager breakfast of tea and bread. This had become the norm instead of the more plentiful meals that were provided when the soldiers and staff still thought that Uday would be returning soon to continue with his planned debauchery that the women were dreading. She ran back into the small bedroom to wake the others. "Wake up!" she whispered loudly as she began shaking Lara, Eman and Eleah. "They're leaving!"

"Who's leaving?" Eman asked sleepily.

"Everyone! I just looked out the front window and only saw a couple of soldiers, and they were putting their gear in a pile. I think they and a few of the staff are the last ones here. Look for yourselves."

The others were wide awake at this news and rushed to the front room to look out from behind the curtains. As Eman and Eleah looked out from each side of the curtain, Lara asked, "What are they doing?"

"Babra is right. They're all getting ready to leave. I can see several trucks loaded with soldiers leaving on the far side of the lake." Eman said.

Eleah stepped back and closed her side of the curtain. "It's hard to see much other than the back of the palace and the side of the lake where Eman is looking."

"I wonder if the Americans have invaded the country. Maybe that's why everyone is leaving," surmised Babra.

Lara stepped up to where Eleah was and peeked out as well. Just then, they could hear the loud rumbling of a truck coming over the bridge toward the palace. "Get back," Lara said. "We need to think of this for a moment." Eman reluctantly closed the curtains and looked at Lara.

"Think about what?" Babra asked. "We need to get dressed and start banging on the door so they don't forget about us."

"Babra's right. If everyone leaves, we'll be trapped here, and then what?" Eman added.

"Maybe not," Lara began. "If we stay quiet, hopefully they will forget about us. Then, when they're all gone, we can get serious about tearing down the sandbags in the back. Remember how they stacked them there?" The others looked at her for a moment as the possibility of escape began to capture their imagination.

"What about the bars?" Eman pushed them back to reality. "The bars are still there. How are we going to break through them?"

"When we tried last time, we were beginning to move one of them before the window broke and we were caught." Lara explained, "This time, if everyone leaves, we won't have to worry about being quiet and we can use the bread knives in the kitchen and whatever else is in this place as tools to break up the mortar and use thicker pieces of wood from the beds to push and pull the bar until it comes out. Then I think we can fit through the opening and start knocking over the sandbags."

They smiled, "Let's go!" Eleah began to walk into the bedroom.

"Wait!" Lara cautioned. "We've got to make sure everyone has left the palace and this area. Otherwise, someone may hear us and take us with them."

"Lara's right. It's still morning. Let's wait until we know everyone is gone." Eman said.

The day dragged on as the soldiers waited for their truck to take the last of them, along with the remaining palace staff. The girls had become accustomed to wearing their night clothes all of the time after it became clear that Uday wasn't coming back and they were not going to be permitted to leave the cottage any time soon. Eman suggested that they change into the clothes that they were wearing on the terrible night they were taken from Baghdad by Uday and his thugs. "Let's be optimistic that tonight, we will be able to escape from here." The others gladly accepted her suggestion. Soon, they were all in their college student attire, though they still wore the slippers that the soldiers provided after they took away their street shoes to make it more difficult for them to run away.Finally, a truck arrived, and the remaining soldiers, along with what appeared to be the last of the palace staff, piled into the back and drove away. "They're all gone," Babra whispered as she watched the truck leave the palace. A moment later, she could see it on the other side of the bridge heading toward the gate. "No, wait! Some of the staff from the palace are walking by carrying their suitcases." This was unsettling. Was everyone gone now? They didn't know.

"OK. Let's get to work," Lara said. "We'll have to take our chances.

Soon they were all focused on the bar in the window. Although the butter knives could chip away only a few flakes at a time, it was a long, slow process. An hour went by and they were able to loosen the bar a little more, but it was clear that they had much more mortar to remove before they would be able to wiggle the bar free. As the light in the cottage started to fade and evening set in, they were just beginning to get the bar to move about a half inch back and forth but the mortar still prevented them from breaking it free.

"Can we take a break?" Eman complained. "I'm starting to get a blister on my hand from this knife." They were all tired and hungry. Although they were glad that everyone had left, they were beginning to miss the food service that was provided by the palace staff.

"OK. Let's take a rest for a while." Lara suggested. The others didn't require any urging as they all took a seat or lay down on the mattress that was now on the floor. Not long after they closed their eyes and began to relax from their work, they heard a boom off in the distance.

"What was that?" Eman asked.

"It sounds like another big storm is coming our way," Eleah responded with her eyes still shut. There had been a couple of thunder storms during the past week, and this sounded like another one rolling in from the east.

"We heard thunder coming from Baghdad last night," Babra surmised. "I hope this will be one of the last for the year. The rainy season is almost over and soon it will be getting hot."

There was another distant boom from the direction of Baghdad. Lara considered the sound of this for a moment and came to a different conclusion. "That's not thunder. The Americans are bombing Baghdad." They all sat up to listen for another ominous boom, and it came within a few minutes. "Those booms are slowly coming this way. We need to get back to work."

They were all back on their feet with a renewed sense of urgency.

While the women continued to chisel through the mortar and slowly move the bar more and more, a formation of two F/A-18 Hornet attack jets were taking off from the USS *Abraham Lincoln* aircraft carrier in the Persian Gulf. Soon, the two jets were on their way to their designated targets with Lieutenant "Smokey" Smith as lead and Lieutenant "Mick" MacDonald as his wingman. "It's always pretty looking at the setting sun," Smokey said as he banked his plane northward toward Fallujah in central Iraq, just west of Baghdad.

"Yeah, the dust from the desert makes the sky almost red," Mick observed. "We'll be on target near one of Uday Hussein's palaces in thirty minutes, just after the last light is gone from the sky."

"We're already nearing Iraq." Smokey looked off to the right and far below to see the fires burning in an oil field near a city in the distance. "There's Basra. Welcome to Iraq."

The thunderous booms coming from Baghdad were beginning to get louder as the women feverishly chipped away at the concrete and continued their effort to move the bar. Boom, BOOM! The explosions were getting much closer, and they started panicking. "We've got to get out of here!" Babra cried as her knuckles began to bleed from scraping them against the bar when she feverishly hammered the knife blade downward onto the mortar. "This blade is beginning to bend like the others!"

Lara was also hammering away on the other side of the bar as Eman and Eleah stood on chairs above them trying to push and pull the bar in what seemed to be a failing attempt to break it free. "Let's all start pushing and pulling this thing. It's got to move!" Usually, Lara was the most calm and level-headed among the four of them, but now she was also beginning to panic.

As she and Babra began to grab the bottom parts of the bar with both hands, Eman began to sob softly. "We're going to die! The Americans will blow up the palace and the cottage with us in it." Soon all four of them had tears in their eyes as they continued to desperately try forcing the bar from its entrenched position in the concrete.

A moment later, they heard someone at the front door as the bar came up and the door opened. "Are you still here?" It was one of the staff from the palace. The girls rushed into the room to see the young man they recognized as one of the servants that brought food to them every day. "Come on, we've got to get out of here! Now!" Another BOOM, BOOM! It seemed as if the explosions were almost on top of them.

Although the girls only had slippers on, they ran out of the cottage with the young man and followed him as fast as they could as he began to run down the road toward the bridge.

Soon the man was on the bridge. He stopped, turned and pleaded with the girls as loudly as he could, "Hurry! The Americans are bombing everything! The palace may be next!" With that, he turned again toward the bridge and began sprinting over it.

"We'll be over our target in five minutes," Smokey said calmly. "Lock and load. Set the coordinates on the cruise missiles for AX98735. Look down below to the left for a visual. We'll circle around to get in position."

"Roger," confirmed Mick as he began to bank his plane to the left in tandem with Smokey's lead.

The man disappeared on the other side of the bridge as the girls looked up to see two jets making a tight circle in the dark night sky. "Run!" Lara screamed.

They began to run like never before, even with their slippers on, as the jets completed their circle and positioned themselves. Soon Lara was on top of the bridge and running toward a guard house on the other side. "Come on! Hurry!" she urged the others on.

Smokey began the countdown as he and Mick covered their thumbs over the fire control switch on each of their planes. "Five, four, three, two, one, fire!" The four cruise missiles were released and the planes banked to the right. The satellite-guided missiles remained on their radar and were tracked as the GPS systems guided each of them toward the palace.

Eman and Eleah caught up with Lara as Babra continued to run as fast as she could toward where they were lying behind the abandoned guard house. "Hurry Babra!" the three pleaded. "We can see the missiles coming!"

Babra was about ten feet from them when Lara screamed one last order to everyone. "Cover your ears!" Everyone except Babra covered their ears as she took the last five steps toward them and the guard house.

BOOM! BOOM! BOOM! BOOM! The missiles found their mark as the palace and the cottage were transformed into a huge ball of fire and rubble that exploded toward the night sky. Babra was knocked to the ground near the others from the concussion. They were all stunned by the force of the explosion and its loud noise but were otherwise unharmed. The others uncovered their ears, "Quick! Let's get in the guard house!" Lara got off the ground and quickly crawled through the door of the tiny building as the others followed.

The noise of the explosions was deafening to Babra. She could see Lara say something and start crawling into the guard house, but she couldn't hear her. The message was clear, however, although she was bruised from being pushed to the ground by the explosions. Otherwise, she thought, she was unharmed. Soon they heard the sound of falling debris from the exploded buildings. It was like a violent and loud hail storm that reminded Lara of such storms back in Michigan. They waited for about thirty seconds as the noise quickly subsided, then stopped.

"Direct hit!" Smokey smiled. "If Uday Hussein was in that place, they'll have a hard time finding him or anyone else near it."

"Yeah," agreed Mick, "That was almost too easy. At this rate, the war will be over in no time."

Let's circle around one more time to get a visual on the glowing embers. Then let's go home."

"Aye, Aye, sir." Mick agreed as he mimicked Smokey's lead by banking his plane in a tight circle around the burning former palace below and headed back to the CNV USS *Abraham Lincoln*.

Lara and the others waited a few moments under the shelter of the guardhouse roof before getting up. When they stepped outside, looked over the bridge and down the short road to where the palace and cottage were standing a moment ago, they could only see flames from what remained of the palace and cottage. They were all numbed and shocked by what had just happened to them.

The rubble across the bridge continued to burn for about an hour before it slowly changed into a pile of glowing embers. The girls stood and watched in silence as they began to recover from their escape from certain death.

"That was close." Eman was the first to speak.

"What?" Babra asked in an unusually loud voice.

Eman was puzzled by her question, but repeated herself in a louder voice, "That was close".

"Thanks. I can't hear very well."

"Babra, didn't you have your ears covered?" Lara asked.

"I was taking the last few steps to the guardhouse when I was thrown to the ground by the explosions." Babra began to understand that she had just lost most of her hearing. "Am I deaf?" She began to cry as this possible new reality occurred to her.

Lara, Eman, and Eleah gathered around Babra to give her a comforting hug. An hour ago, all of them were healthy in every way. Now, one of them might have been maimed for life. Lacking anything else to say, Lara offered some comforting but perhaps not realistic words to Babra and the others. "It will be OK..."

"What?" Tears were streaming down Babra's face.

"Lara began again. "It will be OK Babra. Don't worry. Lots of times, people regain their hearing after a while."

"Do you really think so?" Babra asked as her cry turned to short sniffling breaths.

Lara paused for a moment as she considered her response. She knew she didn't know if this was true or not. Under the circumstances, she decided it would be better to give poor Babra some reassurance than to express doubt or uncertainty. She made up a plausible response; that she hoped would come true. "My dad told me that he's had many patients that lost their hearing because they didn't protect their ears while hunting in Michigan. He said most of their hearing came back after a while. They couldn't hear as well as they used to, but they were almost back to normal after a couple of months."

"I hope so." Babra sighed. Her breathing was returning to normal, with deep breaths, as she calmed down from her initial shock.

"What are we going to do now?" Eleah asked herself and the others.

"What?"

"What are we going to do now?" Eleah repeated herself.

Lara looked around and saw cottages on the other side of the road, then pointed to the nearest one, near the guard house where they took shelter from the missiles. "The place is deserted and the door is open. Everyone is gone." She looked down at their feet and noticed they were still wearing the slippers that were provided for the cottage. "We should leave here as soon as possible in case the Americans decide to bomb this area again."

"Well, at least we're free and I don't think Uday or others will be looking for us. The highway to Fallujah, Ramadi, and Baghdad is over there," Babra observed as she pointed to where smoke was rising way off in the distance toward Baghdad and much closer in the opposite direction toward Fallujah.

The others looked puzzled. "Babra, you're not talking as loudly as you were a moment ago." Eleah said. "Maybe your hearing is already starting to return."

"I hope so." A faint smile came to Babra's face.

Lara returned to her suggestion as she pointed to the cottages across the street and began to walk toward them, "Maybe we can find better shoes in there." When they entered the dark building, they could barely see the several pair of boots and Iraqi Army uniforms that were still there. Two of the girls found boots that were at first loose on their feet but became acceptable with additional pairs of socks. They moved down the row of cottages to look for boots that would fit the others. During their search, they also found some snacks and other items that the soldiers had left behind which they thought may be useful in the days ahead.

It was one a.m. in the morning and everything was quiet. The bombing in the distance had stopped about one hour after their close call with the destruction of the palace. They were in the fifth cottage and didn't see anything useful to take. However, there were six beds with blankets and pillows. All of them were feeling very tired and drained of energy from their desperate attempt to dislodge the bar from the window, their adrenaline-charged run to escape the missiles, and the search for boots and other supplies. "I'm exhausted." Eman said what the others were thinking.

"I think we should be safe here for the rest of the night," Lara suggested.

Babra sat on one of the beds and grabbed a blanket. "I need to sleep," She lay down and covered herself with a blanket.

"I guess that's Babra's answer," Lara said as she shut the cottage door. Eman and Eleah were already preparing their bed and Lara did the same. Soon they were all in a deep sleep.

It seemed as if they had just shut their eyes when they were startled by someone opening the door. In an instant, they were all sitting up, afraid that the soldiers were back. "Who's there?" Lara demanded.

The door was opened just slightly and they could see that it was already day as the bright light of the morning sun shined in from behind the figure standing there. "It's me, Abraham," a man answered. "I was the one that let you out of your cottage last night."

"Abraham?" Lara asked. "Open the door so we can see you. It's all right. We have our clothes on."

The girls were already beginning to stand up as Abraham opened the door. "Remember me? I was one of the palace servants that brought your dinners to you."

When he stepped into the room and away from the open door, the cottage was flooded by the morning sunlight, and the girls could see that it was the young man who always smiled when he dropped off the tray of food prepared in the palace kitchen at five p.m. sharp every evening. He was about their age, perhaps nineteen or twenty years old, with a light beard and short black hair, gentle eyes, and always a warm smile. When he brought the evening meals to them, he wore a white thobe, which Lara recognized as a long white pullover shirt that went all the way down to his ankles. Many men and boys wore this attire instead of the western shirt and pants, since it was more light weight and more comfortable than the western garb in the heat. Last evening and today however, he was wearing pants and a shirt. Instead of sandals, he also had on regular Western street shoes, and instead of a smile, he had a tired and worried look on his face. "I was ordered to stay behind and keep the palace safe after everyone else left on the last truck yesterday," he said as he walked over to one of the empty beds and sat down. "When I heard the bombs coming closer, I knew that it would only be a matter of time before the palace would be bombed as well. I didn't want to be in it. When I was running past the cottage, I thought of you and wanted to check, just in case you were still in there. I didn't know if they had already taken you in one of the trucks, or not....I'm glad that I checked."

"We are too!" Lara said. "Thank you for saving our lives."

Eman, Eleah, and Babra echoed Lara, "Thank you."

"Abraham, we owe you our lives. We will never forget what you did for us." Babra said.

Abraham was a bit embarrassed by their gratitude. "I didn't want to always wonder if you were in there or not. If I hadn't checked to see if you were there and ran over the bridge without knowing...then, watch everything blow up... It would have made me crazy." Abraham leaned forward, rested his elbows on his knees, and held his forehead in his hands. "I'm very tired. After I ran over the bridge, I kept running as fast as I could until I heard the loud explosions and saw the palace and cottage blow up. After that, I've just been walking around the lake and looking in all the cottages. I grabbed some things...but I couldn't sleep. All I could do was worry about what would become of Iraq, my family, me. It feels like the world is coming to an end."

The girls were silent as they listened to his sorrowful voice and gloomy outlook. Actually, they felt the same way. The cottage was quiet for several moments as they all pondered what the future might bring.

"We've got to go to our families to let them know we're still alive," Lara jolted them from their thoughts. "It's still early in the day. Abraham needs some sleep. I suggest that we let him take a nap while the four of us go to the cottage where we saw the food and cook stove. Maybe we can make a warm meal for all of us while he sleeps. We can all eat when he wakes up, and then we can figure out where we go from here."

"Thank you," Abraham said as he stretched out on the bed.

Eman got up, "Good idea. Let's see what we can find to eat." She picked up her blanket and covered Abraham with it as she walked out the door, followed by Babra, Eleah and Lara. The sun was still low on the horizon, and they guessed it to be about eight in the morning. By the time they found enough food that the soldiers had left in several of the cottages, prepared a meager meal and ate it with Abraham, it was probably ten a.m. When they were finished, they picked up their small packs of food and water, and they all began walking toward the gate of the compound that lead to Route One. This main highway in Iraq ran east and west, and north and south in the country. It was this stretch of road that led to Baghdad toward the east, and to Fallujah, Ramadi, and the crossroads to Jordan and Syria in the west. It also intersected with Route 12 in Fallujah, which led north toward Haditha and Mosul.

Outfitted with socks, ill-fitting boots, some water bottles and food, the girls walked with Abraham in silence for a while. "Since my family lives in Haditha, I suggest we all go there. If we can get a ride from here to Ramadi, it is only an hour away from there," Eleah volunteered. "From there my father can help the rest of you with rides for Eman and Lara to Mosul. Babra, we'll figure out how to get you safely to Hilla."

"Thanks, Eleah. Hilla is only about three hours from here, if I can get a ride with a family that is going in that direction. Haditha is about three hours in the opposite direction," Babra replied.

"Babra, traveling alone may not be safe."

"I think everyone is as frightened as we have been." Babra walked a bit further in silence, thinking of her options. "Actually, after what we've already been through, I'm not too worried. Besides, I can't wait to be with my parents and the rest of my family.

"My family lives in Karbala," Abraham offered. "Hilla is not far from there. We can travel there together."

"Both of you would get in trouble if anyone thought that you were not married or related!" Eman cautioned. "Especially in Karbala."

Eman had good reason to be concerned. The citizens of Karbala were devout Shia Muslims imbued with the memory of Imam Hussein ibn Ali and his brother Abbas ibn Ali, who were killed for their strong beliefs in AD 680 and considered martyrs for their faith. The intense religious beliefs in the city reinforced strict cultural norms that frowned on a young man being with an unrelated young woman.

Babra thought about the pros and cons of traveling with a single man and concluded the danger it might create was far outweighed by her desire to go home as soon as possible. "Abraham can be my brother for a day," she suggested.

"When we get to Karbala, we'll go to my parent's home. My relatives have a car. They can take Babra to Hilla and return home the same day."

"OK, Babra," Lara sighed. "I guess Abraham could pass as Babra's brother. Eleah and Eman, what do you think?"

Eman nodded yes as Eleah spoke for both of them, "Under the circumstances, I don't think anyone will be checking very closely to learn if they're related or not."

The walk to the gate for Dreamland did not take long. Soon they were walking on a two-lane road toward Route One. As they approached the divided highway, they saw a steady stream of cars, trucks, and busses, coming from Baghdad, with only a few vehicles, primarily Iraqi Army trucks, going the other way.

"We will need to travel east on Route One toward Abu Ghraib where the road turns south toward Route 8 and Karbala and Hilla," advised

Abraham. "The rest of you will want to head west toward Ramadi, then on Route 12 to Haditha."

"I hope we can find someone who will take us to Haditha." Eleah was anxious to get home to her parents as soon as possible. "Do you think anyone will stop for three girls trying to get a ride?"

This posed a dilemma. In this culture, young women would never stand by the side of a road waving at cars to stop and give them a ride. "You're right, Eleah," Lara sighed. Maybe we need to walk to the Fallujah bus station to see if we can take a bus." The others pondered this plan of action.

"We don't have any money, even if we did walk to the bus station. What do we do then?" Eman pondered.

Abraham was anxious to return to his family in Karbala, but he also understood the dilemma. "I'll try waving down a car that looks like it has room for the three of you," he volunteered. "Perhaps someone will be more interested in helping a young man with his four sisters long enough to stop and talk with us. Then we can explain your situation and you can determine whether or not you are comfortable getting in the car."

"That would be wonderful!" Eleah beamed.

"Is that OK with you, Babra?" Lara asked.

"No problem. I'll feel better knowing the three of you are safely on your way to Eleah's home."

Abraham stepped up to the side of the highway as the cars, trucks, and buses continued to pass by. Several vehicles slowed but immediately sped up when they understood he had four girls with him. All of them were already full of men, women, and children. Sometimes people waved as they went by. Most of the time, people stared blankly straight ahead, as if they were headed into the unknown, which they certainly were.

"Maybe if we get behind Abraham and start waving frantically, someone may take pity on us," Lara suggested as she walked up to the road behind him and began to wave her hands and yell with a sense of desperation in her voice, "*Musaeada*! *Musaeada*! (Help! Help!)" Immediately, the traffic slowed to see what was going on. Clearly, Lara's strategy was working. Eman, Eleah, and Babra lined up behind Abraham and Lara and started waving their arms, "*Musaeada*! *Musaeada*!"

Soon a family with the husband, wife, and two young sons in a Toyota pickup truck, which had a goat in the back, slowed to a stop just past them. Quickly Abraham ran over to the passenger side as the woman opened the window. "My three sisters are trying to get to our parents in Haditha, while my other sister and I must go to Karbala to check on our grandfather. Can you help us?" By this time, the girls were behind Abraham with sad faces and pleading eyes.

"Why are they wearing those clothes," the woman frowned, looking at their formerly fashionable but now shabby and dirty Baghdad college clothes, and the ill-fitting army boots they were wearing. There was a moment of silence as Abraham thought of how to respond.

"My brother brought my sisters to visit with me at the University of Baghdad, then the Americans started bombing us. We got a ride out of town as soon as we could, and were able to get this far. The driver was going to turn off to go to his farm and dropped us off here. Can you please help us?" Lara pleaded.

The woman frowned and turned to her husband, "What do you think?"

The man also frowned as Eleah began to cry in desperation, "Please, sir! I must see my parents!"

He shook his head and looked at this very unlikely group of young people. He really didn't know what to believe of their story. "They look harmless enough," he said to his wife. "We're going to Hit; you can look for another ride from there. Get in the back with the goat."

Immediately the three of them ran to the back of the truck, climbed in, and sat down with the goat. "Thank you!" Abraham and Babra waved as the man began to pull back into the traffic on their way to the town of Hit, which was about 40 miles south of Haditha.

Eleah smiled at Lara as she held onto the side of the truck and the goat, "We don't even look like sisters."

"We had to say something so I said the first thing I could think of," Lara explained. "We're almost like sisters, aren't we?"

"If we weren't being bounced around and didn't have this goat between us, I'd give you a big hug, sister." Eman smiled as the truck picked up speed on the road to Fallujah, Ramadi and then north toward Hit and Haditha.

Abraham and Babra carefully crossed over to the eastward direction of Route One. They began waving their arms and shouting for help to attract the attention of some friendly family that would take pity and offer them a ride. Since there was much less traffic going in that direction it took longer, but eventually another family stopped, and Abraham was able to convince the man and his wife to give them a ride. When they were finally squeezed into the back of a small sedan with two young children and some of the family luggage, the car started down the road. Babra had time to reflect on the all the terrible events that led her to being in a car with strangers on her way home to her family. She wondered if she would ever see her friends again. If she weren't so exhausted from the last twenty-four hours, she would be moved to tears, but she could only close her eyes and pray that things would get better.

Chapter Twenty-Five:
In the Desert and on the Way to Mosul
March 20, 2003

"Bob, what's new?" Joe asked on the morning of March 19, after the men returned from the reconnaissance trip that determined there were no WMD on the trucks or anywhere they had been searching in the Nineveh Province. Phil and Bob were alternating every four hours on their encrypted satellite-connected computers, waiting for an incoming communication regarding the invasion.

Everyone on the team was anxious to know when they could begin making their way back to Mosul and connect with the 101st Army Airborne Division and a flight to the United States for a well-deserved home leave. However, they had all come to think it would be around April 1, during a dark moonless night that the invasion would start. Joe was always nearby the two communicators on his team, waiting to learn when the long silence would be broken, and asked them the same question at the end of each of their shifts. Since they had completed their reconnaissance mission and determined there was no threat to be destroyed in their area of operation, Joe considered the thought that they should return to the barn and meet up with Hakim. There was water nearby that could be treated to make it safe for drinking and they still had a sufficient supply of MREs to last for two more weeks, so he decided they should hunker down and wait for HQ instructions.

Bob shook his head, "No word yet, boss. Maybe we'll hear something tomorrow night."

March 20 was another quiet evening as the nearly full moon appeared in the sky. Then, on March 21, Joe could see a big smile come across the face of Phil as he received his first incoming message. "The invasion began on March 19." Phil said excitedly.

Joe was tempted to let out a loud "Hurray!" But he settled for a much quieter, "Good news!" He patted Phil on the back, "What's next?"

"They're asking about recommended targeting information, which we may have."

Joe was unprepared for this request. Although he was excited to learn that the war had begun, he hadn't thought of what to report back regarding their two-week search for WMD. After a moment, he composed in his head his reply. "Reconnaissance identified a convoy of three trucks and semi-trailers near the Syrian border, coordinates TXR2357. Stacked nearby were racks of pipes for exploratory oil drilling and trailers had large containers of oil drilling machinery and supplies. These all look like WMD material from a distance."

Phil repeated this response on his radio and waited for confirmation that the message was received. It seemed like time passed very slowly as he and Joe waited for a reply. Phil started nodding his head as he received their orders. "Roger. Coordinates have been targeted. Stand by to verify the results of WMD bombardment on March 23. Please confirm." Phil repeated the message that he received on his radio to Joe.

"Damn." Joe exclaimed, "We said they only looked like WMD."

"Yes sir." Phil agreed. "What is our reply?"

"Tell them... confirmed." Joe sighed. What else could he say? That night, Joe had a restless sleep. This was not what he considered an honorable way to begin their role in the war. He also wrestled with the ethical and moral dilemma of directing fire which would almost certainly kill the three guards, who were not Iraqi soldiers and definitely not threatening. The past three days of observations indicated that the men were not armed with any weapons. Killing innocent civilians was not part of the special forces code of conduct, especially if it could be avoided.

The next morning, when the entire team assembled during the rotation from night to daytime shifts at the observation bivouacs, Joe conveyed the news. "The invasion began on Wednesday evening," he began. "I asked Phil to confirm to HQ last night that we will be positioned this evening to watch and validate the destruction of the WMD."

"There is no WMD!" Nick interjected.

"We told them that it was oil drilling equipment that looked like WMD," Joe explained. "They want to bomb it anyway...Those are our orders." Joe continued, "I've been thinking of those three guards. We all know they are not combatants. I've been thinking that we should create a distraction for them so they're not in the bombing zone, near the trucks."

"Sounds good to me," Tim spoke up. "What's the plan?"

Joe frowned, "I don't have one yet. Any ideas?" The men were silent for a few moments, thinking about and rejecting one idea after another.

"I suggest that my team work our way behind the small hill near the trucks, and down the dirt road that leads north for about a mile." Paul began. "We'll have MICHs on so we can hear when the jets are in range. Then we'll set off two concussion grenades. This should attract the guards toward the hill, beyond range of the incoming missiles," Paul suggested. "Then we'll circle our way back to camp."

"Colin, Jared, Jordan, what do you think?" Joe asked.

"Sounds good to us," Jared affirmed as the other two nodded in agreement.

"OK gentlemen," Joe approved. "Thanks." He continued with the plan that he had in mind for after they reported on the bombing results. "We don't know when the attack will take place during the next twenty-four hours, so we'll stay here tonight and tomorrow. Then, we'll head back to the barn where Hakim will be waiting. Our goal should be return to the barn by March 26. That will give us two nights to get there. It should be easier to walk back since the ground has dried out and it looks like the rains are finished. Also, we don't have as many MREs, so our packs will be lighter."

"Yes sir!" The men responded unanimously. They were happy to be nearly finished with this portion of their assignment, happy that their preparation, training, and the hardships they had been dealing with for the last two months were finally producing some real results toward the elimination of Saddam Hussein and the Ba'athists. Although they couldn't take credit for helping destroy any WMD, perhaps somewhere else in Iraq other special ops teams were being instrumental in eliminating the danger.

The following night, everything worked as planned. Paul and his team made their way behind the hill near the trucks and down the dirt road about a mile, where they waited and listened on their MICHs for the lead F/A-18 pilot and his wingman. Joe suggested that, if the team wanted to, they could take extra MREs with them to leave by the side of the road for the three guards that would be desperate for food after their trucks were destroyed. "No problem." Was their reply.

"It sure is dark down there," could barely be heard on their MICHs as the lead pilot talked with his wingman. This was all the special operators needed to hear for them to know that the planes were closing in. That was their signal to set off two very loud concussion grenades and begin their quick retreat back to the rest of the team. Joe and the others heard the loud BOOM BOOM in the distance and saw the three startled guards get up from their camp fire and begin to run in the direction of the noise. Joe smiled. Paul's plan was working.

A moment later, Joe and the others heard the pilot, "We're getting near coordinate TXR2357. There! Off to our left. See the lights? Let's circle around to confirm our target."

"Yes sir," responded the wingman.

Joe and the men looked into the dark sky and could barely discern the lights of the afterburners of the two planes as they circled at about 20,000 feet.

"There they are." The lead pilot was speaking again. "See the three trucks and trailers with large containers on each one, and the stack of missiles nearby?" The lead pilot had a clear visual on what he thought he was looking at.

"It's interesting that those bright lights are shining on them," commented the wingman. "Maybe they figured we wouldn't be looking for WMD this close to the Syrian border."

"Who knows?" responded the lead pilot. "Let's lock and load. On my mark." The lead pilot maneuvered his plane into firing position, with his wingman at his side. "Fire!" At once four Tomahawk missiles were released from the planes and headed toward their targets. Within seconds, the men on the hill witnessed the trucks, trailers, containers, and stack of pipes explode into large fire balls BOOM, BOOM, BOOM, BOOM.

The team watched as the burning rubble slowly turned into several glowing piles of twisted metal and waited for Paul and his team to arrive from their mission. When they returned, Joe gathered his men near Jason's bivouac before heading back to the cave. "Well, that was a good show. Paul, Jared, Colin, Jordan, thanks again for the diversion. It worked. Those three guards were nowhere near the trucks when they all went up in flames."

"No problem," Paul replied for his team, "We're always happy to save a few lives when we can. We even left our MREs along the side of the road where they could find them, so they'll have something to eat on their way to the nearest road."

"We'll all do four-hour rotations, beginning with Tim and his team, then my team, then Paul and his team. That'll give the good guys an eight-hour break as their reward for saving some poor guards," Joe continued, "We'll keep up the rotations until 2000, then we'll begin our walk back to the barn. Good work, men."

The team's journey back to the barn was uneventful. Dried earth made it much easier for the men to walk quickly, and the invasion seemed to have distracted everyone in the area by making them focus on their immediate surroundings and safety. Although the road crossing slowed them down, as before, this time there were no military convoys to contend with, and there was no rain to make it difficult for the men to scurry up the hill on the other side of the road. When they stopped for the night on March 25, Joe used the Hakim's phone to signal that they would meet him at the barn the following night.

They arrived back at the barn at about 2300 the following evening, March 26. Hakim was waiting for them with fresh roasted chickens, bread, and other local produce. He also brought much-appreciated clean village clothes, towels, and other food from the Baa'j market.

Hakim was handing out the food and supplies when Joe asked, "How are things in Baa'j?"

"Everyone is afraid of what may happen next, but there is no panic. I think everyone thinks they are so far away from where the Americans are invading that they are relatively safe. Although some folks came from near the village of Wardiya on Route 47 and said they heard some loud explosions in the distance two nights ago."

"It could have been thunder," Joe smiled.

"Maybe," Hakim also smiled. Plausible deniability was an accepted norm until everyone was safely in the United States. "I should go. Although people are reasonably calm, they are more suspicious about anything unusual, like having my cousin's truck parked by the barn. I don't want to attract attention. Be ready to go by 1300. I'll return then with the bus. We'll load up and hopefully be on our way to Mosul by 1330."

"Did y'all hear that?" Joe asked his men. "Let's get ourselves and our gear cleaned up so we're ready to go when Hakim returns. By then we'll all look like very tired villagers for the trip north."

"We'll beeady to go, sir," Pete said on behalf of the entire team.

By morning, they had all taken a bucket bath at the well and were wearing clean but shabby workers' clothes that Hakim left for them the previous night. Promptly at 1300 on March 27, the old bus turned onto the dirt road toward the barn as the men lined up outside with their gear. Within minutes everything had been piled onto the roof rack, tied down securely, and adorned with cages of chickens that Hakim bought in Baa'j. They were on the small road toward Route 47 and Mosul.

"So, can you tell us now where we are going?" Joe asked Hakim.

"I didn't tell you before, because of the sensitivity." Hakim explained. "We are going about 18 miles northwest of Mosul, up in the mountains, to an ancient monastery, Mar Mattai, where we will stay until we're greeted by the 101st Airborne to take us all home."

Somewhere in America, a family watched the evening news and the unfolding of Operation Iraqi Freedom. "The administration reported that on March 23, the military located the first stockpile of what appeared to be the aluminum tubes used for uranium enrichment near the Syrian border in the Nineveh Province. These were destroyed by air-to-ground missiles. Verification of the WMD cannot be made, however, until the army secures this area. We are told that operations will continue to be focused on the major cities and it will be several weeks before the military will be able to conduct a thorough study of the WMD equipment that was destroyed."

The man watching the news exclaimed to no one in particular, "I knew there were weapons of mass destruction! Thank God President Bush is the leader he is! We'll kick Saddam's ass and wrap this war up in no time!" That's all he needed to know before he changed the channel.

Chapter Twenty-Six: A Return to Mosul at Last April 13, 2003

The pickup truck finally arrived in Hit, where Eleah, Eman, and Lara expected to get out and begin looking for another ride to Haditha on a much less traveled road. Thankfully, the wife talked her husband into driving the additional forty miles to Haditha, but first they stopped for the night at the family's farmhouse. There the girls ate with some food that the wife prepared and were allowed to get some much-needed sleep on the very comfortable sofas in their drawing room.

The following day, on March 22, they left early for Haditha. Since they were going to her family, Eleah was invited to sit in the cab with the man and wife so she could direct them to her home. Eman and Lara were in the back of the truck. During the trip, everyone continued to look into the sky as US helicopters and warplanes flew overhead on their way to assist with the invasion. Occasionally the helicopters would slow to a hover overhead as the soldiers took a closer look at the traffic on the road. When they saw that there were two young women in the back of the pickup, they would continue flying toward the skirmishes that were taking place north toward Mosul and east toward Tikrit.

When they pulled up a dusty road to the walled courtyard and house where Eleah's parents lived, the man slowed to a stop, and Eleah jumped out, ran to the gate, which was bolted from the inside, and started ringing the bell that was near it. "Momma! Papa! This is Eleah! Open the gate!"

Lara and Eman jumped out of the truck and thanked the man and wife for the ride as they were getting out of the cab. The four of them began walking to Eleah, then the gate opened and Eleah's father saw his daughter. "Eleah!" He immediately picked her up off of her feet in an emotional embrace, "We didn't know what happened to you! *Alhamd lillah*! Thank God you are alive!"

Eleah's mother rushed out of the gate when she heard her husband, "Eleah!" is all she could say as she collapsed against the wall in overwhelming emotion. "Thank God! Thank God!"

When her father put Eleah back on the ground after his hug, she regained her composure enough to turn to the others, "Father, Mom, these are my friends, Lara and Eman, and these wonderful people," she said as she turned to the husband and wife, "are Othman and Hanah Al-Goad. We owe them many thanks. They picked us up when we were stranded east of Fallujah. Although they live in Hit, they drove us all the way here."

Eleah's father and mother bowed toward them with their right hand extended over their heart to express their deep appreciation and respect. "Sir, I am Hussein Al-Abad, and this is my wife, Farah. Thank you so much for delivering our daughter safely to us."

"Please come into our home; you have done so much for us. Let us prepare a meal in your honor," Farah offered.

It was an awkward moment. Custom dictated that honored guests should accept such an offer. However, both Othman and Hanah clearly recognized that Farah's offer, although sincere, was made in haste and as custom would dictate. The palpable emotions on the faces of Eleah, Farah, and Hussein made it very clear that their greatest desire was to go into their home and spend time with each other. Eleah had explained the circumstances leading up to their rescue on the drive from Hit to Haditha, so the Al-Goad couple understood the priorities of the moment. Just then, they heard the loud THUMP, THUMP, THUMP of another group of Huey helicopters approaching from the south. They were low enough that everyone could see the machine guns protruding from their sides as they flew overhead.

Everyone paused for a moment, watched them fly by, and resumed their conversation when it was quiet again. "Thank you for your generous offer," Othman said as Hanah shook her head in the affirmative. "It's getting late, and we've already had a couple of very long days. It would be best for us to return to Hit before dark. We don't want the Americans to mistake us for an Iraqi Army vehicle in the dark."

"We understand," Hussein acknowledged as he put his hand over his heart again in a gesture of gratitude.

"Thank you for bringing our daughter to us," Farah said as she and Othman bowed one more time."

"Thank you so much for bringing us here!" Lara said as she spontaneously gave Hanah a big hug and bowed to Othman. Eman and Eleah were more subdued and bowed toward them.

Hanah was startled by Lara's embrace, but excused it as youthful indiscretion. "You're welcome."

Othman was a bit surprised by all of the emotion and gratitude being expressed. He and Hanah lived quietly in the country and were not accustomed to this sort of attention. "All of you are welcome. Thank you. We must go now." With those brief words, he turned to his wife. "Let's go, Hanah." Then he turned and started walking back to the truck.

Hanah looked at everyone for a moment "Bye!" is all she could say as she turned toward the truck. Soon they were leaving a trail of dust as the truck turned onto the road back to Hit.

Immediately, Hussein and Farah embraced Eleah in a group hug, "Thank God! Thank God!" Farah said over and over.

"Come inside. You all look tired," Hussein said as he ushered everyone through the gate, across the small courtyard, and into the sitting room of their house.

"Mom, can we wash and change into something else? We've been wearing these clothes for two days." Eleah asked.

"Of course. Show Eman and Lara to your room and the bath. Your clothes are still in your wardrobe." She turned to Eman and Lara, "I'm sorry, but you will have to make do with Eleah's clothes. I hope that is all right."

Lara smiled and bowed as a sign of respect to Farah, "Thank you for your hospitality. Anything will be fine at the moment."

"When you are ready, we want to learn everything since Eleah disappeared. Your classmates at the dormitory said the three of you simply disappeared on February 8. What happened to you?" Hussein asked.

"I'll prepare a meal and make tea while the girls bathe and get comfortable in some clean clothes," Farah advised. She turned to the girls: "Then you can tell us everything."

"Thank you, Momma," Eleah replied. "We'll be back as soon as we can."

Hussein went into the kitchen with Farah as she began to pull items together for a meal. "Eleah looks older than when she visited with us in January," he observed.

"She's just very tired, Hussein." Farah said as she put a kettle on the stove to boil for tea. Then she paused for a moment as the last half-hour caught up with her again. "I hope she is all right. What has she gone through! Our dear Eleah!" She began to cry uncontrollably as Hussein held her in an embrace as she sobbed. Her fears, constant worry, and now extreme relief that Eleah was safe and back with her finally created an overwhelming outburst of emotion.

"It will be all right, Farah. Eleah is back with us." Hussein comforted her. "Soon we will know everything.

Lara, Eleah, and Eman returned to the sitting room about an hour later. It was late afternoon when they sat down and began to tell Eleah's parents the details of everything that they had endured since the dreadful night of February 8. Although the girls were exhausted from their recent ordeal, they talked late into the evening, occasionally interrupting each other as one or another added more detail to the conversation. Farah or Hussein frequently stopped them to ask questions and seek further clarification, especially regarding the brutality of Uday Hussein. They were also interrupted occasionally by the THUMP, THUMP of more American helicopters.

"Yes, Mother," Eleah answered Farah's question. "The good news is that after Uday rushed off to Baghdad, we never saw him again, and the soldiers and staff at the palace didn't harm us. They were afraid of Uday and what he might do if he came back and learned that one of us had been touched before he had his time with each of us. Thank God he never came back."

"Thank God," Farah sighed.

"The three of you look like you could go to sleep where you are," Hussein observed. "It's time for bed. Tomorrow we'll figure out how to get Lara and Eman safely to Mosul."

"Thank you," Lara said. "We can't wait to return to Mosul and let everyone know that we're all right."

"Normally you could call your families tonight," Hussein began, "but the phone lines to Mosul aren't working. The road from here to Mosul is through the desert on Route 19 and up Highway One. Both are dangerous, so we must find someone with a good car we can trust to protect you. It will take us time to talk with our family and friends to find someone who can take you there safely."

It took a couple of weeks before Hussein was able to find a trustworthy couple that were planning a trip to Mosul. After the invasion, most people in villages farther from the larger Iraqi cities thought it best to stay where they were. It only required a quick glance at the skies to know that the Americans were taking over much of the country. American C-130 Hercules airplanes, Huey helicopters, and an assortment of fighter jets were frequently overhead. Although most Iraqis didn't know what these planes contained, there were enough aircraft to indicate that Americans were arriving in force. Clearly the Americans were going after the cities, not the villages in more remote areas. Finally, on April 12, Farah learned that one of her cousins, Ibrahim, and his wife, Wid, needed to visit Mosul to check on her sister and family, whom they hadn't heard from since the invasion began. Lara and Eman were ready to go and standing outside the gate the following morning with Hussein, Farah, and Eleah.

When the car came to a stop, Farah rushed over to the driver's side of the car as Ibrahim opened the door. "Welcome, Ibrahim. It's good to see you and Wid. Thank you for taking Eleah's friends to Mosul. This is Eman and Lara. Come in, rest for a while before all of you begin your journey."

Lara and Eman glanced at each other and rolled their eyes a little. They were planning to get into the car as soon as the couple arrived.

"Thank you, Farah." Ibrahim bowed slightly as he turned toward Eman and Lara. "It's nice to meet you." Then he turned back toward Farah. "You and Hussein are always very gracious," Ibrahim replied. "It's already later in the day than we had hoped. Perhaps we can stop and visit with you for a while on our return trip."

Eleah noted the expressions on her friend's faces. "You have a difficult ride ahead, and none of us know if there will be delays on the road. I think Lara and Eman are very anxious to return to their families in Mosul," she offered in support of a fast get away.

"We promise to stop for a visit when we return in a few days. Ibrahim is right. We really should go now before it gets to be too late." Wid was also anxious to get back on the road.

Farah shrugged with a little disappointment. "We understand," she said as she looked at Hussein, who nodded yes. "God be with you. Have a safe trip."

Both Lara and Eman gave Farah a big hug and turned to bow slightly to Hussein. "Thank you. Thank all of you," Eman said with deep sincerity.

"We will never forget you," Lara said as she stepped over to Eleah, wiped a tear from her eye, and gave her a hug. "Good-bye, sister."

Eman also gave Eleah a big embrace. "God be with all of us. Please take care of yourself."

Eleah was also crying, "God only knows when we will see each other again."

Lara took a deep breath to stiffen herself and control the emotions welling up inside her. "We will all see each other again," she said, with a forced certainty in her voice.

Ibrahim took stock of the situation and decided that it was time to go before everyone started crying. "Time to go," he forced a smile. "Let's take you to your families in Mosul."

That little prompting was enough to break the somber mood. "Yes. Let's go, Eman. When the phones start working again, I'll give you a call," Lara promised to Eleah. "Thank you again, Hussein and Hanah, for everything."

Hussein smiled, "It was nothing."

"Good-bye Lara and Eleah. God be with you!" Farah said as the two girls climbed into the back seat of Ibrahim and Wid's car.

The doors shut and Ibrahim turned the car toward the road as the windows opened up and everyone started waving and saying one more "Good-bye."

Then they were gone. "God be with us all," Farah said again.

"Yes, Momma. God has protected us so far. We can only pray that he continues to do so." Eleah said.

"Let's go inside." Hussein suggested. "I need to change for work, and the two of you should think about what we will have for dinner later today."

"Yes," Farah sighed. "Life must go on." The three of them walked through the gate.

The ride from Haditha on Route 19 to the highway from Baghdad to Mosul took about four hours due to the numerous potholes and generally poor condition of the road. During the trip, both Ibrahim and Wid wanted to know more about what the girls had been through during the last two months. Farah and Hussein had given them some information when they met to discuss the possibility of taking the girls to Mosul, but they didn't provide much detail.

The girls provided them with an abbreviated version of their sad story. After all of their questions were answered, Lara reiterated her deep appreciation to Ibrahim and Wid. "Thank you again for taking us to Mosul."

"Hussein, Farah, and Eleah are family." Ibrahim replied. "Farah and I are cousins. They would do anything for us. Taking the two of you with us to Mosul is the least we could do. It is a pleasure."

"Yes. Besides, it is always better to have someone to talk with on this long drive," Wid added. "Ibrahim is not much of a talker." She smiled as she looked over to her husband.

"That's true," Ibrahim replied.

The passengers were quiet for about a half hour as the car continued on the two-lane road until they came to the intersection with the north-south portion of Route One. Lara and Eman observed that, like the traffic near Fallujah on that section of the highway, most of the vehicles were headed north, away from Baghdad.

When they approached the intersection north toward Mosul at the town of Baiji, they encountered their first American military check point. The young American soldiers were all business as they held their rifles at their hips. None of them had ever been in a war zone. They were all very serious and a little nervous about who they might encounter during their shift on the checkpoint. One of them held out his fist as a sign to stop the car. They all rolled down the car windows as the soldier asked "*'Iilaa 'ayn tdhhb? Whein?*" It was all the soldier could manage in his attempt to speak the little Arabic that he knew. "Where are you going?"

Lara was on the same side of the car as Ibrahim in the back seat. She looked at the soldier as she rolled down her window. "*Whein*?" she smiled as she repeated his question. Then, to the astonishment of the soldier, Ibrahim, and Wid, she continued the conversation in perfect American English, "We are going to Mosul to return to my relatives there. My friends are also going to their relatives."

The young man with the gun stood still for a moment, listening to a young Iraqi woman answering him in English. "I'm sorry, ma'am. Where are you from?"

"I'm from Ann Arbor, Michigan. My father is a medical doctor working at the University of Michigan." The soldier stood still, processing this very strange information. Lara continued, "My family allowed me to come and live with my relatives in Mosul over a year ago, and I've been attending the University of Baghdad until..." She stopped there, realizing that she was about to share too much painful information. It didn't matter. The soldier was relieved to be talking with an American and happy that, instead of encountering a car of hostile Iraqis, he was dealing with a compatriot.

"No problem, ma'am," the soldier smiled as he motioned Ibrahim to continue on their way. "Hey guys, she's an American! They're OK!" He said as the other soldiers started smiling and waving as they drove by.

There was a deafening silence in the car as Ibrahim continued on the highway toward Mosul. After a while, Lara spoke quietly, "I'm sorry. Eman and Eleah both knew that I'm American, and they promised not to tell anyone."

"We were afraid of what could happen if anyone knew," Eman volunteered.

"It's all right," Wid finally responded. "Ibrahim and I were just very surprised."

Ibrahim took a deep breath and exhaled slowly. "Well, at least we won't have any trouble getting to Mosul." He was conflicted about having an American in the car when Lara's country had just invaded his. However, he was also ambivalent about the Ba'ath regime and would be just as happy if the Americans took out Saddam Hussein and restored Iraq as they promised, making it a more peaceful, safer country. He could only hope for the best.

The rest of the trip to Mosul was tiring but uneventful. There were a few more US Army check points. Each time, Lara responded to the soldiers' inquiries, and they were waved through to continue their journey.

"Where is everyone going?" Lara asked as the heavy traffic continued to stream northward.

"It's hard to say," Ibrahim volunteered. "Probably families who have relatives in Erbil, Mosul, or other towns in the north are going to stay with them until the Americans stop their bombing and finish their invasion. Everyone wants to escape the fighting. The problem is that no one knows which way to go, or where it is safe."

"Do you think the war will end soon?" Eman asked.

"Who knows?" Ibrahim sighed as he turned off Route One onto a road entering a small town.

"What town is this?" Lara asked.

"This is Telol al baj. Wid has a cousin who lives here," Ibrahim responded.

"We're about two-thirds of the way to Mosul. My cousin Mohammed manages the gas station here. He always has some gas that he shares with his tribe and relatives," explained Wid. "We have forty liters of gas in the trunk but we don't know when we'll find gas again. If Mohammed has gas, he'll sell us what we need to fill the gas tank."

"It's good to have a lot of relatives," Lara remarked.

Soon they were back on the road. "There's a historical area in that direction," Wid said as she waved her left hand to the west. "The ancient fortress city of Hatra is sixty-five kilometers west of here, near the small village with the same name."

"I learned about Hatra in my history course when we studied about ancient Babylon and Mesopotamia. It was a major city on the road from Damascus to one of Nebuchadnezzar's cities of Nineveh, near where Mosul is now," Lara noted.

"Yes, there are still many ruins standing near Al-Hatra," Wid replied. "Long ago, there was a small office of antiquities to protect the site, but it's been closed for several years."

"We have so many ancient sites in Iraq," Eman observed. "Maybe someday we can see them before they are totally destroyed by war and looting."

"*In sha' allh,*" Ibrahim sighed.

The car came to a long line of other cars, busses, and trucks about a quarter mile from the next US checkpoint near the turn-off toward the Mosul airport. When Ibrahim slowed to a stop, they were startled by the sound of US jets flying low overhead, the Boom, Boom, Boom, Boom of bombs exploding, and the plumes of black smoke about a mile away toward the east.

They all looked in that direction, toward the explosions and felt helpless in the traffic. "There they go! The American jets just bombed the airfield over there. Our army has vanished. It seems there is no protection for us," Ibrahim exclaimed with mixed emotions. He was happy to be rid of Saddam Hussein, the Ba'ath party, and the terror associated with the regime. However, he wasn't happy about being invaded by the Americans and more than a little disappointed with the poor performance of the Iraqi Army.

"I don't think the Americans are interested in us. Besides, the soldiers are up there," Lara said as she pointed toward the check point at the front of the line. "They wouldn't be bombing us with the US Army so close.

When they arrived at the front of the line, Lara and Ibrahim rolled down their windows to talk with a young corporal. As soon as Lara opened her mouth, the disposition of the soldier went from tense and serious to a more relaxed sigh of relief. During the standard questions from the soldier and the surprise of talking with a young American woman in a car full of Iraqis, another two US jets flew overhead and started shooting at something beyond their field of vision.

"What were they shooting at?" Lara asked.

The young soldier smiled. "Those jets are tank killers, ma'am. They're A-10 Warthog tank killers, clearing what remains of the Iraqi Army tanks that were protecting the airport about two miles from here."

"My family lives in southern Mosul, about ten miles west of here. Is there any fighting in that direction?" Lara asked the soldier with a very worried look on her face.

"No ma'am. Most of the citizens in Mosul have been very cooperative. I think they're happy to see us here." The soldier smiled again as he waved his hand for them to move on through the check point.

"I hope my family is all right," Lara said as she rolled up her window and Ibrahim continued on the highway as it veered left toward the west. "I pray the Americans kill Uday Hussein after what he did to Yasmine and Aziz... I hope the Americans send Uday, Saddam Hussein, and all the Ba'athists straight to hell," she said softly as the car brought them closer to her relatives.

"I pray the Americans leave the rest of us alone," Wid said quietly.

"Yes," Lara replied, "I pray that also."

Ibrahim drove another twenty minutes as all the passengers remained quiet in their own thoughts. Finally, with Lara's directions, Ibrahim turned onto a road with several large villas, including the homes of her mother's brother, Nawaf Al-Zaidan, and his wife Mohassin. On the same street, a few villas up and across the street, Lara pointed out the home of another uncle and aunt, Salah and Wallah , and their son, Othman.

"I hope they're all right. I hope they're still here," Lara said anxiously.

Ibrahim drove up to the gate. "We'll know in a minute."

When the car stopped, Lara jumped out, ran to the courtyard gate, and started ringing the large bell. "Uncle Nawaf, Aunt Mohassin! It's me, Lara!" There was no answer. In a moment, Lara started ringing the bell again. "Auntie, Uncle! Please open the door!"

Ibrahim, Wid, and Eman got out of the car, expecting that they would have to console Lara on the possibility that her relatives were forced to move, or worse. As they approached Lara, the gate opened. Nawaf stared at Lara for a moment, and after getting over the shock of seeing her, he yelled out in a loud and excited voice, "Lara!" Much like Eleah's greeting with her parents, Uncle Nawaf gave Lara a long hug. "Lara! We thought you were dead! Praise Allah! What happened to you?"

Lara's aunt Mohassin and her cousin, Yasmine's older brother Shalan rushed out of the gate to see what the commotion was all about. He stopped in disbelief as she saw Lara standing there with Nawaf.

Mohassin was almost in shock as she put her right hand over her heart, "Oh, my Lara! After February 8, we didn't know what happened to you, Yasmine, and Aziz." Tears welled up in her eyes and she wiped them away as she continued, "Your uncles Nawaf and Salah, Aziz' father Abdullah and his brother went to Baghdad. Your university friends said you all went to dinner and then disappeared! We thought you were dead. Praise God! Here you are!" She also hugged Lara and began weeping with joy.

"Where are Yasmine and Aziz?" Nawaf asked with trepidation. "When I visited Baghdad in February and stopped by Yasmine's work station at the hospital, they said they hadn't seen her since February 8....Are, are they all right?" There was a knot in his stomach as he said this, not knowing, but fearing deep inside, what Lara's answer might be.

"They are both dead," Lara said quietly.

Mohassin collapsed onto Nawaf in loud wails of grief, "No! This can't be! You're here, how can they be dead?" Her tears and voice were sorrowful. "They can't be dead...My Yasmine...Aziz..."

Lara had steeled herself for this moment while they were driving from Haditha. "Uday Hussein killed both of them." Once she said it, she also began to cry and started to collapse in grief. The stress of the last two months caught up with her. Ibrahim and Shalan grabbed her under the arms as her knees buckled.

"Come, let's all go inside," Nawaf urged everyone, as he helped Mohassin walk inside the gate and toward their front door. Soon they were all in the large drawing room, and Nawaf helped his wife sit down as Ibrahim and Wid did the same for Lara.

"It's true," Eman declared when the others were seated. "Lara, Yasmine, and I saw Uday Hussein shoot Aziz. The next day, Uday and his bodyguards killed Yasmine in front of us."

Eman's statement of fact set Mohassin and Lara into another wailing frenzy that lasted for several minutes as the others tried to console them. After a little while, their cries of sorrow began to subside.

"Why?" Nawaf also had tears of grief in his eyes.

"Because she said she would rather be dead than to have Uday defile her. They used a cage to drown her in the lake at Dreamland, which was one of Uday's palace resorts near Fallujah," Eman said softly.

Nawaf stood up and took a deep breath to help control his emotions. "We must tell Salah and Abdullah. Mohassin, please help Lara to her room. She must be exhausted. Let her rest. We'll talk about this tomorrow when she feels better and can tell us the details of what happened to Aziz and Yasmine."

Ibrahim, Wid, and Eman also stood up. "We must go." Ibrahim said. "We're very sorry about your daughter and son-in-law. If there is anything we can do...."

Nawaf bowed slightly and put his hand on his heart. "Sir, madam, Eman, you have all helped us beyond words for bringing Lara safely home to us." He said as he brushed more tears from his eyes.

"We must take Eman home to her family before it gets too late." Ibrahim began to move toward the door. "She lives on the other side of Mosul near where Wid's sister lives."

"How can we repay you for your kindness?" Nawaf asked.

"Keep Lara safe. She's a strong, brave girl," Wid responded.

"Nawaf, you have my parent's phone number and know where we live. Please give me a call after Lara is feeling better. I can also give you the contacts for Ibrahim and Wid." Despite the solemnity of the moment, Eman was also very anxious to return home to her family as soon as possible.

"Nawaf, we don't know each other," Ibrahim began, "but who knows what will happen next? We need to help each other when we can. Please get our information from Eman."

Nawaf bowed again. "I am in your debt. If I can ever help you and your family, let me know."

Ibrahim, Wid, and Eman all spoke as they walked out the door, "*Mae alssalama*. Good-bye."

Chapter Twenty-Seven: A Plan for Uday's Demise

The following morning, Nawaf and Shalan, called all of the male relatives, including Abdullah, Aziz's father, to their home so they could listen to Lara explain what happened to Yasmine and Aziz, herself, and her friends during the last two months.

The conversation lasted two hours as Lara described every event. Frequently, she held her head in her hands as she rested her elbows on her knees, overwhelmed by her memories. Her audience remained silent as she worked her way through the horrific situations that she lived through. Occasionally Nawaf, Shalan, or Abdullah asked for more details or clarification. Finally, Lara finished with, "Thank God Eleah's mother learned that her cousin Ibrahim and his wife Wid were driving to Mosul. They offered to take Eman and me with them." There was a moment of silence as everyone pondered Lara's terrible story and the awful news regarding how Aziz and Yasmine were killed.

The silence was finally broken when Abdullah stood up and spoke in a loud, determined voice, "Uday may be a distant relative, but he must die! He killed my son and disgraced and killed Yasmine. He is a dog, worse than his father and brother!"

"My car is full of gas. Let's go to Baghdad and find him!" Salah volunteered as he stood up. Immediately the other men stood up with them in solidarity, except Nawaf. He remained seated as he thought in silence for a moment as the others looked at him, wondering why he was not one of the first to seek vengeance.

"Where will you find him?" Nawaf spoke quietly, as he slowly rose to his feet and looked at the others. "Since the Americans attacked, Uday and his family will be in deep hiding anywhere. We will never find them."

Everyone pondered this as Lara spoke up, "Maybe the Americans will find him first."

"We must find him and kill him as revenge for my son and Yasmine," Abdullah said again, more determined than before.

There was another moment of silence, then Nawaf gave Abdullah a sly look. "I heard a rumor that the Americans may be offering a $15 million dollar reward each for Saddam, Uday, and Qusay. Maybe we can get our revenge, have the Americans kill him for us, and leave Iraq with our families until this fighting is over."

"How can we do this?" Abdullah was pondering this intriguing idea.

"Abdullah, you are correct when you said Saddam Hussein, Uday, and their family are distant relatives of ours. No one has seen any of them since the invasion began. They're certainly in hiding, probably between here and Tikrit, where they're from. We'll spread the word among the tribe that we have a very safe place for them to hide," Nawaf suggested.

"Why would they stay with us?" Salah queried.

"We all have nice houses, but we don't have palaces. Our families aren't close to Saddam Hussein so we wouldn't be suspected of hiding any of his family. Also, my house has a room under the main floor, which Mohassin wanted me to include when we built the house as a cool room for her sewing work." Mohassin smiled a little when he said this. "If we let others know that we will put our lives and the lives of our families at risk for the sake of Saddam and his family, maybe Uday or others may come to us."

Mohassin frowned: "What if Saddam or someone other than Uday comes?"

"We will all move to Salah's house," Nawaf explained, "and hope that our guests won't stay long. If Uday comes to our house, we will let the Americans know."

Chapter Twenty-Eight:
A Long Way Home to
Fort Bragg, North Carolina

The bus ride from Baa'j in northwestern Iraq was tense, but without incident. It was late afternoon on March 28, 2003 and Hakim navigated the old bus through panicked Iraqis in cars, pickup trucks, and other buses near Mosul. The American invasion was on full throttle, with all manner of their heavily armed jets and helicopters flying overhead. Much of the Iraqi Army melted away as its soldiers changed from military uniforms to civilian clothes to blend in with the population. The goal for most of the Iraqi military was to avoid the murderous hammering from the US Marines, Army, Air Force and Navy as the combined forces continued relentlessly to bomb and destroy any Iraqi military hardware visible from the air. It was especially puzzling to the Iraqis that the Americans were also bombing concealed military installations throughout much of the country with pinpoint accuracy.

They were driving along a relatively quiet stretch of road east of Sinjar, about seventy miles west of Mosul, when Joe leaned over Hakim's shoulder. "I understand why we're going to the Mar-Mattai monastery instead of hiding in Mosul to wait for the 101st Army Airborne to arrive. Other than that it's up in the mountains on the other side of the city, we don't know much about it."

"It's about 18 miles northeast of Mosul." Hakim began. "Compared with the ancient ruins in Mosul, it's a relatively new complex, established in 363 AD. It's located above the Nineveh plain, on the side of Mount

Afar. The evening we arrived in Mosul from Hatra to begin scouting for possible future hiding places that Saddam and his family might consider, I drove my car with your additional MREs and other supplies to station them there, with the priest and monks. The local villagers call them their brothers. It's a safe place, and the supplies may be useful when we get there to keep us fed until the rest of the U.S. 101st catches up with us." Hakim shifted the bus's gears down as they entered the town of Tal Afar to wave at the local police standing near the road, directing traffic. Five minutes later, after slowing as they drove through the small town, he resumed his speed and continued his briefing for Joe and a few more of the men who were at the front of the bus to hear what he had to say.

"Mar Mattai was a Christian hermit who fled Roman persecution. The legend is that he miraculously healed the daughter of an Assyrian pagan king of her leprosy. The miracle was witnessed by her brother and forty companions. It inspired all of them to convert to Christianity. Unfortunately, the king didn't approve of their new religion and sent his soldiers to kill them. After their murder, the king regretted what he did, and as an act of remorse and attempt at atonement, he asked Mar Mattai to baptize him so he could convert to Christianity. The king built a small monastery on the spot where Mar Mattai healed his daughter. Later, the present monastery was built further up the mountain."

"How did the monastery get involved with the US.?" Nick asked.

"It's affiliated with the Syriac Orthodox Church and began providing support to the US in 1988 when Saddam Hussein ordered the bombing of Halabaj, 60 miles from here, with chemical gas bombs that killed over 5,000 civilians. This resulted in a mass displacement of Iraqi Kurds. Many of these people decided to leave Iraq over the mountains and ended up in Turkey as refugees. Many of them eventually made it the US as immigrants with refugee visas and have since become American citizens. This migration was repeated in 1991 when Saddam and the Ba'athists were merciless. They went after people all over the country who followed President George H.W. Bush's suggestion to revolt against the regime. A transit point in their journey was Mar Mattai," Hakim explained.

"It received logistical and humanitarian assistance provided by the CIA and the US Agency for International Development. They used this assistance to help many families survive their journey over the mountains into Turkey. This relationship forged a strong bond with the United States. That's why they've offered their assistance to us by providing their cover until Mosul and this area of Nineveh province is secured by the US Army."

Soon the men on the bus noticed more buildings and a few lights as they entered the outer suburbs of Mosul. Before long, they crossed the bridge over the Tigris River, Hakim took a right turn off of the main road, and after a few blocks, turned left onto a quiet side street. Although there were people and traffic in the city, it was lighter than they expected.

"I'm surprised there aren't more people in the streets," Paul remarked.

"Probably because most people are afraid of what the Americans and their allies, the Kurdish Peshmerga military units, will do next," Hakim suggested. "Look over to your right."

The men looked to see what Hakim was pointing at. Although there wasn't much light, they saw a few stacks of rubble and soon passed a large structure that looked like it had been a grand entrance at one time.

"What's out there?" Nick asked.

"I thought some of you may be interested in seeing what is left of ancient Nineveh." Hakim replied. "The large building, there," he waived his hand toward the right, "is the Hergal Gate. It was the primary entrance into the walled city about twenty-five hundred years ago. It's one of the few buildings that still remain from that era."

The area on their right looked like an empty field in the dim light of the early evening. There was apparently very little remaining in the direction the men were looking, as they drove by what was once the mighty Assyrian city-state of Nineveh.

Shortly, they passed another section of the modern city of Mosul and were soon on a dark road driving into the country. Within a half hour, the bus came to the end of the paved road. It turned into a narrow, rutted dirt lane that led upward toward a few lights that appeared to be halfway up the mountain, which was silhouetted by the moon and stars. "We're here. Welcome to your new resort," Hakim said as he pulled off the road next to the wall of what remained of an old building. The men stepped out and looked up at the lights of Mar Mattai monastery. They also saw a procession of seven lights making their way down the dirt road.

"The good and bad news is that it's located up there, on the side of Mount Afar." Hakim continued, "You'll have to unload the bus and carry everything up the hill for about two miles with steep switch backs that lead to the monastery. The dirt lane is so narrow and treacherous, that it took me about an hour to navigate the car to meet the priest and monks who live there. There is no way that this bus could make it up there."

"Is there room at the monastery for us to stay inside?" Paul asked.

"It's big enough," Hakim responded. "The accommodations are spartan, as you may imagine. It was built for monks, but there are guest rooms. After your previous accommodations in empty houses, barns, and foxholes in the desert, I suspect that you'll be comfortable enough."

Joe turned to his men. "Well, gentlemen, we'll have one more hike before we wait for our ride home."

"We've gone through most of our MREs," Pete noted. "I wonder what we'll be eating while we're up there."

"Don't worry, Pete, there must have been at least 300 of the team's MREs that I delivered to the monastery six weeks ago. That should last us for at least twenty days, if that's all we have," Hakim said. "There is some good news...the monks are very good cooks. Perhaps we will be eating home cooking instead of your meals ready to eat."

"If the hike ends with home cooking and a ticket home, then I think I'll be able to run up that hill!" Jason said as he looked up the trail to see the lights make their way down the switch-back lane that was barely more than a trail. "Who are they?" Jason and the others instinctively took the safety off their rifles.

Hakim smiled, "Calm down. It's OK. It's the senior priest at the monastery, Father Noah Mosa Shimilk, and the monks. They were expecting us. I suspect they began their journey down the trail when they saw the bus. Father Noah will take all of you safely up the trail, and the brothers will carry the chicken cages. I think you'll like your new accommodations and the cooked food, prepared by those gentlemen. Don't worry. You'll be in good hands with Father Noah and the brothers. He's been here since the mid-1980's and was a young man when the monastery started working with the Americans."

The team unloaded the chickens and their gear off the roof rack on the bus. About the time they were finished unloading everything and hoisted their backpacks and other gear onto their backs, Father Noah rounded the last bend in the road and called out to his guests, "I've never seen such poorly dressed Iraqi villagers carry such large backpacks and US rifles," Father Noah smiled as he walked up to them. Although the men had all of their gear from the bus, they were still dressed in the clothes provided by Hakim.

Hakim introduced Father Noah and the brothers to the men. Joe began to reach out to shake hands with Father Noah, then he remembered the customary greeting and bowed f slightly with his right hand on his heart. "Father, we are grateful for your assistance. Hakim told us about your generous offer to provide shelter until our colleagues arrive."

Father Noah's English wasn't great, but it was good enough. "You're welcome. Hakim and I are old friends. We are honored to have you stay with us. First, let me introduce you to my brothers in the Lord." Father Noah spoke Arabic and English as he introduced the team of soldiers to the six monks who worked with him. The monks all smiled and bowed as the men were each identified. Joe and his men returned the courtesy. Father Noah studied the face of Joe and each of his men, as he tried to memorize each name with the man. Then he continued, "Follow me." Soon, they were walking up the hill, each soldier with about forty pounds of weapons, munitions, gear, and remaining supplies, and thirty pounds for their Kevlar helmets and body armor. Each monk led them with a flashlight in one hand and a cage full of chickens in the other.

When they arrived at Mar Mattai, they were escorted to their very small rooms, each consisting of two cots with pillows, sheets, and blankets. The sleeping quarters were near a separate building with showers, sinks, and eastern toilets that were made of ceramic. They had ten-inch holes in the middle leading to an underground septic tank, and molded treads on either side to ensure firm footing for doing business.

After washing up from their long journey, the men were invited to their first prepared hot meal in six weeks. Other than the chickens, vegetables, fruit, and bread that Hakim was able to provide occasionally from the local villages when the team was hiding during their first visit to Mosul and near Baa'j, their diet consisted of the MREs. The soldiers were happy to learn that the monks worked with the villages in the area and benefitted from a supply of fresh vegetables, fruits, and meats. The monks were also good cooks and pleased to show off their culinary skills. Although the soldiers couldn't speak Arabic with the monks, they quickly learned to communicate with gestures and smiles. After dinner, the first team of four began their watch duty on each side of the monastery walls. Joe went with Phil as he set up his radio with the satellite connection in the sleeping quarters. Now they could continue the daily regime of listening for news and directions from their field command in Kuwait

"What's the latest?" Joe asked when Phil had everything up and running.

"No news, sir." Phil replied. "I guess they'll tell us when they need to."

"Probably that won't be until after they've taken Mosul." Paul surmised.

"I'm sure you're right about that," Joe agreed as he looked toward Phil. "Work out a four-hour shift schedule with Bob so we'll know as soon as possible what the next plan is for us."

"No problem," Phil said. "We've already agreed that I'll work this four-hour shift, then Bob will take over and we'll continue the four-hour rotation from there.

"Sounds good," Joe said quietly. "I'm going to check with the men on watch and then go to bed." Except for the four-man team presently posted on the four sides of the monastery, the others had already turned in for the night. "I hope we have a restful time here."

"Yes sir," Phil said. "I'm ready to take it easy for a few days until we head home."

Joe's walk around the monastery compound only took about fifteen minutes, including his visit with each of the men on watch. His last stop was with Tim.

"Look at those stars!" Tim greeted Joe as he walked across the very large balcony to the waist high wall overlooking the steep slope toward the few lights in the villages and farms below them, and in the distance.

Joe looked over the valley then upwards into the night sky. There was almost a full moon providing light. Where they were on Mount Alfaf, the bright moon and abundance of stars was awesome. "Yeah, Gunny. It is beautiful and quiet up here," Joe observed. "It's easy to see why Hakim recommended this place for us to lie low." Joe glanced across the wide balcony toward the monastery and smiled. "And this area is large enough for a helicopter to land."

"That's what I'm thinking," Tim replied, also with a smile as they both contemplated their trip home. "Good night, sir. Sleep well."

"Thanks, Gunny. Keep an eye on things for us. Good night."

The following morning, Father Noah and Hakim walked down the mountain and took the bus to the house where the men camped out previously in Mosul. They wanted to pick up the old car that Hakim used to shuttle the men around during their reconnaissance of the potential safe houses for Saddam Hussein that they identified in the city. Later in the day, they returned to the bottom of the mountain with the car and the bus. Hakim planned to give to them both to the monastery when he and the team departed for America. They parked the vehicles near an abandoned building that may have been a house at one time, then began their walk up the hill. When they arrived at the gate, Joe and the others were there to greet them. "Welcome to the Mar Mattai resort!" Joe grinned. "Thanks to the brothers, we're all rested and fed.

"We're happy to be back," Father Noah acknowledged.

"Things are a bit crazy in Mosul right now," Hakim added. "I thought there would either be Iraqi or US Army soldiers roaming the streets, but it was the Kurd Peshmerga militia instead. That's unfortunate. There's not much love between the Kurds and citizens of Mosul. As we drove out of town, we saw looting and other street violence as the Peshmerga were asserting their authority."

"We thought the US would be the first to enter the city," Paul remarked. "I'm surprised the Peshmerga are there. I hope they're not creating enemies out of possibly peaceful citizens."

"You'll have to ask your colleagues why the 101st isn't there instead of the Kurds," Hakim replied. "Their dislike of the people in Mosul isn't surprising. The city is home to a large Ba'ath headquarters and has the second largest population of Ba'ath Party members, including senior military officers, security, and intelligence service functionaries. I understand about 300,000 Ba'athists live there. The Peshmerga associate those people with gassing the Kurds in 1985."

"I can see why they have a grudge," Tim said.

"So what's the plan?" Hakim asked. He was as anxious to return to his home and family in America as the others.

"Bob just got off his shift looking for some communication from HQ on his computer," Joe said. "I'll let him brief all of you on the good news."

"Hakim is correct with regard to the Peshmerga taking the lead in occupying the city," Bob began. "Presently the 101st is working on securing the airport and other strategic locations in and around the city, including the Mosul Dam. The Peshmerga were given authority to take control of the city. The good news is that the airport in the Kurdish provincial capital of Erbil is less than fifty miles from here and is already being used by the US We should be leaving here within the next few days. When the flights are arranged, we'll be the first to know. There will be about a two-hour notification in advance, telling us when helicopters will land here to take us to a waiting plane and then home for a couple of weeks of administrative duty, training at Fort Bragg, and three weeks of R&R."

This news was greeted with a loud, enthusiastic cheer by the men.

"It's a pleasure to have you with us until your helicopters arrive to take you home," Father Noah began. "We live a quiet and humble existence but it's always nice to have friendly visitors, especially Americans," he said as he turned to the team of men. "Please feel free to use our small library here. Unfortunately most of our books are in Arabic, but we do have a few in English, including a Bible and some history books. It's not much, but these may help you pass the time."

"Thanks, Father. I hope we'll be able to repay the favor someday," Joe said.

Father Noah smiled. "America has already been gracious to us. Over the years, we've received assistance for helping shelter and feed thousands of poor families trying to escape Iraq in the 1980s and 1990s. The sleeping quarters where you are staying, the latrines, and this magnificent balcony and new wall overlooking the valley below were built with funds provided by the US."

"That explains why it's built large enough to accommodate a US. helicopter." Joe surmised. "OK men, we all know the schedule. Keep an eye on the road below. Hopefully, we won't have any unexpected guests."

Fortunately, the next two days passed quietly. Each of the men spent at least an hour a day doing some sort of physical training. Since they were all restricted to the monastery compound, their exercise routine was limited. One of the routines, which they discovered as a win-win for everyone, was to push the heavy handle for the water pump up and down a few hundred times. The water was pumped up from the ground-water table, which was a couple of hundred feet below the monastery. The water would fall onto a half-pipe spout, which led to a 1,000-gallon cistern that fed the sink in the kitchen and the hoses to the several latrines on the complex. Father Noah told the men that the cistern was built thanks to funding from the Americans in the 1980s. Usually it was about two-thirds empty because it was too much work to fill it to the top. Although the monks had a sufficient supply of potable water, the pressure coming out of the cistern was never very strong.

The soldiers discovered that when they put both hands on the pump handle and vigorously pushed it down and lifted it up a hundred times, they would quickly accomplish some of their abdominal and upper arm aerobic exercises as part of their routine and pour twenty or more gallons of water into the cistern as a reward for their hard work. When the priest and monks discovered how useful the soldiers could be, other projects that had been set aside for years were pointed out to the men as opportunities for their exercise regimen.

Several of the men didn't waste any time visiting the library. There was only one shelf of English language books, but it was enough. Manny grabbed the New International Version of the Bible and the others found at least one book that suited their individual interests.

During the next few day, when the sun was warm and there was nothing else to do, several of the men would set up chairs outside, put their feet on a bench to relax and read whatever they had on hand. "What are you reading about?" Tim asked Manny as they both enjoyed their time off.

Manny looked up from the Bible and stretched his arms over his head. "I've read the book of Jonah and now I'm reading Nahum. It's interesting how much God didn't like the Assyrians and Nineveh in particular." Hakim was sitting with the two of them, simply enjoying the warm, clean air on the side of the mountain. He had his hat pulled over his eyes and feet propped on a bench. Manny turned to him and asked, "Hakim, the Bible says that Nineveh would be left in ruins. Was the area that you pointed out to us when we drove through Mosul all that is left of Nineveh?"

Hakim thought for a moment. "The Bible may have been inspired by God, but it was written down by men. I think, despite God's inspiration, men have probably always interpreted God's messages with their own biases, based upon the political, social, or other influencing factors at the time they were written. You know the Old Testament writers like Nahum were under the yoke of the Assyrians during the glory days of Nineveh. The biblical authors of the day were either from Judah or Israel. Their tribes had been crushed by the Assyrian army, and they were under occupation. So the prophesies of Jonah, Nahum, and others had a strong bias for revenge. Probably when the books were written, it was the various authors' wishful thinking, or it may have been God speaking to them. Who knows?" Hakim said, offering his own view of the biblical passages. "To answer your question, yes, we did pass by the Nergal Gate of old Nineveh, and along one side of what was once the seat of the Assyrian empire. Maybe you guys were in the back of the bus and didn't hear me when we were driving by the ruins on this side of Mosul."

"I do remember passing a big old structure of some kind. Then all I saw for about a mile was a large field that had some old ruins," Tim recalled.

"That was it. We had to make a detour in the city, and it took us by what is left of Nineveh, which isn't much."

"The Bible did say that it would be utterly destroyed," Manny said.

"Yeah, it happened about fifty years after the book of Nahum was written," Hakim continued. "Assyria faded away after that, replaced by Babylon. You can read about that in the book of Daniel sometime."

"I'm surprised that you know the Bible so well." Tim observed.

"I was a young man in 1991 when I was a refugee trying to escape the Ba'athist purge after the first Bush encouraged everyone to continue the fight to topple Saddam Hussein. Although the US imposed no-fly zones, the Iraqi Army wasn't restricted from flying their helicopter gunships and using their remaining ground forces and secret police to crush the rebellion. The result was that the Iraqi Army could murder people all over the country, either for taking part in the attempted overthrow of the regime, or whom they considered were a threat by the regime. Unfortunately for about one hundred thousand Iraqis, the Americans didn't provide any support or protection to help with the revolution." Hakim paused for a moment as his colleagues considered this sad chapter of American history. "I decided to leave Iraq during that time. Part of my passage to Turkey, and finally to America, included about a month at Mar Mattai, sheltered by Father Noah and the brothers. That was when Father Noah introduced me to the Bible. It was interesting to compare this with the writings of Prophet Mohammed in the Koran. My interest in understanding and comparing the two religious books has remained a passion since."

"Hakim, I didn't know that bit of history after the Desert Storm operation. I'm sorry," Manny said with sincerity. "I also had no idea that you were a theologian."

"I'm just interested in the history of this region and trying to make sense out of life. Reading the Koran and Bible has given me plenty of food for thought." Hakim replied as he looked into the sky. "I think our trip home is about to begin. Look over there. I think those are two helicopters coming this way."

The three men stood up to get a better look as Bob, Joe, and the other men came rushing out of the buildings. "Bob got the word a few minutes ago" Joe said breathlessly. "We had to confirm the helicopters for ourselves."

Hakim pointed to the two small black objects in the sky. "There they are!"

They all looked toward where Hakim was pointing. "OK men, time to go home. Get your gear, weapons and ammunition and be ready to go in fifteen minutes." Joe said.

Father Noah and the monks also rushed outside to see what was going on. "Father, here's the keys to the car and bus. Now that I know, for sure, that we won't need them anymore, they're yours for use at the monastery to work with the villagers," Hakim said as he handed them over to the priest.

"The remaining MREs are yours as well," Joe said. "Maybe you can provide them to folks who may pass your way someday."

"Thank you!" Father Noah said with sincere gratitude.

"Excuse us, Father, we have to get ready," Joe called out over his shoulder as he and the others hurried to gather their gear as well. It was time to go home, and they were ready.

Within thirty minutes the helicopters landed and picked up Hakim and the twelve special operators. In less than an hour later, they landed at the Erbil airport. They disembarked from the helicopters and were directed to a spot to leave their backpacks, weapons, and other gear for separate transport. Then they climbed onto a bus that delivered them to a tent being used for debriefing all the special operators that had been working in northern Iraq since February 15.

When they entered the tent, they were greeted by the general who had spoken with them at the Ali Al Salem Air Base in Kuwait, and Charlie the CIA agent whom they remembered from their first introduction at Fort Bragg the previous summer when they were first made aware of the covert "Task Force 20 Mission" they just completed. Joe ordered his men to stand at attention and salute the general as he saluted back.

"At ease," the general commanded. "It's good to see all of you," he said with a broad smile. "Thanks for your hard work. We've already begun to use your information regarding the possible Mosul safe houses to inform people in those areas and throughout Iraq that we're offering up to fifteen million dollars for information leading to the capture or death of Saddam Hussein, his sons, and other senior Ba'ath military and party members." He turned to the CIA agent: "Charlie, do you have anything that you'd like to add?"

"Not much, sir," Charlie began. "We appreciate the work you did to locate the prospective WMD in eastern Iraq." Charlie began.

"But..." Joe was going to explain what Nick and his team really saw.

"Yes. I know," Charlie continued. "It was an old oil exploration and drilling site. The satellite images confirmed this. However, at the time, we had your plausible explanation that it could be WMD, and considering the uncertainty about the invasion back in the US, it was useful to inform everyone that we destroyed what might have been WMD."

Joe and his men considered this bit of strategy and remained silent.

"No doubt, the reality of the situation will eventually become known in the history books," Charlie continued. "Right now, we need to ensure that everyone back home is fully supportive of this invasion. The destruction of what may be WMD is as useful to the war effort at the moment as the actual destruction of WMD."

"Permission to speak, sir?" Tim asked respectfully.

"Of course, sergeant," the general replied.

"Thank you for your clarification on this, sir. Have any of the teams found verifiable WMD?"

Charlie looked at Tim for a moment with a small frown on his face. "Off the record, no." Charlie looked at all of the men standing with Joe. "That answer is considered top secret, and not to be shared with anyone else. Do all of you understand?"

Joe snapped to attention, followed immediately by his men. "Yes sir!"

The general directed the men, "At ease." He continued, "We've only begun to prosecute this war. The administration, CIA, and the other intelligence services all strongly believe that WMD will be found. When they are, this news will validate the invasion. Until this happens, however, we all must support the president and do what is in the best interest of the country by deferring to the public announcements made by the administration." The general stopped for a moment to ensure everyone was listening carefully. "This is an order. Don't speculate on whether or not there are WMD to anyone, not even your family or closest friends. Do you all understand this?"

Once again, Joe and his men snapped to attention and, in unison, responded, "Yes sir!"

The general smiled. "Good." He turned to a lieutenant standing in the room. "Please give these men their orders to go home on a well-deserved leave."

The young lieutenant smiled as he walked over to a table and opened his brief case with the requisite orders and travel documents. "Your flight will leave here at approximately 0500 tomorrow morning." He began. "Tonight, you'll be staying in the sleeping tents that you passed when you walked over here from the bus. From Erbil, you'll fly to Incirlik Air Base near the city of Adana, Turkey, and then to Andrews Air Force Base near Washington, DC and home to Fort Bragg."

"One last thing," the general began his concluding remarks. "The sacrifice that all of you made; the risks and hardships that you had to overcome during these last nine months have not gone unnoticed by the army and by President Bush. Your work has substantially improved the success of the invasion and, no doubt, will help lead to a quick resolution with the overthrow of Saddam Hussein and the Ba'athists. This war is really becoming an effort to help the Iraqi people become free, and the development of a peaceful, democratic Iraq, with no more threat of WMD from this country." The general paused one more time. "Now go home, get a good rest, be safe, and we'll see you back here in late June."

The men saluted the general one more time. "Yes sir!" Two days later, Joe and his US Army Delta Force Special Operations team of exceptional men landed in Fort Bragg, North Carolina.

Chapter Twenty-Nine:
Home Life and Worries
April 2003

It was 0600 when the plane stopped in front of the Pope Air Force Base terminal adjacent to Fort Bragg. The morning light was not strong, but bright enough for Joe and the others to see a large crowd waving signs behind a rope. The men were always overwhelmed by this very typical but never subdued homecoming ceremony. Joe scanned the crowd for his family as the pilots turned off the engines and the stairs to the plane were pulled into place. It took him a moment to spot Alice and his two boys off to the right in the large group of cheering, crying, and poster-waving families who were all there to welcome their loved ones home.

Once he found his family, about 100 feet across the runway from where he was looking out the plane window, he noticed something different about the three of them, but he couldn't quite discern what the difference was. Soon he was going down the stairs and first walking, then running the last distance to Alice, Nathan, and Michael. They embraced each other in a group hug, as seamlessly as a drop is absorbed into a small pool of water. Joe didn't consider himself a very emotional man. However, each homecoming always brought tears of joy to his eyes and the eyes of Alice as they hugged each other and the boys in a tight embrace of love and affection. "We only learned three days ago that you were coming home," Alice whispered as Joe continued to hold her in his arms.

"That's when we learned that we were finally coming home," Joe said quietly as he let go of their embrace, took a deep breath and stepped back to look at his family. He was with all of them for short periods, during breaks in training since he was introduced to the Task Force 20 Mission the previous July, ten months ago. However, he did not appreciate how each of them was changing. Alice looked a bit smaller, Joe thought. Perhaps it was because Nathan and Michael, who were six and seven years old last July 4, were now almost a year and more than two inches taller. He also noticed there were a few wisps of gray hair that were not on Alice's head last summer. "Let's go home!" he declared. "We need to plan a vacation!"

"Dad, really!" Nathan, now eight, seized on this idea.

"I want to go to Disney World!" Michael already knew where he wanted to go.

"Spring vacation begins next week," Alice said enthusiastically. The last ten months had been very long, sad, and confining for her at Fort Bragg. She was also ready for a family vacation, with her husband at their side.

"OK! I think we can get discount tickets through the MWR." Joe hadn't been home more than fifteen minutes, yet he was already feeling like a different person. The underlying pressure of the previous assignment seemed to have been lifted from his shoulders as Alice drove them home in the family car.

The first seven days were blissful. Alice would get the boys ready for school and out the door and return to deliver coffee to Joe as he began to slowly wake up. It seemed that he needed much more sleep now that he was in the comfort of his home. They both surmised that he was sleep deprived for most of the last year and his body was finally catching up on the rest that he needed. Their mornings were leisurely. Alice had a full-time job as an HR manager for Fort Bragg's sprawling PX and commissary operations. However, the army ensured that when soldiers returned from lengthy deployments, the spouses working on the base were guaranteed that the vacations days they had earned would coincide with their returning husband or wife, so the families had time together.

Afternoons were spent visiting some of Joe's comrades and friends whom he hadn't seen in a while. Some had also been on the Task Force 20 Mission, working elsewhere in Northern Iraq and Baghdad. When Alice and Joe visited with his friends and their wives, the conversations were all about the kids and stories on what the wives did to stay busy and remain focused on keeping the families moving forward together.

Left unsaid were the conversations that the women had while their husbands were gone about their fears, frustrations, bouts of loneliness, and for some, depression. The men would occasionally meet up in quiet corners of the officers or enlisted clubs or at a local watering hole in Fayetteville to share their experiences and also act as an informal support group for each other.

The next seven days also flew by for Joe and the family as they enjoyed all that Disney World and the surrounding attractions of Orlando had to offer. Joe was surprised that he and Alice had a hard time on their first day in the Magic Kingdom, straining to keep up with his sons as they ran from one attraction to another. Fortunately, the boys' energy seemed to peak by about two in the afternoon. Then the pace was more relaxed into the evening, until they were ready to collapse from exhaustion by the time the fireworks appeared over Cinderella's castle.

Each day was different, as they alternated between the various theme parks in the area, and a day simply resting by the pool at the hotel resort where they were staying. Joe and Alice focused entirely on the family and enjoying their time together. Iraq and Joe's job in the army were purposely avoided as topics for conversation.

Quickly, the time passed and they were back home at Fort Bragg and the three weeks of R&R segued into three more weeks of administrative, medical, and some training requirements before Joe and his team had to report back to the air field for their next deployment to Nineveh Province where they would provide support to the 101st Airborne. "Good news," Joe remarked as he came into the house and gave Alice a hug and kiss on her cheek. "The medical exam went well. The doctors said I'm in great shape and ready to go."

"Good," Alice said quietly. "I want to keep you around for a long time."

"Don't worry," Joe replied. "They said that I'm in better shape than most men my age."

"Joe, you're only thirty-four. Considering your line of work, I'm not surprised that you're in great shape," Alice replied. "Did you hear what I just said a moment ago?... I want to keep you around for a long time." It was clear that Alice was not her usual cheerful self.

He paused to consider for a moment what Alice was trying to say. "You're sad that I'll be going back to Iraq for another three-month assignment, aren't you?"

"Joe, I don't want you to go on another assignment at all." Alice sat down at the kitchen table. "We've lived this army life for almost fifteen years and I'm tired of being the single parent and the lonely housewife."

"What do you want me to do?" Joe asked plaintively. He guessed what she wanted him to do.

"I want us to have a normal life; with you at home to help me raise the boys. I want to live in a neighborhood that includes friends that are not all associated with the army. When can we have this?"

Gunny Tim had occasionally talked with Joe about how his marriage ended in divorce. It was conversations like this, Tim said, that began the downward spiral. Joe felt momentarily trapped in a bad situation. "We had this conversation last summer," he began. "Then, I had seven years before I reached the twenty required for me to retire. Now, I have about six more years."

"In six years, the boys will be thirteen and fourteen. The next six years are their most formative. These coming years will be when they need you with them to shape their lives as much as possible," Alice reasoned. "If we wait that long we'll be six years older. It will be six more years until we can start a new life outside the army." Alice paused for a moment, thinking of this. "I don't want to wait that long."

Joe was conflicted between his deep love for Alice and his family, and his love and commitment to the men in his team and the army. The bonds of friendship ran deep. "Alice, I love you deeply. I know you want me to say something now, but I don't know what to say. Do you mind if I go for a walk?"

"Do whatever you want," she said quietly, with some resignation in her voice. Alice also knew that Joe was not ready to resign his commission in the army and take a desk job somewhere. Joe walked outside and down the sidewalk. Alice laid her head on her arms at the kitchen table and cried. She didn't want Joe to go away again. Her loneliness had been building slowly since the last time they were briefly together before he departed into the unknown in late January. Thankfully, the boys wouldn't return from school for another three hours.

He wasn't sure where he was walking to. The world just went dark for him. He didn't resent Alice for confronting him with this terrible dilemma. After all, only Alice could help resolve the situation that he found himself in. After about ten minutes walking in one direction, he decided that talking with a friend who had gone through this nightmare would be helpful. Since he was already walking toward one of the Fort Bragg gates, and the shops and restaurants just beyond, he called one of his closest friends and colleagues. "Tim, I need your advice. Can you meet me at the Mission Barbeque?....Thanks. I'll see you there in about fifteen minutes." The restaurant was two miles from his home, but Joe figured that the walk there would help him think about what was best for both his family and his commitment to the team. He made one more call while walking to the rendezvous. "Alice, I need a couple of hours. I'm sorry....You don't mind?....Thanks honey...I just need a little time... Thanks. Bye...I love you."

The Mission BBQ Restaurant was popular with the folks working at Fort Bragg and always busy. Fortunately, late May weather in North Carolina was very comfortable, so Joe sat at one of the picnic tables the restaurant had outside, where it was quiet and away from other customers. Tim arrived shortly after Joe, and they both ordered a beer. Joe's request at such short notice had never happened before. Although Tim had other plans for the afternoon, he didn't hesitate to change them for his good friend.

"Alice wants me to quit the army." Joe said in a matter of fact voice as he took a sip of his beer.

"I figured it was something like that. I don't get last minute calls to go have a beer with you that often." Tim attempted a smile. "What happened?"

"This sort of came out of the blue," Joe began. "We've been having a great time, all of us....Then today; Alice told me...in her own way, that she's tired of being alone to raise the boys and wants me to get a job that will allow me to stay home most of the time."

"Been there, done that." Tim empathized. "I was twenty-one at the time and already been married for three years. We got married when I enlisted in the marines, and for a while she was happy with the fact that I had a steady job, a housing allowance, and all the military benefits. Then, after a year, during my first overseas tour, we started drifting apart. Her letters to me began to change. She started talking about going out with her friends all the time. When I returned home, she was different. Or maybe I was different. I don't know. Anyway, when I got orders for another tour she gave me an ultimatum: either stay home or the marriage would be over. I tried to explain to her that with the marines, you often don't have much choice in the matter."

"Yeah." Joe considered his situation. "Well, at least in six months I'll have a choice when my present commitment is over."

"So, Joe, what do you want to do?"

"The war is just starting. I have an obligation to the team and the army to do what I can do."

"Joe, you have a wife that loves you and two young sons that look up to you as their role model," Tim observed. "Think about it this way: Will winning the war in Iraq depend on your being there? Alternatively, will your family and marriage survive if you're in Iraq, or will they be better off if you are here with them?"

Deep down, Joe was more afraid of wasting his life chained to a desk, like his father the accountant, than in a war zone fox hole with his men. But he was even more fearful of losing his family. "The answer is simple. My family comes first," Joe sighed. "I just don't know what I should do."

"Joe, you didn't need me to help figure this out." Tim counseled. "Looking back, I suspect my marriage wasn't going to last regardless of whether I stayed in the marines or not. We were both too young. You, on the other hand, have more than ten years invested in your marriage. Alice loves you and is a great person and mom to Nathan and Michael. Don't mess it up."

"Thanks, Tim. Sorry to interrupt your day."

"No problem, boss. It's what good friends are for. Let's change the subject. What've you been up to for the last couple of weeks?" Tim's diversion was appreciated. Joe knew what he needed to do. A little distraction, talking to Tim about their recent vacation and the fun that he and his family had in Orlando, was a nice way to get into a better, more positive frame of mind.

Despite the two-mile walk each way to meet up with Tim and have their conversation, Joe returned home to discuss a way forward with Alice before the boys returned from school. Alice had recovered from her momentary despair and was puttering around the kitchen, preparing dinner but still troubled by pent-up fears for their marriage and what Joe would do when Joe walked through the door. She looked at him, not knowing what to say.

"Alice, I've decided to quit the army. You're right. The family...You and the boys are more important to me. I've been too concerned with my job to really understand what my deployments are doing to us." He walked up to her and gave her a hug. "I'm sorry."

She looked up at him. "Let's talk." She said as she sat down at the table. Joe slowly followed her lead and sat down across from her. "We all need to be happy and despite the challenges, try to do what is best for the family. I know your commitment to the army is up after this next tour. You've got almost fifteen years invested. We have a lot to lose if you don't stay with the service for five more years. We have one more week before you get on the plane again. We should talk with the marriage counselor just to help ensure we are both on the same page regarding our future."

"No problem," Joe said. He was happy that she wasn't going to object to his upcoming deployment. "I'll talk with the Human Resources Command Assignment Officer to learn if there are options other than leaving the army."

"I'm sure we'll find a reasonable option." She said with confidence. "I've learned a lot working in HR." The remaining time home was more subdued than the first five weeks. Thankfully, Joe and Alice worked together with the resources available at Fort Bragg. Alice's experience in HR helped them to ask the right questions to navigate through what was a very common but extremely sensitive military problem. Their discussions and research renewed a sense of hope that there were promising options. The night before his departure, Joe was organizing his gear and packing his things. "Can I help?" Alice smiled at her husband as she walked into the bedroom where he was working.

Joe stood up from the organized piles of clothes on their bed and also smiled as he admired, again, how attractive she was. "Give me a hug." He walked over and put his arms around her. "You know I don't want to leave you this time, more than ever before."

She stepped back and looked into his eyes. "Promise this will be your last tour?"

Joe gave her another long hug. "I promise, Alice. This will be my most difficult tour, simply because I'm looking forward to our future together when I return home."

The following morning, she drove Joe and the boys to the Fort Bragg air strip for a final family farewell. It was even more emotional than his arrival. The boys were just proud of their dad and understood that this was the life they had experienced since they were babies. However, Alice and Joe knew this time would be different. Their mutual understanding of the future and their prayers that Joe would return safely, more so than ever, increased the intensity of their farewell hug and created tears in both of their eyes as they said good-bye.

When Joe saw his team as they met up to walk toward formation before boarding the plane, he transformed from loving husband and father to the elite commander of men. When the men lined up with several other units that were scheduled to fly to Iraq with them, Joe had a feeling of pride for his special operations unit, knowing that his team would have the best-trained, most combat ready and proven warriors on the plane.

Alice and the boys watched as the plane taxied up the runway and took off. Once again, Joe was gone with his men to do a job that included dangers that she could only imagine.

Chapter Thirty:
The Trap Is Set
Late June 2003

The journey was long: Fort Bragg to Andrews Air Force Base, Maryland to Erbil International Airport in Iraq, then a MH-47 Chinook helicopter to the military air base near Forward Operating Base Marez near Mosul took thirty long hours, including transit stops. When Joe's team left Fort Bragg, it was a warm 90 degrees Fahrenheit. When they walked out the back end of the Chinook, they were struck by a furnace-like blast of 110 degree air.

"Wow! I don't remember this kind of heat!" Jason exclaimed as they walked toward the waiting bus. Each man was loaded up with their duffle bag of clothes, personal items, and was wearing a helmet and body armor on the flight from Erbil to Mosul.

"Welcome to summer in Mosul." The young staff sergeant greeted the men as he stood at attention and saluted the special operators. "As soon as your orders are processed when we arrive at main camp, I'll take you to your sleeping tent and show you around. Considering that we've only begun to build the camp, it's not bad." He said this with a smile and some pride. "Tomorrow, you're scheduled to meet with Colonel O'Connor at 0900.

When they arrived at Camp Marez after the short bus ride, Hakim was there to greet them. "Welcome back!"

"Hakim, when did you get here?" Joe asked as he shook Hakim's hand.

"My flight arrived in Erbil yesterday, and I was able to get a hop over here last night. Our sleeping quarters aren't fancy, but they're better than our last visit to Mosul." He was clearly happy to see his friends and colleagues. The feeling was mutual with the team.

The following morning after a hearty breakfast at the DFAC dining hall near their sleeping quarters, the men walked over to a plywood building known as a SWA hut. This building was pointed out to them by the sergeant previously as the headquarters for their command. When Joe walked in, he was surprised to see Charlie, the CIA agent standing next to Colonel O'Connor. Joe greeted the Colonel with a salute and introduced Hakim and each man in his team. "It's good to see you again Charlie." He said as he shook Charlie's hand.

"Gentlemen! It's good to see you." I was briefed by HQ regarding your reconnaissance mission and read your report. Charlie was telling me about your very thorough exploration of the Mosul suburbs. Good job!"

"Thank you sir, 'Task Force 20" was an interesting assignment." Joe spoke for the entire team.

"Charlie, tell them what we're looking for now."

"Gentlemen, remember the deck of most wanted cards that we gave to you before you began your mission? We have reason to believe that Saddam and members of his family are in the Mosul area. Our Iraqi contacts said they think Uday and Qusay are traveling from one house to another every few days to avoid being caught. They travel at night with two cars and an SUV loaded with weapons. When you were in Mosul last time, you gave us a number of coordinates for houses where Saddam and the others may want to hide. Now we want you to start checking on these places. Do your best to find the most wanted men on those cards for us."

"Take the day rest of the day off and get over your jet lag." Colonel O'Connor advised. "Good Luck!"

The following day, Joe met with his team to describe his plan for surveillance of the houses that were on their list of possible safe-houses. "Gentlemen, you all now have a new MOS to add to your list of specialties. The task described by Charlie and the Colonel will require the best public relations skills that a Civil Affairs Specialist can muster."

"Cool. I always thought I was pretty good at public relations." Jared joked.

"Yeah, too bad the ladies you were chasing didn't agree." Colin retorted. Both men were unmarried and in their mid-twenties. It was well known among the others in the team that they competed with each other as being successful meeting young ladies when they were on R&R.

"Yeah. OK guys. Let's get serious." Joe continued. "We'll divide up as we did when we were here in February, checking out the various locations. Depending on the logistics and availability of Humvees for our mission, I want each team to visit the neighborhoods where you visited before, including the targeted homes. This will be a busy time for Hakim, unless we can get other Iraqi-American advisors to help us out. The goal will be to hand out decks of the 'most wanted' cards and the Fifteen Million dollar reward flyers that Charlie showed us. Talk with everyone to let them know we want them to get the reward money if they help us out. Hakim will also give the owner of each targeted house a cell phone number to call if and when they spot one of the people on the deck of cards.

"I think we may be a bit short-handed for this kind of task." Paul observed. "Hakim and one or two teams can only do so much meeting and greeting in a day."

"I talked with the Colonel about this yesterday afternoon. He said he'll see if Civil Military Affairs personnel will be available to help us out, but he's not optimistic. Especially with regard to fluent interpreters who can help us communicate with the neighbors." Joe answered. "We'll do the best we can. Since we have ten houses and their surrounding neighborhoods to canvas, we will focus on each target house and the houses surrounding them. With Hakim's help, we should be able to cover at least two neighborhoods a day, cycling back through the neighborhoods every five or six days. That way, the people will get to know us and feel more comfortable with helping us out.

"Maybe we can hand out MREs which many Iraqis may appreciate right now, since there's a food shortage in the city," suggested Hakim.

"Good idea." Paul agreed. "If we can give each household one or two MREs and show them the food inside the packets and how to cook them, that would be a good way to earn their trust and friendship. If you agree, Joe, I'll work with our supply guys to see if we can get the MREs for this."

"Sounds good. If they need some convincing, I think I can get a directive from the Colonel to help us out with this request."

The team worked on logistics regarding the use of sufficient transportation for their excursions, and the requisite friendship-building MREs for the rest of the day. The first two teams set out on Monday,

June 30 with Hakim to meet and greet the families and others in each of the targeted neighborhoods.

Nawaf and Salah were contacted on July 5 and again on July 10 by Hakim, Joe, Nick, Phil and Pete regarding their interest in finding Saddam Hussein and his family. Although Lara came to the door with Nawaf she didn't expose her American identity to the soldiers out of concern for Nawaf and the rest of the extended family. She didn't want them to receive more attention than other Iraqis, at least not until Saddam, Uday, and Qusay Hussein were captured or killed.

Chapter Thirty-One:
A Bad Day for Uday and Qusay

On July 15, at about eight in the evening, a slightly dented sports car stopped in front of Nawaf's walled house and a man wearing well-worn western clothes, one considered "business casual" in America, rang the bell at the Al-Zaidan gate over and over again, demanding entry. Nawaf went out to see who it was. When he opened the gate, he recognized the man as one of his distant relatives.

"Mohammed! I haven't seen you in years." Mohammed rushed into the house as Nawaf was speaking to him.

"Nawaf, I'm here to tell you that you and your family must leave your house tomorrow. Very important people want to use the house for a few days. I can't tell you when they will arrive or when they will leave, but they must have complete privacy, and no one can know who they are."

"Mohammed, we're cousins. You can tell me," Nawaf attempted to coax more information from him.

"If I told you and anyone found out, we would both be dead and so would our families. Leave your house tomorrow and don't come back until I tell you it's OK to do so." Mohammed had the look of a hunted man. "I've got to go now, Nawaf. God be with you and your family. Remember, not a word to anyone, or we're all dead." With those final words, Mohammed ran out of the house, through the front gate, and was gone in an instant.

Nawaf went out to shut the gate, then the door to the house. Mohassin and Lara were in the kitchen and they heard Mohammed's warning. "Who was that?" Mohassin asked.

Nawaf stood by the front door and smiled. "Maybe our little trap is going to work. That was Mohammed. He's a distant cousin who lives in Tikrit. He told us to leave the house because some very important visitors will be staying here."

"I wonder who it is." Mohassin thought out loud, "Saddam, Uday, Qusay, or one of the generals?"

"I hope it's Uday!" Lara said with a solemn conviction.

"Nawaf, where shall we go?" Mohassin asked.

"Salah said that we can stay at his house." Nawaf and Salah already considered this possibility. "His roof has a good view of our house, and with the half-wall up there, we can lie low and look through a small opening without being seen. Salah already said we could stay with them if our trap worked."

Nawaf, Mohassin, Shalan and Lara moved in with Salah and his family on July 16. Salah, his son Othman, and Shalan knocked out a few of the cinder blocks that created the half wall on the flat roof of Salah's stately three story house that was similar to Nawaf's across the street and two houses down the road. The small openings provided strategic views of Nawaf's courtyard behind the outer wall and the front and left sides of his house. The walls on the roof of Salah's house were sufficiently high enough for the people to crawl on their hands and knees without being seen from the ground or even Nawaf's roof.

Meanwhile, Nawaf called the phone number provided by Hakim when the soldiers visited their neighborhood. "...Yes Hakim...we are living at my brother's home and can see my house clearly from here...No. No, I don't think it's a good idea. If your team shows up on our street with your Humvees again, others will get suspicious. The neighborhood is quiet now and we don't want the US Army visiting too often. You've already visited our area twice during the last two weeks...I'll call you when we see someone move into our house." Nawaf hung up his phone. "Well, all we can do now is wait."

They didn't have to wait long. Three days later, on Saturday, July 19, it was about seven p.m. The summer sun was just beginning to set in the west over the hill, toward Mosul. Lara, Mohassin, and Salah's wife, Walla, were talking in the kitchen when Othman rushed in after running down two flights of stairs from the roof. "They arrived!" He said as he stopped to catch his breath, "There are two cars and an SUV. Two men are beginning to unload weapons and boxes from the back of the SUV."

Lara bolted for the stairs, "I want to see!"

"Don't be too anxious." Nawaf said as he was coming down the stairs. "When we go back to the roof, we must stay low and quiet. No one must see you or any of us on the roof." He grabbed Lara's arms to look in her eyes and make an important point. "If they see and recognize you, we will all be killed."

"Uncle, what shall we do? If that is Uday Hussein's car at our house, he must be there!"

"Lara, we don't know who it is. We didn't see a Lamborghini. I've known many senior people in the Ba'ath party. I don't want to be responsible for getting another person killed by mistake."

Lara took a breath to calm down from her initial excitement, "Uncle, the Ba'athists killed Yasmine and Aziz, and probably hundreds of thousands of other innocent people. Why worry about whether an innocent Ba'athist is killed? They're all murderers!"

"Not all of them were murderers Lara. We need to be sure who is there before we contact the Americans." Nawaf counseled. "Let's go up and peek through the wall. If you're sure it's the car you remember, then I'll call Hakim."

It was close to dusk but the summer sun was still hot on the roof. When Lara crawled out of the roof door onto the concrete, her hands and knees soon began to burn. Fortunately, Salah, Othman and Shalan had covered the areas near the wall with old carpets to cushion them from the heat. An old bed sheet about a foot below the top of the wall was secured and sloped down to the roof floor behind the carpets by bricks to protect them from the hot sun during the day. It wasn't much but it provided some protection and wasn't visible from the street.

"How will you know if it's Uday?" Nawaf asked Lara.

"Uday's Lamborghini had a large metallic gold racing stripe that accented thc bright high-gloss red finish on the rest of the car. If we see that car, we'll know he is with them." She said, as they positioned themselves so they could each look out of the two holes that were positioned about six feet from each other. Salah was also on the roof looking through a third hole in the wall.

"I see the SUV. Where's the other car and the Lamborghini?" Nawaf asked his brother.

"They left about ten minutes ago, soon after Othman went downstairs to tell all of you."

Lara rolled over onto her back. It was tiring, even for a couple minutes, leaning up on her elbows while she was stretched out on the very warm carpet under the bed sheet. "When do you think they'll return?" she asked.

"Who knows?" Salah replied. "I'm going down for a rest from this heat and will send Othman up with some bottles of water. Do you want to go down into the house with me until Nawaf or Othman tells us they've returned, or wait up here?"

Lara was already beginning to perspire but she was determined to stay there until she saw the Lamborghini and possibly Yasmine and Aziz' assassin. "Thanks Uncle. I'd like some water but I'll stay here." She continued to lay there for a minute and then rolled back on her stomach again to prop herself up to look through the hole. After a few more minutes she rolled onto her back again. Soon, Othman came crawling onto the roof with several bottles of water for Lara, Nawaf, and himself.

They were all hot under the sheet as they waited on the roof. Lara dozed off as the still air and warmth of the afternoon sun acted as a mild narcotic. It must have been fifteen or twenty minutes when she heard the sound of a car. Immediately, she woke up and rolled back into position so she could see who was coming down the street. "Uncle, it's the car!" She whispered, perhaps more loudly than she should have.

"SHHHH!" Nawaf cautioned.

"See the gold stripe? That's the car!" Lara whispered as it came to a stop in front of Nawaf's house gate. The other car pulled up behind it. Four men stepped out and began looking at each of the houses in the vicinity. She panicked as she saw one of the men look directly at Salah's house and upwards at the wall that she and the others were hiding behind. The man slowed his gaze for a moment and Lara almost fainted in fright as he seemed to be looking right through the hole at her. Thankfully, he turned his head toward the house next to Salah's and continued his search for spies or other threats.

The driver of the Lamborghini stepped out of the car and walked toward the gate. "That's Mohammed!" Nawaf whispered in surprise.

When they completed their surveillance of the neighborhood, a man limped out of the gate to talk with Mohammed. He was accompanied by four other men gathered round him to provide a human shield. It was only a few steps to the open gate, but Lara could see by the protected man's movements he was Uday Hussein. His pronounced limp was easy to recognize. "It's him! It's Uday Hussein!" she whispered almost too loud in her excitement. After a brief conversation, Uday and his men went through the gate and Mohammed got back into the Lamborghini and drove off.

"Shhhh!" Nawaf cautioned again. "Othman, you stay here and keep an eye on things. Lara and I will go downstairs and alert the others." He rolled over a couple of times under the sheet to position his head toward the rooftop door and began to crawl in that direction. Lara did the same. Soon the two of them were back in the kitchen and covered in sweat from their hour-long wait on the roof. Lara began to describe the Lamborghini and the man with the limp.

"Now is the time to call Hakim," Nawaf said as he picked up the phone. "This time, Lara, I'll introduce you to Hakim over the phone and you can explain in English what you saw a few moments ago to him and his soldier friends."

"Hakim, Uday and others just moved into my house...Yes. We are sure...I'm handing my phone to my niece, Lara. She can tell you the details."

Hakim looked at Joe and the others in the room. "He's handing the phone to his niece." He shrugged his shoulders.

"Hello. My name is Lara Al Mohammed. I'm an American from Ann Arbor, Michigan. I know for a fact that it is Uday Hussein and his henchmen."

"Lara? Please hold one second," Hakim replied in English as he turned to Joe with a look of surprise on his face. "She's an American from Ann Arbor, Michigan."

"Holy...!" Joe and several of the team all exclaimed at once. "How did she get here?"

"Lara, why are you in Iraq? How did you get here?" Hakim asked. It was if he and the men had just stumbled upon a huge diamond in the desert. The one-sided conversation they were hearing was very surreal and totally unexpected.

"It's a long story and I'll tell it to you after you've killed Uday and the others."

Hakim held his hand over the phone's mouth piece for a moment. "Wow. She really doesn't like Uday." He said to the men. All of them were silent, still trying to get their heads around the fact that an American woman was in Iraq, in the middle of an invasion.

"Can I talk to her?" Joe asked as he reached for the phone, as Hakim handed it to him.

"Lara, my name is Major Joe Keith. We want to take care of Uday as much as you apparently do. What can you tell us?"

"Uday killed my cousin and her husband in front of me and my friends in Baghdad. I know very well what he looks like, and I know the car that he was driving then. The same car just parked across the street from us, and the same man that limped into my uncle's home a few minutes ago."

"How can my team get to where you and your family are staying in a manner that will keep us out of sight of Uday and his men?" Joe asked.

"Major, I'm handing the phone back to my Uncle Nawaf. Let him talk with Hakim about this. Uncle Nawaf and Salah, my uncle who owns the house we are presently staying in, know the neighborhood much better than I do. They can give you better advice."

Joe handed the phone back to Hakim, who put it to his ear. "OK. Yes. Yes. OK. Hold on a minute while I explain this to the major." Hakim turned to Joe. "Remember the hill we were on when I pointed Nawaf's house out to you? He recommends that you park behind the hill and walk around it to the street behind Salah's house." Hakim put the phone back to his ear. "OK. I'll tell them and will call you back as soon as there is a plan. Thanks. Bye."

"So, what's the deal?" Joe asked.

"He said that you and the men you were with when we visited his house should come to Salah's house as soon as possible. At the moment, Uday and his men are in Nawaf's house, but he doesn't know if they're going to stay inside or if some of the men will be posted around the neighborhood."

"OK. Nick, Pete, and Phil, we're going with Hakim to Salah's house tonight if the colonel agrees," Joe directed his men. "I'm going to brief him now. Prepare your kit for five days." Joe walked out of the tent over to the HQ SWA hut. It was about 2030, but, like most nights, the colonel and his staff were still working.

"You're sure that it's Uday?" the colonel asked. Joe explained the unusual communication from the American woman. "I want to take Hakim and three others with me tonight to stake out the target house. I'll report back to you based on our assessment of the threats involved and how we should proceed with taking Uday, if the man is who she said it was."

"Permission granted," Colonel O'Connor approved. "I'll let General Petraeus know what we're doing so we can call in the reinforcements if they're needed."

"Paul, arrange for three Humvees and drivers to take us over to the Al Yarmuk district to drop us off behind the hill. The colonel gave us permission to begin surveillance tonight. Hakim, please call Nawaf and tell him to expect us at his brother's back gate at around 0100."

Joe, Hakim, Nick, Pete, and Phil arrived at Salah's back gate and were surprised to be greeted by the entire household. Lara was the first to step into the alley behind the house and introduce herself. "Sir, I am Lara Al-Mohammed. Welcome to my uncle's home." Once again, the men were surprised to hear an American woman speaking to them in Mosul. It took them a moment to regain their composure. Even in the middle of the night, the men could see that she was an attractive young woman with wavy dark brown hair and eyes, about five feet six inches tall, and very self-assured. After introductions, Joe asked to be taken to the roof.

Salah and Lara escorted Joe and Hakim to the holes in the roof wall under the sheet that remained in place. "When the SUV and cars arrived, I saw the Lamborghini that was being driven by Uday Hussein in Baghdad on February 8. He came out of Uncle Nawaf's house and talked with the man that drove to Uncle Nawaf's house in the Lamborghini. Then he and his bodyguards went back inside, and the man got back into Lamborghini and drove away. I'm sure it was Uday Hussein. There is no one else that walks with such a limp, which that man had." Lara said emphatically.

"When the SUV and cars first parked in front of Nawaf's house, the man with the limp got out of the back seat of the SUV along with a teenage boy. They were escorted into the house by twelve bodyguards from the SUV and other two cars. Then some of the men made at least two trips back to the vehicles to unload weapons and other boxes. I don't know what was in the boxes, but they looked like they were heavy. Several of them required two men to carry into the house." Hakim translated as Salah explained what he saw to Joe as they were led through the roof door, down the stairs, and into the large drawing room in the front of the house.

"It sounds like they were bringing in a lot of ammunition," Joe surmised. "Hakim, tell Salah thanks and also tell him that after we go onto the roof again and review the situation, we'll begin to develop a plan. Ask him if he and Nawaf have any suggestions. We will welcome their ideas."

"Tell him thanks," Salah said to Lara. "You know we haven't made any plans yet."

"Major, my uncle said they haven't made any plans yet."

When Lara stopped talking, Salah assumed she was finished, so he added, "tell the Major that he and his men can sleep anywhere they can find space on the main floor of the house. Show them were the washroom and toilet is, and tell them thanks for coming."

Hakim smiled when he heard this, and translated Salah's offer of hospitality to Joe.

"Joe nodded to Salah and replied, "*Shukraan*." He didn't know much Arabic, but he learned that "thank you" is perhaps the most important expression in any language for building friendships.

Joe organized his team of four, including himself, into one-person two hour shifts. Lara asked her family if they wanted to watch through the holes as well. Everyone said yes. So in their turn, Nawaf, Shalan, Salah, Othman, Mohassin, Walla, and Lara would also be on the roof with the soldiers on one-hour shifts. Hakim also said that he would spend time on the roof at the third hole in the wall. This schedule made the heat of the day tolerable for everyone during their assigned times to keep an eye on Nawaf's house and the people inside of it.

The following morning, Joe and Pete were on the roof looking through two of the holes and Lara was with them looking through the third. It was about ten a.m. when the Lamborghini turned the corner onto the street and parked in front of the house. A nervous man in ill-fitted western style clothes got out of the sports car and fidgeted next to the gate, waiting for someone. The gate of Nawaf's house opened and the man with a limp walked out with two others to greet him. "That's him!" Lara whispered in surprise. "That's Uday Hussein!"

Immediately, Joe and Pete zoomed in their binoculars to study the man that Lara was referring to. Pete pulled his deck of most wanted cards out of his pocket and quickly found Uday's card, one of the top three cards in his deck. He looked at the card and took a long look at the man with the limp, who was standing still, giving the nervous man directions for a few minutes. Sure enough, the man with the limp matched Uday's card. "It's him," Pete told Joe, "that's Uday Hussein." He handed the card to Joe for his verification.

Joe looked at the card then through his binoculars to see the rumpled nervous man get into the Lamborghini as Uday Hussein watched him drive down the street and around the corner before limping back into the house with his two bodyguards.

The rest of July 20 passed without incident. Two men did leave the house and drive away, returning an hour later with food and other supplies, but that was the only activity. Joe was a bit surprised that none of the men ventured into the neighborhood to look around. He surmised that Uday and the others inside did not want to draw any attention. The neighbors all knew that someone important from the Ba'ath party had taken up residence in Nawaf's home, but they dared not inquire who the person might be. Everyone realized that avoiding them on the street was the best policy for living a longer life.

It had been two nights since Nawaf's house was occupied. By Monday, July 21, Joe and the others were becoming concerned. They knew that Uday and his entourage did not stay at one place for too long. They could move on at any time. "Phil, I want to contact the colonel and request permission to bring the rest of the team here tonight, so we can take out Uday and his men before they slip away."

Phil connected his radio phone set and quickly routed Joe to the colonel. "Colonel, we have observed no roaming Iraqi guards or other threats in the area. The team is capable of taking out everyone in the house tomorrow night."

After a few moments of silence, while the colonel consulted with others, he provided the affirmative to Joe: "Permission granted. We'll inform your men and arrange transport to the drop-off point at 2330."

"Good. I'll go in my village clothes to meet and guide them back here," Joe said as he turned to Salah and Nawaf. "Hakim, ask Salah and Nawaf if they don't mind if another eight men join our party."

While Hakim translated the question, the two brothers smiled and replied, "They don't mind at all."

That night, the rest of the team was happy to see Joe meet them behind the hill. They were excited to get into the action. When they arrived at the back gate of Salah's house, they were ushered in by Nawaf and escorted to the drawing room, where Joe and the others made themselves at home. The men were only carrying their night rolls, a change of clothing, their body armor, helmets, weapons, and a lot of ammunition.

Although it was midnight by the time the entire team was in the house, Lara and all the members of the two Al Zaidan families were wide awake with excitement and interest in seeing these other friends of Joe, Nick, Phil, Pete, and Hakim.

When the men entered the room, Lara greeted each of them with a handshake. After Paul, Colin, Jared, Jordan, Tim, Manny, Jason, and Bob introduced themselves, she introduced her extended family. Everyone was smiling and bowing with respect and appreciation for each other's help with the very dangerous firefight they expected would take place the following evening. After the backpacks, weapons, and ammunition were arranged around the drawing room there was sufficient space for the men to sleep. Then, each man was escorted, one at a time, by a member of the Al Zaidan family to take a look through one of the holes in the wall. When they returned from their brief tour, each man found a place on the floor and bedded down for the rest of the night.

Although most of the soldiers and family had less than six hours sleep, everyone was up by 0700 the following morning, eager to eliminate at least one of the Hussein family members and his thugs. Lara and her family were particularly anxious to see justice done to Uday Hussein.

Hakim and Nick were on the roof peering through two holes, and Nawaf was at the third at 0800 when Nawaf saw the Lamborghini stop and park in front of Nawaf's gate. The man in the rumpled western clothes got out and ran inside as the gate opened for him. "I wonder who that was?" Nick whispered softly.

Although he didn't understand English, Nawaf guessed Nick's question. "He's my distant cousin, Mohammed," Nawaf replied in Arabic. "He was the one that visited my house to inform us that we had to move on so 'important visitors' could move in."

Hakim translated this to Nick, "he says the man is his relative and Uday's front man for arranging the next safe house." A few minutes later, Mohammed hurried out the gate, got into the sports car, and drove off.

Nick was watching this through his binoculars. "He seemed to have a worried face."

Nawaf looked to Hakim for a translation, which was provided. He smiled and said something to Hakim. "Nawaf said you would also have a worried face if you worked for Uday Hussein."

Nawaf continued talking to Hakim for a while longer. "He said that Mohammed's arrival probably means that Uday and company are getting ready to move," Hakim translated.

"When?" Nick asked, and Nawaf guessed what his question was.

"Who knows? But probably soon," Hakim translated.

"Hakim, ask Nawaf if he would go with you to tell Joe and the others what he just told me. I'll stay here and keep an eye on things," Nick requested.

When Joe learned the situation from Nawaf and Hakim, he made a decision to take action. "Phil, get on the radio and request HQ to approve a change in plans; that our operation should commence as soon as possible because there is a strong possibility that Uday and company may be preparing to leave the target house."

"Yes sir," Phil said as he started up the radio.

Joe turned to his team: "Are you ready for some action?"

"Yes sir!" Was the unanimous reply.

Joe had been formulating a plan during the last twenty-four hours, based upon what he observed at Nawaf's house. It was clear that there were one or two men stationed at each of the doors and windows on every level of the house. The watch teams noted a regular movement of the curtains as Uday's men frequently moved them to peer out the windows. Thankfully, the house did not have a half-wall on the roof, so there were no men looking out over the entire area. Unfortunately, they could no longer carry out the original plan at night. A day-time operation was always more dangerous.

"Sir, HQ has approved your request and says they are standing by to offer whatever assistance may be necessary," Phil informed Joe and the others.

"Hakim," Joe began, "we don't want to draw attention to ourselves, but we need to get people out of the area so that civilians aren't caught in the middle of the fighting. I know it's risky and you're a civilian, but you will draw the least attention if you go to the houses near Nawaf's villa, where Uday is, and tell the neighbors they must leave the area immediately. Tell them you've been told there may be a fight between the remaining Ba'athists in the area and the Americans. I know you can't do anything to make them leave, but if some of the locals leave the neighborhood through their back doors now, there will be fewer Iraqis to worry about when the fighting begins.

"OK. There are eight houses on this street in addition to Salah's and Nawaf's houses. This will take a while," Hakim observed. "I'll work the row of houses that we're on from the alley behind us, then the houses on Nawaf's side of the street. Assuming there are no obstructions, I'll try to do the same with the house next to Nawaf's. Hopefully, I can contact everyone by their back door. They may see me, but only when I cross the street. Hopefully, I won't appear to be a threat, or a target to any of them."

"Thanks, Hakim." Joe said sincerely. "This type work is not in your contract. Try to make it back here, safe and sound, by 1030. That should give you enough time. We'll be waiting for you.

The situation was also getting tense across the street. "Qusay, we've been here long enough. We've got to move on tonight." Uday advised his brother Qusay, and Mustapha, Qusay's 14-year-old son.

"Calm down, Uday. Mohammed said that the next house is ready for us." Qusay assured his brother. "There are more Americans on the streets now. We've got to wait until this evening so we can go there without being noticed."

They were in the sitting room on the second floor. It was the inner sanctum of the three story house surrounded by three large bedrooms and two bathrooms. The third floor had a master bedroom and bathroom, Nawaf's office, and another smaller room that was used intermittently as a guest room or for storage. The first floor had a large drawing room that took up a third of the floor, spacious kitchen, pantry, dining room, and another bathroom with an eastern toilet, sink, and small shower area. There was also a small cellar room that Nagham and Mohassin included in the design when the house was built. It was used by Mohassin as her sewing and craft room and place of cool, quiet solitude. It was especially appreciated in the summer months when the rest of the house was much warmer.

Uday's senior body-guard, Abdul, and the personal bodyguards for Qusay and Mustapha peered from the drawn curtains of different rooms on the second and third floors onto the street below. Six specially selected members of the elite Iraqi Republican Guard were on the first floor guarding those windows and doors.

Nawaf's house sat on the corner, three doors down and across the street from Salah's house. The left side faced the hill, and the back of the house had an open field behind it. Having a clear field of fire on two sides made the house more desirable as a safe house. The house next door was very close, perhaps only two feet away. There were no windows on that side of Nawaf's house and none on that side of the neighboring house. This made it pose less of a threat than the other three sides. Nawaf and Salah's houses were located on a quiet three-car-wide side street with very little traffic and sufficient width to park cars along one or another side of it.

"I'm going to miss the Lamborghini," Uday sighed nostalgically as he thought of Mohammed driving off in his car. Qusay gave him a stern look. "Yes, I agree. It's a liability, but it was fun to drive."

"Mohammed said that another car and driver will come for us this evening. When it does, Abdul and two others will take the car that is outside now and leave about five minutes ahead of us. We'll get into the car that is coming to get us, and the SUV with the others will follow behind us." Qusay reviewed the brief conversation with Uday that he had with Mohammed minutes before.

"Uncle Uday, can I have your Lamborghini after the Americans leave?" Mustapha asked naively.

"No problem," Uday smiled. "Not likely," He thought to himself.

Mustapha was big for his age and not particularly smart. He led a sheltered life within the confines of his family and enjoyed receiving deference from the people and families that his grandfather, father and uncle regularly socialized with. From this upbringing and his role models, he was developing the unsavory traits of his other male relatives: selfishness, intolerance, violence, and empty bravado.

At the age of two, he learned that he could get what he wanted by screaming, punching, and kicking whoever had what he wanted. The servants of the Hussein family took the brunt of his tantrums and never defended themselves or complained. Since he was big for his age, his mannerisms and violence grew with him. Before the invasion, every subordinate of the Hussein family, which meant everyone in the country who might be in the same room with Mustapha, was terrified of him.

While Uday and Qusay were discussing their plan to move to the next location, Mustafa was looking over one of the sniper rifles in the arsenal of weapons stacked in the room. "Someone is crossing the street and going to the house next door to us." Abdul called from a front bedroom. "Now he's walking up the street."

Mustapha stood up with the sniper's rifle, "Dad, can I shoot him?" He had learned to shoot rifles and other weapons at confined animals near Al-Faw palace, at Saddam's private zoo. He was very serious about shooting and killing the unknown man walking down the street.

Qusay shook his head. "No, let's keep an eye on him and see what he's up to. We don't want to draw attention to ourselves."

Uday smiled again. A little humor helped ease the tension. "Mustapha reminds me of us when we were his age."

"There's something strange going on," Abdul said as he peered out the window from behind the bedroom curtain. "He just walked up the street two houses and turned into the third house. We haven't seen anyone else this morning except him.

Hakim completed his rounds and walked back up the street and through the gate of Salah's house. It was 10:25 a.m.

Uday limped into the bedroom and peered out the window with binoculars from behind the curtains as Hakim went through the gate. Then he began to scan the house very slowly and methodically, from one side to the other, raising the binoculars up slightly to scan back across to ensure nothing was missed. He was finally looking at the top of the house and the half wall. Since the house stood at a slight angle from where he was looking, he could see the right side of the wall facing down the street in his direction and the wall facing directly across the street. His slow sweep stopped near the corner of the house on the front where he noticed a small hole in the cinder block. The binoculars were set on full power so he could determine that the hole was about half a cinder block high and wide, with the remaining block still in place. There were three more rows of cinder blocks on top of the hole. The morning sun was high in the sky, so it shaded the opening of the hole and prevented him from seeing what was on the other side. A knot formed in his stomach as he continued his slow scan to the right side of the wall facing down the street. "There! There are two more holes!"

Qusay, Mustapha, and Abdul were all standing behind Uday as he conducted his search. "What holes?" asked Abdul, with a knot beginning to form in his stomach. He and his men were responsible for ensuring there were no enemies and no threats in the area when they first arrived. Under normal circumstances, this omission could have resulted in his dismissal—or worse.

"Let me see," Qusay demanded as Uday stepped back from the curtains and handed the binoculars to his brother.

"Focus on the right front corner of the wall on the house across the street and three doors up."

"There is no wall."

"The next house up!" Uday directed his brother, with some irritation. "That traitor is working for the Americans. I think they know we're here. Load all the weapons with full magazines."

"Yes. I see them: one hole on the front wall and two on the side.

Mustapha still had the sniper rifle and was the first to snap a magazine of cartridges in place. "Those bastards! Let's kill all of them!"

Qusay shook his head with some pride. "He's definitely from the Saddam Hussein family," he said to Uday and turned to his son. "May you live to carry on the family traditions."

"Abdul, tell the others. Qusay, Mustapha, and I will go to the third floor with the sniper rifles, one of the RPGs, and grenades. Make sure you all have plenty of ammunition," Uday ordered in a voice loud enough to let everyone in the house hear.

"I talked with the neighbors that were still in their homes. Unfortunately, the houses on this side of the street near Nawaf's didn't have back gates so I had to go to their front doors to see if anyone was home." Hakim reported as he walked into the drawing room where Joe and the families were gathered. "They're all very frightened. Some said they would leave immediately, others said they would go to a safe room in their house." Some houses were built with rooms similar to Mohassin's sewing room. "None of them seemed to trust me, but they don't know what to believe at this time. I told the families that wanted to stay in their homes that there will be a lot of explosions and shooting. The family next to Nawaf's house is leaving out their back door. No one was home in the house directly across the street from Nawaf's."

"Good," Joe said, "we will need to use those houses."

Nagham looked concerned. "Those are good friends and neighbors. Do you think their houses will be damaged?"

"Probably." Joe was being realistic. "I will do everything that I can when this is over to ensure they are compensated for whatever damage may be caused."

"Did you notice anyone from the house looking at you?" Lara asked.

"No. After talking with the few remaining families on Nawaf's side of the street I crossed it and walked back here. I didn't want to look at the house because I thought it would spook whoever might be looking at me," Hakim explained.

"Good idea," Joe observed. "I hope if anyone did see you, they thought you were just a friendly neighbor. When I was on the roof looking through the hole in the wall up there, I didn't see anything, but I'm sure they know something is going on. The neighborhood is too quiet for them not to figure it out." He paused a moment to clear his head and begin the execution of their plan. "Paul, call Jared and Jordan down from the roof. When the three of you are here, we'll go over the plan one more time." Joe paused to think for a moment. "Hakim, tell Nawaf and Salah that I think it's time for all of them, including Lara, to go out through the back door and alley. They need to get away from the neighborhood until this is over."

"Where should we go?" Lara spoke for all of them.

"We'll walk over to Abdullah Al-Atwan's house. He lives about a kilometer from here and we can be there in about fifteen minutes."

"Do we need to take anything with us?" Mohassin asked.

"Lara, please tell everyone that we don't think this will take very long, but we want them all to be safe. Going to their friend's house is a very good idea." Lara still hadn't told Joe and his men about the family's relationship to Abdullah and Hana, or the fact that their son was her cousin's husband. After repeating Joe's guidance to them in Arabic, she turned to Joe. "They understand." With that, Salah led the families toward the kitchen and out the back door. Nawaf followed behind everyone to ensure there were no stragglers.

Paul quickly returned with the rest of his team and Joe turned toward Tim. "Tim, let's start with your team."

"Yes sir. Manny, Jason, Bob, and I will take the C-4 explosives, enter through the back door of the house next to Nawaf's, and set the charges near the front left side of the wall opposite Nawaf's drawing room. At 1130 we'll set off the first set of charges, sufficient to blow through the wall of the neighbor's house. As soon as we hear the rest of you complete the barrage of firing at the house from across the street, we'll blow through Nawaf's wall and join the party."

"Good," Joe approved. "Paul, what is your team going to do?"

"We'll go with your team through the back of the house which is across the street from Nawaf's," Paul said, looking at Joe and his team. "We'll take positions behind the front windows facing Nawaf's house. When we hear the first explosions from Tim's C-4 demolition, we'll open fire on all the windows in front of us. Colin will also aim for the hinges on the front gate to break that open. Hopefully we'll take out a couple of men right away. Then, when we hear the second set of explosions, we'll race over to the front of the house and take out as many bad guys as we can and meet up with Tim and his team."

"Good," Joe approved. "Phil, Nick, Pete, and I will go with Paul and his team to the house across the street and take positions on the two upper floors. We'll start firing at the windows on the second and third floors of Nawaf's house." He looked at his other two team leaders. "Paul, Tim, if either of you think the rest of us are required, let us know," Joe directed. "If anyone gets hit and requires evacuation, let us know and we'll join the fight and help everyone with a strategic retreat. The most challenging part will be to take out the men on the second and third floors since there is only one set of stairs in the house. Our goal will be take Uday alive, if we can. If he resists, Phil and I will call in the heavy artillery." Joe looked around the room at his men one last time to ensure that everyone was ready. "Make sure you all have your MICHs connected and your protective glasses on. There's going to be a lot of shattered glass windows in this fight." He paused to ensure the men were nodding in agreement. "Y'all ready? Let's go!"

"YES SIR!" Was the men's enthusiastic and determined response.

The neighborhood had a surreal quiet as the three teams moved to their designated positions. Pete and Nick ran up to the top floor of the house facing Uday's group. Joe and Phil went to the second floor, leaving Paul and his team on the first floor. The eight of them took up positions behind the three large windows facing the street. Tim and Jason made short work out of removing the hinges and door to the back of the neighbor's house and were soon setting the charges next to the wall as planned. Everyone began looking at their watches after they were in position.

"Ten, nine, eight, seven," Joe was counting down as the men on his floor crouched behind the walls next to the windows. This was part of the unspoken excitement that each of the men really anticipated. They were all adrenaline junkies and the count down before the start of an engagement was the same with them as it was for Olympic athletes waiting the last moments before the start of their event. "Three, two, one," BOOM! Immediately, everyone, including Joe and Phil stepped back a few feet and out from the behind the walls to let loose with a deafening roar of automatic fire from their M4A1s. The windows in front of them were immediately shattered and glass flew, mostly away from them, onto the ground below. However, some of the window glass came crashing down precariously close to where they were firing.

The glass in the windows across the street was also being shattered, but the projection of glass chards in that house were directed inward, along with the curtains. In an instant, Abdul was killed near a second floor window, and another bodyguard died in a hail of bullets on the first floor as he stood behind one of the curtains facing a window in front of him. Several of the others were bleeding with multiple wounds from the glass. There were fewer windows on the third floor, so Uday, Qusay, and Mustapha had more protection and more room to escape the mayhem. The four bodyguards positioned on the left and back sides of the first and second floors moved carefully toward the front of the house to help their comrades with the fight.

BOOM! Tim and Jason set off the second charge, blowing a ten-foot hole into Nawaf's drawing room, killing another guard in the blast. The four special operators started firing into the room quickly. In an instant, Manny spun around as he was hit in the shoulder and a bullet slammed into the front of his body armor, knocking him off his feet. Tim and Jason spotted the shooter and simultaneously cut him down as another guard took cover behind the kitchen wall. Bob dropped for cover behind what was left of one of the sofas after it had been blown across the room by the second explosion. He saw that he had a straight shot into the kitchen door, about fifteen feet from where he was. With a single flowing motion, he removed a grenade from his belt, pulled the pin, counted, and threw it into the door opening. Boom! For a moment there was silence. "I guess I got him." Bob said.

Tim was speaking on his microphone. "Joe! Man down! Manny's been hit!"

The torrent of rifle fire began again as Joe was about to speak in response to Tim's urgent message. Paul, Colin, Jared, and Jordan had rushed across the street, through the gate, and were nearing what was left of the front door when bullets started raining down on the inside courtyard wall. It only took a moment for Uday, Qusay, Mustapha and the few remaining men on the upper floors to spot the team and start firing in their direction. Fortunately, they all made it safely to the house. When the shooters on the upper floors started firing, Pete and Nick took aim from their positions across the street and shot two more guards, which scared the others away from the windows.

It was quiet again for a moment. "Tim, can Manny be moved?" Joe asked over his MICH. Tim and Jason were already kneeling by Manny as Bob continued to cover the smoldering opening to the kitchen and the hallway leading up the stairs to the second floor. "He's wounded on his right arm but the bullet to his chest didn't penetrate his armor." Just then, Paul and his team quietly entered the front door and saw Bob near them while Tim, Jason, and Manny were off to one side of the room.

BANG! Either Nick or Pete fired his gun from the third floor above Joe and Phil. They were away from their window opening, but could see out of it enough to watch a man fall back from a second floor window as a loaded rocket propelled grenade launcher fell out of his hands and to the ground. They held their breath for an instant as it fell into a bush next to the house. "Thank God," Joe sighed in relief. He was expecting the grenade to explode on impact. Luckily, it didn't.

"They have RPGs," Phil observed. "That's not good." A moment later, they heard more shots coming from Pete and Nick. They watched someone fall back from the third floor window, into the house with an RPG launcher falling from his shoulder. As he fell, the rocket grenade was launched and, thanks to the good shooting from above, it was propelled upward over the house. BOOM!

"I hope that didn't hurt anyone." Joe said as Phil nodded in agreement. "Tim, you and Jason try to carry Manny through the hole into the other house."

"Yes sir." Immediately, Tim motioned to Jason to help lift Manny and carry him to safety.

"They're in the house!" Uday hissed as Qusay held Mustapha.

"They shot my son!" Qusay said quietly, as Mustapha looked up at him with real fright in his eyes. He had been shot below his right shoulder and was bleeding profusely.

"He shouldn't have gone to the window with that grenade launcher," Uday said calmly.

"Those sons of bitches!"

"Qusay, your son is dying. We still have the bastards in the house." Uday spoke again in a very even, unemotional tone. "I wonder how many of our men are still alive?"

Four of their men had survived the American's assault. All were on the second floor and had taken positions that gave them a protected view of the stairs to the first floor.

"They're still upstairs," Bob whispered to Paul as he and the others crouched behind whatever suitable barricade was available in the drawing and dining rooms. They hid out of view of the second floor landing and stairs. Paul relayed this information to Joe and waited for his directions.

"It sounds like our men are pinned down on the first floor." Joe relayed to Phil. "It's not worth another casualty to press the attack, and it appears that Uday is not very interested in surrendering peacefully." Phil nodded his agreement. "OK, ask HQ for the big guns. Tell them that we're pulling out, and will meet them where we were dropped off, on the other side of the hill."

"Yes sir," Phil complied.

Joe began talking to Paul and Tim through his MICH. "Is everyone OK?....Good. I'm glad Manny will be all right....I want all of you to retreat through the hole in the wall....Yes, I've called in the big guns..."

Phil interrupted Joe's conversation. "Humvees and gunners with TOW missiles are in the area and can meet us in fifteen minutes. If the TOW missiles aren't enough, they will also be sending a couple of Apaches and an A-10 Warthog to finish the job. How's Manny?"

"Tim said he'll survive. Tell HQ that we have a wounded man. I'll be able to meet them as soon as we get all of the team safely away from the target zone. Possibly in fifteen minutes, but perhaps more time will be needed. Bob, Paul, and Jordan are in the drawing room, but Jared and Colin are on the other side of the stairs and will have to cross an exposed area to get to the hole in the wall. We need to get our men to safety before the others begin to flatten the building," Joe informed Phil through his MICH, then switched to another channel on the microphone. "Paul, get everyone out of there as quickly as possible and rendezvous with us back at Salah's place. We will stay here and begin distracting Uday and what's left of his men beginning in one minute."

"Yes sir." We'll lob a concussion grenade upstairs to distract them and make our exit. See you back at the ranch," Paul whispered, just as a few shots were fired from the second floor, probing for the locations of their enemy on the first floor.

"Stay safe." Joe commanded.

Paul signaled Jared, Colin, and the others by miming what was planned for the next minute. His message was that when he stood up and threw his MK3A2 grenade up the stairs, they all needed to run like hell through the drawing room, out the hole in the wall, and into the building next door. They knew that the grenade only had a five-second fuse, so they needed to be fast.

Joe turned his attention to creating the distraction. "Pete, you and Nick spray the third floor windows. Phil and I will do the same with the second floor. I've ordered the men to leave the building and we need to keep everyone else occupied for a minute or two. Put in full magazines, count to ten, and start shooting."

"Yes sir." Ten seconds later, bullets started flying through the window openings as the automatic firing was heard from across the street.

The rapid gun fire created the brief distraction required. Paul yelled to his men, "Go through the hole now!" As Colin and Jared dashed passed the stairs, Paul reached for a concussion grenade and, in one motion pulled the pin and threw it onto the second floor landing. Bob, Colin, Jared, Jordan were already jumping over to the next building. As soon as he heard the grenade bounce hit the floor upstairs, he turned, ran to the hole and jumped to the other side. When his feet hit the floor of the other house he stumbled and fell. The others were already stopped for a moment to recover their balance. When they saw Paul fall, they reached out to catch him.

"Are you OK?" Jordan asked as he helped Paul up.

"Yeah. I think so." As he stood up, his right leg buckled again and they could see blood streaming from his thigh.

"He's hit!" Jared yelled. "Let's get him out of here." He and Jordan each took an arm of Paul's and lifted him off the ground, along with all of his body armor. The others grabbed Paul's weapon and headed toward the back door through the kitchen. Bob grabbed Manny's weapon as Jason and Tim lifted their teammate to his feet and carried him out the back door and up the alley. When they were all out of the house, Tim realized their escape route could also easily become the escape route for Uday and the others.

"Bob, I'll take Manny's weapon. You and Colin take cover away from the back door and shoot to kill anyone that tries to come out of it. We don't want our friends to escape through the hole that we created."

"Yes sir," both men confirmed.

"Keep your headsets turned on. I'll let you know when to clear the area as soon as we know the big guns have arrived."

"Good idea," Colin said as he touched his earphones to make sure they were working.

The rest of the men moved quickly and silently behind the other houses, away from Nawaf's house, until they were at the other end of the block and could safely cross over to Salah's side of the street, down the back alley, and into the house.

"Joe, we're back at the house," Tim spoke into his MICH. "Paul was hit in the leg on his way out. I told Bob and Colin to take cover behind the house to make sure no one else comes out of the back door by way of the hole we blew through the two walls."

Joe stopped shooting when he heard Tim's message. "Thanks, Tim. Good idea. I hadn't thought of that possibility. When you get to the house, take Jared with you to the roof to keep watch in case anyone tries to go out the front door. They can't run far on the other side of the house without being seen. We'll be back in a couple of minutes." He turned to Phil and spoke in his headset to Pete and Nick. "Cease fire. They're all back at Salah's place." The "ratatatatat" of the automatic fire stopped and it was quiet. "Come on down. We need to get back to the house, and I need to get over to the drop-off point on the other side of the hill. They'll be waiting for my directions."

On the third and second floors of Nawaf's severely battered house, it was also quiet. The remaining defenders for Uday and Qusay were all silent as they listened for their attackers on the first floor. No one dared speak and give away his position. Finally, Uday called out, "How many are down there."

"There were four of us before the grenade went off. Now, we're only two."

"Are there any dead Americans?"

"We don't know. We haven't heard anything since the grenade and all the shooting from across the street."

"One of you go and check."

Uday heard someone go slowly down the stairs to the first floor. "There's no one here. They all escaped from a big hole they blew out of the drawing room wall."

The guard was one of the elite fighting men in the Iraqi Republican Guard. He wasn't usually rattled. Although he was well trained and looked the part of a battle-hardened soldier, for the previous five years he had been a bodyguard serving the Hussein family. His experience was always on the giving end of Ba'athist brutality and executions. This was the first time he was on the receiving end of a fierce firefight with America's elite soldiers. "Go through the hole and see if it leads to their escape route. Maybe we can use it for our escape." Qusay ordered.

The guard went through the hole and toward the back door that was left open. He came back into the safe house and shouted up the stairs. "It leads through the kitchen to a back door."

"Go outside and see if anyone is there."

The guard thought this could be a death sentence. What if there was an American sniper back there? The moment that he stuck his head out of the door, he would be shot. He also knew that if he didn't follow Qusay's orders, Qusay would shoot him. The man followed orders.

BANG! A shot was heard coming from the back of the house. "Damned Americans," Qusay sighed.

"One less fighter," Uday snarled.

"Whoever you are, come up here." Qusay ordered. "My son is wounded and I want to take him to that storage room below the kitchen so he'll be safe when the Americans return." The remaining guard came up the stairs. "Ahh, Sidiq. We're glad you're still alive. Help us carry Mustapha down the stairs."

Sidiq looked at Mustapha and the thick patch up blood below his right shoulder. "It doesn't look good," Sidiq thought to himself. The boy had his eyes open but he was barely moving.

Qusay took Mustapha's feet and Sidiq picked him up under his arms. Carefully, they began to carry the 14-year-old down the stairs, stopping frequently when Mustapha groaned in pain. Uday followed slowly behind them.

When Tim and the others carried Paul and Manny into Salah's drawing room and laid them gently on the floor, the two medics began working on them, and Hakim was there to greet them. "Are they going to be OK?"

Hakim asked as he bent down to where Jason was ripping off Manny's body armor and, with his knife, rapidly cutting away the corner of his shredded, blood-stained shirt to reveal and treat the wound. He could see that Jordan was also cutting away the pant leg where Paul was hit. Both men were bleeding heavily.

"Bob, find out when the helicopters will arrive to lift them out of here. They're both going to need a lot of blood," Jason directed. "How's Paul?" He asked Jordan.

"The bullet entered the top of his thigh, below his butt. There's no exit wound. I don't know what's been damaged, but he's bleeding a lot." Jordan said as he quickly tore open the packages for compression bandages. "The blood is oozing right now but, it's coming out fast. I don't know if an artery has been cut or not."

Hakim knew he was in the way at the moment and stepped back from the four men as Joe, Nick, Pete, and Phil ran through the door. Joe looked at Paul, Jason, Manny, and Jordan to see how badly they were hurt. "Are they going to make it?"

Jordan and Jason continued their work as Bob repeated the conversations the medics had with Hakim. "A helicopter is on the way and will be here any minute. As soon as Paul and Manny are stabilized, they'll get them to the operating rooms at the Marez MASH.

"Good. Nick and I are going to meet the convoy with the TOWs and be back with them soon. Jason, Jordon keep up the good work. We want to get Paul and Manny back, good as new." Joe said as he and Nick turned and headed out the door.

Hakim looked at Bob, "I forget; what's a TOW?"

"They're tube-launched optically-guided, wire-controlled missiles," Bob smiled. Hakim was so integrated with the team that the men occasionally forgot that he was a civilian and not as familiar with the US military hardware as they were.

Joe and Nick grabbed two bottles of water and hurried through the alley to the street. There they turned right and up two blocks to the road that paralleled the hill and intersected with the highway. It was a brisk five minute walk in 100 degree heat to where they met the convoy. There was an army captain standing next to the lead Humvee who saluted Joe as he and Nick walked up. The men returned the formality. "I'm glad you're here," Joe began. "We sustained two casualties before clearing the area.

Uday and his men put up a strong resistance, and we don't know how many of them are still alive."

"What do you recommend?" the captain asked.

"Can you pull up the satellite photo of this area?" Nick asked.

"If we can crowd around the front seat of this Humvee," the captain pointed to the lead vehicle. "There's a mounted computer on the dashboard. We can pull up the grid coordinates and look at the area." The men walked over to the Humvee as a soldier handed each of them another bottle of water, and Joe sat in the passenger seat as the captain sat in the driver's seat, turned on the computer ,and punched in the coordinates.

"We're here, beside this hill. The road that Nick and I just came from will take you to the street where the target house is located, here on the corner." Joe put his finger on the computer monitor. "You can see there is one street before you get to the safe house street. I suggest that you split your convoy so that two of your TOW missiles are pointed toward the house from one angle and two of your TOW missiles are pointed at the house from the other angle." Joe was pointing on the computer map as he talked so the captain would have a clear idea of what they should do. "The angles that your men will be firing from will also afford protection because it will be more difficult for them to aim anything at your Humvees from either corner of their house."

"Thank you, major. Anything else?"

"Give me fifteen minutes to get back to my men before you begin the operation. I need to move two of them from near the targeted house, and I want to station four of us in the house across the street to lay down fire as your guys roll into place."

"Sounds good. It's 1236 now. We'll begin rolling at 1300. Is that enough time?"

Joe nodded, "Thanks, captain. We'll put ear plugs on under our headsets. Those TOW missile explosions are loud!" Joe and the captain saluted each other. Then the captain went to explain the plan to his men while Joe and Nick hustled back to the house to take Pete and Colin, a backpack of water, and ammunition back to the house where they were positioned earlier so they could create another diversion for the convoy. They were heartened to see two helicopters overhead landing in the field at the end of the street.

"Thank God!" Nick said as he watched a team of medics jump out with stretchers from each helicopter with as they landed. Bob was running up the alley to meet them. Nick and Joe began running with them back to Salah's house and their wounded friends.

Jordan looked up from where he was pressing hard on a compression bandage on Paul's leg. "We're glad you're here! The bleeding hasn't slowed down and he is slipping in and out of consciousness." Without saying a word, they laid the stretcher down and gently lifted Paul onto it. Then one of the medics worked for a minute to connect a bag of IV fluids to Paul's arm before lifting him up to carry him back to the helicopter. The other two medics were working with Jason to prepare Manny for transport also. "Do you want us to go with you?" Jordan asked as the two teams began to walk out the kitchen door."

"Thanks. The two of you did a good job keeping these guys alive. We'll get them back to the hospital in twenty minutes, then into surgery." They were moving at a fast pace. Jordan and Jason trotted along with them to see their colleagues get loaded onto the helicopters and headed to the emergency operating theaters.

Qusay and Sidiq gently laid Mustapha down on the second floor landing for a moment to rest. "Papa, papa..." Mustapha said quietly. Then he slipped away.

"Those damn Americans! What have we done to them to deserve this? And where are our people to help defend us?" Qusay's son had just died in front of him and he was in despair.

"We knew he was dying, Qusay," Uday said coldly. "We need to focus on those American bastards. We've always crushed our enemies, and we will crush these enemies or die fighting. Let's fight with honor. We will defend the honor of Saddam Hussein and live to tell about it." Uday remained defiant as he slowly stood up from the stairs where he was sitting. "Sidiq, the RPG that Mustapha had is still upstairs. Get it for me and bring the two remaining rocket grenades with it."

Sidiq walked up the stairs on his errand. "Uday, this may be it," Qusay said in a resigned voice.

"Let's see how many Americans we can take with us, Qusay. Our father will be proud." Sidiq returned down the stairs and was handing Uday the RPG when they all heard the rumble of several Humvees. Sidiq looked around and grabbed one of the AK-47s and several magazines that were near one of his dead comrades. Qusay did the same.

"I'm not going to limp back up those stairs," Uday told the others. "Find your best position. I'm going to blast whatever is coming down the road. See you both in heaven."

"In sha' allh," Sidiq whispered under his breath as he ran back up the stairs with his gun and ammo.

Qusay was running to another window on the second floor when the special operators across the street opened fire with four M4A1s set on automatic. He was struck by two of the bullets coming through the window opening and fell to the floor.

The first Humvee pulled into position where the gunner could fire his missile. Uday stepped from behind the corner window and fired his RPG rocket grenade at the Humvee. He missed his target but blasted a big hole in the wall of the house only thirty feet away. When Sidiq heard the grenade explosion, he began firing his AK-47 out of a window while remaining behind the wall. It was his last, desperate fight as an elite Iraqi Republican Guard.

When the Humvees were in place on the two intersecting streets that formed the corner boundaries of the house, the TOW gunners began firing their twelve missiles in rapid succession toward the house. The building started exploding on all three levels. When they were finished, there was only a shell of a house and a large cloud of dust. Then, the sounds of helicopters were heard overhead as the Apaches arrived and fired M2 .50 caliber machine guns into the crumbling structure. When the helicopters finished their work, an A-10 Warthog flew overhead and emptied more rounds into the large pile of smoldering rubble. Then there was silence.

By three p.m., the dust was beginning to clear. The captain and soldiers with the four Humvees, along with two forensic specialists, who were in a fifth Humvee that remained safely at a distance, began to look through the rubble. There was a lot of concrete to sift through, and it appeared they would require specialized heavy equipment to lift the large chunks of wall and upper floors that fell in on the building as it collapsed. Another convoy with the appropriate equipment was requested and granted from HQ. The work continued into the night, with large portable lighting systems to provide good visibility.

"We made it back as soon as possible. Uday, Qusay, and the rest of them are all rolled up into the rubble of Nawaf's former home. How are they?" Joe asked Jordan and Jason as he rushed into Salah's house, followed by Nick, Pete, and Colin.

"They're both in surgery." Jason said. "Bob, you haven't heard anything more, have you?"

"No, not yet. I was told we wouldn't know anything for a couple of hours."

Tim was walking down the stairs after coming from the roof. "We need to keep them in our prayers," he said to no one in particular. "That was quite a finish," Tim continued. "We enjoyed watching the fireworks from the roof."

"Yeah. It's over. The men from the convoy brought two forensic guys with them and they've begun looking for the bodies. I hope there's enough of Uday to identify him." Joe paused to consider if there were any other urgent matters that he needed to think about. "Hakim, please call Nawaf and Salah and tell them they can all return home. Have them come in through the alley and the kitchen door. I want to prepare Nawaf, Mohassin, and Shalan before they see what is left of their house." He wondered how he was going to explain this to the family when it occurred to him that the two Al Zaidan families had earned fifteen million dollars as a reward for leading them to Uday. "Phil, I want to send a message to HQ requesting permission to inform the families that they will receive the reward for targeting Uday for us."

"Yes sir," Phil responded as he turned on his computer.

Joe looked around the room. Hakim, Nick, Pete, Phil, Jordan, Jason, Tim, and Bob were relaxing. Jared and Colin were on the roof on watch. "It's been an exhausting day. Thank you all for the terrific job each of you did to make this operation a success. Tim is right. Each of you, in your own way, please say a prayer for Paul and Manny; ask that they come through their operations and not suffer any lasting damage as a result of their wounds."

"Sir," Phil interrupted. "HQ approves telling the families about their earned reward and says to inform them they will be asked to come to HQ in a few days to sign papers and work with our finance people regarding how and where to deposit the money."

"Good. That will make it easier to tell Nawaf and Mohassin that their house no longer exists." Joe smiled and the others also nodded their approval. "OK. That's all I have to say. Phil, did HQ give instructions regarding our return to FOB Marez?"

"I'll ask."

Joe added one more suggestion, "I suspect that we'll be returning this house back to Salah and his family tonight. Organize your things and take it easy. Hopefully, we'll all have clean bunks and hot water showers later tonight."

"Sir, HQ said that they are sending a convoy to pick us up and be ready to go by 1800." Phil advised.

Joe looked at his watch and noted they only had one hour before their departure. He began to organize his gear along the others. There wasn't much to it, but like the others, his bed roll was out, along with a few MREs that were never touched, and his weapon needed cleaning after its extensive use during the day. He was just finishing up with his M4A1 when Salah led the Al Zaidan and Al Atwan families through the kitchen to greet the team. Salah and the others all looked excited and happy.

He reached out his hand to Joe and shook it rapidly. Nawaf, Shalan, Othman, and Abdullah also reached out to shake the hands of Hakim and the other soldiers as Mohassin, Walla, and Hana bowed to each of the special operators and Hakim. Lara stood in line with the men to shake Joe's hand and smiled. "I told them that the American custom was to shake hands when you want to congratulate someone, that you don't know well, who has done something very special for you." Lara's grip on Joe's hand was firm but she didn't go up and down, as if working the handle of a water pump, like the Nawaf and the others. "Thank you, major.

"Lara, you are very welcome." Joe didn't know Abdullah and his wife Hana. "Who are they?"

"They are the parents of my cousin's husband." She stopped shaking his hand and told him the short version of her extraordinary story. "Aziz and my cousin, Yasmine, were married in 2002 and my friends and I were with them near Baghdad University when Uday killed Aziz in front of us. The following day he killed Yasmine and held my friends and me captive near Fallujah until we escaped when the war started. We are all very grateful for what you did today. Uday and his thugs deserved to die."

"You never told us how you got here."

"I've told you that I was from Ann Arbor, Michigan. My parents, Omar and Nadia Al Mohammed, moved there in 1989 when I was a baby, and eventually we became US citizens. My father is a Doctor and works with the University of Michigan. Last year, when things seemed calm, my uncles and aunts invited me to spend time with them here in Iraq so I could learn who I am as an Iraqi-American, understand my heritage, and connect with my Iraqi family. None of us had any idea at the time that there would be a war with the United States. " Lara paused as she thought about them for a moment and wiped a tear from the corner of her eye. "Major, I want to go home now."

Joe became emotional for a moment as he looked into the eyes of this strong young woman. "We'll get you home as soon as we can, Lara," he promised.

When everyone completed congratulating everyone else, Joe asked the men to step to one side and invited the families to take a seat on the sofas lining the walls around the room. "Lara, I'd like you to translate for me. We'll give Hakim a rest." Hakim and his men smiled. "I've been given approval to inform Nawaf, Salah, and Lara that due to their very proactive efforts to help us find and kill Uday Hussein, your families have earned the fifteen million dollar reward that the United States offered. Within the next few days, the three of you will be invited to the US. Army Headquarters for Nineveh Province near the Mosul airport to sign papers and tell us how and where you would like the money disbursed. Give this serious consideration. It's a lot of money."

Lara had to pause and looked at the floor for a moment to think about this message. She was surprised by the fact that she would also share in the reward. The families waited for her to talk. Apparently, she had pondered Joe's message for what must have seemed like a long time. When she looked up, the room was completely silent and the families were staring at her, waiting for her to speak.

When she completed her translation everyone stood up. The men started shouting "HOORAH!" and the women began to loudly shout "LULULULU!" to show their very enthusiastic approval. Joe, Hakim, and the soldiers all began clapping happily to express their approval and the congratulations around the room began again.

When things settled down, Joe shared the rest of his information as he looked at Lara, Nawaf, Mohassin, and Shalan. "Please sit down again, I have some bad news."

Lara had a knot form in her stomach. "What could be bad news today?" she asked herself.

All of the families sat down except for Lara who remained standing next to Joe as he looked at Nawaf and Mohassin. "Your house doesn't exist anymore."

Lara took a deep breath as she absorbed this. She knew how Nawaf and Mosassin were going to react. Then she translated the sad news to them. Immediately, Mohassin began to wail and cry uncontrollably.

"Why?" Nawaf's question was translated to Joe.

This time, Joe turned to Hakim to help him with this. Lara appeared to be having a problem dealing with this information as well. "Hakim, tell them that we had to demolish the house to make sure there was no one left in it to kill one of us. Paul and Manny were already badly wounded and we didn't want any more of our friends hurt or killed." Hakim translated this and Mohassin's wailing quieted down to a whimper. Walla and Hana came over to sit by, and comfort her. Joe continued, "I know we cannot replace all of you family memories associated with the house, but I will talk with the men who are looking for the bodies buried in the rubble and tell them that if they find photos or other personal family item that are not terribly damaged, they should save them for you." Hakim translated this as Joe thought of anything else he needed to tell them. "Nawaf, you and your family will not be allowed to walk around what is left of your house until all of the bodies have been found and removed. This is important."

Hakim translated, and Nawaf, Mohassin, and Shalan nodded their heads, then Nawaf spoke to Hakim. "He says they understand. All of their lives were invested in that house. Without it, he says, they have nothing."

Joe nodded, "I understand and will explain this to my commander and others. Memories are really all we have to sustain any of us. We'll do our best to retrieve as many of them for you as we can."

Lara took over from Hakim and explained this to her relatives. Nawaf spoke again. "My uncle said that you have given us several days to think about many things. He, Salah, and their families will use this time to consider what they should do now with their lives. He also thanked you and your soldiers again for what all of you did today and said that his family will pray for Paul and Manny."

Joe, Hakim, and the other soldiers breathed a sigh of relief. "Lara, tell them that we sincerely thank all of you for helping us find Uday Hussein and for how gracious all of you were to us. We really appreciate everything that each of you did and hope we can remain friends after this war is over." Lara translated this. Then Joe continued, "The army is sending a convoy to pick us up in about fifteen minutes. I am going now to talk with the men that are looking for the bodies and will tell them about my promise to you so they will be careful to remove any of your things that are still recognizable. When I get back, the convoy should be here. Nawaf, Salah," Joe turned again toward Lara, "and Lara, thank you again for everything. I'll see you in a few days."

Lara translated this and there was silence in the room. It was filled with emotion for what they had gained and lost in a single day. Joe picked up his gear and weapon and turned, this time to the front door and gate toward the quickly developing search party of men, heavy lifting equipment, and very bright lights.

Three days later, Nawaf, Lara and Salah were picked up and driven to FOB Marez to review and sign the necessary paperwork. Hakim and Joe were there as witnesses for when the army finance officers described the terms of the reward. They greeted their friends at the door with other news and big smiles as they shook each of their hands. "Lara, I'll let you translate what I'm about to say for your uncles. They also found Qusay's body in the rubble. Your reward of fifteen million has been doubled to thirty million dollars!"

Lara stood still for a moment, not believing what she was hearing. "You're kidding!"

Joe and Hakim started laughing, "No, we're not. Those men over there will tell you the details of your reward so all of you will believe us."

Lara let out a loud shriek of joy as she gave a big hug to Joe and Hakim. Nawaf and Salah stood still, not knowing what was going on. They had never seen Lara display such affection for two men who were not even in the family and act like a little girl with a new toy. After hugging Hakim, she turned excitedly to her uncles and told them what she just learned. Then they both shouted, "*Alhamd lillah*!" and also turned to hug Joe and Hakim.

It took a moment for them to recover from the exuberant hugs. When he recovered from his surprise, Joe continued, "Let me introduce you to the men who will help you with your reward." He walked them over to a long table where they were introduced and they all sat down. The reward also included visas and transportation to the United States, and the prospect of expedited processing of refugee status, as well as green cards so the family members could apply for .S citizenship. Lara was surprised to learn that the Department of State and army had already contacted her parents, and based on their information, were able to create a new US passport, which they handed to her at the meeting.

"Lara, we can get you on a plane home today, if you like. What have you and the families decided to do with the money?" Joe asked on behalf of the finance team.

Lara conferred with Nawaf and Salah for a moment. "We've been talking about this for the last three days," she began. "Thank you so much for this passport and a flight home. Before I go, I must return to Salah's house and say good-bye to everyone. Can I fly out tomorrow?"

"If not tomorrow, it will be on the next flight out of Erbil," he said. "We'll have to check with our travel office to figure out what will work. Come back tomorrow, ready to go, and we'll give you a helicopter ride to Erbil and provide you with accommodations until the next flight to the States. Is that OK?"

"Thank you Joe." Lara had been overwhelmed with how quickly her life was changing for the better, but was getting more accustomed to it. "That's very OK." She said with a smile and a slight nod with her hand over her heart. Then she continued on behalf of her uncles. "My uncle Nawaf says that he and uncle Salah have discussed this with their families when they first learned of the reward. They frequently dreamed about what they would do if the Americans really did provide the reward money. Both of my uncles request that the Americans help their families, and the family of Abdullah Al-Atwan move to America and protect them from the Ba'athists. The Al-Atwan family is related to the Al Zaidan family by marriage of their son Aziz to Yasmine, my cousin. I told you what happened to them." She looked Joe in the eyes to ensure that he understood the importance of this request.

"I understand, Lara, and I will do everything I can to make this happen," Joe promised.

Lara smiled and continued. "My other uncles—Sabah, Wadhah, and Moeyd Al Zaidan—will stay in Mosul to manage all of the family's businesses and properties.

When the administrative requirements were completed, Joe stepped out of the room and returned with Colonel O'Connor and introduced him to the Iraqis. "The United States is pleased to honor its commitment to pay these rewards and help your uncles and their families, including the Abdullah Al-Atwan family, move to the United States under our protection. We will give them new identities to protect them from the Ba'athists and others who may want to seek retribution." Turning to Lara, the colonel continued. "Your family, I think, would receive favorable consideration if your other uncles, Sabah, Wadhah, and Moeyd, decided to petition for refugee status and immigrate to the United States where they will be safe. Iraq and Mosul will be a very dangerous place to live for a while—especially if others learn that your uncles helped us find the Hussein brothers."

Lara thought about this for a moment and translated this for her uncles. She also mentioned her concerns for their safety.

"Lara, we've talked about this possibility with your other uncles. You know how stubborn they all are," Nawaf began. "They've all been through many dangerous times almost as bad as this. Your uncles are allied with the powerful tribe of Sheikh Abdullah Al-Kalifa. The tribe has never trusted the Ba'athists and will protect our families from any harm. Iraq is their country, and they want to protect their interests and ours. Perhaps, *In'sha' allh*, we can return home someday." Lara translated this for Joe, the colonel, and the other Americans in the room.

"Well, we can only hope that the Iraqis will help us bring peace to this country so that we can leave as soon as possible. But tell them that remaining here is not safe and probably a bad idea," Colonel O'Connor cautioned.

Lara translated this and Salah replied. "My uncle says thanks for your concern but don't worry."

"OK Lara, you certainly come from a brave family," Joe said. "Tell your uncles that Hakim will work with your family and the army to facilitate whatever arrangements that they would like. You will probably be home in Michigan in less than a week. After all of this, what are you going to do back home?"

"I want to be a doctor. With help from Uncle Nawaf and Aunt Mohassin, I began to study medicine in Baghdad last year before all of this happened. I'll begin studies at the University of Michigan. Perhaps someday, when this war is over, I can come back to Iraq to help rebuild this country as a doctor, which is what my father had always dreamed of doing." She looked at Joe, "And you, Major Joe? What are your plans after Iraq?"

Joe smiled at this very forthright, self-assured young woman. "I'm married to a wonderful wife and have two great sons. I've promised her that after this tour, I'll return home and find a job that will keep me there, with my family."

Lara smiled. "Good. Your family probably misses you very much."

"They do, Lara. Perhaps we can all meet again someday in the US"

"I would like that," Lara agreed. "I have one last request. Tomorrow, when I return here, can I see Paul and Manny? How are they?

Joe smiled. "They'll both survive. Manny had his shoulder shattered by the bullet, and his wound will take a long time to heal. Paul was lucky. Although he lost a lot of blood, the bullet didn't sever an artery. They will be very happy to see you. I think they'll also be returning home to Fort Bragg in a day or two."

That is good news!" Lara agreed. "Joe, peace be with you, *Alssalam ealaykum*"

"*Ealaykum 'an alssalam*. Peace be with you also, Lara," Joe replied. "OK, we've got to go. Lara, tell your uncles thanks again and good luck with your studies. I'm sure that you will do very well." He bowed toward Nawaf and Salah and they bowed back. Then he walked out of the building as Hakim told the colonel that their guests needed transportation back to Salah's home.

Chapter Thirty-Two:
A Happy Ending, Almost

Lara's parents were watching the evening news and waiting for the call to tell them that Lara had finally arrived in America. The television was only a distraction to keep them both from pacing around the house in excitement and anticipation. They were informed that Lara was alive and well in Mosul on July 22, when an army officer and representative from the Department of State knocked on their door to tell them the good news. The men were also there to obtain the requisite information to prepare a new passport and deliver it to her in Mosul. "We'll call you when your daughter arrives in the US," one of the men told them as they walked out of the door.

"It has been confirmed in the city of Mosul, Iraq, that on July 22, the elite Army Delta Special Operations Team, supported by a large number of Humvees armed with TOW missiles, Apache Helicopters, and an A-10 Warthog killed Uday and Qusay Hussein, who were the sons of Saddam Hussein. Qusay's 14-year-old son and twelve others were also killed. An Iraqi informant helped lead our forces to a large home where a ferocious gun fight broke out, during which two US soldiers were wounded. News of the deaths of Saddam's sons quickly spread throughout Iraq, and there were spontaneous outbreaks of enthusiastic cheering among throngs of people in the streets of Baghdad and elsewhere in Iraq. Uday and Qusay were responsible for the deaths of tens of thousands of men, women, and children during Saddam's reign of terror. Their deaths symbolize the end of the Saddam and

Ba'ath party era and a new beginning for the country. That's all for the July 30 edition of the evening news."

Omar turned the TV off and looked out the front window. "When will they call us? This waiting is driving me crazy."

"Me too. It's been a week!" Nadia agreed. "Omar, we need to get out of the house. We've been staying home every night waiting for the phone to ring. It'll do us good to get out. It's a nice summer evening, and the weather outside is perfect."

"What if the phone rings and we're not here?"

"We'll only walk around the block and won't be gone more than ten minutes. Take your cell phone. They'll call us on that if no one answers the house phone," Nadia suggested. Omar was still getting used to his new high-tech phone. "Both of us need to get some air and walk off some of our anxiety," she said as she grabbed Omar's arm and pulled him gently out the front door.

The walk around the block wasn't long. It was perhaps ten minutes when they turned the corner and were back on their street. They could see someone, five houses down, knocking on their front door. "Is that Lara?" Omar asked incredulously.

Nadia was already running down the street toward their house. "Lara! Lara!" Tears were running down her eyes as she stopped a moment to catch her breath.

Omar soon caught up to his wife just as Lara began running toward them. Soon they were all embracing each other and crying tears of deeply emotional joy.

"It happened so fast! The army got me out of Mosul on July 27 and I've been traveling ever since. I wanted to call you several times, but I was too emotional and afraid I couldn't express my love and happiness that I was coming home to you over the phone. I only wanted to be here with you. Mom and Dad, I'm sorry. I must have made your lives miserable for the last six months."

Omar was crying without shame as he hugged his daughter. "God! How I've prayed for this day! Lara, now that you're home, our misery is gone! Thank God that you're alive and well!"

Nadia grabbed her daughter's hands and looked into her eyes as both of them had tears running down their cheeks. "Let's go inside, before our neighbors come out to see what is going on," she said half laughing, half crying.

The three of them walked past the last two houses and entered their home as Omar picked up her small travel bag from the door step. "Come sit down. What can we get for you? Nadia, please make some tea for our long-lost daughter. Lara, are you tired? Do you want to rest first?" Omar couldn't stop talking in his excitement.

"Thanks. Dad and Mom, it's so good to be home and to see you again," Lara said as she wiped more tears off her face. "We can talk now. I want to tell you everything," she began as Nadia ran into the kitchen and came out with a pitcher and poured three glasses of water for Lara, Omar, and herself. "You remember: the last time we talked on the phone was in early February, when I was visiting Uncle Nawaf and Aunt Mohassin. After I spoke with you I returned to Baghdad and the university. Then the terrible things began to happen..." She began to relate the entire ordeal as the evening passed quickly. Omar and Nadia were like the others, frequently interrupting Lara for more clarification or details. Omar looked at his watch and noticed it was already midnight. Five hours had flown by before they realized it. "So the other reason I couldn't tell you that I was coming home is because the army and Department of State thought that it may create some danger for us if others knew that I was in Iraq and involved with helping the Americans find the Hussein brothers. They wanted to conceal where I am now, just in case Saddam's people would be looking for us."

Omar and Nadia nodded their understanding. "Where's Nawaf, Salah, and their families? I thought they were coming to America with you."

"They were beginning preparations to leave when I left Mosul. Uncle Nawaf, Salah, and Abdullah had some business matters to discuss with Uncles Sabah, Wadah, and Moyed before they could leave. Also the army needed time to arrange the details and logistics for the families to come to America and settle somewhere safe, with new identities to protect them from retaliation by the Ba'athists." Lara sighed, "Before I left, the army told me they couldn't even disclose to us where they would be settled until the danger passes."

"Who knows when that will be?" Omar also sighed sadly. "I agree. No one wants the Ba'athists and their hired thugs to have a hint of where Nawaf, Salah, Abdullah, and their families will be living. At least they will have plenty of reward money to live on."

"I've asked the army to put my—really, our—share of the reward money into a private bank account so only we will know the code and have access to it," Lara said in a surprisingly matter-of-fact tone.

"It's past midnight. I can't even think about that now. Your mom and I are just thankful and relieved that you are home with us again," Omar said as he yawned. "Let's all go to bed. I just pray this nightmare will end soon. Maybe it will. I saw President Bush on television saying that the mission in Iraq has already been accomplished. Do you think so, Lara?" he asked as he stood up from his chair when Nadia and Lara got up from their couch.

Lara was more exhausted than her parents and ready for a very long sleep in her own bed. They all began to walk up the stairs to their bedrooms when Lara quietly answered her father's question, "No, Dad, I don't think so."

Chapter Thirty-Three: The Violence Continues December 2004

Sadly, Lara's prognosis proved correct. The expanding US occupation of Iraq included the establishment of the Coalition Provisional Authority under the direction of former Ambassador Paul Bremer in May 2003. One of his first mandates was to ban the continuation of the Ba'ath party in all of its forms and functions and to disband the Iraqi Army.

This effectively put millions of middle-income civil servants, people who administered the government of Iraq and many of the municipal services, out of work. Many of the troops that still had some allegiance to the Iraqi Army were demoralized by the invasion and were not sure what they should do. If many of the Ba'ath civil servants and military were unsure about their loyalties immediately after the invasion, Bremer's mandate helped make up their minds when their jobs and means to support their families evaporated with the stroke of his pen. The frustration of being occupied and subjugated to the whims of the CPA, lack of a paycheck, and more time on their hands than if they were gainfully employed swayed many throughout Iraq to join the nascent resistance to the occupation. This was certainly the situation in Mosul and Nineveh Province.

It was also troubling that despite finding and destroying many military installations and munitions, the US did not find all of them. The underground Ba'ath resistance fighters knew where all of the munitions were and wasted no time removing an estimated 380 tons of conventional explosives from the Al Qa'qaa industrial complex, about forty-eight kilometers south of Baghdad. Reliable sources suggested that the stockpile was there at the beginning of the invasion, but by October 2004, the facility was empty. This cache and others around Iraq were removed to new hiding places controlled by the insurgents. These munitions and weapons were quickly used to produce the small but very deadly improvised explosive devices, creating bombs for suicide attacks and landmines that were devastating to US military vehicles, particularly the Humvees. The autumn of 2003 resulted in increased attacks on the US forces and their Iraqi sympathizers.

The gate bell rang for about a minute before Wadah Al Zaidan made his way out of the house to speak with the young man who was anxious to meet with him. When he walked back into his house, his wife Sama greeted him with a question, "Who was that?"

"It's a messenger from Sheikh Faizan Abdullah. He's called a council meeting to discuss cooperation with the Americans. I've been invited to attend. This should be interesting. I'll be home late tonight."

"Wadah, it's already late. I'm worried about the rumors and don't want anything to happen to you." Sama was a young woman married to the youngest of the Al Zaidan brothers, who was in his early thirties. The rumors were that US sympathizers, including their relatives, were going to be targeted. She had no doubt that Wadah would be among those considered for assassination.

"Be careful," she urged. "Everyone knows that Sheikh Faizan is talking to the Americans. There are enemies who want to kill him and everyone associated with him."

"Don't worry, Sama," Wadah smiled and gave her a gentle kiss as he grabbed the keys to his car. "It's been relatively quiet in Mosul for a while. Hopefully, the insurgents are more interested in causing problems elsewhere in Iraq." He gave her a hug and kissed her again as he walked out the door. "Don't worry. I'll be careful."

The meeting was in the Hayy Al Yarmuk district, only a few miles from Wadah's home. It was near the former homes of his brothers Nawaf and Salah. He took a slight detour to see what the neighborhood looked like since he hadn't been there in a while. Although it was only six p.m., the street was lit up with bright half moon in the sky. Nawaf's formerly grand house was now a pile of concrete rubble and broken cinder blocks with only a few tell-tale signs, such as mangled pipes and windows, of what once stood on the corner lot. The house next door to the pile of rubble was also empty. In the dim light, Wadah could see the gaping hole in its side wall that the Americans created when they blasted their way into Nawaf's home to attack Uday Hussein and his bodyguards. Across the street a battered house had shattered windows and a pock-marked front.

He drove slowly toward the other end of the street and saw one or two lights in several of the other houses. "At least some of the neighbors moved back," he thought to himself. However, his brother Salah's home was dark. Wadah had a feeling of loss as he drove by, knowing that it could be a long time before he would see Nawaf, Salah, and their families again.

He turned right at the corner and drove another kilometer to the meeting place. When he arrived, he walked through the building door into a large room. There were perhaps twenty other men dressed in an assortment of western attire and traditional Iraqi robes. Across the room were Ibrahim, Abu, and Azzam, close friends of the family.

Wadah walked across the room to meet his friends, "*Marhabaan*. It's good to see all of you! These dangerous times have made it difficult to get together like we used to."

"Well, Saddam is in prison and the Hussein brothers are dead. Perhaps it's time for the Americans to go home and leave the rest of us alone," Abu said.

"Then what?" Azzam replied. "The country is a mess and the Americans have created a lot of destruction. They should pay for the damage!"

"If we ask them to pay for the damage, they will certainly want to stay here longer. Do we want that? We don't need to be colonized again, like the British did in the 1920s," Ibrahim observed.

"Gentlemen, the fighting is not over. There are still many Ba'athists and others who want to prevent the creation of a free Iraq, and they're becoming very dangerous. I'm sure you've heard the recent rumors. Maybe we should ask the Americans to help us end the violence and rebuild the country," Wadah added his thoughts to the conversation.

"The Americans seem like they're only interested in helping us be free from the Ba'athists and the Iranians, not rebuilding. Since Bremer dissolved the Iraqi Army and fired the midlevel workers who were holding the country together, the country is in worse shape than ever." When Azzam looked up, he saw a portly older man in a white dishdash with gold trim on the sleeves. "There's Sheikh Faizan; let's see what he has to say."

The sheikh walked over to the podium in the front of the room and began to address the small gathering. "Brothers, thank you for coming. I met with the American general. It appears the Americans are genuinely interested in helping us. He said they're not here as occupiers. We'll see. However, they do want to help pay for the war damage and help us in other ways. They've provided me with a list of proposals for American-funded projects that will help the citizens of Mosul and Nineveh Province. The American general wanted me to share these ideas with you."

He looked down at the list for a moment, then gazed into the room of his friends and some of his neighbors. In the back of the room, two men walked in whom he didn't recognize. They wore heavy coats and seemed out of place in this gathering. "Welcome, do I know you?"

The two men continued walking down the center of the room as the others stared at them for a moment, wondering who they were. "Death to Americans, and death to the collaborators!" That was the last thing anyone in the building heard. The men both revealed their suicide vests filled with very powerful RDX explosives and detonated them. BOOM! The room, everyone inside, and building were instantly consumed in a huge explosion.

The sound of the blast was heard for over several miles. At a house not far from where Wadah had driven on his way to the meeting was a sinister man in his mid thirties with a commanding presence. Wearing black clothes and holding an AK-47 next to him, he received a message from a subordinate. "Good! We will strike fear into all Iraqis. Have our people contacted the press to blame the Shia for blowing up the building?"

His comrade smiled. "Yes sir. Tomorrow all the Iraqi and Middle Eastern news channels will be blaming Shia terrorists for this."

The man was Abu Musab al-Zarqawi, the leader of al-Qaeda in Iraq. "Our brother Osama bin Laden helped us begin this fight here in Iraq. Soon everyone will think the Americans are helping the Shia kill Sunnis, and our attacks on Shia mosques will make the Shia believe that the Sunnis are their enemy with support from the Americans. Al-Qaeda will become a powerful force that controls Sunnis and Shia militia against the Americans and each other."

At the Al Mohammed home in Ann Arbor, Lara and Omar were watching the evening news while Nadia prepared dinner. "The Forward Operating

Base Marez bombing took place on December 21, 2004. Twenty-two were killed in an attack on a dining hall at the forward operating base next to the main US military airfield at Mosul, US soldiers, contract employees, and Iraqis allied with the US military were among the dead and wounded. Perhaps related to this, there was a suicide bombing that killed thirty Iraqis attending a meeting near the Al Yarmuk district of Mosul. The cause of both terrorist attacks are being investigated."

"Marez was where Major Joe and his team were stationed. I hope none of them were in the attack, and I hope none of our relatives were hurt in the Al Yarmuk attack." Lara said. "What a mess." She paused a moment as she remembered when she was visiting the FOB eighteen months ago. "Do you think things will get better, Dad?"

Omar shook his head and looked at his daughter as he turned off the TV. "If they don't have a lot of Iraqi-Americans working with them, they will fail. What do Americans from Detroit or Ann Arbor know about Iraq? Nothing—unless they're from Iraq. How are they going to start developing cooperation and build trust in Iraq if the US military doesn't understand the ways and culture of the Iraqi people or can't speak the language?"

Lara looked out the window as the lights reflected the snow that was falling against the dark night. She could see someone walk up the steps to knock on their front door and got up to see who it was. "Danny! Look at you! What a surprise! Come in." Her good buddy from high school was wearing a Marine uniform.

When Nadia heard Lara, she came in from the kitchen and saw Danny. She and Omar came over to greet him. "It appears that the army is treating you well, Danny." Omar reached out to shake his hand. "I'm not familiar with military ranks. Are you a captain or colonel now?"

"Neither, sir. I wish I were. But I just became a noncommissioned officer. He proudly pointed to his sergeant's insignia. My buddies now call me 'Sarge.'" Danny smiled and corrected Omar. "Sir, I'm wearing a marine uniform."

Omar nodded approvingly. "Sorry, I'm not very familiar military uniforms either."

"Please come in, sit down. I knew that you went to Kosovo on your first assignment. Where are you going next?" Lara asked.

"I've spent the last six months training at Camp Lejeune, North Carolina. Next week, I leave for Iraq to join the 24th Marine Expeditionary

Unit, 1st Marine Division in the city of Hilla, near the ancient ruins of Babylon," Danny said with some pride.

"We were just watching the news." Lara looked concerned. "I don't know about Hilla, but there were two terrible bombings near Mosul, where my relatives are from. What will your job be?"

"I'll be attached to the 1st Reconnaissance Battalion." Danny explained. "I'm hoping that I'll get to go with the civil military affairs teams to meet with the Iraqi people. I understand that in civil affairs, the primary responsibility is to learn as much as possible from the people they talk with. It helps the officers do a better job planning how to keep the peace.

"It sounds like you've memorized the marine handbook on this," Omar smiled. He was only kidding. "Will these teams have civilians who can speak Arabic and be familiar with the Iraqi people to help them?

"I don't know," Danny said.

"It sounds like your colleagues will have a real challenge," Omar replied. "I hope they can find some Arabic-speaking translators and Iraqi-American advisors who can help them understand the attitudes and culture of the people they'll be meeting with."

"Yes sir, I think the marines are trying to recruit Iraqi-Americans and others who can speak Arabic to work with the teams and units like mine. Hey, Lara, you've been to Iraq and speak Arabic. You'd be a natural for this kind of work. I have the name of the recruitment company for these jobs. You've never told me much in our emails about your time in Iraq. I'm guessing it wasn't very exciting; otherwise, I would have heard more about it. Come on, this could be a real adventure."

Lara wasn't smiling. Her university studies were going well and the memories of her experience in Iraq were still too fresh and painful for her to consider such a possibility. "No, Danny. I saw many very terrible things in Iraq that I don't want to think or talk about."

Danny was embarrassed by her response. He had no idea what she had encountered there. "I'm sorry," he paused for a moment, not knowing what else to say. "Well, it will be a new adventure for me."

"Danny, we know how friendly you are with everyone," Nadia changed the subject away from Lara's sad recollections. "This, I'm sure, will help with your new job, but be very careful. We want you to come back safely."

"Thanks Mrs. Al-Mohammed, I'll be careful. Actually I'm looking forward to this assignment. I've had time with the marines to think about what I want to do some day. I think that I'd be good at helping people overseas. This may be a good opportunity that will help me learn more about how to do this."

"Yes Danny, I'm sure you'll do very well in public relations, which I assume is the same as the marine civil affairs," Omar surmised. "I've always admired your friendly and cheerful nature. This assignment may be very interesting for you." Omar became very serious as he looked Danny in the eyes. "Just stay safe."

"Most of the time, I'll be part of a convoy, driving around Babil Province and reporting back to HQ on what we see. I understand that region has been pretty quiet compared to other parts of Iraq." Danny paused again to drive out any trepidation that he was having. "I'll be OK."

"South Iraq is a big area, but like all of Iraq it has a lot of history. You may want to read the Old Testament of the Bible if you have time. You'll learn that many things in the book of Daniel happened in Babylon," Omar advised. "Actually the ancient Tower of Babel was located near the Babylon ruins. Let me know if you see it."

"Yes sir. If I go there and see it, I'll definitely let you know," Danny said with a smile.

Lara repeated her parent's concern and their advice. "Just be safe. Do you want to have dinner with us?"

"Thanks Lara and Mr. and Mrs. Al-Mohammed. I only have this weekend to visit with my folks before returning to my unit and deploying to Iraq. I just wanted to stop by and say hello before I leave. Lara, if you change your mind about applying for an interpreter's job in Iraq, let me know. It would be really cool to work with you over there."

"Thanks, Danny. I promised my folks that I would finish my undergraduate degree and apply to medical school in a couple of years."

"Danny, we want to keep our only daughter safe and sound. You take care of yourself and come back to Ann Arbor safe and sound too." Nadia said, speaking as a mother and a friend.

"Yes ma'am, I will. I'll see you in September when I get my first R&R and will tell you all about my adventures then." He reached out to shake Omar's hand and give Lara and Nadia a gentle hug good-bye before walking out the front door.

"I can't imagine going back to Iraq. Things just seem to go from bad to worse there," Lara said, with sadness in her voice, and worry for the safety of her good friend.

"Yes dear, we're glad to have you stay with us and become a doctor like your father." Nadia was very glad that her daughter had no plans other than her studies.

"Lara, you belong here now. Iraq is a long way from being a place where you should go at this time. Danny and his colleagues will need lots of help from friendly Iraqis and Iraqi-Americans. I hope they find the right people with the right skills." Omar said as he motioned everyone toward the dining room. "Let's eat."

"*In sha' allh*. Let's pray that it will all come to a peaceful end." Nadia said hopefully. "I think we're all ready to eat. Dinner's ready."

The end

Postscript

The role of the USAID as the development agency for the US government continues in Iraq, Afghanistan, and many other troubled countries around the world.

The Task Force 20 Delta Team and other highly dedicated and skilled soldiers from other branches of the military were crucial to the early successes during the war and continue to be an essential but highly classified tool of the US government.

The Army 101st Airborne Division provided the ground and air support to the Task Force 20 Delta Team to demolish the villa where Uday and Qusay were hiding. They were also responsible for the security of Nineveh province and Mosul after the invasion.

The story of Uday Hussein is based upon real events, and the time periods are approximately correct. There are many documented reports of Uday Hussein's merciless killing of Saddam's servant Kamel Gegeo, torturing members of the Iraq soccer team, raping and killing Iraqi university coeds and other women, and killing anyone else that displeased him or got in his way. Uday, Qusay, and Qusay's son Mustapha were killed in Nawaf al-Zaidan's villa by Task Force 20 special forces, aided by Humvees with TOW missiles, Apache helicopters, and an A-10 Warthog.

Qusay Hussein was in charge of all Iraqi intelligence and security services, the Republican Guard, and the Special Republican Guard. He played a significant role in crushing the Shiite rebellion after the first Gulf War in the mid-1990s and directed the mass murder of thousands of men, women, and children. He also directed the murder of thousands of prisoners in the late 1990s to make room for more prisoners. His reputation as a cold-blooded murderer was probably equal to his brother's.

Saddam Hussein and his first and second wives were very real people.

Nawaf Al-Zaidan did own the villa where Uday and Qusay were hiding. His reward for turning them in was $30 million and secure escort to the United States, where presumably his identity has been changed and he is living a comfortable quiet life.

Salah Al-Zaidan was not as lucky. Assassins attacked and killed him in Iraq and wounded other members of his family.

Abdullah, Aziz, Lara, Babra, Eleah, and the rest are all fictitious characters in the story.

Wikipedia and Google Search and Maps engines were essential for providing background information, historical, and geographical context. Search Google Maps for geographical details associated with the region, provinces, cities, and towns described in *Surviving Dreamland – Escape from Terror*.

Arabic-English Expressions (from Google translate):

Alhamd lillah—Praise be to God
Ahlaan wasahlaan bikum!—Welcome!
Alssalam ealaykum – Peace be upon you
Ard al'ahlam—"Land of the Most Important" is the literal translation. It was popularly known as the Dreamland palace and resort complex.
Ealaykum 'an alssalam—Upon you be peace
In sha' allh—If God wills.
Iilaa 'ayn tdhhb?—Where are you going?
Marhabaan—Hello, Hi!
Musaeada!—Help!
Shukraan—Thank you.
Qad sallam alllah maeakum—May the blessings of God be with you.

Characters:

Saddam Hussein Family and Associates

- Uday Hussein— Older son of Saddam Hussein and
- Qusay Hussein—Younger son of Saddam Hussein
- Saddam Hussein—Ruthless dictator of Iraq and father of Uday and Qusay.
- Sajida Talfah—Mother of Uday and Qusay and first wife of Saddam. She was very protective of her sons and vengeful to anyone who crosses her.
- Samira Shahbandar—Saddam's mistress who became his second wife.
- Kamel Hana Gegeo—Saddam's personal valet and food taster, killed by Uday Hussein.
- Abdul—Lead guard at the Dreamland Palace.
- Mohammed—Messenger for Uday and Qusay and cousin of Nawaf.
- Tamara Stetsenko—Pretty Ukrainian woman killed by Uday at Dreamland.

Al-Mohammed and Al-Zaidan Families and Relatives

- Lara Al-Mohammed—Heroine and niece of Nawaf and Mohassin, and cousin to Yasmine.
- Omar Al-Mohammed—Lara's father and Nadia's husband, brother-in-law of Nawaf and Salah Al-Zaidan.
- Nadia Al-Mohammed—Mother of Lara and wife of Omar Al-Mohammed and sister to Nawaf Al-Zaidan
- Nawaf Al-Zaidan—Father of Yasmine and uncle to Lara.
- Mohassin Al-Zaidan—Mother of Yasmine and Aunt to Lara.
- Shalan Al-Zaidan—Yasmine's brother, son of Nawaf and Mohassin.
- Yasmine Al-Zaidan—Twenty-something daughter of Nawaf and Mohassin and cousin of Lara, wife to Aziz. Killed at Dreamland by Uday.
- Salah Al-Zaidan, Wallah, and Othman—Brother and neighbor to Nawaf, his wife, and son.
- Wallah Al-Zaidan—Wife of Salah and mother of Othman.
- Othman Al-Zaidan—Teenage son of Salah.
- Sabah, Wadhah and Moeyd Al-Zaidan—Three other brothers of Nawaf Al-Zaidan and Nadia al-Mohammed (Omar's wife).
- Ibrahim, his wife Rinad, and their ten-year-old daughter, Nagham al-Zaidan—Nawaf's cousin and his family from Hillah in Babil Province.
- Aziz Al-Atwan—Twenty—something Iraqi Army officer; husband of Yasmine and son of Abdullah Al-Atwan
- Abdullah Al-Atwan—Father of Aziz and long-time friend of the Nawaf and his family.
- Hana Al-Atwan—Wife of Abdullah and mother of Aziz.
- Azzam Al-Atwan—Brother to Abdullah Atwan.

Friends of Lara

- Sergeant Danny Rodriguez—High school friend of Lara
- Melanie—High school friend of Lara
- Eman—University friend of Lara.
- Babra—University friend of Lara
- Eleah—University friend of Lara daughter of Hussein and Farah Al-Abab

Other Iraqi Characters

- Abraham—Servant at Baharia Palace and friend of the girls
- Hussein and Farah Al-Abad – Father and mother of Eleah.
- Othman and Hanah Al-Goad—Husband and wife who drove Eleah, Eman, and Lara from Fallujah to Haditha.
- Ibrahim and Wid – The man and wife who drove Lara and Eman from Haditha to Mosul.

Special Operations Team

- Joe Keith—Commander and leader of Task Force 20 Delta Team of commandos.

- Nick—Operations/intelligence sergeant.
- Pete—Weapons sergeant.
- Phil—Communications sergeant.
- Paul—Assistant commander (warrant officer).
- Colin—Weapons sergeant.
- Jared—Engineering sergeant.
- Jordan—Medical sergeant.
- Tim Jones—Sergeant Major, Noncommissioned officer in charge (NCOIC).
- Manny (Emmanuel or "Reverend")—Weapons sergeant.
- Jason—Medical sergeant.
- Bob—Communications sergeant.
- Hakim – Iraqi-American guide and translator for the Delta Team.

- Alice—Joe's wife.
- Nathan—Older son.
- Michael—Younger son.

- Charlie-CIA Agent
- Father Noah Mosa Shimilk – Priest and director at Mar Mattai monastery.

Military Terms and Acronyms

M4A1—One of the standard issue rifles used during Operation Iraqi Freedom, especially in urban settings. Although the basic weapon was standard, there were many accessories that were available to special operators to enhance and specialize their use.
CPA (Coalition Provisional Authority) The US Civilian authority in Iraq with the significant power conferred by President George W. Bush in 2003.
Delta Force—Under the command of the US Army Special Operations Command (USASOC), which fell under the command of the Joint Special Operations Command (JSOC).
DFAC—Dining facilities administration center. DFAC is a common military term for "Dining Hall"
JSOC—Joint Special Operations Command. According to Wikipedia, the known units under this command are the US Army's Delta Force, the 75th Ranger Regiment: Regimental Reconnaissance Company, the US Navy's SEAL Team Six, the US Air Force's 24th Special Tactics Squadron, and the US Army's Intelligence Support Activity.
HR—Human Resources
Humvee—High-mobility multipurpose wheeled vehicle (HMMWV), a four-wheel drive military light truck.
IED—Improvised explosive device.
IV—Intravenous fluids, used to stabilize a patient who has lost a lot of blood.

MASH—Mobile army surgical hospital.
MICH—Modular Integrated Communications Helmet communications component. It includes protective hearing and headphones with a small microphone that can be fastened on the soldier's neck. The system is integrated with the special operator's custom-designed helmets and had extensive communications capabilities.
MOS - Military occupational specialty.
MWR – Military welfare and Recreation.
PTSD—Post-traumatic stress disorder.
PX—Post exchange: an assortment of military stores and services.
RDX—Highly explosive compound used for suicide and other bombs. A small quantity of RDX used as a component in an explosive can produce a blast forty times greater than a car bomb.
RPG—Rocket-propelled grenade. The kit consists of a hand-held tube launcher and the RPGs.
SWA Hut—Southwest Asia hut. The name became common during the Vietnam War and became the lexicon for wooden structures with four walls, roof, and no windows, which were well suited for arid, dusty regions like Iraq.
TOW—Tube-launched, optically tracked, wire-guided (missile). It is an American anti-tank missile.
Thawb (Thobe)—Customary men's attire in the Middle East. It is a long tunic reaching from the shoulders to a length somewhere between the hips and the ankles.
USASOC—US Army Special Operations Command.
USAID—United States Agency for International Development.

Military time:

0000.......12 a.m.	0600.........6 a.m.	1200........12 p.m.	1800..........6 p.m.
0100..........1 a.m.	0700..........7 a.m.	1300..........1 p.m.	1900..........7 p.m.
0200.........2 a.m.	0800.........8 a.m.	1400..........2 p.m.	2000.........8 p.m.
0300.........3 a.m.	0900.........9 a.m.	1500..........3 p.m.	2100..........9 p.m.
0400.........4 a.m.	1000........10 a.m.	1600..........4 p.m.	2200........10 p.m.
0500..........5 a.m.	1100.........11 a.m.	1700..........5 p.m.	2300.........11p.m.

Approximate distance conversions:

U.S. Customary	Metric
3.3 feet	1 meter: 1,000 meters = 1 kilometer
1/2 mile	.8 kilometers
1 mile	1.64 kilometers

Acknowledgements

Web reference:
Nawaf Al-Zaidan: http://www.theguardian.com/world/2004/jan/24/iraq.rorymccarthy

Book Cover Credits:
Cover Design by Natalie Penoyar & John Sellards
Photos by Bill & Phil
Eyes provided by Sama

Special thanks to my family, friends, others who have, over this very long project, have offered suggestions, encouragement, and technical advise: Sandi Penoyar, Rhea Penoyar, Enas Al-Wawi, Karen Benson, and the Department of Defense, Philip M. Strub, Director of Entertainment Media for the Department of Defense and Lt. Cmdr. Renee Soltes, USN Deputy Director, NAVINFOWEST.